ASHLEY HERRING BLAKE is an award-winning author and teacher. She holds a master's degree in education and loves coffee, arranging her books by color, and cold weather. She is the author of the romance novel *Delilah Green Doesn't Care*, the young adult novels *Suffer Love*, *How to Make a Wish*, and *Girl Made of Stars*, and the middle grade novels *Ivy Aberdeen's Letter to the World*, *The Mighty Heart of Sunny St. James*, and *Hazel Bly and the Deep Blue Sea*. She's also a coeditor on the young adult romance anthology *Fools in Love*. She lives on a very tiny island off the coast of Georgia with her family.

CONNECT ONLINE

AshleyHerringBlake.com
🐦 📷 AshleyHBlake
📌 AEHBlake

BY ASHLEY HERRING BLAKE

Delilah Green Doesn't Care
Astrid Parker Doesn't Fail

ASTRID PARKER
DOESN'T FAIL

Ashley Herring Blake

PIATKUS

PIATKUS

First published in the US in 2022 by Berkley Romance
An imprint of Penguin Random House LLC
First published in Great Britain in 2022 by Piatkus

7 9 10 8

A CIP catalogue record for this book
is available from the British Library.

ISBN 978-0-349-43258-8

Printed and bound in Great Britain by Clays Ltd, Elcograf S.p.A.

Papers used by Piatkus are from well-managed forests
and other responsible sources.

Piatkus
An imprint of
Little, Brown Book Group
Carmelite House
50 Victoria Embankment
London EC4Y 0DZ

Hachette Ireland
8 Castlecourt Centre
Castleknock
Dublin 15

An Hachette UK Company
www.hachette.co.uk

www.littlebrown.co.uk

For everyone who figured it out a little later in life.

ASTRID PARKER
DOESN'T FAIL

"It's a helluva start, being able to recognize what makes you happy."

CHAPTER

ONE

ASTRID PARKER LOOKED perfect.

Well, as perfect as she *could* look, which these days meant a lot of concealer smoothed over the purple half-moons that had taken up residence under her eyes. But other than that bit of smoke and mirrors, she was pristine.

She hurried down the sidewalk, the April morning light lengthening her shadow along the cobblestones of downtown Bright Falls, Oregon. She couldn't believe the sun was out, warm on her pale skin, that she'd actually been able to leave her umbrella and galoshes at home in her front closet. This was the first rainless day they'd had in two weeks.

Born and raised in the Pacific Northwest, Astrid was used to the spring rains, used to gray and drizzle, but the fact that the clouds had deigned to part—today of all days—was encouraging, to say the least. Had Astrid actually believed in signs, she might've gotten a bit dramatic about the timing. Instead, she stopped in front of Wake Up Coffee Company and gazed at her reflection in the large picture window.

This morning, she'd woken up an hour earlier than she needed to, washed and blown out her hair, making sure she styled her recently trimmed blond fringe exactly the way Kelsey, her stylist, had shown her. The result was . . . well, it was perfect. Her wavy locks fell just past her shoulders; her bangs were shaggy and chic and shiny. Her makeup was minimal yet elegant—concealer notwithstanding—and her jewelry understated and tasteful, just a pair of gold hoops swinging from her lobes.

Her dress was the real star, her favorite outfit and the most expensive thing she owned—she still didn't dare tell her best friends Iris and Claire how much she paid for it last year after she and Spencer broke up. It was a necessary purchase, a power buy to make her feel confident and beautiful. As she took in the ivory pencil dress now, sleeveless and midi-length, her reflection confirmed it had been worth every penny. She'd paired it with her favorite strappy black three-inch heels, and even her mother couldn't complain about the vision Astrid saw in the window right now. She was elegant and poised. Prepared.

Perfect.

Everything she should be for this meeting and first filming at the Everwood Inn. A wobbly smile settled onto her mouth as she thought about the historic inn, which was now hers to re-create. Well, not exactly *hers*. But when Pru Everwood, longtime owner of the nationally beloved Victorian, had called last month and said that she was ready to renovate—and that Natasha Rojas's super-chic HGTV show, *Innside America*, wanted to do an episode on the whole transformation—Astrid had nearly bitten her own tongue to keep from screaming with glee.

Glee and a good bit of terror, but that was just nerves, or so Astrid had been telling herself for the last month. Of course she was excited. Of course this was the opportunity of a lifetime.

The Everwood Inn was famous—there were countless books and documentaries about the legend of the Blue Lady, who purportedly haunted one of the upstairs bedrooms—and being featured on *Innside America* could change everything for Astrid. This was her chance to go from small-town designer with a failed engagement to something more. Something better. Someone her mother actually *liked*.

Plus, the old mansion-turned-inn was a designer's dream—three stories of intricate eaves and gables, a wide front porch, an exterior that was currently the color of cat vomit but would shine beautifully under some lovely pastel hue, lavender or maybe a cool mint. Inside, it was a maze of dark-paneled rooms and cobwebs, but Astrid could already envision how she would lighten and brighten, the shiplap and accent walls that would replace the cherry wood wainscoting, transforming the rotting back porch into a sun-drenched solarium.

There was no doubt, the Everwood Inn was a dream project.

And currently, it was her only project.

She sighed, pushing her recent financial woes to the back of her mind, including the fact that just last week she'd let her assistant *and* her receptionist go because Astrid could no longer afford to pay them. Not that she'd ever tell her mother that Bright Designs was officially a one-woman show. She'd rather chew on a cactus, thanks very much, so she certainly didn't have time for doubts or inconsistency.

Since taking over Lindy Westbrook's design business nine years ago when the older woman had retired, Astrid usually had the perfect amount of work to keep her busy and solvent. But lately, things had been slow . . . and boring. There were only so many design jobs to go around in a town as tiny as Bright Falls, and if she worked on one more doctor–slash–lawyer–slash–real estate agent's office, filling them with uncomfortable seating and abstract paintings, she was going to tear her own eyelashes out.

Not to mention, if she let the business go under now, particularly after her disaster of a failed engagement last summer, Astrid's mother would not only tear her eyelashes out for her but would make absolutely sure Astrid knew the failure was one hundred percent her own fault, warping her professional deficiencies into intimately personal shortcomings.

Lately, this endearing quality of her mother's had kicked into overdrive, Isabel's lip literally curling whenever Astrid had a hair out of place or reached for a bagel. Astrid was exhausted, had slept like shit for months, her mother's constant scrutiny and unattainable expectations playing like a film on repeat every time she closed her eyes. Surely, if anything would appease Isabel—maybe even draw out a proud hug or a glowing declaration like *I had every faith in you, darling*—and give Astrid a few months of peace, it was appearing as the lead designer on a prestigious show and bringing the beloved Everwood into the modern age.

She offered her reflection one more smile and was straightening the buttery linen of her dress when a fist banged on the glass from inside. She startled, stumbling back so that her ankle very nearly buckled from the height of her heels.

"You look hot as fuck!"

A pretty redhead grinned at her through the window, then made a show of waggling her eyebrows at Astrid's form.

"Jesus, Iris," Astrid said, fingers pressed to her chest as she tried to calm her galloping heart. "Could you *not* for one day?"

"Not what?" Iris yelled through the glass, arms propped up on the back of a turquoise-painted wooden chair.

"Not . . ." Astrid waved her hand around, searching for the right word. When it came to her best friend Iris Kelly, ever the middle child vying for attention, the right word rarely stuck for very long. "Never mind."

"Get your cute ass in here already," Iris said. "Claire and Delilah are whispering sweet nothings in each other's ears—"

"We are not!" Astrid heard her other best friend, Claire, call from somewhere behind Iris before she appeared in the window too, her brown hair up in a messy bun and her dark purple–framed glasses catching the sunlight.

"—and I'm slowly losing my will to live," Iris went on, shoulder knocking into Claire's.

"Don't even pretend you don't love it." This from Delilah, Astrid's stepsister and Claire's girlfriend for the last ten months, whose presence Astrid was still getting used to in her life. She and Delilah had had a fraught childhood together, filled with resentments and misunderstandings. The healing process was long and, honestly, exhausting. They'd come a long way since last June, when Delilah arrived in town from New York City to photograph Astrid's doomed wedding and fell in love with the maid of honor instead. Since then, Delilah had moved back to Bright Falls and proceeded to make Claire happier than Astrid had ever seen her.

As though to further prove the point, Delilah glided into view and draped a tattooed arm around Claire's shoulder, and Claire promptly beamed up at her as though Delilah created coffee itself. Astrid felt a pang deep in her chest. Not jealousy necessarily, and she'd long realized the problems she and Delilah had growing up were just as much her fault as they were her stepsister's, so it wasn't discomfort or worry on her best friend's behalf either.

No, the feeling was more akin to . . . nausea. She'd never, ever admit it to Claire—or Iris and her brand-new girlfriend, Jillian—that the sight of a happy couple gave her the urge to vomit, but it was true, and her roiling stomach was the proof. Ever since she and Spencer had broken up last summer, she felt physically sick just thinking about romance and dating.

Which was exactly why she *didn't* think about romance and dating—much less engage in them—and had no plans to do so in the future.

"Come on inside, honey," Claire said, tapping at the window gently. "It's a big day!"

Astrid smiled, her nausea dissipating, thank goodness. When

she'd told Claire and Iris about Pru Everwood's call—about *Innside America*, Natasha-freaking-Rojas, and Pru's grandkids coming into town to help the older woman manage the whole affair—her best friends had promptly squealed with glee right along with her and helped her prepare for today's first meeting and filming with the Everwood family. Granted, *prepare* entailed several nights at Astrid's house, open wine bottles littering her coffee table while she worked on her computer and Iris and Claire grew increasingly giddy and obnoxious, but still. It was the thought that counted.

Today, they'd insisted on meeting her for breakfast at Wake Up to fuel her with, as Iris put it, "bagels and badassery." Astrid would be lying if she said she didn't need a little badassery right now. She nodded at Claire and moved toward the front entrance, hand reaching for the tarnished brass handle. Before she could give the first tug, however, the turquoise wooden door flew open and something slammed into Astrid, yanking all the breath from her lungs and sending her flying backward.

She landed hard on her butt, palms scraping on the cobblestones, and a burning sensation grew in the center of her chest before slithering down her belly.

"Oh my god, I'm so sorry."

She heard the voice right in front of her, but she was frozen, her legs splayed in a most inelegant fashion, the right heel of her favorite shoes hanging on by a literal thread, and—

She squeezed her eyes closed. Counted to three before opening them again. Maybe it was a dream. A nightmare. Surely, she was not sitting on her ass on the sidewalk in the middle of downtown. Her pencil dress—her gorgeous, lucky, just-shy-of-a-grand pencil dress that made her butt look amazing—was not covered in very hot, very wet, very dark coffee right now. Three soggy paper cups were not spinning on the ground around her, a drink carrier was not upturned in her lap, pooling more liquid all over the dry-clean-only linen, and there was most definitely not a woman with pale skin, a tangle of short golden-brown hair, light denim overalls cuffed at the ankles, and rugged brown boots standing over her with a horrified expression on her face.

This was *not* happening.

Not when she was about to meet Natasha Rojas. And certainly not when she was about to appear in front of a camera for the project of her life.

Not. Happening.

"Are you okay?" the woman asked, holding a hand out to Astrid. "I was in a hurry and I didn't see you there and wow, that dress really took a hit, huh?"

Astrid ignored her babbling, ignored the hand. She concentrated instead on breathing. In and out. Nice and slow. Because what she really wanted to do right now was scream. Loudly. In this woman's face, possibly accompanied by a nice, firm shoulder shove. She knew she shouldn't do any of those things, so she breathed . . . and breathed.

"Are . . . are you hyperventilating?" the woman asked. "Do I need to call someone?"

She knelt down and peered into Astrid's face, her hazel eyes narrowed. Her face was almost elfin, all delicate features with a sharp nose and chin, and her short hair was shaved on one side and longer on the other, swooping over her forehead and filled with messy tangles like she'd just woken up. She had a nose ring, a tiny silver hoop through her septum.

"How many fingers am I holding up?" she asked, presenting two fingers.

Astrid felt like responding by holding up just one important finger, but before she could, Iris and Claire and Delilah spilled out of the café, their eyes wide when they spotted her on the ground.

God, was she *still* on the ground?

"Honey, what happened?" Claire asked, hurrying over to help her up.

"I happened," the woman said. "I'm so sorry. I was coming out and not watching where I was going, which is just so typical of me, and I feel so horrible and—"

"Will you *please* shut up?"

The words fell out of Astrid's mouth before she could think better of them. The woman's eyes went wide, perfect winged eyeliner arching upward, her raspberry-red mouth falling open in a little *o*.

"At least she said *please*," Iris muttered out of the side of her mouth. "Peak Astrid. Polite, even when rude."

Claire cleared her throat and tugged on Astrid's arm, but Astrid waved her off. Goddammit, she was going to get up on her own, preserve what dignity she had left. Passersby on their way to work or out for coffee stared at her, all of them probably thanking the gods or whoever that their mornings weren't going as badly as that poor lady with the ruined dress and scraped-up palms.

She hobbled to her feet, the woman rising with her. She twisted her hands together, wincing as Astrid whipped off her broken shoe and inspected the ruined heel.

"I'm really—"

"Sorry, yes, I got that," Astrid said. "But your sorry isn't going to fix my dress or my shoe right now, is it?"

The woman tucked her hair behind one ear, revealing several piercings lining the delicate shell. "Um. No, I guess not."

Something that felt like despair, as irrational as it might be, flushed Astrid's cheeks and clouded into her chest. This one thing. That's all she wanted, this *one* morning to go perfectly, but no, this disaster of a woman with her cute hair and her nose ring had to come barreling into her life at the worst possible moment, obliterating any chances at perfection. Her fingertips felt tingly, her stomach cramped with nerves, and her words flowed forth in a panoply of venom and annoyance.

"How could you possibly not have seen me?" Astrid said.

"I—"

"I was right there, in *ivory* no less." Astrid fluttered her hands down her currently *not* ivory dress. "I'm practically glowing."

The woman frowned. "Look, I—"

"Oh, forget it," Astrid said. "You've already ruined everything." She dug her phone out of her bag, tapped into her contacts, and shoved it in the woman's face. "Just put your number in here so I can send you the bill."

"Oh shit," Iris muttered.

"The bill?" the woman asked.

"Run away," Iris whispered at her, but the woman just blinked at both of them.

"The dry cleaning bill," Astrid said, still holding out her phone.

"Sweetie," Claire said, "do we really need—"

"Yes, Claire, we do," Astrid said. She was still breathing hard, her eyes never leaving this walking hurricane who couldn't seem to pass through a door without causing mayhem.

The woman finally took the phone, her slender throat bobbing in a hard swallow as she tapped in her number. When she was finished, she handed the phone back to Astrid and bent to pick up the now-empty coffee cups and drink carrier, dumping them all into a large trash can near Wake Up's entrance.

Then she walked away without another word.

Astrid stared after her as the woman hurried about half a block down the sidewalk. She stopped at a mint-green pickup truck that had most certainly seen better days and all but threw herself inside, peeling out of the parking space with a squeal of rubber, engine rumbling north and out of sight.

"Well," Delilah said.

"Yeah," Iris said.

Claire just reached out and squeezed Astrid's hand, which jolted Astrid back into what was actually happening.

She looked down at her dress, the coffee drying to a dull brown, her shoe dangling from her fingers. Fresh horror filled her up, but now, it wasn't from her ruined outfit, her destroyed perfect morning on the most important day of her professional life. No, she was Astrid-goddamn-Parker. She could fix all that.

What she couldn't fix was the fact that she'd just ripped a complete stranger a new one over some spilled coffee, a fact that settled over her now like tar, thick and sticky and foul.

"Let's get you cleaned up," Claire said, trying to pull Astrid toward Wake Up, but Astrid wouldn't budge.

"I sounded just like my mother," she said quietly. She swallowed hard, regret a knot in her throat, and looked at each of her friends in turn, then let her gaze stop on Delilah. "Didn't I?"

"No, of course not," Claire said.

"I mean, what is *just like*, when you think about it?" Iris said.

"Yeah, you really did," Delilah said.

"Babe," Claire said, swatting her girlfriend's arm.

"What? She asked," Delilah said.

Astrid rubbed her forehead. There was a time when sounding exactly like Isabel Parker-Green would've been a good thing, a goal, an empowered way to manage the world at large. Astrid's mother was poised, perfectly put together, elegant and educated and refined.

And the coldest, most unfeeling woman Astrid had ever known. Astrid often feared her mother's over-involvement in her life would have severe repercussions, Isabel's essence seeping into her daughter's blood and bones, becoming part of her in a way that Astrid had no control over. And here was the proof—when shit went down, Astrid Parker was entitled, arrogant, and an all-around bitch.

"Shit," she said, squeezing her temples between her thumb and forefinger. "I threatened her with a dry cleaning bill, for god's sake. I need to apologize."

"I think that ship has sailed," Delilah said, waving toward where the burned-rubber smoke from the woman's tires still drifted through the air.

"You'll probably never see her again, if it makes you feel any better," Iris said. "I didn't recognize her. I would've remembered someone that hot."

"Iris, Jesus Christ," Claire said.

"Oh, come on, she was empirically gorgeous," Iris said. "Did you see the overalls? The hair? Total soft butch."

Delilah laughed, and even Claire cracked a smile at that. Astrid just felt a dull sense of loneliness she couldn't explain.

"We all have bad days," Claire went on. "I'm sure she gets that."

"You are too pure for this world, Claire Sutherland," Iris said.

Claire rolled her eyes while Delilah grinned and pressed a kiss to her girlfriend's head. The whole scene caused Astrid's stomach to roil even more—the PDA, Claire's constant positivity, Iris's snark. The only one who gave it to her straight anymore was Delilah, and Astrid couldn't bear to look her in the eye right now, not after going all Isabel Parker-Green.

"I need to get cleaned up at home," she said, slipping off her other shoe to avoid limping down the sidewalk in one three-inch heel.

"I'll come help," Claire said.

"No, that's okay," Astrid said, untangling her arm from Claire's grip and moving toward where she'd parked her car. She needed to be alone right now, get her head on right. Disaster of a morning notwithstanding, she was still the lead designer for the Everwood Inn, she was still going to be on *Innside America*, and she was still about to meet Natasha Rojas. No way in hell was one collision with a clumsy coffee drinker and a moment of extreme bitchiness going to ruin that for her now.

She'd kissed her friends goodbye and was halfway to her car when she thought to look at her phone for the woman's name. Maybe she could send her an apologetic text, tell her, at the very least, that of course she would not be sending her the dry cleaning bill. She unlocked her phone, her bare feet coming to a halt as she stared down at the woman's contact information.

There was no name.

There was only a number, saved under **Delightful Human Who Ruined Your Ugly Dress**.

CHAPTER

TWO

JORDAN EVERWOOD MADE it about a mile down the road before she had to pull over. She tried to hold off, swallow around the thickening of her throat, but fuck it, really, because who was she trying to keep it together for? Certainly not herself. She'd been a complete mess for a year straight and counting—longer if she started from Meredith's diagnosis—so it was a state of being she was well used to by now.

She was about five miles from where she was staying at her grandmother's. Simon was already blowing up her phone asking when she'd get back with his precious hipster coffee, and she didn't want to arrive with mascara tears leaking freely down her face.

She pulled her truck, Adora, onto the side of the road leading out of Bright Falls, a two-lane with nothing but rain-soaked evergreens as far as she could see, some mountain she didn't know the name of in the distance.

So different from Savannah.

Though she supposed that was the point.

She threw Adora in park, the gear shifting reluctantly—the drive across the country a week ago had thoroughly exhausted her precious truck. She and Meredith had named the vehicle after the leading lady in their favorite show, *She-Ra*, back when Jordan first started doing carpentry for Dalloway and Daughters Homes four years ago.

Jesus, had it only been four years?

It felt like a lifetime.

Jordan leaned her head against the pleather seat and let the tears dribble down her face. This was a disaster—this move, this second chance, as Simon loved to call it. Her twin brother had been hassling her for nearly six months about moving out of Savannah.

"It's haunted, Jordie," he'd said more than once.

"Of course it's haunted," she'd always retort. "It's one of the most haunted cities in America."

"You know what I mean, smart-ass."

And she did, but fuck if she wanted to admit it. Still, in the months that had passed since he started sending her postcards in the mail, all of them featuring some exciting new city—San Francisco! New York! Chicago! Los Angeles!—her life in Savannah had steadily declined. Her work at Dalloway and Daughters had grown sloppy, accompanied by several client complaints, dozens of custom-built cabinets and one-of-a-kind furniture pieces ruined by her miscalculations, this fogginess in her head she couldn't seem to get rid of.

Even her therapist said it was time for a change.

"I thought the point of therapy was to face your problems, not run from them," Jordan had said in a session two months ago, when Angela had finally suggested, ever so gently, that maybe Simon was right.

"There's running *from* something," Angela said, "and there's running *to* something new. You need the something new, Jordan. You're not living your life. You're living a life that died a year ago. Or you're trying to, and it's clearly not working. It's a life that can't be lived."

Jordan had all but stomped out of Angela's office after that tidbit of wisdom, no goodbye or fuck you or anything. Still, her therapist's words had haunted her—more than any of Savannah's famous ghosts—until the day things had come to a head at work.

Okay, maybe *come to a head* was putting it mildly, considering she'd set a small fire in a multimillion-dollar renovation on Chatham Square.

On purpose.

It was a *small* fire.

She'd just fucked up installing a set of gorgeous oak cabinets—and by fucked up, she meant dropped a corner piece after refusing help from her assistant Molly, shattering the lovely wood all over the floor—and she was frustrated, to say the least. Apparently, according to witnesses, she found a box of matches in her toolbox, struck a handful to life, and dropped it on the pile of wood while yelling something akin to *Fuck, fuck, fuckity fuck you* at the top of her lungs.

The spark barely caught. One couldn't just start a raging fire out of professionally finished cabinets, wood or not, but it was the spirit of the act that sealed Jordan's fate. Bri Dalloway, matriarch and Jordan's highly accommodating boss, had had enough, as had her two daughters, Hattie and Vivian.

Freshly fired—no pun intended—and without anything to fill her hours, she spent the next two weeks on her couch with Catra, her tuxedo cat, ignoring her phone and eating Lean Cuisines while binge-watching every romantic comedy she could find on Netflix. This continued—and she would've kept on in this state very happily, thank you very much—until Simon showed up on the doorstep of the tiny ranch house in Ardsley Park she'd shared with Meredith, all the way from where he'd been living in Portland, with his phone pressed to his ear and Jordan's most favorite person in the world on the other end of the line.

Their grandmother.

Who could convince Jordan to do just about anything, including moving across the country to help with renovating the Everwood, the inn that had been in their family for over a century. All Pru had to do was say, "Come home, honey," in her soft, sweet voice, and suddenly Jordan was twelve years old at Everwood in the summer, the only place Jordan had ever felt truly at ease. No sick mother to worry about. No kids at her school in the small Northern California town where she grew up looking at her sideways for coming out as queer when she was eleven. Nothing but the creaky stairs and secret passageways of the inn, wild roses and Oregon's soft overcast skies, and the sweet scent of rosewater lotion when her grandmother gathered her in a hug.

So now here she was, three thousand miles from the home she'd shared with the love of her life, crying on the side of a country road with absolutely no coffee and the memory of an extremely irate woman's screeching echoing in her ears.

Yes, excellent plan, Simon.

God, what a disaster. She couldn't even execute a simple coffee run. Pru only drank tea, and her tiny cottage kitchen didn't have a coffee maker. Hence the coffee run, hence the disaster. She should've just bought a damn Keurig when she'd arrived in town last week, or at least made Simon get one. God knew he could afford it with his book money. But no, in all his preciousness, he said nothing beats Wake Up coffee first thing in the morning, and goddamn if he wasn't right. It was the absolute best coffee she'd ever tasted.

Unfortunately, Simon's nectar of the gods—and the third cup she'd bought for this designer they were meeting about Everwood Inn renovations, along with *Innside America*'s host and crew (though hell if she was going to buy coffee for everyone)—was currently soaking into the lush cotton or linen or whatever the fuck of Little Miss Bitch's dress.

She heaved a hiccupping breath. She didn't like calling other people bitch, not when she meant it in a negative sense. She usually only used the word around her girlfriends. Not that she had those anymore. Her friend group back in Savannah had been her and Meredith's friend group, and she simply didn't know how to interact with them without her partner, nor they with her.

Apparently, she didn't know how to interact with anyone.

And, of course, the woman she'd barreled into like a bull chasing red just had to be pretty. No, not pretty. She was goddamn gorgeous. Soft curves and shaggy hair, thick brows—perfectly shaped, of course—and just enough shadows under her dark brown eyes to make her interesting. She was stunning, and for the first time in over a year, Jordan had found herself momentarily dazed, a feathery feeling swooping through her belly.

Until the woman opened her mouth and all those delicate feathers had turn to stone.

"Fuck," Jordan said out loud, curling her fingers around Adora's steering wheel as a wave of fresh tears spilled over. She was literally crying over a run-in with a mean girl, like she was that queer kid with the weird hair back in high school all over again. She felt suddenly ancient. She was barely thirty-one. She'd already met, courted, married, and lost the love of her life. She was too young to feel this goddamn old.

She sniffed and wiped under her eyes, shaking her head to clear it. Then she grabbed her leather messenger bag, the one Meredith always called the bottomless pit, and dug around until she found the silk pouch that held her Tarot. She tugged on the drawstring and spilled the cards into her hands. She loved this set. The cards were colorful and modern, and best of all, they were feminist and queer as hell. Each card, even the Kings in each suit, featured either a woman or nonbinary person. Jordan had gotten them shortly after finding herself all alone and without Meredith, a comfort purchase, and she'd used them every day since. They were the one healthy habit she maintained, each card grounding her to herself, keeping her from floating away.

Except lately, they were pissing her the hell off.

"Come on," she whispered as she shuffled the glossy cards in her hands. "Come on, come on, come on." She knew one was supposed to ask deep and profound questions while shuffling the Tarot, things like *What do I need to know today to live my best life?* But that hadn't been working out for her so well lately.

In fact, in the past month, these cards had right and truly betrayed her.

She stopped shuffling and divided the cards into three stacks on her lap, then quickly piled them back into one. Shoving her bag against the passenger door, she fanned the cards out along the bench seat. She eyed the bright blue pattern on the backs of the cards, ran her hand above them and waited for one to catch her eye.

One did. She didn't hesitate. She just went through the motions as she always did, operating on instinct, and pulled the card. She held it to her chest for a second and breathed. There were seventy-eight damn cards in the Tarot, twenty-two in the Major Arcana and fifty-six in the Minor. What were the chances of her pulling the same card again?

Very slim.

And yet—

She flipped the card over.

The Two of Cups stared back at her, just as it had most mornings for the past month. The cheeky little bastard was in on some sort of prank against her. Every now and then she'd pull something different, a random Wand or Pentacle or a good old Fool or Hierophant or Moon.

She'd even take the disastrous Tower right now. At least it would fit with the state of her life. Anything instead of this little asshole, this bright card with two women standing on a beach, each holding a large goblet. They were facing each other, smiling, happy, full of hope and possibility. The Two of Cups whispered of romance and love, of new relationships.

A perfect pairing.

Matched souls.

She wanted to rip the goddamn thing in half. She couldn't believe she'd pulled it again. Each time she did, she was shocked anew, angry, and, honestly, terrified. The Tarot wasn't meant to be predictive. The practice was about insight, knowing yourself. The cards guided you to a deeper understanding of what you wanted, what you were going through, what you needed. So it wasn't like she took the card to mean her soul mate was right around the corner.

How could she?

Her soul mate was long gone.

She didn't know what this card meant, honestly. Not for her. It could indicate friendship, a deep need inside of her to connect with . . . *someone.* Anyone.

But she'd already proven, time and time again, and *again* this morning, she wasn't the greatest at that.

She took a shuddering breath and slipped the Two of Cups back into the deck. As she placed the silk pouch in her bag, her phone buzzed loudly in the cupholder. She picked it up, the screen revealing a text from her brother.

Where the hell are you?

She'd just started to type when another message came through.

Hello?

And another.

Jordie.

And again.

Are you okay? Seriously, this isn't funny. You've been gone for over an hour.

She rolled her eyes and called him.

"I'm fine," she said before he could even finish his panicked greeting. "You can stop lambasting me via text message now."

"Hey, as your older brother—"

"Oh yes, those three and a half minutes you spent as an only child really infused you with unsurpassed wisdom."

"—I'm entitled to check up on you and make sure you're not lost or severely maimed or—"

"Setting things on fire and driving what's left of my sorry life into the ground?"

"I was also going to add ensuring your cat hadn't eaten your face."

She gasped in faux shock. "Catra would never."

"Cats are nature's perfect predator. If you cracked your head on the bathtub and she had no one to feed her, she would totally eat your face after a few days."

"Can we stop talking about how my cat is going to turn into a murdering psychopath?"

"I'm just saying, if I'm going to have to deal with filming this show our grandmother locked us into alone, I'd like to be prepared."

Jordan sighed. She still couldn't believe they were going to be on *Innside America*. One of HGTV's most popular shows, it featured Natasha Rojas, a woman who'd built her career on bespoke interior design, created and edited a very chic design magazine called *Orchid*, and spent much of her time traveling around the country to oversee the renovations for historic inns. The team was always local—

especially the designer—and Natasha was famous for her extremely direct feedback, not to mention her flawless style.

If she was being completely honest, Jordan was a bit intimidated. She hadn't exactly been doing stellar work lately, and Natasha Rojas would expect nothing but perfection. Still, the show's interest in the inn finally pushed her grandmother to renovate, something Jordan and the whole family knew needed to happen, like, twenty years ago.

"It'll be interesting," Jordan said.

"Yeah. To say the least." Simon huffed a laugh. "Seriously, though. You okay?"

"Yes," she said, because it was the right answer for her overprotective brother, if not a completely truthful one.

"Okay," he said, relief clear in his voice. "Okay, good. Take a sip of that coffee, it'll help."

She opened her mouth to explain there would be no morning-saving coffee, but then the whole altercation in front of Wake Up would just confirm what he already feared, already *knew*, really.

Jordan Everwood was a walking catastrophe, and she needed careful handling.

"Yeah," she said. "Great idea."

Then she ended the call and shifted Adora's gear into drive.

***

TEN MINUTES LATER, Jordan turned onto a single-lane gravel road. Officially, the Everwood Inn belonged to Bright Falls's zip code, but it was actually just outside the city limits in no-man's-land, tucked away in the evergreens like a secret. The Queen Anne Victorian home was an Everwood original, built by Jordan's great-great-great-grandparents, James and Opal Everwood, in 1910, with elegant spires and gingerbread trim and half a dozen hidden passageways inside she loved exploring as a kid with Simon during the summer and other holiday visits.

Their grandmother, Prudence Everwood, was the one who'd converted it into an inn in the 1960s, along with her younger sister, Temperance. It was an instant success, first for its beauty and idyllic location, and second for its famed Blue Lady.

Or maybe it was the other way around. Everyone loved a ghost story, that connection to the Great Unknown. Jordan certainly couldn't resist the tales when she was younger. Pru hadn't lived in the main house since the inn opened, choosing instead to reside in the carriage house just behind the property that had been converted into a charming—if very tiny—three-bedroom cottage. Whenever Jordan and Simon visited, they would stay up late and sneak into the inn, desperate for a peek at the ghostly visage of their long-dead ancestor, Alice Everwood, the infamous Blue Lady.

They never got one. But they did have plenty of moments when a squeak on the stairs or a whip of wind through the eaves caused the young twins to scream their bloody heads off, resulting in irate guests and their extremely annoyed elders.

Jordan couldn't help but smile at the memories as she rounded the corner and the Everwood Inn towered into view. She loved this place, loved that it was her family's, that she could always count on it to open its doors to her. When she and Simon were kids, their mother, Serena, had dealt with undiagnosed depression, so the twins had spent most summers with their grandmother while their father tried to help Serena "get it together," as they always called it. Jordan would usually arrive at Everwood in a tangle of knots, but between her grandmother and the soft Oregon rain, she slowly unfurled, resembling the carefree person all kids were meant to be by the time August rolled around. Eventually, when Jordan and Simon were sixteen, Serena was properly diagnosed with major depressive disorder. She went to therapy and got on the right medication, and things improved, but the twins kept up their Oregon summers until they went off to college.

While Jordan wasn't quite sure about being in Bright Falls in and of itself, had no clue what the hell she was going to do with her life considering she couldn't perform even the most basic of carpentry skills right now, this place was still magical for her. Always would be.

Granted, the house had seen better days. The exterior wood and stone, once a gleaming ivory, were now the color of dull, yellowed bone. Paint peeled from the gingerbread trim around the windows and porch, and the turret's tiny balcony was sagging on the left side. Rosebushes, once lush and perfectly pruned, blooming into a riot of color every summer, were scraggly and overgrown, threatening to take over the porch. The inside wasn't much better, the *haunted* element unintentionally taking precedence over *charming Victorian inn* in the last few years or so, all dark corners and uncomfortable, creaky furniture. Jordan was pretty sure the four-poster beds in each of the guest rooms were original to the very first owners.

Including their mattresses.

She shuddered at the thought.

When the people at *Innside America* contacted Pru a few months ago about a possible renovation episode, their grandmother had only hesitated for a moment. She was old, approaching eighty. Aunt Temperance had died back in the nineties, so Pru had been running this place largely on her own for the better part of twenty years. Serena was Pru's only child, born out of a torrid affair Pru had in her late twenties with a semi-famous painter who'd lived in Bright Falls for a time. He'd never been part of their lives, and Pru had never married. Jordan and Simon's parents were still madly in love and now ran a tiny, struggling vineyard in Sonoma County, a project they dived into headfirst just ten years ago after they both grew dissatisfied with their corporate jobs.

As a result, there was no one to help Pru manage this beast of an inn as it fell down around her head, much less the stress of a televised renovation. No one except Simon, who could work remotely

and live anywhere. And who better to help with a huge project, pro-
viding free labor and insight, than Simon's lost and brokenhearted
twin sister?

She heaved a sigh as Adora bumped into the circular front drive.
Simon and her grandmother were standing on the front porch. He
was pointing to this and that, while Pru nodded along and sipped on
what Jordan assumed was a strong cup of English breakfast. They'd
closed the inn to guests just last week and didn't plan to open up
again until the reno was done, which, by Jordan's estimation, would
take at least six weeks, and that was at a fast clip. Because they
planned to keep most of the bones of the house intact—as an inn,
open floor plans were not only unnecessary but detrimental to guests'
comfort—a lot of the work would be cosmetic, with some structural
issues to deal with on the exterior. Granted, she wasn't sure how
much slower things might go with a film crew constantly in the mix.
Preliminary emails had indicated Natasha Rojas strove to keep things
as authentic as possible, but Jordan had no idea how all this would
really go down. Natasha was due to arrive with her crew any minute
now, so Jordan supposed they'd go over the details then.

"There you are," Simon said, bounding down the rotting steps as
she stepped out of the truck. He wore dark jeans and a maroon T-shirt,
his feet shoved into a pair of worn gray Vans. Jordan and Simon were
twins, but they looked nothing alike. While she had her mother's
bronze hair, her brother's inky locks were all their father's, messy on
the top and short on the sides. Their eyes were the same though, the
Everwood eyes, hazel with more gold than brown streaking through
the green.

Now, those eyes widened behind Simon's black-framed glasses.

"I know, I know," she said, presenting her coffee-less hands. "I'm
sorry, but—"

Simon grabbed her arms and peered into her face, cutting her off.
"What happened? I thought you said you were okay."

She frowned at his worried expression, but then remembered she'd spent a good twenty minutes sobbing in Adora on the side of a road. Apparently, she'd forgotten to clean up the evidence. Her beloved winged eyeliner and vegan mascara were probably tracking down her cheeks as though she'd done her makeup for a Halloween party.

"Oh." She touched her face. "That."

"Yes, that."

"Darling, what happened?" their grandmother said, heading toward them from the porch, her short silver hair gleaming under the sun. She was dressed in a green-and-black color-block sweater, dark blue jeans, and white Keds. Her glasses were grass-green today, perfectly matching her top. For as long as Jordan could remember, her grandmother's glasses had always complemented her clothes. God only knew how many pairs the woman owned at any one time. At least two dozen, Jordan would guess.

"Nothing," Jordan said.

"You didn't ruin that gorgeous eyeliner over nothing, love," Pru said, swiping some black smudges from her granddaughter's cheek.

Jordan sighed, leaning into Pru's touch. She really didn't feel like getting into the whole mess—the collision with Little Miss Bitch, the dressing down she received as a result, the crying. Her entire family already thought she was barely able to function. The last thing she needed was to admit a little social altercation had her hiccupping like a hormonal preteen.

"I spilled all the coffee as I was leaving the shop," she said. "Some splashed on my face and I didn't pay attention to how I was wiping it off."

"Shit, did you burn your face?" Simon said, now grabbing her cheeks and scanning for burns.

For Christ's sake.

She wiggled out of his grip.

"No, it was just a few drops." She backed up toward the pebbled path that led to her grandmother's cottage. "I'll just go get cleaned up. What time is everything supposed to start?"

Before Simon could answer, tires crunched over the gravel driveway.

"Um, now?" he said, wincing.

Jordan groaned. "You really need me for this?"

"You're the lead carpenter, Jordie, and a family member. They want you on film."

She blew out a breath. An honorary role at best. No way her brother actually trusted her with this job. She already knew he'd hired a contractor—some guy named Josh Foster out in Winter Lake—and contractors had their own carpenters on staff.

She should know; she used to be one of them.

Still, Simon had promised he'd already worked it out with Josh, how *Jordan* would lead, *Jordan* would work closely with the designer, *Jordan* would be the point person for all carpentry work. The thought both excited and terrified her. There was a time when carpentry was more than a job, it was a passion. She loved woodworking, loved creating, dreamed of producing her own line of furniture and opening up her own shop.

Or she used to, at least, before an electric saw in her hands turned into a literal occupational hazard.

"Fine," she said to her brother. She'd play along. She *did* want to be involved in the reno, after all. She just wasn't sure how much control she'd actually have here. But whatever. Anything to wipe that *are you okay* look from her brother's face.

A silver sedan flashed into view, and Jordan maneuvered behind her brother to set about wiping her cheeks clean. She may or may not have had to use her own spit, but desperate times and all that.

"Hello, dear," her grandmother said as a car door opened and shut.

"Pru, how are you?" a voice said.

"I'm just fine," Pru said. "Oh, you do look lovely."

A laugh. "Thank you so much. But look at you! Those glasses!"

"Grandma could give us all some fashion tips, I think," Simon said.

Another laugh.

Jordan took a breath, steeled herself to be professional, and turned around.

She blinked.

Blinked again, because . . .

There, a few feet away and smiling at Jordan's precious grandmother, was Little Miss Bitch herself. Granted, she was no longer covered in coffee, her eyes were now soft and friendly as opposed to wide and rage-infused, and she was dressed in a stunning form-fitting black suit and white blouse, complete with dark burgundy heeled oxfords that gave her legs for days, but yeah, it was absolutely her.

"Astrid Parker," she said, holding out a hand to Simon. "Bright Designs. We've been emailing quite a bit."

"Yes, hi, great to meet you finally," he said, pumping her hand. "Simon Everwood. And this"—he turned and nudged Jordan out from behind him—"is my sister, Jordan. She'll be the lead carpenter on the job and your primary contact with the family."

The woman's—Astrid's—eyes went wide, and her pretty, light pink mouth fell open in shock.

CHAPTER

THREE

ASTRID DIDN'T USUALLY employ the work *fuck* on a regular basis, but *oh holy fucking fuck*.

The woman from Wake Up.

The woman.

"H-h-hi," Astrid managed to say. She held out her hand. She had no clue what else to do.

The woman—Jordan Everwood—lifted a dark brow. Astrid held her breath, pasted on a smile. If there was anything she was great at doing, it was executing a convincing smile. She even let it reach her eyes.

"It's lovely to meet you," she added.

Jordan's mouth twitched, and Astrid knew she was doomed. She'd lose this job, she'd lose Natasha Rojas, lose her last bit of sanity when it came to her mother, all because of a few cups of coffee and a dress.

A goddamn *dress*.

She felt her throat thickening, which meant that on top of ruining her career in one go, she was also going to cry in front of this beautiful Everwood. No, make that all three beautiful Everwoods.

Astrid was just about to lower her hand when cool, calloused fingers slid over her palm.

"Oh, it's *lovely* to meet you too," Jordan said.

Astrid's belly swooped in relief. Jordan held onto her hand a bit longer than was necessary, but right now, Astrid would probably let this woman toss her into Bright River if she was so inclined.

"I'm so excited to get started," Astrid said once Jordan released her. "The Everwood Inn has long been a design dream of mine."

"Has it now?" Jordan asked, her voice dripping with sarcasm.

Astrid saw Simon shoot his sister a *what the hell* look, but Jordan ignored it. She was too busy watching Astrid with an unreadable expression. Mischief? Interest? Pure unadulterated evil? Astrid couldn't tell, but whatever it was, it made Astrid feel the need to vomit into the weed-riddled flower beds.

"It has," Astrid said, pushing forward. "I received the specs you sent me, Simon, but I haven't been inside the Everwood in some time."

"You've never stayed here?" Jordan asked, those expressive eyebrows lifted once again.

Astrid opened her mouth. Shut it again. She should be able to say yes, but Christ, this inn wasn't famous for its luxury. Looking up at it now, overgrown thorns from the rosebushes creeping up onto the porch, faded lace curtains in the century-old windows, it looked like something out of a horror movie.

"I—"

"She lives in Bright Falls, Jordan," Simon cut in, saving her. "She wouldn't need to stay at an inn in her own hometown."

Astrid smiled and nodded.

"Mmm" was all Jordan said in reply, earning another look from Simon.

"Well, I, for one, am thrilled about rejuvenating the inn," Simon said, clapping his hands together and beaming at Astrid. "Time to take this old relic into the twenty-first century, right, Grandma?"

Pru's eyes seemed to dim a bit, but she nodded. "Of course. Yes."

"Granted, we'll be doing it all on camera," Simon went on, "which should be interesting."

"Speaking of," Jordan said, chin-nodding toward the driveway.

Astrid turned to see two white vans crunching over the gravel, *Innside America* printed across the sides in a bold burgundy, the *I* of *Innside* in the shape of a turret. Her stomach flipped and flopped like it was the first day of school. The Everwoods—well, Pru and Simon— came to stand beside her, and she felt a strange sense of camaraderie as people spilled out of the vans. She felt Jordan hovering behind her somewhere, but she forced herself to breathe . . . smile.

There were seven people total, and most of them immediately went to the backs of the vans, pulling out equipment and slinging giant black bags over their shoulders.

Only two headed toward the Everwoods and Astrid, one of whom was Natasha Rojas.

She was magnificent.

That was the only word Astrid knew to describe her. Her brown skin glowed in the morning sunshine, and her long dark hair was pulled into a low side ponytail only so many people could pull off. She wore a long navy maxi dress and espadrilles, a few gold chains looped around her neck, one of which had a strange charm that looked like a double wishbone.

"Hello!" she called, waving and flipping her sunglasses onto her head. She glided toward their group as if on a cloud.

Okay, it was possible Astrid was a bit starstruck, but in her defense, Simon looked a bit dazed too.

"Hey, there," Simon said, reaching out a hand when Natasha got close. "Simon Everwood."

"Simon, it's so wonderful to meet you." Natasha clasped his hand in both of hers, then turned to Pru. "And this must be Pru Everwood. It's an honor. I've long admired your inn."

"Oh, thank you so much, dear," Pru said.

"And may I just say," Natasha said, "your glasses, that sweater." She held both of Pru's hands out, taking in her outfit. "Classic."

Pru beamed. "I try to keep up with these two," she said, elbowing Jordan, who had come up next to her grandmother.

"I can see that's a tall order," Natasha said, shaking Jordan's hand.

Astrid dutifully waited her turn, smoothing her black pants as surreptitiously as possible as Natasha turned toward her.

"That leaves our intrepid designer!" Natasha said.

"Yes, hi, Astrid Parker," Astrid said, proud when her voice came out smooth and even. Years of etiquette training as a girl—literally, there were lessons conducted by a pinched-mouthed woman named Mildred—had prepared her for moments like this. "I'm a huge fan of your work."

Natasha narrowed her eyes, but not in an unfriendly way. "I'm excited to see what you have in store for us, Astrid."

And with that, Natasha turned to the person standing next to her. "This is Emery, our brilliant producer."

"Hey, great to meet you all," Emery said. "They/them."

"Good to know," Jordan said, shaking Emery's hand. They were Black, with a halo of dark curls around their face, and wore jeans, a soft-looking green sweater, and rugged brown boots. "She/her." Jordan pointed to her chest.

"He/him," Simon said, grasping Emery's hand as well. "Nice to meet you."

Pru also shared her pronouns (she/her), as did Natasha (she/her). Astrid almost felt redundant when she smiled at Emery and said "she/her," which was ridiculous. A person's pronouns were their pronouns, but the storm in her belly had her questioning every word.

"Okay, so a few logistics," Emery said as crew members went in and out of the inn to search for the best lighting for the first scene, which would feature Astrid sharing her design plan with the Everwoods.

"We'll take a look around first, get acquainted with the space. At some point in the next few days, we want to shoot the Everwoods, Natasha, and Astrid meeting as if for the first time. I know it's tedious, but it's an important opener for the show."

"But that will be the only inauthentic scene," Natasha said. "After that, your goal is to act as though there aren't at least four people at any given time standing in the room with you, pointing lights and cameras in your face."

"Should be a piece of cake," Jordan said sardonically.

Natasha laughed. "It takes some getting used to, but just focus on your work, and you'll be fine. Don't worry about messing up. If you stumble over your words, just start over like you would in any situation. If you drop something, pick it up. We want real people doing real work here. Humor is a must. Plus, editing exists for a reason."

Astrid nodded along, her mind whirling. Humor was a must? She wasn't exactly known for her jokes. Oh, god, this was real. This was actually happening. And so quickly. She knew they were filming today, but after the morning she'd had, after *Jordan*, she'd kill for a few hours to regroup.

Hours she clearly wasn't going to get.

"Shall we take a quick tour while the crew sets up?" Natasha said, holding her arm out to Pru.

"Of course," Pru said, looping her hand around the inside of Natasha's elbow. The two of them started toward the house, Emery and Simon trailing behind them.

Astrid hung back for a second so her usual brisk walk wouldn't overtake them. Plus, she could use a second to get her thoughts organized, her emotions in check.

And there were a lot of emotions. The altercation outside Wake Up flashed in her mind again, threatening to overwhelm her. She couldn't believe her luck. Or lack of luck, rather. Of all people. Of all jobs. And now here was Natasha Rojas, looking every bit the gorgeous goddess

Astrid always knew she was, Emery all collected and cool, people dressed in black carrying cameras.

It was very nearly too much.

But Astrid could handle too much. She could handle anything. She had to.

She took in a slow, deep breath through her nose, just like Hilde, her therapist, had taught her. Held it in her lungs for four, released it over a count of eight. She was about to repeat the process, just one more time, when she realized Jordan had not moved toward the house with the crew and her family. Instead, she was leaning against her battered truck, arms folded over her chest.

"That helping?" she asked.

"Is what helping?" Astrid asked.

"The breathing."

Astrid sighed. "No, not really."

"I wonder why."

Astrid frowned, not sure what to say to that, but she knew she had other things she needed to say. Several things, in fact.

"Look," she started. "About this morning, I—"

"Yes, that was quite the experience."

Astrid's mouth hung open, her words cut off. She took a step closer to the woman, determined to get this apology out. If she didn't, her work would be compromised, as would her client relationship.

Her career.

Plus, it was just plain human decency to apologize for acting like a tyrant.

She forced herself to look Jordan Everwood in the eyes. The other woman was beautiful, there was no doubt. Had Astrid simply seen her on the street or sitting in a restaurant, she would've studied her, watched her move through the world, wondered about her life.

As it happened, their current situation was very different. Astrid noticed that Jordan's winged eyeliner from this morning was gone, smeared in fact, a bit of black streaking toward her temple. On her cheeks, there were a few tiny tracks of lighter skin, as though tears had carved a path through her makeup. Her lipstick was still perfect— a bold raspberry shade expertly applied to full lips—but the rest of her face seemed . . . tired. Worn.

A flood of guilt spilled into Astrid's chest. Had she actually made this woman cry?

Shit.

"I'm sorry," Astrid said before Jordan could stop her. "Truly, I acted abysmally this morning, and I won't offer up an excuse—"

"Oh, I'd love to hear it."

Astrid blinked. "Hear what?"

"The excuse." She flourished her hand as if to say *Please, do go on.*

Astrid's heart was solidly in her throat now. She tried swallowing a few times, but it didn't help all that much as paltry excuses rushed into her mind.

I was in a hurry.

That was my favorite dress.

I didn't get enough sleep last night.

Well, none of those would do. Not at all, no matter how true they might be.

Jordan's brows shot up. "Do you actually have one? Or do you just treat people like shit on any given day?"

"No, of course not. That's not what I—"

"Then you must have an excuse. Or are you only apologizing now because I'm your client?"

Astrid looked down and rubbed her forehead. Tears gathered in her throat. Again. Goddammit, how had this day gotten so far away from her? It was supposed to be perfect. It was supposed to be empowering and successful.

She gazed back up at Jordan, who regarded her patiently. Astrid let herself stare, searching for the right words when, suddenly, she didn't have to search. She knew the right words, her excuse—or rather, the reason for this whole horrible morning. It came so easily, words she'd never been able to say in the past year to her best friends, as though this woman's intent golden-green gaze just pulled truths out of her.

I'm terrified of failing.

I'm terrified of everything.

Jesus Christ. Astrid shook her head a little, swallowed down all the horrifying, embarrassing words that had swelled so suddenly into her chest.

Several seconds passed before she realized Jordan had taken a step closer to her, her crossed arms released, hands now stored in her overall pockets, her head tilted.

Astrid tucked her hair behind her ears, rolled her shoulders back. No way she could say *that* to this woman, but she had to say something. "I—"

"Jordie!" Simon called from the porch. "Can we get started already?"

Jordan blinked, took a step back. "Yeah. Yeah, absolutely. Sorry." Then she turned and hurried toward her family, leaving Astrid with a mouthful of worrying truths she was suddenly very glad she didn't get a chance to say.

CHAPTER

FOUR

JORDAN PRACTICALLY RAN up the steps, taking her place next to Simon. Emery, Natasha, and Pru meandered to the other side of the porch, discussing structure. Pru fiddled with a dying fern hanging from the ceiling, a deeper-than-normal crinkle between her eyes.

"So, Natasha seems great," Simon said.

"Yeah," Jordan said. "She's wearing a clit necklace, so I'd say she's pretty awesome."

Simon blinked. "She . . . what?"

Jordan motioned to her neck. "Her necklace. Looks like a funky wishbone? It's the clitoris."

"I . . . hadn't noticed."

Jordan smirked. "The clit, my darling brother, is something you really should notice."

He rolled his eyes and shuddered at the same time. "Can you never say *clit* to me again, baby sister? Thanks."

She laughed, but his eyes grew serious.

"What I did notice was some tension," he said.

"What are you going on about now?"

He nodded his chin toward Astrid, who was paused at the bottom of the steps, looking at something on her phone.

"You and Astrid. You know her?"

"No." She said it quickly, making her eyes wide and innocent. The decision to refrain from telling her brother and grandmother about how she and Astrid actually met seemed to make itself.

Well, *met* was a stretch.

She watched Astrid walking toward them now, her gait elegant and purposeful, perfectly poised. But a second ago, she hadn't been so put together. Not at all.

And Jordan . . . liked it.

The way Astrid had fumbled over her apology sparked something in Jordan. Interest, perhaps, a less-than-charitable desire to watch the woman sweat. Either way, she'd wanted to hear what excuse Astrid was about to reveal for her behavior. That glimmer in her eyes as the two of them had regarded each other, the way Astrid's mouth parted like she'd realized something earth-shattering, it was—

Jordan squeezed her eyes closed.

Intriguing.

That was all it was.

Astrid might be gorgeous—standing there under the morning sun in a tailored suit and looking like a younger Cate Blanchett, biting her full bottom lip in a way that made Jordan clench her legs together—but she wasn't a nice person. That much was clear, so her *attractiveness* was irrelevant.

Jordan certainly hadn't been immune to pretty women and nonbinary people since Meredith. She perceived them, just as she perceived the humidity in the air during a Savannah summer or that her coffee had gone cold. It was simply that, most of the time—aside from a single ill-fated one-night stand about six months ago—she felt nothing beyond observation, nor did she want to.

And she certainly didn't feel anything now.

Astrid climbed the steps, and Pru called her over to the plant cemetery. She slid by Jordan without a word or a glance, something Simon apparently noticed, because he pulled Jordan to the other side of the porch and picked at the peeling paint on the railing. A huge slice of wood came away in his hand.

"Jesus, this place is falling apart," he muttered.

"Hence the reno," she said, but she knew how he felt. Looking around at the once-lush yard, now practically barren, the one she used to bolt into every morning, picking roses for the guest rooms and searching for snails in the garden, her heart felt soft. Too tender.

"Look," Simon said, sighing heavily, "we need this to go well, okay?"

"Need what to go well?"

"The renovation. The redesign. Grandma's been worried about it, about the inn in general."

Jordan frowned. "What do you mean, Grandma's worried about it?"

He shook his head, but Jordan knew her brother.

"Simon," she asked, "what's going on?"

He sighed and raked a hand through his hair. So there was definitely something going on. Dread pooled in Jordan's gut.

"What is it?" she all but snapped when he did nothing but project angst at the peeling railing.

"Grandma didn't want to tell you. You've got enough on your plate."

Oh, for fuck's sake.

"Simon, I swear to god, if your tongue doesn't start spitting out some sense, I'm going rip it out."

He presented his palms. "Fine, fine, Jesus." He turned toward her, his voice low. "The inn's in trouble. Real trouble."

"Like . . . money?"

He nodded. "Guests have been few and far between for over a year now. Grandma's tired, Jordie. She owns the house outright, but without any revenue, she can't run the place. She doesn't want to lose the inn, but if something big doesn't change . . ."

"Hence the televised reno," she said.

"Hence the televised reno. Unfortunately, the network doesn't pay for the reno itself, so Grandma took out a huge loan to fund this whole thing, counting on the boost in business to make it all back and then some. If this doesn't go well, if we don't get a lot of eyes on this episode that'll bring in a shit ton of guests, then—"

"Fuck."

"Exactly."

She pressed a hand to her stomach, trying to keep her insides in place. "Why didn't you tell me?"

He gave her a look. "You know why, Jordie."

She clenched her teeth and turned away. Yes, fine, she'd been a bit off-kilter for the last year. Maybe she'd let a lot of things in her life go off track. What of it?

"You think I'm going to fuck it up," she said. It wasn't a question.

His mouth fell open, but no protestations fell from his lips. Not right away, at least. The words sat there between them for a good five seconds, a thundercloud ready to drop rain.

"That's not it," he finally said.

She sucked at her teeth as she gazed out into the side yard, a mess of overgrown flower beds and weeds.

"I just need you and Astrid to work together," he said. "Work well. She's the only design gig in town and Grandma likes her. Plus, she's good, so just—"

"Don't start any fires, is what you're saying."

He winced. That was exactly what he was saying, and they both knew it. He wanted her on this job, but only to a point, is what he was saying. They could joke about her cat eating her face, about how Jordan's life was a mess, but when it came down to it, her family was *worried*. They loved her, she knew that, but that didn't mean they believed in her talents.

"Got it," she said, then turned away before he could see the hurt in her eyes.

He reached for her hand, but she pushed off from the railing and headed toward their grandmother, looping her arm through hers. When Jordan spoke, she made damn sure her tone was laced with sugar and sunshine. "Let's go inside, shall we?"

Simon frowned at her, but she ignored him. More than that, she resisted the urge to present her middle finger, a feat she was very proud of in that moment. Pru patted her arm, and Jordan breathed in the older woman's scent, rosewater and mint, the smells of her childhood. She relaxed, just a little, and squeezed her grandmother closer. Jordan didn't want her to worry about anything, and dammit, she would not give her any reason to.

"Yes, I can't wait to see inside," Natasha said, then she gestured to a white woman with bright pink hair who had a large camera perched on her shoulder. "We want to get some footage of the tour to document what the inn looks like before the reno. This is Goldie. She'll be following us around a bit. But again, just act natural."

"Hi, all," Goldie said, and everyone offered their greeting. An Asian woman named Darcy came over and cleaned up Jordan's fucked-up eyeliner, then dusted powder all over her face. Jordan caught Astrid fidgeting, straightening her blazer, smoothing a hand over her hair.

Astrid's eyes met hers, her mouth parting in a split second of vulnerability before a poised mask dropped down over her lovely face. Jordan had the sudden urge to do something to yank it off again.

Once they were settled and Goldie gave them a thumbs-up, Simon opened the front door and a stale smell rushed out to greet them, like century-old wood and unused rooms, which was odd considering they'd only just closed to guests right before Jordan arrived last week.

Now she wondered if maybe they'd been closed a lot longer, and her family hadn't bothered telling her because she was oh-so-fragile.

"This entryway is breathtaking," Astrid said, gazing up at the vaulted ceiling.

And it was. The vestibule was dark and musty, granted, but the bones were incredible. It was a large space, the stairs spiraling to the second floor in front of them. Crimson-pink floral wallpaper covered the walls, meeting the deep cherry wood wainscoting rising up from original cherry floors. If you looked up, you could follow the staircase to a small balcony on the second floor that looked down on the vestibule.

Several floral couches and wingback chairs took up most of the living room, where the rest of the *Innside America* crew was currently setting up cameras and lighting. The parlor was to the left, now used as the concierge room, a huge oak desk equipped with an ancient computer and . . . god, was that a Rolodex?

Jordan knew her grandmother employed exactly two people to help her with the inn: Evelyn, a woman only about a decade younger than Pru herself, who handled all the booking and guest services, and Sarah, a woman in her fifties who acted as the cook-slash-housekeeper. There were only eight guest rooms upstairs, which was a huge number of bedrooms for a residential house, but not so many for an inn. The three of them had gotten along nicely for as long as Jordan could remember . . . but now, in light of Simon's revelation and looking at that sad Rolodex and dinosaur computer, she felt concern bloom in her chest.

"Now, we'll want to brighten this up," Astrid said, waving her hand across the foyer. "Make sure that the Everwood experience begins as soon as guests walk in the door." Her voice was perfectly calm. Elegant, even.

"Yes, I agree," Natasha said.

"Perfect," Simon said. "We know it's a little dark."

Everyone was playing their part just perfectly. Wasn't it all so nice?

"And what is the Everwood experience?" Jordan asked, eyeing Astrid. She folded her arms for extra effect.

Simon shot her a look, but it was a fair question. All renos had a vision—Jordan simply wanted to know Astrid's.

She tilted her head at Jordan and smiled. "Luxury."

"Everyone likes luxury," Simon said, clapping his sister a bit too hard on the back.

"I think so," Astrid said, her tone methodical, almost scientific. She began to circle the area. "These hardwood floors are beautiful and in pretty good shape, so I'd love to refinish them and replace any carpet throughout the house with a similar product. We'll remove the wallpaper, use a cool gray paint and bright white trim throughout."

"Gray paint and white trim?" Jordan said. "That's it?"

Astrid cleared her throat. "Of course not."

"Interesting," Natasha said, shooting a glance at Emery that Jordan couldn't parse. Emery simply lifted their brows.

"Okay, let's see the rest of the house, and then we'll all sit down in the living room to go over the design," Natasha said.

Goldie trailed them through the dark and cluttered kitchen, the one guest room on the main floor that had literal cobwebs in the corners, the upstairs rooms, including the famously haunted Lapis Room, where Alice Everwood's ghost purportedly still resided. And all the while, Astrid talked of white this and gray that, so that by the time they all came into the living room to look at her actual design plan, Jordan already knew she was going to hate it.

"I'm so excited to show you what I've come up with," Astrid said, once they were back downstairs. She took an iPad out of her fancy bag and tapped its leather cover.

"Oh, goodie," Jordan said.

Simon muttered something that sounded suspiciously like *Jesus*

Christ under his breath as they all headed into the living room and sat in the musty chairs circling the coffee table. Astrid set her iPad on the surface, carefully pushing aside some ancient *Better Homes and Gardens* magazines, and tapped a few things on the screen. Emery chatted with the crew, and they all fiddled with lighting and angles for a few minutes while Astrid and the Everwoods waited. Jordan pulled one leg up on the chair she was in, bouncing her knee. Every now and then she and Astrid would lock eyes, but it never lasted long.

Pru placed a calming hand on Jordan's undulating leg. Jordan stopped immediately, and Pru winked at her. Jordan took a deep breath, trying to focus on her grandmother's happiness. Simon was right—this had to go well. They couldn't lose the Everwood.

"Okay, we're all set," Emery said. "Whenever you're ready, Astrid."

She nodded, and opened an interior design app Jordan recognized from her time with Dalloway and Daughters on her iPad.

"Okay, based on the ideas Simon and I discussed"—here Jordan shot Simon a *What the fuck* look, one she very much hoped Natasha didn't notice—"this is what I had in mind for this floor." Astrid handed the device to Pru.

"Here we'll throw the design onto the viewers' screen, just so you know," Emery said.

Astrid nodded, and both Jordan and Simon stood to hover over their grandmother, who clearly didn't have much of an idea of what to do with the iPad. Jordan knelt beside her and helped her zoom in and out and rotate the 3D images of the rooms, seeing them from all angles.

They might as well have been exploring the Pottery Barn website. Everything was white and gray, textured with rough woods, stripes, a random floral print throw pillow here and there. There were subway tiles in the kitchen, white-and-gray marble counters, stainless steel appliances. Modern Farmhouse, Jordan knew the style was called. It was luxurious and classic all at once. It was lovely.

But it wasn't the Everwood.

The Everwood was eaves and secrets, wavy glass and copper pots, cozy nights spent in front of a fire, walls of dark wood bookcases all around. Jordan took in a slow breath, trying to keep Simon's words from earlier at the forefront of her mind.

"Wow," Simon said. Jordan waited for him to go on, but he didn't. He just gazed at the images on the iPad, his hand covering his mouth as though in deep thought over the accent wall in the dining room. White shiplap, oh how original.

"You asked for this?" Jordan finally said, glaring at Simon.

He reared back. "We have to modernize, Jordie. 'Creepy haunted house' isn't cutting it anymore in this day and age."

Jordan saw Astrid glance at the crew, but Emery rotated their forefinger, a clear sign to keep going.

"I'm not saying it is, but this isn't us," Jordan said.

"It's what we *need* to be," he said. "To compete."

She shook her head, boggled at his attitude. This design didn't modernize the Everwood. It didn't update it. It flung it into metamorphosis, transforming it into something Jordan didn't even recognize.

"Grandma, what do you think?" she asked.

"Ah," Pru said. "This is . . ."

The older woman frowned. Blinked. Jordan felt relief rising up in her. Her grandmother didn't like it. She could tell from the way her brows were shoved together, her red-lipsticked mouth pursed.

"This is lovely," Pru finally said.

"What?" Jordan said. Blurted, really. Simon shot her yet another look. Jordan shot him one back, one that she hoped said, *Are you fucking serious right now?*

Apparently, though, he was. He squeezed their grandmother's shoulder and said, "It's very modern."

"It is that," Natasha said, and Jordan met her eye. There was something there, some question, but Jordan couldn't tell what the hell their host was thinking.

"It's very calming," Natasha added. "Spa-like, which a lot of inn-goers are looking for."

"Luxury," Astrid said, nodding at Natasha.

Pru nodded, her mouth pressed flat.

Fuck my life, Jordan thought.

"I can make any adjustments you'd like, of course," Astrid said, motioning toward the iPad. "These are just preliminary ideas. As we move forward, I'd love your involvement in choosing fabrics, furniture pieces, appliances, and the like."

"Of course, dear," Pru said. "Though I'm sure whatever you pick will be wonderful."

Jordan opened her mouth to protest—this was *not* her grandmother. Her grandmother was highly involved in every aspect of the inn. Always had been. It was her baby, after all, her *life*.

This wasn't right. None of this felt right.

Jordan placed her hand on Pru's arm. "Grandma—"

"How about we see the plan for some guest rooms," Simon said. He didn't even bother to level Jordan with a look this time. He simply didn't look at her at all while their family home dissolved into a Crate-and-fucking-Barrel.

Jordan kept her mouth shut as the rest of the design plans flipped by in a blur of white and gray, porcelain and glass. After all, that was clearly what her family wanted from her, even if the design, lovely and modern and bright as it might be, was horribly wrong for the Everwood. But at the end of the day, what did she know? She was simply an out-of-work carpenter with a penchant for setting things on fire.

CHAPTER FIVE

FINALLY, THE CAMERAS shut off, the lights went down, and Emery declared they were done for the day.

Astrid was sweating, her pits like a Florida swamp. She just hoped that no one could tell. She wiped at her forehead, taking her time putting her iPad into her bag. Everyone around her stood up, chatting about plans for the rest of the afternoon, but she needed a minute.

She needed days.

Granted, the sooner she got out of here, the sooner she could fall onto her couch with a bottle of wine. She wasn't even sure she needed the glass.

"Demo starts on Wednesday, people," Emery called out. "Lots to do before then, including cleanout with the family on Monday."

As the crew gathered to discuss details, Astrid couldn't help but think this was all so surreal, everything edged with a dreamlike haze. Granted, Jordan Everwood and her clear dislike—hate?—for Astrid's design wasn't helping.

No one had ever hated her designs before. True, the Everwood was unlike any home she'd ever worked on. Most of her clients were of her mother's ilk, and they wanted their spaces to reflect what they saw in magazines and on TV. They wanted Reese Witherspoon's living room and Nicole Kidman's bedroom.

Luxurious. Bright. Modern.

Astrid had always delivered. She'd grown up in that exact kind of house, after all, decorated by Lindy Westbrook herself. But more importantly, this style was what Simon and Pru wanted. Jordan could just shut up and build the cabinets.

Astrid winced at the uncharitable thought, but honestly, she was running out of steam here, and quickly. She stood up and swung her bag over her shoulder. She was heading toward Pru to say goodbye when Natasha called her name.

"Astrid. Jordan. Could we have a moment?" the host said, nodding her head toward where she and Emery were standing next to the truly heinous fireplace, all brass and soot stains.

"Yes, of course," Astrid said, walking their way. She felt Jordan behind her and braced herself.

"What's up?" Jordan said, spreading her legs wide and folding her arms. Jesus, the woman exuded confidence. Astrid would adjust her posture, but she knew it was already ramrod straight.

"So," Natasha said, smiling at the two of them, "how do you feel about the first shoot?"

"Fine," Astrid said automatically, because she certainly wasn't going to say what she was really thinking, which was somewhere along the lines of *shit show*.

Jordan, however, had no such reservations. "Meh," she said.

"Tell me more about that," Natasha said, and Jordan laughed.

"Okay, Dr. Rojas."

Astrid clenched her jaw, the familiarity in Jordan's tone setting her on edge. This was *Natasha Rojas*, for god's sake.

But Natasha just laughed back. "Nothing wrong with therapy."

Jordan held out her fist for a bump, and Natasha happily reciprocated.

Astrid's jaw tightened again. She'd be sleeping in her mouth guard tonight, no doubt.

"The design isn't what I expected," Jordan said when all the warm and fuzzy camaraderie was finished.

"You don't like it," Natasha said.

"No," Jordan said, glancing sideways at Astrid. "I don't."

Astrid's fingers tightened on her bag. If she were a rubber band, she would've snapped into several pieces by now.

"It's what Pru and Simon asked for," she said firmly.

"Am I not also an Everwood?" Jordan asked.

Astrid met her eyes then. Searched for some softness, but she didn't find it. All business it was, then. "Yes, but you're not the one who signed my advance check, nor, I'm assuming, the one who will sign my final check when all is said and done."

Jordan's mouth dropped open, her tongue popping out to lick at her full lower lip. Astrid had to force herself not to follow its path. She turned back to Natasha, who was watching them both with a hand over her mouth and—Astrid frowned—a *delighted* expression in her eyes.

"This is perfect," Natasha said, then slapped Emery's arm gently. "Don't you think this is perfect?"

"Perfect," Emery said, their light brown eyes all but glowing. "This will make for very interesting television."

"Sorry," Astrid said, shaking her head. "What?"

Natasha waved her hand between Astrid and Jordan. "This tension between you. This . . . shall we say, light enmity? It's gorgeous."

"Gorgeous." Astrid could only blink.

Natasha nodded, then pressed her hands together like she was praying. "I pride myself on authenticity. I don't like to fabricate emotions on screen, and I won't censor my own from this point forward. But . . . well, we're running a show here. And conflict sells."

"Meaning . . ." Jordan said, a question in her tone.

"Meaning don't hold back," Natasha said. "Feel what you feel. I would say play up this tension, even, but that's up to you. It sounds like there might be enough here already to make this whole process very intriguing. Lead carpenter—an Everwood, no less—and lead designer at odds."

"We're not at odds," Astrid said.

"It's delicious," Natasha said, apparently ignoring Astrid's protest. "All I'm saying is lean into it."

Bile rose up Astrid's throat. This could not be happening. This was not how she conducted business. She went in, did her job, and got out. She didn't engage in drama. She barely let her emotions into a project at all. They clouded judgment and had no place in a professional relationship.

"Look," she said, ready to explain why this was absolutely not going to work for her. "I don't think—"

"I'm in," Jordan said, shooting Astrid a sideways glance. "Let's do this."

THAT EVENING, ASTRID had barely locked up the Bright Design offices at promptly five o'clock when her phone started buzzing with texts in the group chat.

> Stella's, anyone? Jillian and I are already here.

Iris. Of course it was Iris, beckoning them to Bright Falls's only bar for a night of bad country music and beer.

I'm in, Claire texted. Plus we need to hear about Astrid's big day!

As long as there's bourbon, Delilah chimed in.

Of course there's bourbon, baby, Claire said.

You say that like it's a matter of course, but I distinctly recall Stella's running out of Bulleit back in October, Delilah said. It was a dark day.

BYOB, Del, Iris said.

To a bar? Delilah asked. The audacity.

Claire sent a laugh-crying emoji while Astrid watched the words fill up her screen. She knew her friends wanted to see her, wanted to know how the shoot and meeting Natasha Rojas went, but as she dug into her bag for her keys, the idea of sitting in a noisy bar and reliving her shitty day word for word—particularly that the coffee woman ended up being Jordan Everwood—felt like an anvil on her chest.

She got into her car and started her drive home without replying. She had to think of how to play this, because if she hinted at how awful she was feeling right now, all three women would land themselves in Astrid's living room before she could even chuck her heels off her sore feet.

By the time she made it through her front door and flipped on a few lamps, her phone was vibrating almost incessantly in her bag.

Astrid?

Are you on your way?

I'll order you a Riesling!

Astrid?

ASS.

She sighed, her thumbs poised over the keyboard. Exhaustion? Iris would never let her get away with that. Period cramps . . . no, she could almost feel Iris shoving a few ibuprofen into her hands.

Migraine. That could work. She'd never had one before, but if any day was going to bring on searing pain behind her eyes, it was today.

I think I've got my first migraine, she typed out before she could overthink it.

Oh no! Claire immediately replied.

So it went badly? Delilah said, because of course she saw through Astrid like a sheet of cellophane.

It was fine, Astrid said. I just need some quiet and a dark room.

Boring, Iris said.

Ris, Jesus, Claire texted back.

Sorry, Iris said. Need anything?

Astrid quickly tapped out a serene No thank you and then turned her phone off before they could text her back. She wasn't completely lying. Her head *was* pounding and her dark living room, complete with its brain-quieting neutral tones, seemed to beckon her like heaven's pearly gates.

After changing into a tank top and a pair of yoga pants, she poured herself a glass of white wine and settled on her couch, exhaling as her body sank into the cushions. The day settled with her, everything that happened spilling into her chest, thick and uncomfortable. She replayed the events over and over again, from Jordan's horrified expression this morning as Astrid lit into her outside the coffee shop to the woman's clear disdain for Astrid's work.

She lingered there for too long—Jordan's rolling eyes, her pursed mouth at Astrid's design, the way her lean but toned biceps flexed when she folded her arms across her chest.

Astrid shook her head, hoping to clear Jordan out of her thoughts, but everything Astrid should have done differently flipped through her brain like a gag reel, failure after failure. Her chest tightened even more, that familiar panicky feeling she first experienced as a ten-year-old trying to get her grief-stricken mother to smile.

Trying, and failing.

She rolled her shoulders back. Lifted her chin. She just needed to focus. She dug her laptop out of her bag and opened it up, the light from the screen filling the room like an unwelcome ghost. She clicked into her email, ready to answer all the messages that surely had poured in throughout the day while she'd pored over her Everwood designs.

She blinked at the lone new email in her inbox.

One.

And it was from her mother.

Business hadn't been great lately. She could admit that—or, she could admit it to the quiet of her own mind—but this was getting dire. She was used to at least twenty emails a day, contractors asking about her next project, potential clients inquiring about their drab living rooms, current clients linking Pinterest mood boards and sending photos of some antique candleholder they spotted at the flea market in Sotheby.

She slumped back onto the cushions, panic and something else clouding into her chest. She exhaled, closed her eyes. Relief. That's what it was. Which couldn't be right, because she loved work. Thrived on it. These days, aside from her blissfully in-love best friends, work was all she had.

She sat up and fixed her posture, determined to spend the night hunting for potential projects she could pitch, when she spotted her mother's email again. The subject line read "Interesting."

Dread quickly replaced every other emotion.

She took another sip of wine—no, two—just to steel herself. Maybe it was a possible job. Maybe it was a link to a dress her mother thought would look good on Astrid. Maybe . . .

She opened the message, ready to get this over with. The message said nothing, but it did contain a single blue-underlined link. She clicked on it and a photo bloomed onto the screen, so large and in such high definition, Astrid's entire body shot back in alarm.

"Jesus," she said to her empty house as she stared at a white man with perfect teeth, golden hair, and a crisp blue button-down. He was standing next to a blond white woman who had clearly undergone just as much expensive orthodontia in her youth. Her hair shone in soft waves around her pristinely made-up face, blue eyes like a summer sky. Astrid couldn't tell where her ex-fiancé was, exactly—a restaurant, perhaps, or maybe a vineyard—but the familiar rock on the woman's left hand was crystal clear.

This time last year, that same diamond had sparkled on Astrid's own hand.

The photo sat at the top of an article in the Lifestyle section of the *Seattle Times*, a collection of text beneath it.

> Few people understand the travails of true love better than
> thirty-three-year-old Dr. Spencer Hale. After enduring a
> crushing breakup with one Astrid Parker of Bright Falls,
> Oregon, Dr. Hale fled to Seattle to tend to his broken heart.
> "I came here to heal," Dr. Hale said. "I didn't expect to
> discover what true love actually was."

Astrid felt all the color drain from her face. Her wine sloshed in her empty stomach, an acidic mix threatening to come right back up. She knew she should slam her laptop shut. Get up. Go take a bath. Better yet, get her ass to Stella's and maybe do a few shots of hard liquor for the first time in her life. She should not, under any circumstances, continue reading this article. And Astrid was very, very good at doing what she should.

Usually.

Her fingers scrolled on the track pad, revealing more of Dr. Hale's journey to everlasting love.

> Dr. Hale, a successful dentist in Capitol Hill, met his
> bride-to-be on a blustery day in September, when Amelia
> Ryland (24) walked into his office in need of a cleaning.

"Her teeth were perfect," Dr. Hale said, laughing as he wrapped his arm around Ms. Ryland. "I should've known right then she was the one for me."

After the couple weds in June, Ms. Ryland, a recent graduate of Vassar equipped with a family fortune that rivals the Vanderbilts', plans to volunteer and prepare for the couple's already budding family—

Astrid finally slapped her computer closed. She was breathing so heavily she could feel her nostrils flaring.

. . . discover what true love actually was.

. . . already budding family.

She poured more wine, but then just held the glass in her hand, unable to choke it down as she tried to parse her feelings. She wanted to observe Spencer's new fiancée in all her poreless skin and perfect-lipstick beauty, and feel nothing but a wave of relief that the woman in the picture wasn't Astrid herself.

She *wanted* to feel nothing so badly.

But she didn't. She felt something. A lot of somethings, in fact. Regret, thank god, wasn't one of them. She didn't envy Spencer's fiancée either. In fact, she felt a tiny twinge of worry over the woman's future—Spencer was the worst kind of controlling asshole, gaslighting and smiling his way through his relationships. So, no, she didn't envy this woman.

Still, her heart and mind weren't blank slates when she thought of Spencer. They weren't impartial observers. As Astrid sat in her dark living room, thinking about how her lone email of the day was from her own mother, bearing news of her ex-fiancé's blissful happiness with another woman, she tried to figure out why.

Or, rather, she tried to *ignore* the reason why. Because she knew. Oh, she knew all too well this feeling of inadequacy, this constant push in her chest to be more, make the right choices, land the big account, marry the right man.

Interesting, her mother had said of Spencer's news. But as Astrid opened up her laptop again, closing out of the article and starting a search for recent real estate sales in the area, she knew that's not what her mother truly wanted to say at all.

———

THAT SUNDAY, ASTRID stood in front of Wisteria House, the purple flowers that had earned her childhood home its name curling over the terra-cotta brick. Funny, how something as simple as walking through a door could feel extremely complicated, a web of knots she wasn't sure she would ever untangle. She would worry her mother was watching her pace on the front walk, but that wasn't Isabel's style. Isabel Parker-Green didn't seek anyone out. People came to her.

Astrid rolled her shoulders back, put a heeled foot on the bottom step. She could do this. It was brunch, for god's sake, not a root canal, though the two seemed to conflate in the dread pooling in her gut.

She put her foot back down on the sidewalk.

Taking out her phone, she texted the only person she could think of who would understand her ridiculous predicament right now.

Tell me how you do this again? she tapped out to Delilah.

Do what? Delilah wrote back immediately.

Walk into our house.

Oh, that. Easy. I try very hard not to.

Astrid huffed a breath. But if you had to.

Those three little dots bounced on the screen. Disappeared. Then resurfaced again before a bourbon emoji popped up, followed by the wine emoji, then the martini emoji, and finally, the beer emoji.

You hate beer, Astrid texted.

Desperate times.

Astrid nearly cracked a smile. I don't exactly have a flask in my bag.

I'd suggest getting one.

You're not exactly helping.

orders you a flask

Astrid laughed. Oddly, this bizarre conversation *was* helping a little. Her chest felt a tiny bit looser—loose enough to get a deep breath and put her foot back on the bottom step at least.

Baby steps.

Claire wants to know if you need us to come over, Delilah texted.

Astrid smiled. Leave it to Claire to offer reinforcement for Astrid's long-standing Sunday brunch with her mother. For a second, Astrid considered it. She hated that interactions with her mother had become this convoluted. After Astrid called off her wedding last June—a wedding Isabel had poured tens of thousands of dollars into and invited everyone on god's green earth she'd ever rubbed rich elbows with—their relationship had gone from companionable to frigid and cordial.

Because Isabel Parker-Green was nothing if not polite, even to her disappointing daughter.

That's okay, Astrid texted back. She certainly didn't want to subject her best friend to this horror. She didn't even want Delilah to have to deal with it, and she barely liked Delilah.

Tell Claire thanks anyway, she typed.

Tits up, Delilah texted back.

Astrid rolled her eyes as she tucked her phone back into her bag, but she found herself actually sticking out her chest a little as she climbed the steps and all but flung herself into the house in one hurried motion.

Inside, the house was quiet and freezing cold, as always, the lavender-slash-bleach scent and white walls weirdly comforting and disarming at the same time. She meandered into the huge kitchen, all gleaming white and stainless steel, before spotting her mother on the back deck, fake-blond bob shining under the late morning sun as she sipped a golden mimosa.

"You're late" were the first words out of her mouth when Astrid stepped outside.

"Sorry," Astrid said, sliding into a chair across from Isabel. A full mimosa awaited her—thank god—and an incredible spread of eggs Benedict, fresh fruit, and buttery croissants Isabel would never eat in a million years.

"Work kept you?" Isabel asked, pouring herself some coffee from a stainless steel carafe.

"Yes," Astrid lied. "It's been busy lately." Another lie. Though she had spent the entirety of her Saturday dissecting her design for the Everwood, searching for the flaws. *Something* in her plans had caused Jordan Everwood to frown and huff the way she had, but damned if Astrid could find it. Her current mockups were exactly what Pru and Simon had asked for. Clean. Modern. Elegant. Exactly what Astrid excelled at.

She glanced around, through the French doors that led back inside, taking in all the *modern* and *elegant* in her mother's home. For a split second, a splinter of doubt worked its way under her skin— that sudden panicked feeling she got sometimes even in her own *modern* and *elegant* house, like she'd suddenly been dropped into a life she didn't recognize—but she flicked the feeling away.

"Oh, I'm sure," Isabel said, sitting back in her chair. She had on a huge pair of sunglasses, which was unnerving because Astrid couldn't tell if she was being scrutinized or not.

Better to assume that she was and act accordingly.

"Lots of projects going on?" Isabel asked.

Astrid sipped her mimosa politely. "Quite a few," she said, nodding vigorously. "Interesting designs."

Isabel's lips pursed. "Or is it just one project, which you seemed to have started off by publicly humiliating the client's beloved granddaughter in the middle of downtown?"

Astrid froze, champagne flute cold against her mouth. Goddamn small towns. Her mother had spies everywhere.

Isabel sighed and spooned a heap of brightly colored berries onto her plate. "Astrid."

There it was. The labored sigh paired with her name, which always indicated some calmly delivered dressing down was forthcoming, disguised cleverly in motherly concern.

"You know I want what's best for you," Isabel said.

"Of course," Astrid replied, as was their custom. She kept her face impassive, but inside, her stomach felt like a writhing pit of snakes.

"If you want to be taken seriously, you have to act seriously."

Nod.

"Screaming at another person in public is never appropriate, I don't care what the little urchin did to deserve it."

"I understand that." Astrid reached for a croissant, Isabel's eyes following her hand's journey. Astrid dropped the bread on her plate.

"I've known Pru Everwood for a long time," Isabel went on. "Her grandchildren—twins, I believe they are—were notoriously unkempt when they were here during the summers, running around barefoot with tangled hair and dirt under their fingernails."

Oh no, not tangled hair and dirt.

Astrid took another demure sip of her drink. She didn't remember Jordan and Simon at all from her childhood, but that wasn't a surprise. The way Isabel spoke of them now, with a curl to her lip and disdain lacing her voice, there was little chance of her mother letting her play with anyone who might neglect to slip on a pair of shoes before leaving the house.

"Be that as it may," Isabel went on, taking a squirrel-like bite of a strawberry, "your behavior reflects on your business and it reflects on me. I don't have to tell you that this project is important. This could make or break you. I expect better and so should you."

Wait for it . . .

"Particularly after last year's unpleasantness. You can't afford to lose the Everwood job, and we both know it."

Isabel leaned across the table and patted Astrid's hand. On her way back, she slid the croissant from Astrid's plate back onto the serving dish.

"Lindy built that company with her own two hands," her mother went on, and Astrid fought an eye roll. Lindy Westbrook was one of her mother's dearest friends, if Isabel was truly capable of friendship, which Astrid doubted.

Regardless, when Lindy, at the age of fifty-one, decided to leave the business to pursue other real estate ventures with her fourth husband up and down the western seaboard, Astrid had just returned from college with a shiny new degree in business administration. Before Astrid even knew what was happening, she'd agreed to step in to run Bright Designs. She was a twenty-two-year-old millennial, so at the time, she'd felt nothing but gratitude that she had a job, and an interesting one at that. She liked interior design. Seemed to be decent at it, if her first few weeks working alongside Lindy were any proof, and had a good head for details and organization.

She also knew how to smile prettily and please a client, which, as Lindy told her more than once, was half the battle.

So she'd smiled. She'd pleased. She'd kept the business afloat, and whenever Lindy glided back into town with her chic silver hair and power suits, the older woman seemed happy with Astrid's work, with her clientele and design plans, most of them extremely *modern* and *elegant*.

Officially, Lindy no longer owned any part of the business, but that didn't mean she wasn't a legacy. Her approval, Isabel said, was important, even though Astrid owned forty-nine percent of Bright Designs.

Isabel, of course, owned the other fifty-one percent. While Astrid could've afforded to buy the company outright at twenty-two with a bit of finagled paperwork—she had money in a trust, left to her by her dead father, but which Isabel had made sure wasn't fully hers until she turned thirty-five—her mother claimed she wanted to help.

"I can provide some cushion while you get your feet wet" is what Isabel had said at the time. "No need to dip into your nest egg unless you really need to."

Of course, Astrid soon learned it was just another way for Isabel to maintain control over her life. But Astrid was fresh out of college. She was new at running a business. And Isabel was her mother, her only parent for most of her life. She wanted to please her. She wanted Isabel to smile at her, put her arm around her shoulders and squeeze.

She still did, if she was being honest.

"The Everwood Inn is a national treasure," Isabel said now. "And it's in trouble, so if you were the one to help—"

"What do you mean 'it's in trouble'?"

Isabel lifted a single brow—a skill Astrid did not inherit—and pursed her lips. Her mother didn't like being interrupted, and Astrid suddenly felt like she was eight years old undergoing etiquette lessons.

"Sorry," Astrid said. "I didn't know the Everwood was having problems."

Isabel nodded. "Business is bad, from what I've heard. Pru closed it down a month ago."

Astrid blinked. "I had no idea."

"You can see why success is so integral here. Bright Falls doesn't want to lose the Everwood to some hotel chain or a family who won't honor its history. It's part of the town's legacy. Bright Designs needs to be the one to help save it. Don't throw away this opportunity for the life you were meant to lead over a brief moment of temper."

Astrid just nodded and drained her mimosa, the bubbles burning her throat on the way down. *The life you were meant to lead* was one of her mother's favorite catchphrases. The words had always filled Astrid with a sense of purpose, of destiny, but lately, they just made her sort through every major point in her life and wonder, *When the hell did I choose that?*

"So tell me," Isabel said, finally slipping off her sunglasses and smiling at her daughter expectantly, as though she hadn't just served up all of Astrid's past failures and current expectations on a platter and invited her to dig in. "Did you see the article I sent you about Spencer? Quite interesting, if you ask me. Amelia Ryland is lovely, isn't she? You do know what sort of Ryland she is, don't you? As in Ryland drug stores? So much money in that family, it's frightening. I believe Amelia herself is . . ."

Astrid tuned out the rest of her mother's words about Amelia's charms, grabbed the croissant before Isabel could blink, and took a huge, incredibly unladylike bite.

CHAPTER SIX

JORDAN KNEW THAT preparing a house for demolition was nearly as labor-intensive as the demolition itself, except this particular work was filled with wandering through countless memories, deciding what to keep and what to give away, all with an eighty-year-old woman who decidedly did not want to give away anything.

And a full camera crew.

It was just the family on this Monday morning, along with Emery, Goldie behind the camera, and Patrick working lighting for this scene. Natasha was in the house but working on her laptop in the kitchen. Astrid, blessedly, wasn't here at all.

"I can't sell this wardrobe," Pru said as she, Jordan, and Simon stood in the famous Lapis Room, cameras and lights pointed in their direction. The show didn't plan on filming the clean-out process of every room, but they sure as hell would for this one. "It's original to the house."

"It's also really ugly, Grandma," Simon said.

Jordan backhanded him on the chest, even though he was right. The piece looked like something out of *Beauty and the Beast* that might spring into song at any moment. It towered above even Simon, who was a good six feet two, and sported several embellishments over its solid oak surface, including but not limited to curling patterns that Jordan thought were supposed to resemble leaves, and a giant lion's head at the top that seemed to survey their conversation with obvious disdain.

"It belonged to Alice Everwood," Pru said, caressing the piece's creaky door. "And when—"

"—news came of her lover's betrayal," Simon said, "she closed herself inside this very armoire and refused to come out for three days. We know, Grandma. But we can't keep every ghostly relic if you want to modernize."

"So we don't modernize," Jordan said.

Simon shot her a look that could cut through a soda can.

"Good," Emery said softly from off camera. "Really great stuff, everyone, keep it up."

"What?" Jordan said, looking at her brother, not missing a beat. The cameras everywhere were strange, but she found what Natasha said to be true—focus on the work, and everything would be fine. In this case, the *work* just happened to be annoying the shit out of her brother. "This is history, Simon."

"It's a sad story," he said. "That's it."

Alice Everwood was the daughter of the original owners of the Everwood house, James and Opal. She was also the Blue Lady, the infamous ghost of the inn, who, when she found out that her beloved—most likely some privileged asshole who simply wanted to get underneath her petticoat before his own parents married him off to someone richer—was set to marry another, she never left the house again, and always wore a stone of deep blue lapis lazuli around her neck. She was eighteen then and ended up dying of tuberculosis at the tender age of twenty-three, but most of Bright Falls agreed she really died of a broken heart.

Sweat beaded on Jordan's upper lip, the similarities between herself and Alice Everwood suddenly washing over her. They'd both been left alone by those they loved the most. They were both heartbroken. They were both reclusive. At least, Jordan had been a mere two weeks ago, her Savannah house like a tomb for empty Ben & Jerry's cartons and moldering pizza boxes. Granted, Jordan hadn't locked herself in a wardrobe, but who knows what sort of measures she might have resorted to had Simon not dragged her ass to Oregon.

Jordan reached out to touch the wardrobe. As soon as her fingertips met wood, a little zing of electricity sparked between them.

"Shit, ouch," she said, yanking her hand back. "Sorry," she said, wincing in Emery's direction.

They laughed. "Don't worry about it."

"See?" Pru said, waving toward the monstrosity, apparently oblivious to their audience. "Alice doesn't want this taken."

"Grandma, be serious," Simon said.

Their grandmother looked affronted. "I'm always serious about Alice Everwood."

Since Alice's death in 1934, there had been . . . occurrences—noises in this very bedroom, like bare feet sliding over the hardwoods, the wardrobe door opening and closing in the middle of the night, and a very shut and very locked window somehow ending up wide open by morning. Word was, Alice liked fresh air and gazing at the stars, mooning over her lost love.

Alice's history and her alleged haunting were more than just a sad story. They were the bread and butter of Jordan's and Simon's childhood. For him to be fine with sweeping it all away now was nearly unforgivable.

Now more so than ever.

Pru sighed and glanced up at the wardrobe. "I guess I could see if Bright Falls's historical society wants it."

"Grandma, you can't give away Alice's wardrobe," Jordan said.

"What will she . . . I mean she . . . she *opens* that thing. Or something. She needs it."

"'Or something?'" Simon asked. "Jordan, come on."

But Jordan couldn't budge on this one. The Everwood wasn't the Everwood without the Blue Lady. Alice was the heart of his place. She was half the reason anyone came to stay here anyway, and the entire reason for *Innside America*'s interest in the first place. Sure, this room—all the rooms, to be honest—was outdated and gaudy with its heavy velvet-and-fringe drapes and giant four-poster bed, ugly furniture, and eye-gouging floral wallpaper, but removing all remnants of history was not the answer.

Gray paint and fucking subway tiles were not the answer.

"Jordan," Simon said softly. "This is happening. Okay?"

Jordan ignored him and focused instead on her grandmother. "You really think this is the way to go?"

Pru's mouth dropped open, but no answer came. She gazed up at the wardrobe, then around the room in general. Jordan could swear she saw a bit of shine in her eyes, but then her shoulders seemed to tighten and she nodded.

"Yes," Pru said. "Your brother's right, honey. I know it's hard, but we need to get this place up to modern snuff. I have to learn to let go, and so do you."

She didn't want to upset her grandmother if this was what she really wanted, but deep down, Jordan knew this wasn't the way.

Plus, Natasha had said lean into it, right? Emery had said that her defiance—if Jordan read between the lines a little—was what made interesting TV. And interesting TV could save the Everwood.

"We can update and modernize without erasing everything the Everwood stands for," she said. "Let me have the wardrobe. I'll refinish it. Rework it to fit what"—here she nearly choked on the name, but pressed on when she noticed Emery throwing her a very surreptitious thumbs-up—"Astrid has planned."

"Jordan," her brother said, "we can't rework every single—"

"Okay," Pru said, cutting Simon off with a gentle pat on his arm. "Let's see what you can come up with."

Jordan let out a breath. "Thank you." She stuck a blue sticky note on the wardrobe, indicating to the movers coming tomorrow that they were keeping this piece. She'd have them move it out to the dusty shed behind the carriage house she'd already started cleaning out to be her workshop.

As they continued to meander through the house, labeling things with different-colored sticky notes, Jordan pressed a blue one on more things than not.

"Your workshop isn't the Louvre," Simon said when she affixed a note to an antique desk in the master bedroom, a truly atrocious oak beast. "It'll only fit so much."

She simply stuck her tongue out at him, a plan slowly coalescing in her brain.

She was lead carpenter, and she was not going to let Astrid-fucking-Parker, or even her own family, ruin the only place she'd ever been truly happy.

Natasha and Emery wanted tension?

She would give them some goddamn tension.

CHAPTER
SEVEN

TUESDAY MORNING, ASTRID found herself piling into an *Innside America* van with Natasha, Emery, Regina from the crew to run the camera, and Jordan, heading to the flea market in Sotheby to film some local shopping before demo would get fully underway the next day. She knew the flea market wouldn't have anything she wanted to use in her design—while always packed with lots of interesting antiques, the market wasn't exactly Astrid's style—but Natasha always liked to pull in some local shops and artisans for the show.

Astrid was prepared for this. She'd been prepared for this scene from the moment Pru called her about being the lead designer. But now, with her style clashing with Jordan's and this new tension theme Natasha was pushing, she had no clue what to expect.

Once they arrived, Regina hoisted a camera on her shoulder, Emery carried the boom mic, and Natasha simply shoved Astrid and Jordan into the fray and said, "Go get 'em." No direction, nothing.

Jordan, dressed in a pair of gray jeans and a fitted navy button-up covered in tiny clouds dripping rain, looked at Astrid expectantly.

"This is your town, Parker," she said. "Lead on."

Astrid nodded, choosing not to point out that Sotheby wasn't her town at all, that she'd been to this flea market only once, when Iris first moved into her apartment six years ago and wanted to fill it with an amalgam of bohemian colors and fabrics.

She flipped her sunglasses over her face and looked out across the large, grassy space. Multicolored tents spread out before them, shoppers roaming with tote bags and sun hats, arms bared to the long-awaited spring warmth. The air smelled like coffee and butter, and Astrid remembered that there were always a few food artisans here: coffeemakers and microbrewers and bakers, even a few local winemakers.

"Let's head this way," she said, nodding her head toward the main thoroughfare, as if there were really any other option. Still, she was determined to look like she knew what the hell she was doing.

She stopped at a tent that sold candles, and while the strong scents of patchouli and sage were nearly overwhelming, she made a show of picking up one of many white candles in Mason jars, twine curling around the glass.

"These might be nice on some end tables," she said.

Jordan took the candle and sniffed, nose wrinkling in disgust. "It smells like a school cafeteria."

Astrid took a whiff, the candle still in Jordan's hands. She inhaled something pungent and bright with a warmer undertone not unlike baked chicken. "Oh my god, you're right."

Jordan inspected the label. "Look, it's even called 'Horrible Memories from Your Youth.'"

Astrid rolled her eyes, taking the candle to look for herself. "It is not."

"Might as well be."

"Though 'Summer Nights' isn't quite nailing it on the head."

"I think that's supposed to say 'Summer *School*.'"

Astrid laughed and set the candle down. She felt herself relax as they moved on to the next stall. She could do this. She *was* doing this. She was smiling, and she and Jordan were getting along and—

"Okay, now, *this* is what I'm talking about." Jordan stopped in front of a stall draped with dark fabrics, its table littered with all manner of Victorian kitsch. She held up a truly monstrous clock, all tarnished brass and ornate embellishments. Tiny fairies ran amok across the entire clock's surface like a scene out of *A Midsummer Night's Dream.*

Astrid just blinked at her.

"Oh, come on," Jordan said. "This fits the Everwood."

"It fits the Everwood *now,*" Astrid said. "Not the Everwood we're trying to create."

"*You're* trying to create."

"Good," Natasha said from somewhere behind Astrid. "Perfect."

Astrid tried to breathe normally, but this was not good, and it most certainly was not perfect. She'd rather go back to sniffing the lunchroom candle.

"This clock is wrong," Astrid said, standing her ground.

"Again, for *you,*" Jordan said.

"Are we really going to do this every single time we need to make a decision?" Astrid asked. "Me against you, old against new, spooky and outdated against clean and modern?"

Jordan smirked. "Nice choice of adjectives there, Parker."

"I'm just saying."

"Yes, I hear what you're saying. I just don't like it."

"We have a job to do."

"So let's do it."

They stared at each other, facing off while Natasha uttered infuriating encouragements.

"We're not getting this hideous clock," Astrid said. She was going to win this argument, goddammit, if it was the last thing she did.

"And I say we are."

Okay, so apparently Jordan was set on winning too.

"We can find a place for it," Jordan went on. "Surely, there is some room, some corner where your precious virgin eyes won't have to look at it too often, where we can—"

"I'm sorry, *virgin eyes?*"

Jordan shrugged. "I wouldn't want to deflower your delicate sensibilities."

Astrid's blood felt hot, and not in a good way. In a *someone-just-spilled-coffee-on-my-favorite-dress* kind of way. How dare this woman treat her like she was some weak-willed child in need of handling?

"My sensibilities aren't delicate, thank you very much," she said through gritted teeth, "and you can keep your god—"

"Okay, cut," Emery said, pulling off their headphones. "Let's take ten. I think we could all use some coffee."

Astrid nodded but turned away so she could get a few deep breaths and stuff all the swear words tumbling through her head right now back into her mouth. Her limbs were trembling, and her eyes felt like they might fill with tears at any moment.

"Are you all right, dear?" A woman from the clock stall appeared from behind a curtain and was now peering at Astrid with concern.

"I'm fine," Astrid said, forcing a smile. "Thank you."

"Can I show you anything?" the woman asked. Her long red hair was streaked with gray.

"No, thank you. I was just—"

"Actually, how much is this lovely clock?" Jordan asked, sidling up next to her, the fairy timepiece still in her hands.

Astrid didn't wait to hear the answer. She simply turned and stalked off toward a stall, any stall, that wasn't hocking tacky wares for Jordan to root through like a rat.

She ended up at a bakery tent from a few towns over called Sugar and Star. She'd never been there, but she knew it was run by a queer couple, and they specialized in seasonal offerings. The space was crowded, but she didn't mind waiting a few minutes for a view of their selection. She could already smell that warm, yeasty, buttery scent of baked goods, and she felt her shoulders immediately loosen.

"Hi," a round woman with wild curly hair said when Astrid finally made it up to their table. She wore a nametag that read *Bonnie, she/her.* "Can I help you?"

"Oh, just looking," Astrid said, but her mouth was already watering at the display of cookies, muffins, and breads. Her eyes landed on a scone with the tiniest bits of purple baked into the pastry. Could be blueberries, but they looked too delicate for the round fruit. She bent as close as was hygienically appropriate and took a deep breath in, trying to figure out the ingredient.

"Is that . . . lavender?" she asked.

Bonnie beamed. "It is. I'm impressed."

"Me too."

Astrid swung her head to the left to see Jordan standing next to her with her eyebrows in her golden-brown hair. Astrid swallowed but ignored her and turned back to the baked goods.

"Would you like a sample?" Bonnie asked.

"That would be lovely, thank you," Astrid said.

Bonnie slid a scone from the basket onto a white plate, then cut it into bite-sized pieces.

"How do you keep it from crumbling?" Astrid asked as Bonnie's knife slid easily through the pastry. "Butter?"

Bonnie laughed. "Well, you can never have too much butter, in my opinion, but I have another little trick."

"Do tell," Astrid said.

Bonnie placed the scone pieces in tiny cups and handed one each to Astrid and Jordan. "I set them really close together on the baking tray. When they butt up against one another, they don't dry out as much."

"Really?" Astrid said. "I never would've thought of that. I love scones, but whenever I make them, they're always so dry."

"You're a baker, then?" Bonnie asked.

Astrid shook her head. "Oh. No. I—"

"If you're making scones on the regular and can sniff out ingredients in a baked good, you're a baker," Bonnie said.

Astrid blinked. True, she used to bake all the time as a kid. It was her go-to comfort activity, especially in the quiet months after Delilah's father died and her own mother was lost in a haze of grief. She'd find herself in the kitchen, a cornucopia of baking supplies surrounding her. She loved the science of it, the precision. But within those rules, there was so much room for creativity and invention.

College changed a lot of that. There wasn't much space in her freshman dorm for culinary experiments. But even more than that, there simply wasn't time. She was a grown-up now. She had to move on to grown-up things.

Now, Bonnie was smiling at her so warmly, the word *baker* still hovering in the air between them, Astrid suddenly wanted to cry.

Which was ridiculous.

"Are you a baker?" Jordan asked, startling Astrid out of her thoughts. She'd nearly forgotten the carpenter was there, but Jordan was gazing at her with something like wonder in her eyes.

Astrid didn't answer but simply turned away and smiled back at Bonnie, then took a small bite out of the already bite-size piece of scone.

"Holy shit," Jordan said, doing the same. "That's amazing. Doesn't even taste like soap."

Bonnie laughed. "I did try to cut back on the lye."

Jordan waved her hand, still chewing. "Sorry, it's just that lavender tastes like soap to me."

"It can," Bonnie said. "But you can avoid that by—"

"Grinding the buds and mixing them with the sugar." The words were out of Astrid's mouth before she could stop them. She remembered reading about the technique years ago, but she'd never tried it.

Bonnie just grinned. "See? A baker through and through." Then she winked and moved on to another waiting customer, leaving Astrid feeling strangely achy and nostalgic.

"That was . . . interesting," Jordan said, crushing the little paper cup in her hands and looking at Astrid expectantly.

"What?" Astrid said. "You've never eaten a scone before?"

"I'm not talking about the scone," Jordan said, her voice so low and gentle, Astrid sucked in a breath, her throat suddenly thick. "I'm talking about lavender sugar and the way—"

"It's just sugar."

"—you looked like a kid on Christmas when you were talking about it."

Astrid shook her head. "It's . . . it's just something I used to do."

"Used to?"

"Yeah, used to. I'm not . . ."

"The flour-dusted-cheeks type?" Jordan said, her head tilted, eyes narrowed softly.

"Exactly," Astrid said, except her desire to cry multiplied tenfold. It didn't make any sense. Jordan wasn't wrong. Astrid certainly *wasn't* the kitchen wench type. At all. She'd made damn sure of that her entire adult life.

She met Jordan's curious gaze, green and gold and one hundred percent maddening.

"Exactly," she said again and cleared her throat, wiping the scone's crumbs on her jeans before turning away. "We should go. I'm sure Natasha and Emery are ready to start again."

"Fine," Jordan said, the snark back in her voice, which was exactly what Astrid needed right now. "But we're getting that damn fairy clock and that's that."

"Like hell we are," Astrid said as they started across the grass together.

Jordan grinned, but said nothing.

Forty-five minutes later, Astrid sat in the back seat of the van next to Jordan, a monstrously ugly clock on the lead carpenter's lap.

CHAPTER

EIGHT

ASTRID DIDN'T USUALLY attend demo days. She hated the dust, the chaos, the crew tearing cabinets out of walls and wielding sledgehammers haphazardly. But the Everwood Inn wasn't just any design project, and everything had to be documented for *Innside America*, including her overseeing parts of the demo—or at least pretending to. Plus, with her reputation already on shaky ground with the lead carpenter, Astrid knew she needed to be involved. Maybe peeling off a segment of wallpaper or two might go a long way to repairing things with Jordan. All she had to do was be her usual collected self.

Except when she pulled up to the front of the inn and spotted Jordan and Natasha standing on the porch, laughing, Astrid's nerves quickly rebelled. With the giant dumpster situated in the front yard, coupled with the show's crew mixing among the demo crew, things were getting real.

"You're here," Jordan said when Astrid got out of her car and headed toward the porch, her work bag hooked onto her elbow.

Astrid made sure her smile reached her eyes. Jordan's short hair was flaked with dust and god only knew what else, clear safety goggles perched on top of her head. A worn tool belt encircled her waist, fastened around another pair of overalls, these a dark gray denim, with nothing but a bright pink sports bra underneath.

Astrid felt her stomach flip—public displays of skin always made her uneasy, an unfortunate by-product of three decades of Isabel's etiquette lessons. Logically, she knew revealing certain parts of one's body in a situation that didn't involve water and a bathing suit was perfectly normal and acceptable for some people, but her gut instinct couldn't shake off the years of crossing her legs at the ankles, right over left. Still, she found herself tilting her head at the other woman, admiring the smooth skin showing through the sides of her overalls, wondering what it would feel like to be that free.

"Hello?" Jordan said, waving a hand in front of Astrid's face.

"Sorry, hi," Astrid said, slipping her sunglasses over her eyes. She felt better with a barrier between herself and this woman, an extra wall of protection. "How's everything going?"

Her eyes searched for Josh Foster, the contractor the Everwoods had hired and whose crew handled the demo. When they met on jobs, Astrid interacted with the man as little as possible, emailing him design schematics with a curt "Here" in the body of the message and leaving it at that. As her best friend Claire's ex and the father of Claire's daughter, Ruby, Josh was an inevitable presence in Astrid's circle, but she didn't have to like it. He'd crapped out on Claire enough in the past that his newfound responsibility—complete with contracting business and permanent home in Winter Lake—did little to endear him to Astrid. His crew was here, though, dumping ancient sinks and cabinets into the large green dumpster on the front lawn, so she had to give him that.

"Things are going fine," Jordan said. "Destroying my childhood home is fully underway."

"Dammit, Jordan," Natasha said, mirth filling her tone. "Save that sort of snark for the cameras."

Jordan laughed too, and Astrid forced herself to join in, though the action felt desperate, like she was a tween asking to sit at the cool kids' table. Still, Natasha wanted her to play a role? She'd play a role. She was fantastic at playing roles.

Astrid let her laugh fade. "So, you *want* to keep that clawfoot tub with the rust ring and the . . . " She squinted at the details on the bathtub two crew members were carrying to the dumpster. "What are those, cherubs on the faucets? Then again, you do love gaudy dancing fairy clocks, so."

Jordan continued to gaze at her coolly, one eyebrow lifted. Goddammit, Astrid wished she could lift one eyebrow.

"Oh, this is going to be so much fun," Natasha said. Then, placing a hand on Jordan's shoulder, she turned and called into the house's open front door for Emery. Jordan kept her eyes on Astrid, a tiny smirk on her raspberry red mouth.

"Hey, what's up," Emery said, appearing on the porch with their own safety goggles and wearing a gray T-shirt with six horizontal bars printed on it, each one in a different color of the rainbow. "Oh, hey, Astrid."

"Hey," she said, smiling.

"Okay," Natasha said, clapping her hands. "Our two stars here are fired up and ready to go, so I say, let's get something really interesting."

"What'd you have in mind?" Emery asked.

Natasha turned to Jordan. "You'll feature more prominently for the demo shots—we already have some planned with you and Josh, as well as one or two with Simon and Pru, if you think they'd be up for it."

"Absolutely," Jordan said. "My grandmother would love to hit the shit out of some kitchen cabinets."

"Actually," Natasha said, her voice curling mischievously as she turned toward Astrid. Then she just grinned at her.

"What?" Astrid asked. "Actually what?"

"No way," Jordan said, shaking her head.

"Oh, come on," Natasha said. "Emery, am I right?"

"You're right," Emery said, winking at Astrid before tapping something out on their phone.

"What are you right about?" Astrid asked.

"That has disaster written all over it," Jordan said, ignoring her completely and still looking at Natasha.

"It'll be fine," Natasha said. "It'll be like a teacher-student moment."

"I don't know," Jordan said, finally glancing at Astrid. She slid her eyes down Astrid's crisp, fitted white tee, dark skinny jeans, and white sneakers. Astrid squirmed under her gaze, fighting the urge to make sure the cuffs of her short sleeves were rolled up evenly. "That's a lot of white."

"Even better," Natasha said.

Astrid's pulse roared in her ears. "Will someone please tell me what the hell is going on?"

Everyone's eyes went wide. Astrid's voice had bordered on a yell. And she'd sworn. She'd sworn in front of Natasha Rojas.

Natasha, for her part, looked delighted. "We have the perfect task for you."

"Why do you say that like you mean the exact opposite?" Astrid asked.

Jordan grinned—a Cheshire cat kind of grin. "Look at us. We all know each other so well already."

Astrid sighed and hoisted her bag higher on her shoulder. Whatever this was, she had to be game. Anything else would come off as . . . well, elitist and bitchy. "Fine. Lead on."

Natasha beamed and shot a thumbs-up to Emery, who disappeared into the house ahead of them, calling Regina's name. Jordan watched Astrid for a split second before turning and heading up the rickety front porch steps. Astrid followed, the sounds of demolition growing louder as they walked through the open front door.

Jordan and Natasha led her through a dark oak swinging door and into the kitchen. It was a large space with a bank of windows along the back wall, surprisingly bright for a century-old house. Still, Astrid couldn't wait to change out the dark cabinets for white shakers, remove the peeling laminate counters and replace them with smooth marble.

Regina and Emery were already inside, setting up lights and cameras, as was Darcy, whose job was setting up the aesthetics in each shot, everything from hair and makeup to debris on the floor.

"Let's get you settled," she said, sitting Astrid on a stool in the back of the room. She inspected Astrid's face, while Astrid focused on Darcy's eyebrow piercing and her purple eye shadow. "Well, you already look pretty damn fabulous."

"Oh," Astrid said. "Thank you."

"What about me, Darce?" Jordan said, looking affronted.

Darcy laughed, her asymmetrical bob swinging. "Please, you could probably do my job with that eyeliner work."

Jordan laughed, catching Astrid's eye. For some reason, Astrid felt a blush creep into her cheeks. How was Jordan so friendly with everyone already?

Darcy fluffed Astrid's hair, added a swipe of blush over her cheekbones, and then patted her shoulder before releasing her. Astrid stood up, set her bag on the stool. She still had no idea what they wanted her to do in here.

"The network is cool with you wearing that necklace on screen?" Jordan asked, motioning toward the single gold charm around Natasha's neck, that same double wishbone Astrid remembered from their first meeting last week.

Natasha laughed and picked up the charm, looking down at it. "Most people have no clue what this is."

Jordan rolled her eyes. "I'm gay. Of course I know what it is."

"What is it?" Astrid asked and immediately wished she hadn't. Both women's eyes flew to her, then back to each other. Clearly, she *should* know what this was.

"Point," Jordan said, nodding at Natasha.

Natasha, at least, was a bit more polite and smiled warmly. That is, until she opened her mouth. "It's the clitoris."

"It's the . . ." Astrid trailed off. Blinked. She didn't think she'd ever said that word out loud.

"The clit," Jordan said.

"Yes, yeah, I got that," Astrid said.

"Those who have them have to prioritize their pleasure, am I right?" Natasha said.

Another fist bump between Natasha and Jordan. Darcy let out a little woot from near the back door where she was moving a pile of broken wood farther into the corner.

"Right," Astrid said. Was she sweating? Shit, she was sweating. It wasn't that she was appalled or offended. Quite the opposite, actually. Iris Kelly was her best friend, for god's sake. She simply felt . . . lost. The crew—Natasha and Emery and Jordan, everyone—was vibrant and funny and brazen.

Everything Astrid wasn't.

Everything she sort of wished she was.

"Okay, we're ready," Regina said, face still hidden by the camera. "Five . . . four . . . three . . ." Then she simply held up her fingers for two and one, and before Astrid knew it, the camera's light was green.

"Oh," she said. "Um—"

"Here."

Something cool and smooth pressed against her arm. She looked down at the steel head of a sledgehammer pressing against her bare arm, the long wooden handle in Jordan's hands.

"What do you mean, 'Here'?" Astrid asked.

Jordan quirked a brow. She pulled the sledgehammer back and choked up on her grip, hands sliding toward the steel head as she held it up. "This, my sweet summer child, is a sledgehammer. It smashes stuff. Big crash, big boom."

Natasha, who was off-screen for this shot, laughed into her hand, eyes sparkling. Astrid squared her shoulders. She was going to do this right, goddammit. She was going to sit at that cool kids' table.

"Oh, so you're a smart-ass?" Astrid said, and Jordan grinned. Astrid was pretty sure her mouth was trying to do the same, but hell if she wanted to give Jordan the satisfaction.

"You're a quick learner," Jordan said. "I'll show you. Here." With her free hand, she tossed Astrid a pair of clear goggles, which Astrid fumbled but managed to hold on to. "Protect those baby browns."

Something about the way Jordan said "baby browns" sent a surge of blood to Astrid's cheeks as she slipped the goggles over her head. She had no clue why. Eye protection was a basic requirement on renovation sites, and she'd worn them enough to expect them here as well.

Jordan settled her own goggles on her face, causing a longer piece of hair to tangle in the strap and stick out from her head in a golden-brown loop. Astrid doubted she noticed or cared as she hoisted the sledgehammer onto her shoulder, planted her booted feet on the plastic-covered floor, and let the tool fly.

A huge crack resounded through the kitchen. Even though Astrid was prepared for it, she startled, stepping back a couple of feet as chunks of wood catapulted into the air. Jordan's lean arm muscles rippled as she reared back and did it again. She had abs—actual defined abs visible between the denim of her overalls that contracted each time she reset herself for another swing.

It was fascinating. Jordan's body was efficient, quick, like a finely tuned machine that knew exactly what it was built for. Astrid had only ever seen men do this kind of work, which was probably why this—Jordan, exhibiting such power—was so enthralling. Astrid felt like a horrible feminist. Of course she knew women and nonbinary people worked on construction sites all the time, but she still couldn't pull her eyes away. Score another point for internalized sexism.

She shook her head to clear it, shoving any and all *fascinated* thoughts from her mind. This was a woman doing her work and doing it well. That was all.

Once the bank of cabinets was clear, Jordan stopped. She shoved her goggles on top of her head, pressed the steel head to the floor and leaned on the handle as she turned to face Astrid.

She was sweating.

Arms glistening. Droplets on her chest.

Astrid felt like slapping herself for noticing these details. True, she was a detail-oriented person. Type A, organized to a fault, eyes keen and constantly searching for flaws. She was the friend who always spotted the piece of fuzz in Claire's hair or noticed that Iris had missed a button on her shirt, but still. She was in a professional setting, for god's sake—on camera, no less—and here she was noticing beads of perspiration trailing into her carpenter's cleavage.

"And that's how you do it," Jordan said.

"Looked thrilling," Astrid deadpanned. "Now where's a steamer? I'm great at removing wallpaper."

"Oh, no," Jordan said, laughing. "It's your turn."

Astrid's stomach tightened. She probably couldn't even lift that sledgehammer, much less send it flying toward a collection of wood. She'd rather not have Jordan-the-sexy-carpenter—not to mention half the show's crew—witness her flailing with the tool. She'd probably end up breaking a toe or finger or something else she was most definitely not supposed to be destroying. No thanks.

"What's wrong, Parker?" Jordan said, taking a step closer to her, sledgehammer in tow. "Scared?"

Astrid got the distinct feeling Jordan knew the answer to her question, but hell if Astrid was going to admit it. The carpenter was even closer now. Astrid could see a circle of darker green rimming the center of her hazel eyes. She'd never seen eyes like that before.

"So?" Jordan said, that shit-eating grin on her face again.

Astrid swallowed and set her jaw. "Fine."

Triumph—that was the only to describe it—flooded Jordan's expression.

Astrid followed the other woman to a still-intact row of cabinets.

"Put these on," Jordan said, taking off her gloves and handing them over. They were still warm as Astrid slid the rough material over her fingers. "Okay, now here's what you're going to do . . ."

Jordan proceeded to explain how to hold the sledgehammer, how to use your legs for leverage, how to grip it firmly before letting it fly toward the intended target.

"Once you hit the cabinet, don't loosen your grip," she said. "Keep it tight, pull back, and go again. Got it?"

"Got it," Astrid said, but she felt anything but confident. Her hands shook as she took the handle, suddenly terrified that she truly wouldn't be able to lift it.

"No time like the present, Parker," Jordan said, watching her with what could only be described as a smug expression. Did she . . . want Astrid to fail?

The thought was a punch in the gut. Then again, it wasn't like Astrid didn't deserve whatever attitude Jordan felt like dishing out, but Astrid's whole body suddenly felt like a healing bruise—the gentlest press was bound to hurt.

She sucked in a lungful of air and lifted the sledgehammer into the air. The weight was substantial, falling heavily on her shoulder and pulling at her neck muscles, but she did it. She squared herself in front of the nearest cabinet while Jordan took a few steps back.

Probably wise. God only knew where this thing was actually going to land. She set her body to mimic exactly what Jordan had done, eyeing her target like a bull's-eye. She breathed in slowly through her nose but couldn't seem to move beyond her current position.

"I always picture something I really despise," Jordan said from behind her.

Astrid turned. "What?"

Jordan gestured to the cabinet. "Imagine it's something you hate. Or someone. The forty-fifth president. Racists and homophobes. Brussels sprouts."

Astrid cracked a smile. "Brussels sprouts?"

"Loathe them entirely."

"Is that what you do? Picture brussels sprouts?"

Jordan's wry expression dimmed, just a little, and when she spoke her voice was softer. "Something like that."

Astrid turned back around but felt suddenly empowered. Something she hated. Jesus, where did she even start? Clutter. Victorian-era furniture. Berry-flavored sparkling water. Shape wear. Four fork choices at dinner. Her mother's eye twitch. Her mother's sigh. Her mother's pursed mouth when Astrid ate a goddamn carb.

Her ex-fiancé's face appeared in her mind. Spencer Hale's perfect, chiseled, golden-boy face with his new perfect golden-girl fiancée. She didn't hate him. Not exactly. She certainly didn't hate *her*. More like she hated who she was when she'd been with Spencer, hated how she believed she needed to marry someone like him. Hated feeling powerless to make her own choices, live her own life.

Astrid heard a grunting noise, a growl almost, and it took the sledgehammer actually flying through the air for her to realize the sound was coming from her. The steel end slammed into the cabinet with a crash, splinters flying everywhere. The action and resulting consequence surprised her so much, she loosened her grip and the sledgehammer plummeted to the ground, taking her arm with it.

"Whoa, killer," Jordan said, suddenly right next to her. "Keep it tight, remember?" She slid her fingers over Astrid's bare wrist and helped her lift the tool back up.

Astrid shivered. Her whole body was shaking, adrenaline coursing through her veins. Goose bumps erupted along her arms.

"Again," she said, and Jordan's brows lifted. The other woman said nothing, though, stepping back and flourishing her hand for Astrid to proceed.

And proceed Astrid did. She forgot all about the cameras, about Natasha Rojas watching. She demolished the cabinet until it was nothing but a husk of wood hanging from the wall by its brackets. Then she pulverized the one next to that, swinging the sledgehammer over and over until she was out of breath and her fingers stung despite the gloves protecting her skin. She felt wild, alive, like every bit of her will had been poured into this tool and she alone was calling the shots.

She didn't think she'd ever had so much fun on a jobsite.

When she finally stopped, her arm was sore, bits of wood and dust speckled her white tee, and she didn't even want to think about what her hair looked like.

She shoved her goggles on top of her head and turned to face an open-mouthed Jordan Everwood. "Damn, that felt good."

CHAPTER
NINE

JORDAN STARED AT Astrid, an mixture of amusement, irritation, and . . . fuck, *arousal* churning in her gut.

"You're surprisingly good at that," she said, stepping toward Astrid and taking the sledgehammer before the woman could go on a bashing spree.

Astrid laughed and shook her hair, dust cascading from her shaggy bangs like snow. "I had no clue it would be so therapeutic."

"See? You resisted me over nothing."

Astrid frowned. "I didn't resist you."

Now Jordan laughed. "I'd love to see what you actually consider resisting, then. Poor guy."

Jordan watched Astrid's reaction carefully. Yes, she said *guy* one hundred percent on purpose. Yes, she was looking for any sign that Astrid wasn't straight, because goddammit, she was getting vibes. One didn't date women and nonbinary people exclusively for nearly two decades and not pick up on these kinds of things. First, there was that whole long look they shared yesterday at the flea market, with Astrid looking all soft and vulnerable over a baked good. Then, today, that little hitch in Astrid's breath when Jordan had touched her wrist, a sound that had the potential to completely wreck Jordan for the rest of the day. And she couldn't even think about the way the designer had legit checked out Jordan's entire body in the driveway— mouth open, eyes scanning skin—without grinning.

Then again, Jordan had seen all of these things from straight women too. The curious ones, the bored ones, the repressed ones who longed to show off their midriff without feeling like they were going against their mama's wishes. Astrid could most definitely fall into one of those categories, and if she did, Jordan was most definitely not going there.

What the hell was she thinking? She wasn't going there even if Astrid ended up as queer as a glitter-covered unicorn. Astrid was the enemy, the purveyor of white and gray, the ruiner of character and atmosphere. A fact Jordan would do well to remember when teaching her to wield a sledgehammer.

Now, though, Jordan noticed a distinct blush creeping into Astrid's cheeks as she looked down, long lashes brushing along her cheeks.

Well, fuck.

"I don't think my ex-fiancé would use 'poor guy' to describe himself," Astrid said.

Yes. Good. Himself. Ex. Still didn't mean she was straight, or that the fiancé in question even identified as a man, but Jordan was going to take what she could get here. Anything to cool her suddenly heated skin down a little.

"Is that who you were picturing?" she asked. She couldn't help it. She was curious. Astrid had come alive when she was swinging the tool, her teeth gritted, her slender arms taut. And that growl. No, Jordan would not think about the growl.

Jesus, she needed to get laid.

And not by Astrid-fucking-Parker.

She made a mental note to close herself in her tiny bedroom to-night and spend some quality time with the contents of her bedside table. Which was trickier than one might think with her brother and grandmother always just a wall away in the cottage. But she'd figure it out. She had to—it'd been a while since she'd gotten off, her two-week-long couch fest after being fired quelling her libido, and now living with her *grandmother*, for god's sake, as much as Jordan adored her. Her situation didn't really fan the flames of desire.

But watching Astrid breathing heavily, the sledgehammer still in her grip, her flame felt sufficiently fanned.

Astrid nodded. "That's who I was picturing."

"He's a dick?"

The other woman sighed. "He's . . . no. Well, yes, he is, but that's not really why . . ."

There she went again, lowering her eyes, lashes for days. This time, she even bit her lower lip. Jordan needed to get out of here. Now. She glanced toward Natasha and Emery, Regina behind the camera, but they were all watching the interaction as though view-ing an intriguing film, mouths parted, eyes widened just a little.

"Who do you picture?" Astrid asked.

She blinked and turned back. "What?"

"Who do you picture?" Astrid asked again, then nodded toward the sledgehammer still in her hands.

And just like that, sadness and anger fell over her like a curtain. So sheer she didn't see it descending until it was too late. She never saw it coming, the grief. It was tricky like that, surreptitiously trail-ing her until it found the perfect moment to leap at her like a predator.

"It's not a who," she heard herself say.

"What is it then?" Astrid said, her eyes wide and curious. She even took a step forward, leaning in a little.

Jordan took a step back. Leaned away.

"Cancer," she said quietly. "I picture cancer when I'm bashing the shit out of those cabinets."

"And cut," Emery said.

About goddamn time. Jordan exhaled, but Astrid's eyes were still fixed on her, mouth open, her thick brows dipping low in concern. Shit. Jordan didn't want to hear any more questions, and she damn sure didn't want to hear the horrible and inevitable "I'm sorry." She didn't even know why she told Astrid the truth. Or half of the truth, at least. She'd gotten really great at never saying that horrible word out loud, at rolling around in her pathetic behavior all by her lonesome.

But now, here was Astrid, along with a fucking television crew who'd just captured every single moment of her patheticness on film.

Fucking great.

No way they were getting any more out of her right now, which was exactly why she turned and left out the back door before anyone could offer up any useless words.

———

NO ONE WAS allowed in Jordan's workshop, not even Natasha Rojas. Jordan had made that clear before demo officially began, claiming it was currently unsafe and she was still getting things in order for the job. Josh Foster had set up a tent in the backyard for his own employees to work in, complete with everything they'd need to hack, saw, and hammer, so they shouldn't need access to the lead carpenter's private workshop anyway.

Josh's group had frowned at this, already sizing her up and grumbling about how she was technically in charge. Josh didn't react, though. Well, he did, but he simply said, "Sounds like a plan," and went on with work. Jordan expected a certain level of sexism on the work site—it was inevitable in her line of business, but so far, Josh had treated her with nothing but deference and respect. Not that he got a cookie for basic human decency, but still. She was thankful Josh didn't question her privacy decree. In reality, the old shed behind her grandmother's carriage house was in perfect shape as of last night, when Jordan finally finished working to get the space ready for what she had planned.

She just didn't want anyone seeing what that plan was.

Now, she burst out the inn's back door and hurried across the too-long grass toward the shed. She keyed in the combination to the padlock she'd placed on the door the day after she'd met Astrid Parker and let herself inside. The space was large, plenty big enough for a one-person workshop. It already smelled of aged wood from the several pieces of furniture Jordan had stored in one corner, including Alice's wardrobe. Her workbench, the shining jewel of any workshop, sat in the middle of the room, an L-shaped wooden table with close access to the power saw at one end.

A corner kitchen cabinet, cut to Astrid's design specifications, was already sitting on the surface.

Jordan unclipped her tool belt and let it thunk onto the cement floor. She walked to her workbench, braced her hands on the thick wooden surface. Breathed. It had been a year. She didn't understand why losing Meredith could still feel so . . . fresh. So new.

And here she was, pining after her wife once again, very nearly with the same breath she'd just used to lust after Astrid Parker and her infernal sledgehammer-growl.

"Jesus," she said out loud, pressing the heels of her hands into her eyes.

It wasn't that she felt guilty. After everything, she knew guilt didn't factor into her and Meredith's story at all. There was anger— as evidenced by how she'd pulverized one cabinet with only three swings of the sledgehammer—but mostly, there was fear.

Lots and lots of fear. Jordan had lived with it long enough to recognize it. She wasn't deluded. She just didn't know what to do about it.

She'd had one lover since Meredith, a bar hookup named Katie after a rough day at work and enduring a particularly loud silence in her house. The loneliness had gotten to her, and she just needed another voice in her house other than her own. But as soon Katie was in her bed, as soon as they'd right and truly fucked and Katie was ready to leave, Jordan felt that *need* rise in her.

Don't go.

That's what she'd wanted to say to a complete stranger, the desperation for someone to just *look* at her so strong she gave in, let the words tumble out of her mouth.

Katie had looked at her then, but not in the way Jordan wanted. She'd smirked, pulled on her clothes, and said, "We both know that's not what this is," and left without another word.

Jordan spent the next week in bed, Bri Dalloway blowing up her phone and finally roping Simon into the mix, and he'd left Jordan a voice mail threatening to come and kidnap her cat if she didn't go to work.

That was six months ago. Suffice it to say, Jordan was no longer built for casual sex. And anything *other* than casual would surely just lead to more evidence that Jordan wasn't anyone's idea of a life partner, which pretty much left her alone with her fingers.

But if Jordan was honest with herself, that's what she really wanted. A partner. She always had, the solidity of a family around her, creating the kind of life with and for someone else that her grandmother and brother had created for her. But after Meredith, she didn't think that was possible anymore. She was terrified to even dream about it.

After Katie, she'd invested in numerous sex toys—three different vibrators and two different clitoral stimulators, a couple of dildos—and she'd been fine ever since. At home, she always had music on, a show or a movie, always had another voice in there with her. With regular orgasms—and pretty damn great ones, thank you, technology—she hadn't thought about hooking up in a long while. Even when her senses noticed an attractive person, she simply observed, imagined a nice long session with her Satisfyer 3000 later that night, and moved on.

Until Astrid-fucking-Parker.

Until her shaggy bangs and buttoned-up outfits and adorable ignorance over what a clitoris looked like.

Jordan could educate her. She could teach her all about how the clit—

Sweet Jesus, *no*.

That was sure as shit not going to happen.

She scrubbed her hands over her face, most likely smearing her eyeliner, and looked down at the cabinet she was building. A lot of times, she ordered the cabinets the client wanted. There were several great local manufacturers in Savannah that Dalloway and Daughters had used, and Josh had mentioned one he often employed up in Winter Lake, even for his Bright Falls jobs.

But Jordan had a plan.

And if they ordered the white shaker cabinets Astrid wanted, her plan was fucked.

So she'd convinced Josh that she could build a better cabinet—that was true, she could—and it would save them money on the budget—also true—and he'd agreed. He was so trusting, a good old boy raised in a small town, and Jordan was fully prepared to take the brunt of Astrid's wrath when the cabinets were finished and installed.

In fact, Astrid's wrath was half the draw here.

She set to work, sliding on her goggles again, measuring and cutting the doors to make room for the vintage mullioned glass she had on order. The Everwood kitchen was huge, so this was a big job. An assistant would be nice, she wasn't going to lie, but it would be worth it.

For the next hour, she lost herself in the work. She loved this part of her job, the creating. She hadn't built something from scratch in so long, she'd forgotten the thrill of it, the way her whole body felt alive as she watched something take shape and come into being. And this project was even more invigorating, picturing the kitchen that actually fit what the Everwood was, modernizing while honoring history and story.

She paused, switching off her saw and shaking off her gloves to open up her laptop. Astrid had emailed her digital plan to both Jordan and Josh just last week. Jordan had promptly made a copy in her design program, then used all the same schematics so she could redesign the Everwood room by room, the way it should be. Now, she smiled at her plan for the kitchen.

It was beautiful. Jordan let Astrid keep her precious gray paint. She left the stainless steel appliances, left the rough-hewn wooden table Astrid had included for texture. Everything else though . . . well, let's just say it wasn't white and gray. It was darker than Astrid's design, with sage-green cabinets and inlaid mullioned glass, copper pots dangling from the iron pot rack above the ceiling. There was a farmhouse sink, just like Astrid wanted, and Jordan could admit that white fit nicely here, but instead of white marble counters, Jordan had instead ordered butcher block throughout.

The effect—at least in her mind and in the image on her computer— was vintage and cozy. It was the Everwood.

She smiled at the room on her screen, shoving away everyone's reactions when they saw the finished product. She didn't think this was exactly what Natasha meant when she said lean into the tension between carpenter and designer. Natasha meant snark, banter, which she and Astrid seemed to be handling pretty well, but these cabinets, her whole redesign . . . well, this was something else altogether.

Jordan wasn't sure if she would be able to carry any of it through. With everything on film, she'd have to work at night, off camera, but once the cabinets were in, once the paint was on, what could anyone really do? She was counting on that ratings factor, the fact that Natasha wanted authenticity and tension to increase the excitement for the show.

She was also counting on Astrid's very obvious pride. The woman was practically vibrating with . . . well, it wasn't passion, necessarily. It was dimmer than that, a desperation for approval, for success maybe. Whatever it was, Jordan was ninety-nine percent positive it would prevent Astrid from ever admitting that she'd lost control of her carpenter or her design.

Honestly, Jordan didn't really care how it got done, as long as the Everwood didn't become a West Elm showroom and the episode still aired, so she had to be careful here. Very careful. Walking on eggshells kind of careful, not letting her brother—who already thought she was a bit of a fuckup—find out what she was doing.

For now, though, her heart slowed, that curtain of loss had lifted, and Astrid Parker was nothing but a nuisance in the very back of her mind.

THE NEXT WEEK went by just like any other job. Well, mostly. If Jordan completely ignored the cameras, the lights, Darcy fluttering around to make sure she exuded the right mix of glamorous and work-worn, Natasha and her clit necklace directing and comment-ing, the infuriating way her stomach fluttered like a nervous preteen when she heard Astrid click-clacking through the halls, it went by like so many jobs before it.

Jordan lost herself in the work, in saws and drills and the slow forming of a kitchen cabinet, in surreptitious trips to the home store in Sotheby for paint that was most definitely *not* on Astrid's design plan. She spent long nights scouring Pinterest for ideas, constructing her own plan in her design software, room by room—a copper tub in the master bath, white-and-silver damask drapes, built-in book-shelves in the exact same shade of sage as the kitchen cabinets.

While she'd always offered her input about a room's aesthetic design during her time with Dalloway and Daughters, and she'd certainly designed her share of furniture, she'd never really gotten into the nitty-gritty details of a room—the paint and fabrics and rugs.

She loved it. The colors, the textures, the idea that she was creating the entire feel of a room in a home—her home—felt important. It felt right, more right than any other job she'd ever worked on, particularly in the past two years.

Granted, all of this was still mostly imaginary, existing only in her workshop or on her computer. In the house so far, she and Josh and his crew were simply carving out a space for the design, priming the walls for new paint, the floors for refinishing, consulting with electricians and plumbers, all with Astrid hovering and monitoring in her pressed jeans and blouses, a camera occasionally capturing some conversation or another.

But tonight, all that would change. Demo was finished. They were set to start refinishing the original wood floors, which meant all the painting—Astrid's homogenous gray—needed to get done this coming week. Tomorrow, they were filming in the Lapis Room, Alice's bedroom, as Natasha wanted to capture a good "before" scene with the whole family, talk about how Astrid's plan would lace through the house's history.

Which, as Astrid's plan stood now, it wouldn't at all.

But it would. After tonight, it most definitely would.

At five o'clock, as the crew's sleek vans rolled out and Josh's team skidded down the gravel driveway in their mud-covered trucks, Jordan peeked under a drop cloth, eyes surveying her supplies.

Blue painter's tape.

A fresh roller and brushes for edging.

Two gallons of indoor paint.

Twilit Stars the color was called, which was perfect. The shade was dark, but with a sheen to it, a little whisper of something otherworldly.

Some magic.

She pressed a hand to her belly, anxiety spiking. Before she could second-guess her plan—or, if she was being honest, third-, fourth-, and fifth-guess—she let the cloth drop over her stash, went home to help her grandmother with dinner, and waited for night to fall.

CHAPTER

TEN

ASTRID EYED HER ivory pencil dress, still enveloped in the pink dry cleaning bag and hanging in her closet. It had been two weeks since the coffee incident and, miraculously, the stain had come out. Before that disaster, she'd worn this dress whenever she needed to feel powerful.

Today was just such a day.

She carefully peeled back the wrapping, like she was opening a precious gift, and slipped the smooth material off the wooden hanger. Sliding it up her body, she rehearsed what she would say when they filmed the "before" scene in the Lapis Room later this morning.

In the last few days, she'd been brushing up on the room's history. She'd watched two documentaries that featured Alice Everwood's ghost, as well as several articles online. Of course, she'd leave most of the history discourse up to the Everwoods, as it was their family's legacy, but she was sure she'd need to talk about how her design accentuated Alice's story . . .

. . . except her design didn't accentuate it at all. She hadn't really realized it while creating the look for the room. She was focused on *modern* and *elegant*, but now that it came down to the day where she'd have to talk about her inspiration, she was coming up blank.

The choice of fabrics is reminiscent of the early twentieth century . . .

Sure. Maybe.

See how the position of the furniture highlights a cozy, almost ghostly atmosphere . . .

Not even close, but perhaps, if she said it with enough conviction, they'd buy it. Poise and confidence could convince anyone of anything—that, and a carefully chosen outfit. At least, that's what her mother had always taught her, and, in Astrid's line of work, she'd found it to be mostly true.

She breathed in . . . out. She could do this. Her plan was *good*. It was beautiful, and it was what her client wanted. Everything with the inn was ready, and today would be perf—

She wondered if she should even think the word, but as she slipped into a new pair of black heels and gave herself another once-over in the mirror, she couldn't imagine what could possibly go wrong.

Just as long as she steered clear of Jordan Everwood and her morning coffee.

⁓

"I'M EXTREMELY EAGER to talk about the famous Lapis Room," Natasha Rojas said.

Astrid climbed the Everwood stairs, Natasha beside her, the Everwood family bringing up the rear.

Cameras were positioned above them on the second floor, below on the first, and down the hall outside the Lapis Room, where Emery also hovered out of sight.

"I think it's really going to be lovely," Astrid said, trying to match her calm tone to Natasha's.

"These floors are classic," Natasha said as they reached the top landing. "They're original to the house?"

"Yes," Jordan piped up from next to Pru. She had her arm threaded through her grandmother's, her usual raspberry-red lipstick perfectly in place, winged liner, and a button-up denim shirt over skinny black jeans. She looked adorable, just like she always did. It was irritating, really.

"James and Opal Everwood installed them when they built the house in 1910," Jordan went on.

"They're in wonderful shape," Natasha said, squatting down to run her hands over the deep amber wood. Her long dark hair was in a low ponytail and looped over her shoulder, the perfect kind of carefree look that Astrid could never quite pull off. "You're preserving them?"

"Oh, absolutely," Astrid said.

The group continued down the hall, the Lapis Room the first destination of the tour, being the most famous room in the house.

"So has anyone ever seen anything supernatural in here?" Natasha asked. They stopped in front of the closed oak door, and her brown eyes glittered mischievously as she turned the ancient crystal knob. "Please say yes."

"I haven't," Simon said, "but not for lack of trying. When we were little, Jordan and I—"

But before he could finish whatever he was going to say, Natasha swung the door open, blue sunlight spilling into the hallway.

Blue.

Astrid blinked.

Blue sunlight.

She blinked again, but there was no denying what she was seeing. The April sun from another cloudless day streamed through the windows, reflecting off the blue walls.

"Blue," she said out loud, though she didn't mean to. She, as the designer, should not be surprised by the color of the room, but damn.

It was blue. Actually and literally dark blue. Not quite navy. More like the deepest parts of the sea when the sun shone on its surface. There was a sheen to it as well, a shimmer that made Astrid feel like she was trapped underwater.

But the painters weren't due to start until tomorrow, and when they did start, this sure as hell wasn't the color they had on their job list.

"Oh my god," Simon said, moving past a gaping Astrid to the middle of the room. He spun in a slow circle, as though making sure he was seeing correctly. He looked just as surprised as Astrid.

Natasha was quiet. She walked farther into the room, her head canted at the silver-and-white damask drapes that framed the window. They actually went quite well with the deep color of the walls, but right now, Astrid didn't care. All she cared about was that she did not pick out those drapes, no matter how lovely they were.

The crew filled the room. Regina behind the camera, Chase holding up a boom mic, Patrick adjusting the lighting, Emery watching it all with their eyebrows raised.

"Interesting," Natasha said.

Astrid had no clue what to say in response. If she agreed, she would clearly be admitting that she didn't make this choice, and a good designer knows what's happening on her projects at all times. If she said *Thank you*, she'd be taking credit for something she didn't plan and didn't even like.

Dark blue? Who in hell did this?

"What do you think, Grandma?"

At Jordan's soft and gentle voice behind her, Astrid turned around. Slowly, as though the other woman had a gun pointed at her back.

Simon turned too. Natasha. Every bit of energy in the room gravitated toward Pru Everwood. The old woman's hazel eyes glowed behind her sunflower-yellow glasses, her mouth open just a little.

Astrid's heart rocketed to her feet. She'd been in this business for almost ten years, and she knew that look.

The look of love.

The look of *home*.

The look of a client one hundred percent satisfied with the work.

"It's lovely," Pru said. She pressed a shaking hand to her throat, eyes shiny with what definitely looked like tears. "It's perfect, Astrid."

Astrid.

"It feels like her," Pru went on. "Like Alice. I can't wait to see the finished product."

"Me too," Jordan said, still squeezing Pru's arm and smiling at Astrid. "It's really a beautiful color."

Astrid opened her mouth to say something—the truth would be preferable, she knew, but she couldn't get it out. *I didn't do this* felt like impossible words to speak in front of her clients, in front of Natasha Rojas and the cameras.

"I remember your plan being quite different for this room," Simon said, hands on his hips. Astrid turned to face him, but noticed he wasn't even looking at her.

He was looking at Jordan.

Some sort of twin-talk was going on silently between them, but Astrid didn't have time to figure out what. Natasha fingers were swiping over her iPad, brows furrowed.

"Indeed," Natasha said, frowning at the screen. "No blue here." She held up the iPad, silver-gray walls on the 3D image, immaculate white duvet over a wrought-iron queen-size bed, a herringbone-patterned feature wall behind it created from distressed pine, drapes and accent pillows in browns and blues and grays.

It was an oasis, just what guests in small-town inns were looking for.

"I will say, though, I like the change," Natasha went on, pinching the iPad screen between her thumb and forefinger to inspect something closer. "Your original plan is actually a bit . . . uninspired."

The word was like a bomb dropped into the middle of the room.

At least, that's what it felt like to Astrid. She blinked as Natasha Rojas continued to frown at the screen, swiping and zooming, mouth pursed in scrutiny.

Uninspired.

Uninspired?

Astrid repeated the word in her head so many times, it started to sound like gibberish. She knew she needed to say something, but, in all honesty, she was terrified tears would leak out with any words right now. Plus, if she agreed with Natasha, she'd pretty much be shitting all over her own design plan in front of her client. If she balked, fought for the work she'd actually done, she undermined a design legend *and* the blue walls that Pru Everwood clearly adored.

Fucking fuck, she thought. If there was ever a great moment for some internal f-bombs, it was this one.

"Okay. Um, well," Astrid said when she'd finally gotten herself together enough to speak. Still, the right words seemed to fly right out of her head, and she wondered how many more fillers she could utter before she made a complete fool of herself. "I—

"*We* decided to go in a different direction," Jordan said, as calmly as if she was talking about a chance of showers that afternoon. It took Astrid a few seconds to really process Jordan's meaning.

"You did?" Simon asked, eyes flicking between Astrid and his sister. "You and Astrid together?"

Jordan simply tilted her head at Astrid, one eyebrow lifted in her direction. A challenge, if Astrid were to put a name to the expression.

Astrid had to make a choice then, and it happened almost without her knowing it. They were all waiting for her, Natasha Rojas included, who of course was more than okay with letting this little bit of carpenter-client-designer drama unfold. So she schooled her features, pressed her shoulders back.

"We're working through some ideas," she finally said, smiling without her teeth. There. That wasn't technically a lie, as she planned to work out a number of ideas with Jordan Everwood when they were next alone.

"Exactly," Jordan said.

"Interesting," Natasha said again while she and Emery eyed each other. *Interesting* seemed to be Natasha's favorite word, and, honestly, Astrid was getting sick of it.

"Isn't it?" Jordan said, clapping her hands together once, then turned toward Natasha. "Now, how would you like to see a secret passageway or two? We can go from the master bedroom all the way to the library downstairs through the walls, if you can believe that."

Natasha's eyes lit up. "I thought you'd never ask."

Jordan grinned at her, and Astrid had a fleeting thought that the two women were flirting, then pushed it away. She didn't care if Jordan flirted with a lamppost. What she did care about was this disaster of a room, her *uninspired* design plan, and what she was going to do about whatever Jordan was up to.

"Why don't you all go ahead," Astrid said, perfect smile still firmly in place, her hands clasped in front of her. "I'm just going to check a few things in the bathroom."

"No problem," Natasha said. "I think we've got all we need from you, right, Emery?"

"Good to go," they said.

"I'm very excited to see how this room progresses," Natasha said.

Astrid smiled and revealed just the right amount of teeth, catching Jordan's eye over Natasha's shoulder. "Yes. As am I."

⌇

ONCE THE GROUP had moved off toward the still unblemished master bedroom—well, as far as Astrid knew—she let out a breath that sounded like a mix between a sigh, a growl, and a sob.

Uninspired.

Un-fucking-inspired.

She paced the room in circles. Her bag, hooked on her elbow, batted against her hip over and over. She couldn't believe this. Her design plan for this room—for this house—was good.

This is lovely.

That's what Pru had said when she first saw the design plans two weeks ago. Surely, the inn's owner wouldn't be shelling out a hundred grand for a renovation she hated.

Would she?

Still, Astrid couldn't get Natasha's assessment out of her head, as though her teacher had just smacked a dark red F onto the paper she'd spent weeks pouring her heart and soul into.

Astrid froze, her own thoughts jolting her pacing to a stop.

Heart and soul.

She'd never used those terms to describe her designs. She worked hard, listened to her clients, created spaces they loved, but it had always felt like just that—work. She didn't think *heart and soul* described anything in her life.

Jesus, what a depressing thought.

Astrid took a deep breath through her nose. In for four . . . out for eight. She repeated this a few times until the rising panic ebbed enough for her to focus on something else.

Something far less depressing and far more rage-inducing, but rage was good.

Astrid couldn't believe Jordan had turned out to be this . . . this . . . conniving. A little tension on-screen was fine, a little salt, but this was unprofessional. And why? It was clear she hadn't loved Astrid's design, but this is what her own family had asked for.

Except now, Pru very clearly loved the blue currently marring the walls of the Lapis Room.

Astrid closed her eyes. She could figure this out. She could still save this project, save her reputation, and impress the hell out of

Natasha Rojas. She and Jordan just needed to have a little chat, that was all.

She started for the door when her phone buzzed. Digging it out of her bag, she read a text from Iris.

I'm on my way! I'm craving fries.

Astrid had almost forgotten that Iris wanted to take her out to lunch, a little celebratory meal for having survived the famous Lapis Room "before" filming. Though, Astrid was sure *celebratory* wasn't quite the word for the kind of morning she'd had.

CHAPTER ELEVEN

THE MORNING COULD not have gone better.

Pru loved the wall color, just like Jordan knew she would, which was all that really mattered. But other things fell right into place too. Exactly as Jordan suspected, Astrid was way too concerned with saving face in front of Natasha Rojas to question the blue walls. Even Simon bought that Astrid knew all about the paint color.

Granted, Natasha's proclamation about Astrid's designs being uninspired was a little rough, but Jordan had to agree. Honestly, she wasn't certain Astrid even *liked* designing all that much. Sure, she got the job done, but the only times Jordan had ever seen a spark of passion in Astrid's eyes were when she'd swung that sledgehammer at the kitchen cabinets and mooned over a scone at the flea market. Every other time she'd been at the house, on camera or not, the woman's manner was staid, clinical, like a doctor delivering treatment.

After a little trek through an incredibly musty, dusty secret passage, which started in the master bedroom's closet and wound through the middle of the house, emptying out through a bookshelf in the library, Natasha excused herself for some phone calls, and Emery had to work on setting up the next scene's shoot. Pru was ready for lunch anyway, and Jordan needed a minute to process what her next move would be now that Astrid very obviously knew Jordan was engaging in design shenanigans.

She walked Pru back to their cottage, Pru burbling happily about the Lapis Room the whole time, much to Jordan's delight. After wolfing down half a turkey sandwich Pru insisted she eat to get her through the afternoon, Jordan headed to her workshop. Outside, clouds slid across the sky. The morning had started bright and sunny, but Jordan actually liked the clouds, the softness of the gray sky. It felt right, comforting, whereas the sun in Savannah always felt like it was mocking her. *Look*, I'm *happy, why can't* you *get your shit together?*

Clouds were kinder.

She rolled her shoulders, ready to work on her kitchen cabinets, which were about halfway finished. All she wanted was some peace and quiet, wood under her hands and a beautiful design plan inside her mind.

But of course, because the universe hated her, she ran smack into Astrid Parker as she rounded that infernal overgrown rosebush between the cottage and her workshop.

"Shit," she said as their shoulders collided. She bounced backward while instinctively reaching out to grab Astrid's arms to steady her.

"Sorry," Astrid said. "I didn't see you."

They stood awkwardly for a second. Astrid appeared to be taking several deep breaths, her knuckles white on her bag's straps.

"Okay," Jordan said, "Well, I'll see—"

"What the hell was that today?" Astrid asked.

Jordan froze, her mouth still open. Astrid's dark eyes were fixed on her in a way that could only be described as intense. Really intense. And a little angry. Jordan's stomach clenched. She knew she'd have to face Astrid about the whole painted-the-room-blue-without-telling-you thing sooner or later.

She'd been hoping for later.

"I don't know what you mean," she said.

Astrid huffed a single laugh, which held absolutely no mirth whatsoever. She stepped closer, and Jordan got a whiff of some clean scent, like sea breezes and fresh laundry.

"Really? Gaslighting?" Astrid said. "I thought you were better than that."

Jordan deflated a little. Astrid was right on both counts.

"Unless Alice Everwood painted her own room blue," Astrid went on.

Jordan lifted her brows. "Perhaps she did?"

"Can we cut the shit?"

Jordan tilted her head at Astrid. "You don't strike me as the swearing type."

Astrid lifted a hand and let it fall back down, slapping against her leg. "Why does everyone always say that? I swear just like anyone else."

"Not quite like anyone else. That *shit* had a very refined lilt to it. Nice dress, by the way."

Astrid glanced down at herself, as though she'd totally forgotten she was wearing the infamous ivory dress. She looked suddenly vulnerable—mystified, even—and Jordan felt her hackles settle down. Okay, so Astrid had yelled at her on a bad day. Big deal. Jordan had dealt with worse, that was for damn sure. And now, the woman was just trying to do her job with the redesign. A *bad* job, but still.

"Look," Jordan said, releasing a breath. "You know I don't like your plan for the inn. My brother might not give two shits about our family home, but I do. Your style isn't the Everwood, plain and simple. It's not personal."

She very seriously considered bringing up Natasha's assessment too, but that just felt mean.

Astrid stared at her with a somewhat awed expression on her face. And not the good kind of awe. The *can you believe this bitch* kind.

"Except it is personal," she said. "This is my job. My business. My reputation on the line. And I was caught completely off guard today."

"You handled yourself pretty well."

"Only because you gave me no choice in the matter."

"So make a choice, then. I know Natasha and Emery want us to be all dramatic with each other, but for me, it's really simple. I want the right design for the Everwood, and yours isn't it."

Astrid groaned and sliced a hand through her hair, causing her bangs to stick up. Jordan had the sudden and ridiculous urge to smooth them down, send her fingers through all that shaggy blond.

She cleared her throat, curled her hands into fists to keep them in place. She kept her face impassive, but the pounding of her heart right now couldn't be ignored. If she were being honest, she quite liked this. Not putting Astrid's job at risk, necessarily. Despite their first encounter, Jordan didn't have any energy to spend on trying to ruin the woman's life, and Jesus, what a horrible vendetta to hold on to anyway—*She yelled at me, so I fucked her over.* No, that's not what Jordan was after here. She simply wanted her family home righted, and Astrid just happened to be the person standing in her way.

Well, Astrid, and Jordan's own brother's complete lack of faith, but potatoes, potahtoes.

Still, in this moment, sparring with this gorgeous woman, she felt suddenly . . . alive. More alive than she'd felt since Meredith got sick, at any rate.

There was also the fact that this whole renovation would be a lot easier if she could get Astrid Parker on her side, despite *Innside America*'s thirst for drama. Hell, Jordan could act affronted at anything if they wanted her to. But if she was really going to pull this off, not just dream about it, she needed Astrid Parker.

"Listen," Jordan said, stepping closer, "we don't have to be at war."

"War?" a voice said right before a gorgeous redheaded white woman rounded the rosebush. "Who fired first?"

"There's no war," Jordan said at the same moment Astrid said, "She did."

The woman nodded, lips pursed. "Well, I'd be on your guard. Astrid is a hell of an opponent."

"Iris," Astrid hissed.

"What?" the woman—Iris, Jordan supposed—asked. "Do you remember the time you hip-checked Piper Delacorte into her locker so hard she fell down, all because you found out she'd spiked your soda at Amira Karim's party just to see what you acted like when you were drunk?"

"That was high school. Everyone's horrible in high school."

Iris smirked. "And she deserved it?"

"Of course she deserved it." Astrid actually flipped her hair, albeit theatrically, which hinted at a humorous tone. "You don't just put alcohol into people's drinks without permission."

Iris laughed and Astrid actually cracked a smile and dear god, what sort of sorority hell was this? Jordan narrowed her eyes at the cackling friends, something in her chest stretching tight—something years old and years gone.

She shook off the feeling and focused. Iris looked familiar. She had long red hair, little braids woven through here and there, and was dressed like she was about to go frolic in a field of wildflowers— a flowy floral dress that fell to her knees, cognac-colored sandals, and dangly gold earrings that featured a cloud with raindrops drizzling down toward her shoulder. Total bohemian bisexual vibe, if Jordan had to put a name to it.

She was one of the women fawning all over Astrid after the unfortunate coffee incident outside Wake Up, because of course she was.

"Excuse me," Jordan said, very ready to get the hell away from them both. She tried to sidestep them, but Iris stopped her.

"I'm sorry, we're being so rude." She smiled, showing a row of perfect white teeth. "I'm Iris. I came by to take Astrid to lunch."

Jordan sighed inwardly but capitulated. "Jordan."

"You look so familiar," Iris said, tilting her head. "Have we met?"

Her tone dripped with sarcasm, which, from the way Iris cut her eyes to her friend, Jordan assumed was meant for Astrid.

"Before five seconds ago?" Jordan asked. "Not officially, no."

Iris nodded. Astrid squirmed, lifting her eyes heavenward as if an alien abduction would be preferable to this conversation.

Jordan could relate.

"Well, I'm glad it's official then," Iris said. "Do you like putt-putt?"

"Putt—I'm sorry, did you say 'putt-putt'?" Jordan asked. She must've heard wrong. Either that, or Iris was a master of non sequiturs.

"Putt-putt," Iris said, nodding.

Okay, master of non sequiturs, then.

"Iris," Astrid said.

"You're going," Iris said. "Deal with it."

"All right, fine, but don't subject Jordan to the ridiculousness that is boozy mini-golf."

"Boozy . . . mini-golf?" Jordan said. Had she tumbled down a rabbit hole?

Astrid sighed, her cheeks flushing an adorable shade of pink.

No, not adorable. *Goddammit, Jordan.* Just plain old pink. A ruddy pink at that. It was one hundred percent unattractive.

"It's nothing," Astrid said.

"It's delightful," Iris said. "There's this putt-putt place over in Sotheby called Birdie's, and it's twenty-one and up. They have the wildest courses. Like entire shipwreck scenes with mermaids and deserts and jungles. Plus, they serve booze. It just opened up a few months ago, and we're all going tonight. Want to join?"

Iris talked fast, her hands flying all over the place, leaving Jordan feeling like she was watching a show where the sound wasn't linking up with the actors' mouths. It took her a second to realize she'd been invited to an outing. A boozy putt-putt outing.

"Oh," she said.

But before she could form an actual sentence, her brother appeared around the rosebush. She was starting to really hate that damn rosebush.

"Hey, there you are," Simon said, that ubiquitous worried crease between his brows smoothing out for a second. "Everything okay?"

Jesus, she was tired of that question.

"I'm fine," she said. "Just chatting it up with Astrid and Iris here."

Simon frowned at her overly bright tone but turned to face the other women.

"Hi," he said, smiling widely at Iris, "I'm Simon, Jordan's twin brother."

"Simon Everwood," Iris said, pursing her mouth as she looked him up and down. "The author."

His charming grin shifted into his *Oh, you've heard of little old me* expression. "That's what they tell me."

Iris's brows lifted. "Who's *they?*"

Simon just laughed and rubbed the back of his neck. "Good question. Some days, I'm still figuring that out."

Iris laughed. "Well, I'm sure Violet could give you a hint."

Violet was one of the main characters in Simon's debut novel, *The Remembrances*, a sweeping family saga set in LA filled with dysfunction and existential crises aplenty. Last fall, the book sat on the *New York Times* best seller list for nineteen weeks. Since then, though, he'd been struggling to finish his next novel.

Simon's face took on an expression that could only be described as elated. "You've read it?"

"I tolerated it."

Simon clutched his chest but laughed and said, "Ouch," which just made Iris smile even broader.

Jordan caught Astrid's eye, an expression like *Can you believe these two?* passing between them. Jordan started to smile, but then Astrid yanked her gaze away.

"Anyway," Jordan said loudly. "I'm off to do some work."

"Hang on," Iris said, reaching out and actually grabbing her hand. "Say you'll come tonight. Both of you."

"Iris, for god's sake," Astrid said.

"Come to what?" Simon said, and Jordan groaned inwardly.

"Oh, we'll be there," he said after Iris explained the event, just like Jordan knew he would. He slung an arm around Jordan's shoulders and grinned. "Most definitely."

Jordan had never considered fratricide before, but suddenly, the concept sounded incredibly enticing.

CHAPTER
TWELVE

ASTRID SAT IN the back of Claire's Prius, Iris stuffed next to her in the middle seat, while Jillian, Iris's very new, very beautiful girl-friend who currently lived and worked as an attorney in Portland, occupied the other side. She had short blond hair that seemed to have a mind of its own, but made up for the mess with her power suits and butch style. Tonight, she'd left the suit at home—or Iris's apartment—and instead favored jeans, brown dress shoes, and a navy blazer over a white tee. She rarely spoke, but when she did, it was always some-thing devastating, like "My firm has box seats at the Met, we should all fly out some time," as though that was something their group just *did*.

Even Delilah thought Jillian was a bit much at times, and she'd lived in New York City for twelve years.

The relationship was new, and Iris was extremely smitten. After a relatively calm breakup with Grant this past fall, her boyfriend of nearly three years, Iris had laid off the dating scene until Jillian walked into her shop a month ago. The woman said she found Iris on Instagram and was willing to pay top dollar for a custom planner.

Iris had made the planner in record time—a power lesbian planner, she'd called it—and she and Jillian promptly fell into bed once the job was done.

Of course, Astrid knew every detail of their romance, how Iris wanted to tear off Jillian's bespoke suit the moment she saw her, because Iris had absolutely no verbal filter.

About anything.

Now, Astrid listened while her friends chatted about their day, about how Claire had never put it together that *the* Simon Everwood was a Bright Falls Everwood.

"I hadn't either," Iris said. "Honestly, I never gave it much thought. His book is total white dude navel-gazing."

"It is not," Claire said. "I liked it. And, like, half his characters are queer."

"Fine, I'll give you that," Iris said. "But it still rang a bit too Franzian for me."

"Oh my god, you're terrible," Claire said, laughing. "Simon writes cis female characters way better than Franzen. And he didn't even have any gratuitous sex scenes where a woman's breasts quiver like sentient beings."

"Why the hell read it, then?" Delilah piped up from the passenger seat.

Claire giggled and took Delilah's hand, pressing a kiss to her fingers. "Simon doesn't write romance."

"Sentient boobs are romantic?" Delilah asked.

"God, I'd love to see him write romance," Iris said.

"I highly doubt he could pull it off," Jillian said in her smooth voice.

"Exactly, babe," Iris said, beaming like the woman invented sex itself. Astrid had the sudden thought that Jillian probably owned a clit necklace.

A laugh bubbled out of her mouth.

"What's so funny?" Iris asked.

Astrid waved a hand and turned back toward the window.

Claire cleared her throat. "I'm glad you invited the Everwoods along tonight, Ris."

Astrid gritted her teeth. She'd already told Iris she most definitely was *not* glad for her impromptu invite more than once over lunch earlier that day, which was pretty much all Astrid had said about her morning. Iris, of course, wanted to know every detail of filming with Natasha, as well as why Jordan Everwood was talking about war when Iris first joined them outside the inn. Astrid managed to satisfy her with effusive statements like "Natasha's amazing" and "Oh, just a few creative differences," but the truth was, all Astrid could think about was that blue paint and how *the* Natasha Rojas had called her much more modern design "uninspired."

"Speaking of the Everwoods," Iris said, waving her hand between the front seat and herself. "I still can't believe you didn't tell us that you were working with the very woman who spilled coffee all over your precious dress."

"I heard about that little encounter," Jillian said, leaning forward so she could see Astrid. "Rough go."

"Yes, the roughest," Astrid said, and Iris elbowed her in the ribs. "And I see them daily on a professional basis. I'd rather not hang out with them in my free time, thanks."

"I had to invite them," Iris said. "We take care of our own."

"Who's *our own*?" Astrid asked.

"Queer folk," Iris said, again flinging her hand to the front seat and then toward Jillian.

Astrid had heard that Simon Everwood was bisexual. That was public knowledge, and he was a semi–public figure—he'd talked about it in interviews more than once. And she already knew Jordan was gay. It made sense that her entire friend group—all of them queer except for her—would be drawn to the Everwood twins.

"Okay, fair," she said. "I'd still rather keep my personal and professional lives separate."

Iris made an exasperated sound. "Sweetie, try to unclench. Just for tonight. You've been working hard and you deserve it."

Astrid said nothing, but her throat felt suddenly tight. She knew Iris meant well, that she really just wanted Astrid to have some well-earned fun, but Astrid had always hated this view of herself—uptight, unable to let go, cold.

Everything Isabel Parker-Green embodied.

Everything Astrid didn't want to be but felt trapped into being anyway.

The feeling wasn't new, but it had been growing as of late, ever since her breakup with Spencer. Well, no, before that even. Maybe it had always been there. Hell, she didn't know.

Ending things with her fiancé last summer was supposed to be a step forward, the beginning of Astrid understanding, finally, who she was and what she wanted. But if anything, she'd only felt more lost since her engagement ended. She didn't regret not marrying Spencer. Not for a second. But she couldn't seem to find her footing since then.

And now with this Everwood Inn mess . . .

"Yeah," she said, taking a deep breath, "you're right. I just need to relax."

As Claire pulled into Birdie's parking lot, the neon lights of the course brightening the night sky, Astrid smiled at her reflection in the window, forcing the corners of her mouth a little wider so it looked real.

THE PUTT-PUTT COURSE was like something right out of Disneyland. Each of the eighteen holes had a theme—pirates, deserts, mermaids, jungles, futuristic cities—and was elaborately designed and executed. Inside the building, where you paid and got your clubs and balls, there was also a full bar named Bogey's where golfers could order beer, wine, and cocktails, all served in convenient plastic cups with handles, lids, and straws.

Astrid had to admit, the place was pretty amazing, if a bit tacky—Isabel would never be caught dead at a place like this, much less alive and in her latest Jimmy Choos. The thought made Astrid feel all warm and fuzzy inside.

A feeling that quickly dissipated when she spotted Jordan and Simon waiting for them by the bar. Fairy lights strung from hooks in the ceiling, along with backlit shelves full of bottles, cast them and the few other patrons in a soft amber glow. Jordan had on a pair of black skinny jeans cuffed at the ankle and a blue, short-sleeved button-up shirt patterned with little lemons. Her hair was amazing—the buzzed side looked freshly shorn, the longer locks swooping over her forehead in golden-brown waves. She had on her customary raspberry-red lipstick and perfect winged eyeliner.

She looked amazing. Had Astrid ever looked that effortlessly cool? She glanced down at the russet blouse she'd tucked into her high-waisted jeans, her cognac ankle boots that went with everything, and felt suddenly like she was back in high school again, questioning every single thing she put on her body.

"Hiya," Iris called, and waved, pulling Jillian along by the hand toward the Everwoods. Simon had on a hunter-green long-sleeved Henley and dark jeans, his glasses and messy hair making him look every bit the literary author that he was.

Introductions were made—Iris taking the lead, of course—drinks were ordered, balls and clubs rented. Astrid sipped her white wine and ambled toward the French doors that led outside to the course. They were thrown open, letting in the unseasonably warm April night air.

She knew she needed to talk with Jordan more about the inn, but the very idea of being alone with the woman again made her stomach feel like it was packed full of lightning bolts. Still, their almost-argument earlier had left her unsettled and anxious, two feelings she knew far too well lately, and if she was ever going to *unclench*, as Iris so decorously put it, she needed to clear the air.

She squared her shoulders, determined, and took another gulp of courage-giving alcohol before she spun on her heel to face her group.

And smacked right into Jordan Everwood.

Again.

Jordan's beverage—red wine, by the looks of it—burst right out of her flimsy plastic cup and splashed over her lemony shirt.

"Oh my god," Astrid said. "I'm so sorry. Here, let me get you some napkins." She hurried over to the bar where the rest of the group was still gathering their drinks, totally unaware of what just happened. She grabbed a handful of brown napkins and rushed back to Jordan, who was just standing there with a sort of resigned look on her face.

"Well, I guess this is what karma looks like," she said, dabbing at her possibly ruined shirt.

"What?" Astrid said.

Jordan waved between them. "I spill on your favorite dress, you spill on my favorite shirt."

Astrid winced. "It's your favorite?"

Jordan shrugged. "Second favorite."

"I'm really sorry." So much for proving she was a decent human. "I'll pay for the dry cleaning."

Jordan snorted a laugh at that, then waved a napkin through the air before uselessly blotting at her chest again. Her shirt had three buttons undone at the top and Astrid caught a glimpse of purple lace. A few drops of red wine disappeared into her cleavage.

Astrid swallowed and looked away, eyes searching for her best friends to come and save her from this hell. Claire was busy whispering with both Iris and Delilah in a tight little circle, while Simon and Jillian stood off to the side and talked about who-the-hell-even-cared-what as they sipped their beer and bourbon respectively. She was on her own here, which was just as well. No need to embarrass herself even further in front of the entire group. She just needed to figure things out with Jordan about the inn.

Trouble was, she had no idea how to handle anything about this situation. Her anger from this morning had faded, leaving her equal parts embarrassed that Jordan had witnessed Natasha calling her designs *uninspired* and clueless about how to fix it. She felt suddenly lost and overwhelmed. She knew it was juvenile—she was thirty years old and a professional, for god's sake—but she was starting to believe you were never too old to feel lonely, to wonder where you belonged in the world.

She turned back to Jordan, who had finished cleaning up and was proceeding to down the rest of the wine in her broken cup.

"You could get me back by kicking my ass at putt-putt," Astrid said. She didn't know where the idea came from. She hadn't even wanted Jordan here tonight, but suddenly, a mini-golf challenge seemed like the only way forward with Jordan Everwood.

Jordan finished knocking back her wine and eyed Astrid. "Oh?"

Astrid nodded. "I'm terrible. Truly."

Jordan narrowed her eyes, then glanced over at her brother. She watched Simon talk with Jillian for a second, before she turned back to Astrid and grabbed her club from where she'd set it on the floor to clean up.

"Okay, Parker, let's do this." Then she tossed her ruined cup into the trash and flourished her arm toward the French doors, indicating Astrid should go first.

Astrid swung her own club onto her shoulder, much like she'd done with the sledgehammer during demolition, and walked onto the course without a backward glance.

CHAPTER
THIRTEEN

JORDAN HATED TO admit it, but she wasn't one hundred percent miserable right now as she watched Astrid Parker struggle with the par three on hole number four.

"God, you really are terrible," she said.

"I told you," Astrid said. She was attempting, for the fifth time, to get her lime-green ball over a tiny Golden Gate Bridge that was in the process of being damaged by a city-ruining earthquake. Every ten seconds or so, the iconic red metal bridge rattled and undulated, causing Astrid's ball to slip and slide everywhere except where she wanted it to go.

Jordan would have thought that the way Astrid huffed and muttered a quiet "goddammit" under her breath was a little bit cute, if she were allowing herself those kinds of thoughts at all.

Which she wasn't.

Nor was she letting herself check out Astrid's surprisingly curvy ass in her jeans as she bent over her club. This little tête-à-tête with Astrid was just good business sense. That's all it was.

"So," Jordan said loudly—a little too loudly, as Astrid startled and knocked her club into her ball before she was ready—"that's quite the group you have with you."

She waved her own club toward the rest of their group, who were only on hole two because they kept stopping to talk, or someone ran back to the bar to get refills, or Delilah—who was evidently even worse at mini-golf than Astrid—accidentally tossed her club into hole one's chemically blue pirate lagoon.

Astrid reset her ball but then straightened up and sighed, eyes narrowing softly on her friends. "Yeah. They're one of a kind, that's for sure."

"Are they always so . . ."

"Loud?"

Jordan laughed. "I was going to say *spirited.*"

"You're polite."

They fell silent as Astrid hit the ball—the bridge burped and rumbled and spat it right back to her—while Jordan watched her brother and the others.

Simon was laughing while Iris laid out her case for why she should get an extra swing, which apparently had something to do with the full moon and the fact that her drink didn't have enough ice.

"Are you always so maddening?" Simon asked.

"You have no idea," Iris said, grinning at him and slurping at her cup.

Simon laughed even louder, his eyes glowing, his smile bright, his posture relaxed and confident. Jordan loved her brother, probably more than she loved anyone else on earth other than Pru. But sometimes, a little twinge of jealousy flickered to life in her chest. Her twin truly loved life, and it loved him back.

Fiercely.

A bestselling debut novel, undeterred faith in true love despite getting his heart crushed more than once, coming out. Deep in her heart, she knew she wasn't being completely honest with herself—Simon had experienced some very real heartache in his life, and he was bullied pretty heavily when he came out as bi their freshman year of high school. Still, as soon as the quarterback on the football team came out as pan a mere three weeks later, the bullying magically stopped. Not that she wished it had been harder for him. Of course she didn't. But sometimes she just . . . she didn't know. His smiles, his success, his endless search for a great love that kept him so goddamn *hopeful* all the time—it all made her feel like she was on an island by herself.

The feeling had gotten worse since Meredith. Everything had gotten worse, of course, her whole life imploding, while Simon glided into a feature in the Sunday *Times*. She could charm the *Innside America* crew, but that was work. She had a context there. Drop her in the middle of this boisterous group, and she was lost.

"They make it look so easy," Jordan said now.

Astrid had halted her journey across the bridge and gazed at her friends.

"Make what look easy?" she asked.

A tiny smile lifted the corners of Jordan's mouth. "Life. Fun."

Astrid lifted her brows. "You have a hard time having fun?"

Jordan looked at her then. Shit, her eyes were pretty—a brown so dark Jordan could hardly make out her pupils. Juxtaposed with her sandy hair and thick dark brows . . . well, Astrid Parker was stunning. There was no doubt about it.

"I wouldn't say that," Jordan said.

Astrid shot her a look. "Really? You're here with me, the person who treated you like shit over a coffee spill, and you hate everything I'm doing to your family home to the point that you're pretty much trying to sabotage me."

Jordan opened her mouth to protest but . . . well, shit, when the woman was right, she was right. "Fun" was not a word she would use to describe any part of her existence lately. She worked. She fucked up work. Her brother tried to save her. Rinse and repeat.

She hadn't always been like this. She felt as though her recent lack of faith in anything at all had carved a hole right in the center of her chest where her heart pulsed the brightest, the strongest, and all that was left was a tiny ember she didn't have the strength to fan most of the time.

"Goddamn," she said, running a hand through her hair. "I mean, what am I even doing with my life?"

Astrid's eyebrows popped up at first, but then she laughed—a real laugh that crinkled her eyes and showed off her incisors, which were a little bit sharp, like a vampire's. "I'm not much better. After all, I'm choosing to hang out with someone who no doubt thinks I'm a garbage human and hates my taste rather than spend time with my lifelong friends, so." She looked away, biting her lower lip with those sharp teeth.

Jordan shivered, then tilted her head at the other woman. She figured her line was something to the effect of *You're not a garbage human*, but for some reason, she knew Astrid wasn't fishing for reassurances, so she didn't offer any.

"Well, then," Jordan said instead, "I guess we really need to make damn sure we have some fun tonight. Just to prove to ourselves that we can."

Astrid's brows lifted, just a little.

Just enough.

"What did you have in mind?" she asked.

Jordan paused. She didn't know what the hell she was doing. She should really just go back to her grandmother's, binge-watch something on Netflix, and fall asleep after a nice long session with something battery-powered. Still, she couldn't help closing her eyes and reaching back . . . back . . . years ago to a time she was actually happy—or at least, as happy as any human who had a loving partner and a steady paycheck. She searched for a different Jordan altogether, one who wasn't scared of screwing up all the time, who wasn't planning on sabotaging this woman's plans for the inn. A Jordan who slept easy, loved easy.

That Jordan knew exactly how to have fun. Granted, her brand of fun wasn't the raucous kind going on behind them. It never had been. But somehow, she knew Astrid Parker would be more than okay with that.

"What I had in mind," she said, leaning on her putter and into Astrid's space, "is going to require a change in venue."

CHAPTER

FOURTEEN

IF ANYONE HAD suggested to Astrid that she'd be riding down a dark state road in a beat-up truck with Jordan Everwood that night, she would've thought that person was drunk.

Or high.

Or any other combination that would explain the ridiculous notion.

Yet here she was in the truck Jordan called Adora, the speakers blasting some moody indie folk music Astrid had never heard before while the wind blew her hair into her face.

"Where are we going?" she yelled, turning down the song. Astrid had asked the same question twice already, and every time, Jordan just grinned and turned the music back up, singing along.

She flipped the knob to the left again. "Jordan, seriously. I don't do well without a plan."

Jordan laughed. "I noticed."

"So?"

"Your fiancé never surprised you with anything? Your friends?"

Astrid opened her mouth to say *absolutely not*, because everyone in her life knew she hated surprises. But that didn't stop Spencer from buying a whole house in Seattle without telling her a week before their wedding last year. And it hadn't stopped Iris and Claire from colluding with Delilah behind her back to break up her wedding. Granted, their intentions were good and their instincts were spot-on, but that was beside the point.

"They have," she said. "And I didn't love it."

Jordan tucked a piece of tawny hair behind her ear, revealing a bevy of silver hoops, moons, and stars curling up the shell. "You'll like this. I promise it's not scary."

"Does it involve tattoos or bungee cords?"

Jordan shot her a look. "What the hell kind of surprises have been sprung on you?"

Astrid laughed. "Okay, they didn't involve needles or leaping to my death, but they still weren't very fun."

"Then I guess it's a good thing the whole point of tonight is fun. That is, if you're up for it."

Their gazes met, just for a second, before Jordan looked back at the road. Astrid realized, in the past hour since they'd left Birdie's— no, even before that, since she'd stepped onto the mini-golf course with Jordan—she hadn't worried about her job, the show, the way Jordan Everwood had gone behind her back with the paint, how they were going to fix that blue room.

She hadn't thought about anything, really, at least not anything serious. And it was fun.

That was it. She was having actual fun.

Even more surprising, she realized she didn't really want to know where they were going—she was enjoying the mystery, the teasing tone to Jordan's voice when she denied Astrid any knowledge. Just experiencing a moment where she wasn't constantly thinking about why and when and how was exhilarating.

This woman next to her didn't even feel like the same Jordan Everwood from earlier today. She felt like . . . well, Astrid wasn't sure. Whatever this feeling was, it was new and exciting, and Astrid didn't want to ruin it by bringing up the inn and what happened with the Lapis Room today. That could all wait. The whole world could wait and give her one night off, one night where her whole goal was to smile and laugh and not care so damn much.

Besides, Astrid really, really wanted to know what this woman had up her lemon-dappled sleeves.

THEY ENDED UP in downtown Winter Lake, a small town about thirty minutes from Bright Falls, but nearly an hour from Birdie's in Sotheby. Even though she'd grown up in Oregon, lived here all her life with the exception of four years at Berkeley, Astrid had only ever passed through this particular hamlet. Josh Foster lived here now, she knew that, which did not increase its appeal.

That is, until Jordan pulled up in front of a movie theater.

Not just any movie theater. An old-timey movie theater called the Andromeda, like something right out of the Golden Age of Hollywood. It was beautiful. All pinks and reds and oranges, a tiny carnival on an otherwise quiet street, the shops around it already closed up for the night. A fluorescent-lit marquee advertised a silent movie marathon and three-dollar cocktails.

"Wow," Astrid said when Jordan shut off the ignition. She gazed up at the towering marquee.

"See?" Jordan said. "No bungee cords."

Astrid smiled. "No bungee cords *and* cheap drinks?"

"It's even better inside."

Jordan opened her door and slid out, Astrid following close behind. They paid the attendant in the burnished gold-and-glass booth by the front entrance for the eight o'clock showing before stepping into what felt like another era. The lobby was all red carpeting and gold accents. Everything was vintage, from the soda machine to the popcorn maker to the crimson outfits with gold tassels the employees wore while they directed guests to their seats. The bar was ornate, with gleaming bottles on green-lit shelves, a lacquered bar top, and fringed, red velvet stools already occupied by patrons, several of whom were costumed like it was the 1920s.

"We're underdressed," Astrid said, pulling at her blouse.

Jordan waved a hand. "It's fine. I've been here plenty of times in costume and not. Anything goes here. It's whatever you want it to be."

"How have I never heard of this place?" Astrid asked. She knew her mouth was hanging open, but it was all so intoxicating. The air smelled of butter and maraschino cherries and good liquor. Glasses clinked. Voices laughed.

"It's a hidden West Coast gem," Jordan said, her voice suddenly soft. "My grandmother would bring Simon and me here in the summers when we were kids. Sans the cocktails, of course. Lots of popcorn."

In that moment, Astrid's stomach growled so loudly, she was surprised Jordan didn't hear. She hadn't eaten since her lunch with Iris. "Popcorn sounds good. So does an old-fashioned."

Jordan lifted a brow. "I would've pegged you for a strictly expensive wine kind of gal."

Astrid shrugged. "This seems like the kind of place where you order a drink with a name."

"Oh, it definitely is."

After securing a huge bucket of buttery, glistening popcorn, an old-fashioned, and a Manhattan, they settled into two plush velvet chairs in the very middle of the theater. Astrid couldn't stop looking around at the heavy drapery, the dazzling crystal chandeliers, the antiqued brass tiles on the ceiling that made everything feel glamorous.

The space was . . . *inspired*.

Astrid stuffed some popcorn in her mouth, bitterness rising like bile at the thought. Still, the theater *was* inspired. Tonight, she just wanted to enjoy all this beauty and majesty around her without constantly thinking about how she could achieve the same effect.

"I've never seen a silent movie before," Astrid said after a deep, calming breath.

"Oh, okay," Jordan said, turning toward Astrid with one leg propped up on the seat. "Here's the best part, a game Simon and I used to play. Every time an actor does this"—she launched into a series of comically affected expressions with her lips curled and then pursed, her eyes wide before narrowing again, hand clutching at her chest and then her cheek—"we have to take a drink."

Astrid tilted her head at her. "Let me see that one more time?"

Jordan laughed, but she obliged, really hamming it up just like a silent movie actor reacting to a villain with a dagger.

"You and Simon played a drinking game when you were kids?" Astrid asked when she stopped laughing, rattling the huge square ice cube in her glass.

"Well, drinks might've taken the form of Sour Patch Kids, and our tongues may or may not have been raw by the end of the movie. Simon may or may not have puked in the back of my grandma's car."

Astrid leaned against their shared armrest, toying with the tiny straw in her whiskey. "Just Simon?"

"I have a stomach of steel." Jordan patted her belly. "And, okay, I may or may not have insisted on the front seat so I didn't barf."

"What was that like? Growing up with a sibling?" Astrid asked.

Jordan's brows dipped. "Isn't Delilah your sister?"

Astrid blinked for a second. Shit. It wasn't that she'd forgotten about Delilah—one didn't easily forget Delilah Green—it was simply that playing games, vying for the front seat, eating candy together until you spewed . . . these were not things she ever did with Delilah.

"Stepsister," she said. "And it's complicated."

Jordan nodded, eyes searching Astrid's in a clear invitation to keep talking.

So Astrid did.

She told her all about growing up with Delilah—her father dying of cancer when she was three, her stepfather dying of an aneurysm when she was ten, how both Delilah and Astrid spent the bulk of their adolescence believing the other one hated them, when really, they were just kids who had lost too much and didn't know how to process it all.

"And my mother . . ." Astrid said. "Well, let's just say I'd need about ten more of these before getting into all that." She jiggled the ice in her glass.

"Shit," Jordan said softly. "That's . . . that's rough."

Astrid said nothing, then stuffed another handful of popcorn in her mouth. She'd never been comfortable talking about her grief, her loneliness as a kid. In fact, she hated it. The only reason Claire and Iris knew any of it was because they were there for it. She couldn't possibly hide her past from them, but that didn't mean she chose to wax poetic about everything she'd dealt with on a regular basis.

And, sure, maybe it was just the whiskey—she didn't make a habit of drinking hard liquor—but as Jordan took all of this in, pointedly offering zero placations, Astrid felt her shoulders loosening up a little.

"What about you?" she asked.

Something flickered in Jordan's eyes. "What about me?"

"Come on," Astrid said. "I shared my mess, you share yours."

"Oh, is that how it works?" Jordan's tone had turned sardonic.

"I mean, it's been a while since I've had a heart-to-heart, but yeah, I'm pretty sure it is."

They both fell silent at that, *heart-to-heart* shimmering in the space between them. Astrid hadn't really meant to call it that, but she couldn't think of another word for their conversation right now.

Still, unease crept in slowly, the fear that Jordan was just going to leave her hanging here with a good bit of her emotional baggage on the proverbial table, offering her nothing to balance the load.

"You know I have a twin brother," Jordan started.

Astrid breathed out as quietly as possible. "Yes, I know this."

"And a grandmother."

"Jordan."

Jordan laughed and leaned a little closer. She smelled like the woods, an almost piney scent shot through with something softer, like jasmine.

"Okay, okay, fine," she said, exhaling. Then she told Astrid about her mother's untreated depression when they were kids, how Jordan spent most of her childhood worried and blaming herself for not being able to make her mom happy.

"I know now it wasn't my fault," she said. "But you know, as a kid, with my undeveloped frontal lobe and all."

"Yeah," Astrid said softly. "I get that." When grief had taken over her own house as a child, she hadn't known how to process it as anything less than something she'd caused. She and Delilah had spent the last few months trying to untangle their relationship as kids— one founded on rejection and anxiety—from this new life where they were trying to be halfway functioning stepsiblings.

"Anyway," Jordan went on, "Simon and I would come to the Everwood in the summers to give my parents a break, and it was the only time of the year I felt really happy, felt like me."

Realization settled over Astrid, both warm and heavy. "That's why the inn means so much to you."

Jordan nodded, took another sip of her drink. Then she laughed and slid a hand through her hair. "That and my entire life fell apart about a year ago, and this project is literally all I have."

"Oh," Astrid said, curiosity replacing any twinges of guilt she was currently experiencing. "What happened?"

"Shit," Jordan muttered, then waved a hand. "Never mind. It's not important."

"No." Astrid put a hand on her arm, just the very tips of her fingers. Jordan's skin was warm, smooth, dappled with a random freckle here and there. She pulled her hand back. "It's obviously really important."

Jordan gulped back a large mouthful of bourbon, winced as she swallowed it. "Remember how I said I picture cancer when I beat the shit out of a kitchen cabinet?"

Astrid got a horrible sinking feeling in her stomach. "Yeah." She found herself placing her fingertips back on Jordan's arm, the barest brush of skin on skin.

Jordan sighed, eyes flicking to Astrid's fingertips before focusing on the space in front of her. "My wife. Meredith. Diagnosed with breast cancer two years ago."

Astrid reared back as though she'd been slapped. "My god. When did she . . . I mean . . . how long ago did she . . ." She couldn't seem to get *die* out of her mouth.

"Oh, she's not dead," Jordan said.

Astrid blinked. "She's . . . she's not." It wasn't a question, but Astrid was completely confused all the same.

Jordan shook her head, then knocked back another glug of liquor. "She survived. Been in remission now for, oh, I think she must be going on fourteen months?"

Astrid had no idea what to say. Jordan was married? She had a whole wife? Conflicting feelings swirled in Astrid's gut—surprise, confusion, and . . . no, that couldn't be jealousy in there too. Absolutely not. She shook her head, swallowed, and just said what she was thinking. "I don't understand."

"Join the club," Jordan said, huffing a little mirthless laugh. Then she seemed to settle, her ruffled feathers smoothing out. She sighed and let her head drop back against the seat, throat exposed, eyes on the gilded ceiling. "Okay, I'll say it fast."

Astrid didn't dare utter a word, didn't even breathe as she waited for Jordan.

"She left me," Jordan said. "After she got better, once she was officially in remission. Said cancer made her realize she wasn't living the life she really wanted. She said she loved me, but as her best friend, and, apparently, she didn't want a best friend for a partner. She wanted a destiny."

Jordan lifted her head and looked at Astrid then. "Can you believe that?" she said. "A fucking *destiny*. And I guess holding her hair back while she puked from the chemo, scouring the Internet for real human hair wigs, setting my alarm for every two hours at night so I could wake up and make sure she was still fucking breathing, wasn't quite the *destiny* she had in mind."

Astrid could only blink at her.

"Don't get me wrong," Jordan went on, sighing. "I'm thankful as hell she beat it. Cancer is a bitch, and I would never wish that on anyone. It's just . . . after we went through all of that together, things didn't quite turn out the way I thought they would."

"Yeah," Astrid said softly.

"And the best part? She still texts me, oh, every couple of months, just to"—Here Jordan shot finger quotes into the air—"*check in*, because apparently, she's taking that best friends bullshit all the way."

Words escaped Astrid. Fled from every brain cell in her head. Crowd noise grew louder around them, laughter and chatter, the rattle of ice in glasses.

"Oh, and here's a little cosmic twist for you," Jordan said, sitting up suddenly and grabbing her bag from the seat next to her. She rummaged around in the brown vegan leather, then came out with a colorful paper rectangle a little bigger than a playing card. "How's this for fucking destiny?"

She held the card out and Astrid took it, peering at the image. It featured two women, both with different shades of brown skin, one with long black hair and one with short. They faced each other, and each held a golden cup in their hands. *Two of Cups* was printed across the bottom of the card.

"A Tarot card?" Astrid asked.

"Not just any Tarot card," Jordan said. "The Tarot card I drew this morning. Oh, and yesterday. Three days ago. Four times last week, and so on and so on for the past month."

Astrid looked from Jordan to the card, from the card back to Jordan.

Jordan laughed and snatched the card back, glaring down at it. "It's the soul mates card. Perfect pairs. True love."

Realization spread through Astrid. "Ah."

"Yeah. Wife leaves me for a greater romantic destiny, I start drawing the fucking romantic destiny card. The universe has a hell of a sense of humor, doesn't she?"

Jordan stuffed the card back into her bag and dropped it on the empty seat next to her, then took another gulp of liquor. She slumped in her chair, one ankle propped on her knee, arms on the seat rests as she leaned her head back.

Instinctively, Astrid's fingers found their way back to Jordan's arm. Well, no, not instinctively. Her instinct rarely included physical comfort, but somehow, her fingers didn't seem to belong anywhere else right now.

Jordan rolled her head, eyes meeting Astrid's. Her gaze was a little hazy, but from the alcohol or her story, Astrid wasn't sure. When Jordan didn't move her arm, Astrid pressed her fingertips into Jordan's skin a little more firmly.

"If you fucking say you're sorry," Jordan said softly, "I'm going to dump the rest of my drink all over your pretty hair."

Astrid cracked a smile at that. "I was not going to say that I'm sorry."

Jordan glanced at her skeptically. "Oh, really? Then what were you going to say?" She lifted the cherry from her drink to her mouth and bit the fruit off the stem with a vicious snap.

Astrid let her mouth hang open again for a second. "I . . . was . . . going to say that I can tie a cherry stem into a knot with my tongue."

Jordan blinked.

Astrid blinked.

The whole theater seemed to blink.

Holy shit, did she just . . . ? Yes, Astrid Isabella Parker really did just pull out a frat house party trick in response to news about Jordan's cancer-surviving wife leaving her for a greater destiny than the one she already had.

"Well, this I have to fucking see," Jordan said, sitting up straight—which dislodged Astrid's fingers—and holding out the cherry stem.

Astrid dropped her face into her hands. "Oh my god. I have no idea why I said that."

"What's done is done." Jordan waggled the cherry stem at her. "Get that tongue ready, Parker."

Astrid took the stem while Jordan folded her arms, drink still in one hand.

"I haven't done this since college," Astrid said, flicking the stem between her thumb and forefinger.

Jordan grinned, flourishing her free hand as if to say *Go on, then*.

Astrid groaned, but popped the stem into her mouth. She worked her tongue around the waxy matter, her jaw moving back and forth and up and down while she tried to keep her lips pressed together so her mouth wasn't hanging open like a gutted fish. She knew she probably looked like a complete idiot, and laughter bubbled into her chest.

Jordan leaned forward. Slowly, eyes flicking to Astrid's mouth, her own parting just a little. Jordan watched her so intently, as though everything Astrid was doing was fascinating.

As though Astrid herself were fascinating.

Something about the whole scene made Astrid's stomach flutter, warmth blooming in her cheeks. She couldn't remember the last time anyone, regardless of gender, had looked at her like that. Suddenly overwhelmed, she stopped working the stem and made to spit it out, but Jordan grabbed her arm.

"That better be coming out of your mouth in a knot, Parker," she said, brows lifting in a challenge. Her thumb traced a circle over Astrid's wrist—just once as Jordan pulled her arm back, but it was enough to make Astrid want to . . . what?

Succeed?

No, that wasn't quite right, though, of course, now that the gauntlet had been thrown, the thought of giving up was unbearable. But it was more than that. As her tongue curled and coiled, maneuvering one end of the stem under the other, she realized what the feeling was.

She wanted to impress Jordan Everwood.

And goddammit, she would.

Once she was sure the stem was knotted, she lifted a lackadaisical hand, plucked it from her mouth, and handed it to Jordan.

The other woman took it, twirling the perfectly tied stem between her fingers. Her gaze dropped to Astrid's mouth one more time, and Astrid found herself doing the same. Jordan had a nice mouth—top and bottom lip equally full, perfectly ruby red despite her drink and the popcorn. Astrid always envied women who had a rosebud mouth like Jordan Everwood. Her own mouth was thinner, her bottom lip bigger than her top, and she could never quite pull off red lipstick.

It took the house lights dimming for Astrid to realize she'd been staring at Jordan Everwood—at her *mouth*—for at least ten seconds.

Astrid cleared her throat and straightened in her seat. "Told you I could do it."

"You sure did," Jordan said, but her voice was softer, all teasing gone. Her tone made Astrid feel itchy, anxious, not unlike that restless feeling she got when she was turned on, which was ridiculous. Granted, everything seemed to make her horny lately—a body wash commercial, a whiff of cologne in the coffee shop, the feel of her own bare thighs against her expensive cotton sheets.

Sheets, for god's sake.

In her defense, she hadn't had sex in . . . well, a while. Her last time had been with Spencer, about a week before they broke up last June. Ten months wasn't that long, but with Claire and Delilah pretty much publicly humping each other every time they were all together and Iris's constant mooning over Jillian, her dry spell felt more like a dry era.

And she wasn't even going to think about the last time Spencer— or any guy she'd been with—had actually made her come. The whole scenario felt like such a cliché—the repressed only daughter of a controlling mother had a hard time getting off with other people, because of course she did.

Jesus, why was she even thinking about this right now? Sheets in the privacy of her own bedroom were one thing, but Jordan Everwood's husky voice? She had two queer best friends and a queer stepsister, so it's not like she wasn't aware these things happened . . . they'd just never happened to her.

Surely—*surely*—they weren't happening now. Not in this gilded movie theater with a bucket of popcorn between her thighs and the taste of a waxy cherry stem in her mouth.

She glanced at Jordan, who tucked the cherry stem into the front pocket of her wine-stained shirt, dark brows drawn together like she was thinking her own deep thoughts, probably about her abandoning wife.

Her wife.

Jordan Everwood had had a wife. Vows and rings, for better or worse, till death do them part.

Or not.

Astrid fixed her eyes straight ahead, her throat suddenly swelling. She took another sip of her drink, and her head went a bit fuzzy as she sucked a piece of ice into her mouth. She rather liked the feeling. Astrid hardly ever drank past a slight buzz, but right now, she sure as hell needed something.

She shoved yet another fistful of popcorn in her mouth while the velvet curtain pulled back from the stage, revealing a pair of golden cherubs, flowers, and birds bordering the movie screen. The opening credits started to roll, and *City Lights* flashed across the screen.

"Hey," Jordan asked, holding up her bourbon. There was an impish gleam in her eye that, for some reason, made Astrid want to exhale in relief. Jordan nodded toward the screen and then held up her drink. "You in?"

Astrid barely hesitated before clinking her glass with Jordan's. "I'm in."

CHAPTER

FIFTEEN

AS IT TURNED out, Astrid was a very fun drunk. Jordan worried a silent movie wouldn't hold her attention, but the woman was like a tiger hunting an antelope, catching every over-the-top facial expression any actor exhibited ever. The result was two very tipsy women by ten o'clock, when they spilled out of the theater and into the warm April night.

Jordan knew she should've cut herself off after two drinks so they could drive home, but dammit, she just hadn't wanted to. It had been so long since she'd been with another human like this. After Meredith left, the friends Jordan and her wife once shared tried to include her, but Jordan's heart hadn't been in it.

Her heart hadn't been in anything.

And still wasn't, she told herself, a default message that didn't sit right in her spinning brain right now. Goddamn bourbon. She never made great decisions when she drank bourbon. Hence spilling her guts about Meredith leaving her—and not even for someone else, just flat-out leaving—to a person who was essentially her enemy.

But as Astrid spread her arms wide under the Andromeda's glowing marquee, the lights painting her skin pink and gold, she didn't feel like Jordan's enemy. Not one bit. This was certainly a different woman than the one who'd ripped into Jordan over some spilled coffee a week ago, but not so different than the one from earlier tonight, or even the one who swung the sledgehammer a week ago. No, this Astrid was just a little softer, that stiff outer shell she wore cracked ever so slightly.

Jordan wondered if her own shell was cracked too.

"Ready to go?" she called to Astrid, who was still spinning like an ice skater while other moviegoers angled around her, amused expressions on their faces.

Astrid stopped, out of breath, eyes sparkling from the fluorescents as she blinked at Jordan. "Not even a little."

Jordan laughed. "Well, good, because there's no way either of us can drive yet. I guess we could call a Lyft."

"And then you'd have to come all the way back out here to get your truck tomorrow."

"A trip you'd most certainly take with me, Mistress Let's-Have-Another."

Astrid giggled—legit *giggled*—and spun around a few more times. She was making Jordan nauseous just watching her twirl.

"You're not one of those awful people who never gets hangovers, are you?" Jordan asked.

Astrid shrugged. "Not sure."

Spin, spin, spin.

"Hold up," Jordan said, walking—albeit a little crookedly—over to Astrid and stopping her by closing her hands around her upper arms. "Have you never been drunk before?"

Astrid scrunched up her face, pretending to think. It was fucking adorable, except it wasn't, because Astrid Parker was *not* adorable, goddammit.

"Inebriation is not Isabel Parker-Green approved," Astrid said, tapping Jordan's nose once with her forefinger. "Obviously."

"'Inebriation?'"

"Isabel Parker-Green would never say the work *drunk*."

Jesus, her mother sound sounded like a real piece of work.

"What about college?" Jordan asked.

Astrid swayed, and Jordan realized her hands were still around Astrid's arms. She let go, but then Astrid tilted to the side a bit more than was safe, so she grabbed this infernal woman again and held on.

"College was . . ." Astrid waved a sloppy hand through the air. "Too much to do. Straight As, dating golden boys."

"Sounds fucking horrible."

Astrid laughed. "It was. Iris always tried to . . ." But then she trailed off, her eyes focusing on something over Jordan's shoulder. "There's a playground over there."

Jordan laughed. "A what?"

"A playground," Astrid said, lacing her fingers through Jordan's and tugging her toward a tiny park at the end of the street. "We can't drive right now. Might as well swing."

Might as well swing was a phrase she'd never expected to hear from Astrid Parker, much less coupled with the action of drunk-stumbling to a park at the edge of the lake.

She also never expected Astrid's hand to feel so warm and soft, fingers squeezing Jordan's just tightly enough.

The park was small, a lot of green space bordered by a walking path, a minimalist playground about fifty feet from the water. There was a swing set, a seesaw, and a bright orange slide that coiled around a large oak tree. Once they arrived, Astrid dropped Jordan's hand and promptly fell into a plastic blue swing, her movements so wobbly, Jordan was amazed she made it into the seat.

"How high do you think I can go?" Astrid said, starting to pump her legs like a fourth grader.

Jordan couldn't help but smile. "Not as high as me."

"Want to bet?"

"Oh, you're on, Parker." She settled into the swing next to Astrid, who was already soaring through the air. "Though I'd be remiss if I didn't mention that swinging motions and alcohol don't always mix."

Astrid just grinned, and soon they were flying through the night air. The sound of Astrid's laugh as their swings synced up made Jordan feel . . .

Young?

Hopeful?

Happy.

That was it. She was happy—a little drunk, sure, but not so much that she couldn't tell that her laughter, the fizzy feeling in her chest, were real.

Astrid reached out a hand, her smile bright and wide, and gripped Jordan's fingers. They stayed like that, their bodies swinging this way and that, hands entwined under the Oregon sky.

CHAPTER

SIXTEEN

THE SUN WAS trying to kill Astrid Parker.

At least, that's what it felt like when she woke up the next morning, light streaming in through the gauzy curtains of her bedroom window and knifing its way under her gummy eyelids.

Something buzzed loudly to her left.

Something horrible that surely hated her guts.

This something turned out to be her phone, which, admittedly, didn't have the sentience to despise her, but the emotion remained all the same. Astrid grabbed the thing off her nightstand and squinted at the screen, only to find a picture of Iris puckering her mouth at Astrid in an air kiss.

It took her a good five seconds to figure out this meant Iris was calling her.

"What?" she said when she finally managed to slide her finger over the screen.

"Oh, so you *are* alive."

"Why are you calling me?" No one called anyone anymore, and Iris hated talking on the phone.

"The forty billion texts didn't seem to have any effect," Iris said.

Astrid pulled the phone back from her ear and blinked at the device. An amalgam of *Where the hell are you* texts filled her messages.

"Ugh, sorry," she said, flopping back onto her pillow and rubbing her temples with her thumb and forefinger.

"Where have you been?"

Astrid paused on that one, images of last night coalescing in her foggy brain. She caught a whiff of her hair, which smelled like a weird mixture of popcorn and pine trees. Her mouth tasted like a swamp.

She was also completely naked.

She sat up.

Fast.

Way too fast.

Room spinning, horrible feeling in her stomach.

And she was naked.

As in . . . *naked*. Astrid never slept naked.

She took a few deep breaths, pushing the nausea back down, and tried to puzzle together what happened last night. The movie, that ridiculous cherry stem, the drinking.

Had they . . . gone to a playground? She vaguely remembered a cold plastic seat, the metallic smell of the swing chains. Holding Jordan's hand as they soared through the air.

Her stomach swooped at the memory.

Was it even real?

The swoop turned into a lurch as she distinctly remembered bolting off the swing so she could puke into a juniper bush.

After that, Jordan had sobered up a lot quicker than she had. She vaguely remembered getting in the truck, Jordan shoving a water bottle into her hands, windows down and cool night air on her face. Then . . .

Nothing.

She looked around the room for signs of what she did when she came home. Her clothes from the night before were folded on the overstuffed armchair in the corner, but not the way she herself would've folded them, sleeves all tucked in nicely. No, her blouse's sleeves were visible, like someone cut the shirt in half lengthwise first, which Astrid never did. Plus, the garment was most likely filthy and belonged in her dry cleaning bag.

There was also a glass of water on her nightstand she had no memory of obtaining, along with a bottle of ibuprofen.

Okay, fine. So maybe Jordan had come in and helped her out a little. Gotten her into bed. No big deal.

But why was she completely naked and where the hell were her bra and underwear? She scanned the floor, the chair, but didn't see them anywhere.

"Hello?" Iris said.

Astrid startled, having totally forgotten her friend was on the phone. "Um . . ." She finally spotted her bra . . . hanging off one corner of her fabric headboard, as through she'd flung it off in the night.

God, please let her have flung it off in the night as opposed to whenever Jordan put that glass of water by her bed.

"Astrid, I swear to god," Iris said.

Astrid ignored her, on a mission to find her undies. They weren't on her headboard—thank god—and they weren't on the floor anywhere that she could see. She pushed her bedding back to get up and check more thoroughly, but then spotted the damn things under the covers near the foot of the bed.

She exhaled and went to grab them, swearing never, ever to drink that much again, when something pink caught her eye. Peeking out from underneath her plain cotton briefs was . . .

. . . oh god.

"Astrid," Iris said. "Are you dying? What the hell is happening?"

"Let me call you back."

"Oh no. If you hang up, I'm coming over there and—"

Astrid ended the call and stared at that flash of pink.

Surely not.

She picked up her underwear, flinging it across the room like it was on fire to reveal the California Dreaming Malibu Minx vibrator Iris had gotten her over two years ago. She'd never used it. Not once. It sat in her nightstand next to a silk sleep mask and a bottle of lavender oil. It wasn't that Astrid never got herself off. She did. A couple of times a week, in fact. She just preferred using her fingers most of the time. Honestly, the California Dreaming was a little intimidating. It was . . . well, it was goddamn huge, is what it was, and Astrid had never felt the need.

Why the hell was it in her bed?

She gingerly picked it up, using only the very tips of her fingers around the base, and inspected the toy. It looked like it always did, bright pink and smooth, a little curve to the tip. She couldn't tell if she'd actually employed its services last night, but as she stared at the thing, little pieces came back to her, like waking slowly from a dream.

"Oh, okay, then," Jordan had said as Astrid flung her clothes off in her bedroom, desperate for her bed. Jordan had picked up the garments after her and folded them—albeit wrongly—before placing them on her chair.

"Sleep," Astrid had said.

"Yeah, I'd say that's a good idea," Jordan said. "But first, take this." She held out two liquid blue pills and a glass of water. "Trust me."

Astrid had obeyed. She remembered blinking up into Jordan's hazel eyes as she sat on the edge of her bed in her bra and underwear and gulped the water down while Jordan held the glass.

She'd flopped onto her pillow after that. Covers secured around her chin and then . . .

"I should be the one tucking you in."

That's what she'd said to Jordan when the other woman had literally tucked the sheets around her arms and legs.

"Why's that?" Jordan had asked.

"Because," Astrid had mumbled. "She left you like you didn't mean anything. And you do. You mean something."

Silence. A smooth, cool hand on her forehead, hair looped around her ear. Astrid saw it all unfold in her mind like she was watching a movie for the first time, witnessing the main character make cringe-worthy, booze-infused choices.

After that, she'd slept, she supposed, but then she remembered waking up in the middle of the night because—

Oh god.

She'd had a dream.

A sex dream.

About Jordan Everwood.

In the dream, they'd been in the Andromeda, sitting in the red velvet seats. Just like the night before, Astrid tied a cherry stem into a knot—seriously, what the hell had she been thinking?—but in the dream, instead of Jordan slipping the stem into her pocket, she'd continued to twirl it between her fingers, her eyes on Astrid's mouth. And Astrid had . . . well . . . something otherworldly must've taken over her body, because she—Astrid Isabella Parker—had climbed onto Jordan's lap.

Straddled her.

As in, one leg on each side of Jordan's hips.

She had no clue what happened to the cherry stem. Jordan couldn't possibly be holding on to it, because she'd drawn Astrid closer, gliding her hands around Astrid's ribs and under her shirt. Jordan hadn't gone straight for her breasts though. No, she'd taken her time, fingertips ghosting down Astrid's back, cupping her ass, then sliding around to her hips. Dream-Astrid panted—*panted*, for god's sake— desperate for Jordan to touch her.

In fact, that's what she'd said in the dream.

Touch me.

And Jordan had obliged. Her thumbs swept over Astrid's already hardened nipples, and Astrid had moaned, tossing her head back.

Astrid never *moaned*.

Jordan licked a stripe from her neck to her ear before kissing her properly, tongue and teeth and rosebud mouth closing around Astrid's bottom lip and tugging. Then Jordan had unbuttoned Astrid's jeans and—

"Oh shit," Astrid said now, staring down at the vibrator.

She remembered waking up in a daze, hornier than she'd been in a long time, ripping off her undergarments before grabbing the California Dreaming from her drawer and turning it on. Then she'd pressed it to her clit and . . . well, she'd come. She remembered that very clearly now. Harder than she had in months.

"Oh shit," she said again.

She didn't think. Couldn't. Panic was filling her up like water in her lungs. She simply dropped all the evidence of last night's Jordan Everwood–fueled orgasm and tripped into a clean bra, underwear, a pair of yoga pants, and an off-the-shoulder sweatshirt. Her head pounded, her stomach still considered rebelling, but she couldn't stop to take care of them right now. Iris was probably on her way over here, and Astrid needed to talk to someone.

Someone else.

The only someone else she trusted to treat this whole experience with the dispassionate who-gives-a-shit attitude she needed right now.

DELILAH GREEN OPENED her apartment door with a quintessential greeting.

"What the fuck, Ass?"

"I'm sorry," Astrid said. "I know it's early."

"Early?" Delilah said. "It's the middle of the night."

"It's seven-thirty."

Delilah's eyes narrowed. Her curly hair was piled on top of her head, tendrils sneaking out of the silk scrunchie and looping around her neck. "Oh. Well, that's practically the middle of the night."

Astrid's stepsister was not a morning person, to say the least.

"God, you look like shit," Delilah said.

Astrid touched her hair, a total rat's nest after all her tossing and turning. While she hadn't dared look in a mirror that morning, she had no recollection of washing off her makeup last night, which meant she probably looked like a hungover raccoon.

"Yeah, well, rough night," she said.

"Are you okay?"

Astrid nodded, though she wasn't sure if she was being truthful or not. "Claire's not here, is she?"

Delilah frowned. "She and Josh have a conference with Ruby's teachers before school, so we slept at our own places last night. Why?"

"I just . . . I need to talk to you."

"About what?"

"Something important."

"Sleep is important."

"Delilah."

"Ass."

"I had a sex dream about Jordan Everwood."

This was not exactly the way Astrid envisioned dropping the news, but it shut Delilah up at least. Her stepsister blinked a few times, then scrubbed her hands over her face before opening her door wider to let Astrid inside.

"Coffee," Delilah said, shuffling toward the kitchen. "I'm going to need a lot of coffee for this conversation."

Astrid didn't respond. Instead, she plopped down onto the gray couch in the living room, breathing heavily as if she'd run here, and glanced around to distract herself. She'd been here only a few times, but Delilah's apartment was nice, simple, grays and blues and greens. Lots of black-and-white photographs of Claire on the walls. Claire's daughter, Ruby. The three of them together. Family photos.

There were also several boxes littering the space, some of them already labeled "Books and shit" and "Old-ass photos" in true Delilah style. With everything going on at the inn, Astrid kept forgetting that her stepsister was officially moving in with Claire and Ruby next week. While Claire had been taking things pretty slow because of her twelve-year-old daughter, everyone knew she and Delilah were the real deal. The forever kind of love.

Something ached in the center of Astrid's chest. She wasn't sure what it was specifically, but her mind went to Jordan, the look in her eyes as she'd told Astrid about her wife.

"Here," Delilah said, holding out a large mug.

"Thanks." Astrid took it, noticing with a tiny jolt of happiness that Delilah had added a splash of cream and a little sprinkle of cinnamon, just the way Astrid liked her coffee. She took a sip, and the caffeine soared through her bloodstream, life-giving and healing. Her head instantly felt less like a balloon filled to capacity.

Delilah settled in on the other end of the couch and tucked her legs underneath her. Then she just stared at Astrid, waiting.

Astrid cleared her throat, totally unsure what to say now that the reason for her visit was out in the open already. What did she expect here exactly? Advice? Reassurance? And for what? She wasn't ashamed that she had the dream. She wasn't even confused. She was just . . . she didn't know.

Overwhelmed.

That was it.

She was violently overwhelmed by every single thing that happened last night.

"Do I get details?" Delilah finally asked.

"Details?"

Delilah waggled her eyebrows. "Details."

Something about Delilah's expression and tone, the lightness of her simple question lifted a weight off Astrid's shoulders.

"Absolutely not," she said.

"But it was hot?"

Astrid's smile faded. She swallowed hard, could only nod in response. No way she was bringing up the vibrator and subsequent real-life orgasm, but her cheeks flushed warm anyway.

Delilah grinned. "Nice."

"You don't seem surprised."

Delilah canted her head. "What do you mean?"

"I mean . . . I'm me. I'm not . . . I mean, I've never . . ."

"Okay, hold up," Delilah said, sitting up and leaning a little closer to Astrid. "*Never before* doesn't mean *never ever*. You know that, right?"

"Yes. Of course, I just . . . I mean, I have Claire and Iris. I have . . . I have *you*. I'm surrounded by queer friends and family. Wouldn't I have known by now if I was attracted to women?"

Delilah shrugged. "Sexuality is complicated. It's not static. People change and sexuality can change too." She took a sip of her coffee. "But this *is* you we're talking about here. You're pretty much the poster kid for compulsory heterosexuality."

Astrid frowned, that old defensiveness rising. "What? What the hell are you talking about?"

"Don't get your undies in a knot. I'm not insulting you. I'm just saying . . . well, think about it. If you'd been attracted to a woman or anyone who wasn't a cis dude in the past, oh, eighteen or so years since you hit puberty, what would Mommy Dearest have done?"

Astrid opened her mouth, then snapped it shut. Isabel would've lost her shit. Her mother had never said a negative word about Claire's or Iris's queerness. She'd never even said anything against Delilah's queerness. When her stepdaughter came out back in eighth grade, Isabel had simply lifted a single eyebrow at the news and moved on, so Astrid didn't think homophobia played a huge role in Isabel's mindset so much as expectations. Delilah was Delilah. But Astrid . . . well, Astrid was a Parker, Isabel's blood, and she was expected to wed a rich golden boy, pop out some golden kids, and join the Junior League.

Which was a kind of homophobia, Astrid realized. She'd just never thought about it that way before. But now, as she searched back for any evidence that she'd ever been attracted to women before, she found little clues.

Her keen attention to every detail of Amira Karim's jeans in high school. She'd simply been fascinated by the way they fit her thighs, her butt. Then there was the way her eyes always seemed to notice how a woman's chest filled out a shirt. Back in college, sophomore year, some drunken frat boys had dared her and Rilla Sanchez to make out at one of the few parties she'd attended, and she remembered a distinct and strange flare of disappointment when Rilla had told them all to go fuck themselves.

There were other memories, countless moments she'd long ago chalked up to admiration or envy. Just good old-fashioned jealousy. She wanted to *be* those girls, or maybe even compete with them, as horrible as that sounded, not make out with them. And maybe that really was all it was sometimes. Simple observation. But maybe those tiny clues actually added up to a whole lot more, and she'd simply never let herself face it.

She liked guys, so she focused on guys. It was easy to ignore anything else.

"Shit," she said, dropping her face into her hands.

"Yeah," Delilah said. "You were expected to only see men as potential romantic partners, so that's what you did."

"Like, really, holy shit."

"Look," Delilah said, setting her mug on the coffee table full of photo thumbnails and lacing her hands together. "The big question here isn't about a sex dream. It's a dream. Dreams happen. Hell, I'm pretty damn sure I had a dream last year during that camping trip to Bagby Hot Springs that I was a vampire and full-on seduced your ex-fiancé so I could bleed him dry while he was distracted by my tits."

Astrid's eyes widened, setting her own mug on the table. "And you don't think that *meant* something?"

Delilah's upper lip curled. "I don't do cis men."

"Yes, fine, but the vampiric murderess out for Spencer's blood?"

Delilah scrunched up her face in thought. "Okay, you make a strong point, but the sex dream is still not what's important here."

Astrid groaned and fell back onto the couch pillows, flopping her arm over her eyes.

"What's important," Delilah went on, "is whether or not you like Jordan Everwood. I mean, aside from wanting to fuck her brains out."

Astrid sat up. "I do not want to . . . to . . ."

"It's okay. You can say it."

Astrid rolled her eyes. "I do not want to *fuck* her brains out. There, are you happy?"

Delilah grinned. "Very. And sure you do—you had sex dream about her."

Astrid lifted her hands and let them fall back to her legs with a loud slap. "But you just said that wasn't the important part!"

Delilah shrugged, picked up her coffee, and took a smug sip.

"You are infuriating, you know that?" Astrid said, picking up a pillow embroidered with the words *To be quite queer* and tossing it at Delilah, who caught it deftly with one hand and threw it right back.

"Which is exactly why you came to me about this and not your BFFs," she said.

Astrid opened her mouth to protest, but her stepsister had a point. She did go straight to Delilah, never even considered taking this to

Iris or even Claire first. She already knew exactly how they'd react. Iris would squeal and pop some bubbly, even at this early hour, going on and on about how Astrid completed their queer coven. And Claire—gentle, cinnamon roll Claire—would simply be too sweet about the whole thing. She'd soothe and ask soul-probing questions, and Astrid didn't want any of that.

She wanted the hard stuff, the complicated truth, and she knew Delilah was the only one who would give it to her.

"So, do you?" Delilah asked.

"Do I what?"

Delilah just lifted her brows.

She left you like you didn't mean anything. And you do. You mean something.

Astrid didn't speak—she couldn't. Her throat felt suddenly tight, too big for her body. It had been so long since she'd actually liked someone. She wasn't even sure she'd *liked* Spencer—he'd just fit the right mold at the right time.

Jordan, one the other hand, was a puzzle, one that Astrid was pretty sure she wanted to figure out.

"She's trying to sabotage my design plan for the Everwood," she said. "So that's a problem."

Delilah's eyebrows lifted, but a little smile settled on her face. "So solve it. That's what you do best, isn't it?"

Astrid sighed. Before her broken engagement with Spencer, yeah, she would have said she was an excellent problem solver. But in the past year, she couldn't stop thinking about how close she came to marrying a man she didn't even like, and all for what? Well, that was the question, wasn't it? She'd let herself *be made* instead of deciding what kind of life she really wanted. And while she'd gotten out of that mess, she hadn't quite felt like herself ever since. She wasn't altogether sure she'd ever felt like herself, to be honest.

As she sat there in her stepsister's living room—the stepsister who left Bright Falls at eighteen because she wanted more, created beautiful art because she loved it, because she couldn't *not* create it, and then came back home for a woman she didn't want to live without—Astrid had the sudden and horrible thought that maybe, just maybe, every single detail and quirk that formed who she was had *been made*.

The thought was a firework in her chest, and she suddenly had a hard time breathing.

"You okay?" Delilah asked, brows dipping low in concern.

Astrid nodded, swallowed one more sip of coffee and got a grip, because that's what Astrid Parker did—she got herself together.

"I should go," she said, standing and smoothing out her yoga pants, which couldn't be wrinkled anyway, the motion so practiced, such a habit.

Delilah nodded and stood too. "Well, you can always come find me here at two in the morning if you have any more dirty dreams."

Astrid laughed, but it felt like one of those that verged on the edge of tears. "Until next week."

Delilah looked confused for a split second, but then a blissfully dopey expression settled on her face as she gazed at the boxes. "Yeah. Next week."

"You two are having a party to celebrate, right? Next weekend?"

Delilah nodded.

"Cute."

Delilah flipped Astrid off. "Yes, it's all super wonderful and perfect. Now get the hell out of here. You really do look like shit, and it's freaking me out."

Astrid laughed, because when her stepsister was right, her stepsister was right.

CHAPTER

SEVENTEEN

THE TWO OF Cups.

There it was again, staring up at her in all its true love, queer, fuck-you-naysayers glory. Jordan sat cross-legged on her bed, a hangover headache pressing against her eyes despite the gallon of water she drank when she got home last night, and glared down at the card.

This was the third day in a row this card had reared its head at her. In the last week, she'd had several pentacles and a few wands, all of which she embraced for their respective material and creative meanings. But of course, the universe loved to laugh, so here she was, the morning after tucking an unbearably adorable and very drunk Astrid Parker into her bed, staring down at this lovefest.

She should've known right then the day would go from bad to worse. Half an hour later, when her phone buzzed in her back pocket while she poured her coffee in the cottage's kitchen, she already knew who it was.

There were only two other people in the entire world who ever texted her, and they were in the room with her at this very moment. Her grandmother sat at the round breakfast table in a purple button-down and matching glasses, sipping Earl Grey tea out of her *I love my queer grandkids* rainbow mug while reading the *New York Times*, just like she did every morning. Simon was whistling while frying up thick slices of bacon to go with the cheesy eggs he'd already scrambled, Jordan's preferred hangover food. Times like this, she was thankful to have a twin who only had to look at her to tell she needed a greasy breakfast.

But now her phone was putting a real damper on her excitement for homemade diner food. Every time this happened, she told herself she wouldn't even look at the text. She hadn't responded to any of them, not once in the last twelve months, but she always read them, puzzled for days over each word, then inevitably gave in and stalked Meredith's Instagram, which was filled with images of her raven-haired ex-wife all bright-eyed and bushy-tailed in San Francisco, Nashville, floating in a crystalline Lake Michigan, posing outside the Eiffel Tower, for fuck's sake.

From there, Jordan's emotional state would spiral, usually ending in a couple pints of Ben & Jerry's, a drained bottle of Bulleit, and a lot of empty delivery cartons.

Suffice it to say, Simon had been right to worry that she wasn't coping with the fact that the love of her life dropped her like a load of garbage at the dump. Problem was, Meredith kept coming back to sift through the trash bags for things she'd left behind.

Jordan sighed, her hand moving on its own to grab her phone out of her pocket. Simon eyed her, but she ignored him as she glanced down at the screen.

Hi, how are you?

Same question every time. And then, without fail, approximately three minutes after the first text, came the long block of words describing Meredith's wonderful life.

I'm in Colorado and thought of you. Remember that road trip
we took right after college? What was it, thirteen other girls?
Emma, Kendall, Ava, and honestly, I can't even think of who
else. All I can remember is that the biggest blizzard to hit
Colorado in like a decade rolled in and I have never been so
cold in my entire life. We stuffed ourselves into one subzero
sleeping bag, hot water bottles at our feet, and still weren't
warm. I'd always wanted to go back when the weather was
decent. Estes Park is truly breathtaking, and I . . .

And on and on she went.

"Seriously?" Simon said, now reading over her shoulder, pan of
sizzling bacon in one hand.

Jordan pressed the side button, turning the screen dark.

"She was 'thinking of you'?" Simon said, his voice incredulous.

"What's going on?" Pru asked, looking alarmed.

"Nothing, Grandma," Jordan said, then glared at her brother. "Simon, don't."

"Has she been doing that a lot?" he asked, finger jutting toward
her phone.

"I don't respond," she said, stuffing her phone back into her pocket.
She was suddenly so tired.

"I sure as hell hope not!" Simon said, his voice growing more
stressed by the second, which was exactly why Jordan never told him
about Meredith's little text intrusions. Simon wasn't her ex-wife's
biggest fan, though Jordan supposed that was to be expected. It wasn't
like she was singing Meredith's praises lately either, but still. The
woman survived cancer. She had been Jordan's wife. There was a
part of Jordan that could never hate her, no matter how much she
wanted to. It wasn't Meredith's fault that Jordan wasn't the one.

That she wasn't *destiny* material.

"Honey, sit down," Pru said, concerned eyes on Jordan. She patted the spot next to her, but Jordan shook her head. She couldn't handle the sympathetic look on her grandmother's face right now, the way Simon rubbed his jaw like he did when he didn't know what to do.

She was so tired of being the one they all worried over. She didn't need their concern anymore, that anxious crease between their eyes that only made her feel weak and useless. She needed . . .

I can tie a cherry stem into a knot with my tongue.

A laugh bubbled into her chest, but she pressed it back down. Still, there was no stopping the smile that pulled at the corners of her mouth.

Simon's eyebrows went up in surprise.

"I need to get to work," she said, jutting her thumb toward the back door before refilling her coffee cup to the brim and heading outside, her smile still fixed on her face.

BY THE TIME five o'clock rolled around and Josh's group and the show's crew headed out for the day, Jordan's sunny smile had darkened into a storm cloud. She'd made a lot of progress on her kitchen cabinets and a table for the dining room, fielded some deliveries for items that were definitely not on Astrid's design plan . . . but she hadn't seen Astrid herself at all.

It was driving her fucking bananas. And the fact that Astrid's absence was driving her fucking bananas was worrisome, to say the least.

She kept replaying their entire night together over and over again in her mind, like her life itself was a silent movie, complete with over-the-top facial expressions and dramatics. Specifically, her brain kept getting hung up on helping Astrid into bed. The way she'd thrown off her clothes with total abandon and snuggled into her high-thread-count sheets with a happy groan, her hair fanning out over her pillow.

And then . . .

She left you like you didn't mean anything. And you do. You mean something.

Jordan had felt all the air fly out of her lungs in that moment. Honestly, eighteen hours later, she still wasn't sure if she'd taken a normal breath. She didn't know what to think of Astrid's words, the gentle way she'd said them—albeit, with a slight slur—and how Jordan couldn't properly swallow for a good five minutes afterward.

And then Astrid had dared to not even show up at the inn today. Not that she was there every day, and she wasn't on the call sheet, but a person couldn't simply say a thing like that to another human and then disappear. Then again, maybe Astrid didn't even remember saying it. She'd been drunk and tired and had recently vomited into a bush.

You mean something.

Jordan's electric saw buzzed through her thoughts. Wood shavings drifted through the air, filling the space with that clean, rugged smell she loved, like trees spilling secrets. She spent another half an hour on the custom vanity she planned to work into the master bedroom, trying to drown out Astrid's soft voice with her work.

BY MIDNIGHT, JORDAN gave up on sleep. Shoving the covers back, she pulled on the same pair of jeans she'd worn that day and a soft hunter-green Henley with the neck a bit too stretched out. She grabbed her bag and sneaked out the back door, heading straight for her workshop.

She never got there.

A light was on in the inn.

Or rather, a light was *present* in the inn. As Jordan paused in the grass, she watched a white glow swing this way and that on the second floor.

A flashlight.

Goose bumps erupted down Jordan's arm. She spent about two point five seconds wondering if she should get Simon or call the police, but the latter didn't seem to be a safe solution for anyone these days, and the former . . . well, she could probably take care of an intruder more efficiently than her brother could. She was almost positive he'd never thrown a punch in his life, whereas at least Jordan knew how to wield heavy tools.

She ducked into her workshop, heart pumping adrenaline, and set her bag on the sawdust-covered cement floor as quietly as she could. Using her own phone as a light, she rooted around on her workbench until she found it—her three-pound, hardwood-drilling hammer.

Slipping out of her workshop, she stole across the lawn, eyes searching in the dark for a car. But aside from the dumpster, the front drive was completely barren, grass torn up from work trucks. She glanced up at the inn.

The light had settled in the Lapis Room.

Jordan squeezed her eyes closed, fear spilling into her chest. She took one . . . two . . . three deep breaths, sent out a little plea for help to Alice Everwood, and then hurried around the back of the house where she used her key to let herself in.

The house smelled like fresh paint, the gray that Astrid had ordered covering the walls in the kitchen. Something *thumped* above her head. She tapped on her phone's light and hurried to the stairs, taking them slowly, avoiding that spot on the twelfth step she knew squeaked, and tiptoed her way to the Lapis Room.

The door was closed, white light swinging underneath the thin strip near the floor.

Jordan circled her hand around the crystal doorknob. There was no way to do this gingerly as she knew the door would creak like an old person's bones as soon as she opened it. She had to choose—the phone light or the hammer. It wasn't a question, really. She turned off the light and tucked her phone into her back pocket, then shifted so she could be ready to swing the door open with her left hand, wielding the hammer with her right.

She paused, listening for movement inside. There were light footsteps, the scuff of what sounded like wood scraping against wood, then . . . a voice. A softly uttered "Shit," if Jordan wasn't mistaken.

Counting to three in her head, she turned the knob and pushed, hammer raised like Thor as she charged into the room. But before she could get any heroic words off her tongue, she barreled into something soft, ricocheted backward, and landed on her ass.

"Oh my god!" a voice screeched.

"Jesus Christ!" Jordan screeched back. The glow that had filled the room snuffed out, whoever-the-hell's phone or tablet landing with a crack on the hardwoods.

Jordan scrambled back to standing, grabbing for her hammer that she'd dropped in her fall. She held it with both hands, ready to swing. "Who the fuck—"

She froze, eyes adjusting to the dark, a familiar silhouette coming into focus.

"Parker?"

Astrid just sighed from where she'd landed on the floor, her iPad in its leather case next to her.

"Hi, Jordan."

"What the hell are you doing here?" She was breathing hard, both relief and anger swirling in her chest. And a little bit of excitement, if she was being honest, but she squashed that feeling down. Way down.

"Well?" she asked when Astrid said nothing.

Astrid picked up her iPad and turned the flashlight back on, pointing it downward as she slowly got to her feet. She was wearing yoga pants—very tight yoga pants, not that Jordan noticed—and a slouchy, off-the-shoulder sweatshirt.

"I . . . well, I was just . . ." Astrid said, but she didn't finish her sentence. Instead she just stood there, her fancy black bag at her feet, an expression on her face that reminded Jordan of a kid trying to figure out a difficult math problem.

Jordan waited. She had absolutely no intention of making this interaction easy for Astrid, not after she'd nearly given Jordan a heart attack at the age of thirty-one.

And ignored her all day after an amazing fucking night, but no need to bring messy emotions into this.

Finally, Astrid sighed and rubbed her forehead. "I couldn't sleep, so I thought I'd come here and do some work."

"As opposed to coming to the inn during regular working hours to do some work?"

"I didn't say it was a logical choice."

"Where the hell is your car?"

"I parked it on the street."

Jordan lifted a brow. "Sneaky."

Astrid looked horrified. "I just didn't want to wake anyone. And Simon gave me a key to the back door."

"Of course he did." Jordan took a step closer to her. "So how's that going?"

Astrid frowned. "How's what—"

"The work." Jordan motioned to her iPad. "Planning to paint it all white tomorrow?"

Astrid didn't say anything, but her eyes finally rested on Jordan's, something soft and a little vulnerable behind them. A feeling like hope swelled in Jordan's chest, but she pushed that back down too.

Or, at least she tried. The feeling persisted, burgeoning and pushing her feet closer to this woman she couldn't stop thinking about.

"Parker?" she asked quietly.

"I don't know," Astrid said. "I get why you want to preserve this place, Jordan. I really do, and I don't want to hurt you, but this is my job. And you're making it really hard for me to do it."

Jordan nodded. "What if I didn't make it so hard?"

"You don't strike me as the kind who surrenders."

"You're right, I'm not."

"Then how do you plan on making this easier?"

Jordan flicked on the overhead light. The blue room exploded into color, the shade even darker now at night and under the glow of the weak, amber lightbulb in the ancient crystal-globed fixture.

"What do you think about the color?" she asked. "Honestly."

"Honestly?" Astrid looked around, one hand on her hip. "I hate it. It's too dark, it shrinks the room, and I can't visualize any sort of end product that would be pleasing to the eye."

Jordan sent a hand through her hair. "Well, I did ask for honesty."

"I'm sorry," Astrid said, taking another step, the gap between them growing smaller and smaller. "It's just not me."

"But *you* are not this inn. Your job is to create a space for your client, not yourself."

"That's what I'm doing, Jordan," Astrid said. "My plan is what Simon said he wanted, what Pru wanted."

Jordan shook her head. "They don't know design. They don't know what they want until they see it, and my grandmother loved this color. You know she did."

Astrid folded her arms, iPad tucked against her chest. "I need this project to go well, Jordan. Natasha Rojas's opinion could make or break my career, my business is already hanging on by a very thin thread, my mother can barely stand to look at me without sneering, and a person can only redecorate so many dentists' offices before they start to question their life choices."

"So go on and question them, Parker." Jordan tapped her chest. "*I* need this project to go well. This place is my home. Do you get that? Not to mention that I'm barely past thirty and divorced, I'm living in my grandmother's house and sleeping in my childhood twin bed, my brother thinks I'm an epic fuckup, and I—"

"You're not a fuckup."

Astrid said it so softly, but it felt as though a bomb went off somewhere around Jordan's heart.

You mean something.

"You don't know me," Jordan said back, just as quietly. "You don't know anything about me, Parker."

Astrid frowned, her eyes leaving Jordan's to scan the room. Her throat worked like she was having a hard time swallowing, and Jordan found herself hoping Astrid would come back with a rebuttal, a *Sure I do*, even though it wasn't remotely true. Besides, what would knowing Jordan really accomplish? Meredith had known her better than anyone, better than even Simon, and she'd still left.

Apparently knowing Jordan Everwood only sent people running in the other direction.

"Then show me," Astrid said.

Jordan blinked, took a second to steady her breath. "What?"

"Show me," Astrid said again, waving her hand at the room. "Surely you have something planned beyond this hideous paint color."

"By all means, don't hold back," Jordan said.

"I won't," Astrid said, a challenge in her eyes.

Jordan felt it then, that spark she used to get so often before Meredith got sick. That drive toward creating, toward making something that another person loved. Granted, it had always been furniture up to this point, shelves and cabinets and tables, but Jordan knew her design plans for the Everwood were good.

And goddammit, she was going to prove it to Astrid Parker.

CHAPTER

EIGHTEEN

TONIGHT HAD NOT gone as planned. Astrid had wanted to come to the inn, spend some time in the rooms by herself, and figure out her next move. All day long, she told herself she wasn't avoiding the Everwood on purpose, that she'd be totally fine to see Jordan on a professional basis after their night together, after the dream and everything she and Delilah had talked about. But each time she thought about being in the same room with the woman, her skin flushed, her belly flopped around like she was a tween with her first crush, and she genuinely felt like she was going to throw up.

Not unlike how she felt now, but there was nothing to be done about it. Jordan had caught her, and Astrid was doing her level best to keep from actually vomiting in front of her.

Jordan rubbed the back of her neck, thinking. Something about the motion—the way Jordan's skin smoothed over her delicate collarbone, one hip popped out a little farther than the other—set Astrid's stomach ablaze again.

Jesus, this was ridiculous. Astrid didn't do this. She didn't go all gaga over a crush. She didn't *get* crushes, period. Spencer definitely never brought out these kinds of feelings. She'd have to go all the way back to middle school, when crushes were a complete novelty, to liken anything to what her body was doing right now as she watched Jordan's golden-brown hair swoop over her forehead.

Shit, she was in so much trouble.

"Can I see your iPad?" Jordan finally asked.

"What?" she asked.

"Your iPad." Jordan nodded toward the device in Astrid's hand. "So I can show you."

Astrid handed it over without a word, then watched as Jordan tapped and walked at the same time, finally settling on the creaky wooden window seat. Astrid followed, sitting down and tucking her legs underneath her so as not to brush against the carpenter.

An attempt that turned out not to matter one bit. After a few more taps, Jordan leaned into Astrid's space so they could both see the iPad, bringing with her the scent of that intoxicating floral pine, a shoulder just barely resting against Astrid's, and the heady press of body heat.

Astrid breathed in slowly through her nose, but suddenly, her dream started playing on repeat in her brain, and dear god, she had to get a damn grip.

"Okay, here's the Lapis Room." Jordan angled the iPad a bit more, and Astrid saw that she'd signed into the same design program Astrid used for her own plans.

Except now the screen showed a completely different design.

In the 3D image, the dark, almost shiny blue was on the walls, of course, and the silver-and-white damask curtains framed the windows. The bed was against the right wall and had an off-white, buttoned fabric headboard. The sheets were white, but the coverlet nearly matched the walls—a deep, silky blue—and the accent pillows featured the same shade shot through with white, gray, and goldenrod, all swirling in a mosaic pattern.

A large rug covered the wood floors, white with a similar blue-gray-white-goldenrod twist of circles. Two goldenrod accent chairs sat in one corner, pillows of white and gray perched on their cushions. The furniture—a table between the chairs, two bedside tables, a dresser, and an armoire—was all dark oak, and little amber-colored sconces dotted the walls, along with placeholders for art that seemed to be mostly whites and grays.

To lighten it up, Astrid thought.

She thought a lot of things as she took in the design, from the colors right down to the ornate chandelier that hung from the ceiling. She thought about how the room needed a bit of texture, something to help it feel truly bespoke. She thought about how she usually despised dark wood furniture.

But mostly, she thought about how inspired this design was.

She knew she just needed to say it, but all the letters kept getting tangled on her tongue. Even more than being inspired, Jordan was right—the room fit the Everwood far better than anything Astrid had come up with. It was elegant and modern and beautiful, yet felt slightly . . . she didn't know. *Spooky* might be the right word here, but not in a cobwebbed, haunted house kind of way. In a mysterious kind of way, full of intrigue and history and story.

But underneath all of that, a new, more confusing emotion rolled through Astrid like a wave.

Relief.

It was relief.

She had no idea where it had come from. It made no sense. She must've simply been worried Jordan's design would be horrible, because if that were the case, what would she say?

Still, there was a tug somewhere deep inside her, one that she'd been feeling more and more lately, like it was trying to pull her clean apart.

You can't afford to lose the Everwood job, and we both know it.

Her mother's words barged into her brain. They did their job too, pushing out all sense of wonder and filling her with dread, with a sense of complete failure.

Her job was all she had.

Her job—*succeeding* at her job—was all she was.

"I used the lapis lazuli stone as inspiration," Jordan said from next to her, startling Astrid out of her spiraling thoughts. She glanced up, meeting Jordan's hazel gaze. Her expression was so open, so . . . eager.

"According to the story," Jordan went on, "Alice Everwood wore a lapis lazuli necklace every day after her lover left her. Never took it off."

"That's why she's called the Blue Lady," Astrid said. She'd honestly never thought about it before.

Jordan nodded. "Some sightings of her ghost report a glowing stone around her neck."

Astrid nodded and looked back at the design. Of course she understood about incorporating history into designs, but most of her clients in the past nine years had wanted ultramodern rooms like the ones they saw in magazines or in their friends' houses, and Astrid had delivered. She'd never had an unsatisfied client.

And she didn't intend to start now.

But this room that Jordan had created—she didn't know how to compete with it. She already knew Pru would love it and Simon would do whatever Pru wanted. Deep down, she knew that's what mattered here—a happy client, especially one as beloved as Pru—but she couldn't let this job go. She couldn't walk away and let Jordan take over. She couldn't let her name be associated with *not good enough*—not in Bright Falls and sure as hell not with Natasha Rojas.

She couldn't endure one more brunch with her mother's disappointed sighs filling the space between them.

Plus, logistically, she didn't even think it was possible to walk away without ruining their episode of *Innside America*. They already had a ton of footage with Astrid as the lead designer—pretty much all the preliminary work—and her business needed this show.

Moreover, the Everwoods needed this show. Jordan might not be aware that Astrid knew about the inn's financial struggles, but sometimes, Isabel's nearly preternatural knowledge of everything happening in Bright Falls worked to Astrid's advantage.

She and the Everwoods were in this together, whether they wanted to be or not.

"Well?" Jordan asked, leaning a little into her space and dipping her head to catch Astrid's eye. "What do you think?"

Astrid held Jordan's gaze, her stomach filling up with that nervous, fluttery feeling again, a feeling that unsettled her but also intrigued her, drew her in.

She couldn't let that feeling go either. And if she walked away now, she'd probably never see Jordan Everwood like this again— makeup-free face, hair a mess from her attempt to sleep earlier in the night, lovely collarbone exposed through the stretched-out neck of her Henley.

"I think it's gorgeous," Astrid said softly. "Truly, Jordan. It's wonderful."

A slow smile spread over Jordan's elfin face, lifting her mouth, her cheekbones, lighting up her eyes. It was like watching a sunrise.

"Really?" she said, her voice small and happy.

Astrid nodded. "Really." Her own voice came out in a whisper, and something about her tone must've been off or given away the tender way her heart beat in her chest right now, because Jordan's sunrise smile set just as slowly as it had risen. Her eyes flicked to Astrid's mouth, sending a wave of want through Astrid so surprising and strong, she sucked in an audible breath and clenched her legs together.

Still, she didn't look away.

She felt her breathing grow shallow, felt her mouth part, and her own eyes drifted down to Jordan's lips and back up again. Her gaze traced the other woman's face like an artist would study a subject, and . . . Jordan did the same. The air between them grew thick, taut, a push and pull so intoxicating Astrid felt a little drunk. She leaned in, just a little.

Just enough.

Jordan's eyes widened, an expression that could only be described as an amalgam of wonder and confusion and lust.

Astrid could relate.

But she still didn't look away.

Neither did Jordan and oh, holy shit, this was happening. She was going to kiss Jordan Everwood, and what's more, she wanted to. She needed to. She had to know if this was real, if she actually felt all of these . . . *feelings* that had been swirling in her gut since last night.

No. Before that. If Astrid was being honest, since the day she watched Jordan swing that sledgehammer. Or . . . Astrid remembered the way she'd studied Jordan during the demolition work, the way she'd let her eyes trace her exposed midriff, her toned arms.

Jordan had taken her breath away from that first coffee-filled moment. Astrid could see it now—she could admit it.

She leaned a little closer, eyes never leaving Jordan's. Jordan placed a hand on Astrid's knee—more for bracing herself as she leaned in too, but Astrid felt the press of her fingers like an electrical storm, heat pooling between her legs.

Oh my god, was all Astrid could think. *Oh my fucking god*.

They were inches away when the bedroom door slammed shut.

Both women jolted backward. Astrid's heart catapulted into her throat as her shoulder blades hit the window, a little yelp falling from her mouth. The iPad slid off Jordan's lap and landed with a crack on the floor as she shot to her feet, palms up and presented to the door like she was trying to block some unseen evil. They stayed like that for a good ten seconds, nothing but the sound of heavy breathing filling the room, before Jordan finally lowered her arms.

"Holy shit," she said.

"Yeah," Astrid said, unfurling from the ball her body had instinctively curled into and setting her feet on the floor. She stared at the closed bedroom door. "What was that?"

Jordan shook her head. "I don't know. I didn't leave any doors open downstairs to cause a draft."

"Maybe someone left a window open today," Astrid said.

Jordan nodded, but all Astrid could think was *ghost*, which was ridiculous.

Or was it? They were in the Lapis Room, after all.

"I think we'd better call it a night," Jordan said, bending to pick up the iPad. She handed it to Astrid without meeting her eyes.

Astrid felt her heart sink into her stomach. She didn't want to call it a night. She wanted to find out what was about to happen between them just now before Alice Everwood so rudely interrupted them.

Jordan walked to the middle of the room and picked up her hammer, then she started for the door. Panic rose up in Astrid's chest, and for once she was going to do what she wanted.

She was going to *act* instead of all this constant, exhausting *thinking*.

"Jordan, wait," she said.

Jordan froze but didn't turn around. Astrid set her iPad on the window seat—she might need both hands for this—and walked over to Jordan so they were facing each other. Jordan lifted her eyes to Astrid's, but those green-rimmed irises weren't filled with lust and wonder anymore.

They were filled with fear.

Astrid frowned. She wanted to reach out and take Jordan's hand, but she didn't dare.

"Hey," she said softly, the way she'd speak to a spooked animal. "Maybe we could—"

"Have you ever kissed a woman, Astrid? Or anyone who wasn't a cishet man?"

Jordan's question settled between them. Astrid's mouth fell open. *Astrid.* She'd called her Astrid. In the short time they'd known each other, Jordan had only ever called her Parker.

"What?" Astrid asked after her throat started working again.

Jordan closed her eyes briefly, raked a hand through her hair. "You heard me."

Astrid felt her face move through a million emotions—eyebrows dipping then lifting, mouth opening and closing. "I . . . no, but—"

"Okay," Jordan said, releasing a resigned breath. "Then I don't think tonight is the night to start."

Astrid shook her head. "I don't understand."

"Don't make me say what we both know was about to happen," Jordan said. "Don't put that all on me."

"No!" Astrid said, and this time, she did take Jordan's hand. "I didn't mean that. I just meant . . . yes, okay, I know what was about to happen. But I don't understand why it can't happen."

Her intonation lifted at the end, like she was asking a question, and she nearly cringed at the needy sound of her voice. But another part of her didn't care.

Jordan sighed. "Look, there's clearly something between us. I'll admit that. But this is all new for you, and while that's not your fault, and I'm all about people figuring out their sexuality at any age and experimenting, *I* can't be your experiment. I've been there, done that, and I'm not in any kind of emotional place right now to be that person for you. I'm just not."

Astrid dropped Jordan's hand and took a step back.

"I want to kiss you," Jordan went on. "Dammit, I really do, but if that's ever going to happen, I need the same from you."

Astrid shook her head. "What do you mean? I thought it was pretty obvious that I want—"

"No. You want to kiss a woman, and I happen to be the first one you find yourself really attracted to. I need you to want to kiss *me*."

Astrid could only blink, any sort of right words for this situation flying out of her head. Jordan watched her for a second, but then she nodded, stepped around her, and opened the door, leaving Astrid with nothing but her thoughts in the middle of a haunted blue room.

CHAPTER

NINETEEN

JORDAN BARELY SLEPT and was in her workshop by seven a.m. the next morning. Rain sluiced down the windows, hammered on the steel roof, mucked up the already ruined yard around the inn, which was just as well.

Rain felt right. Heavy rain felt even better.

The weather matched Jordan's mood perfectly, the rhythm of her nail gun creating a constant barrage of noise to fit with all the thoughts in her head.

Thoughts about Astrid-fucking-Parker.

Thoughts about Astrid-fucking-Parker's mouth.

Thoughts about the look on Astrid-fucking-Parker's face when Jordan told her she wouldn't kiss her.

What the hell had Jordan-fucking-Everwood been thinking?

Last night, her decree had felt like such a smart solution. Hell, it seemed as though even Alice Everwood hadn't wanted them to kiss, what with the theatrical door-slamming and all. But now, after mulling that moment on the window seat over and over (and over), Jordan's chest ached with that feeling she swore she'd never again let herself feel—that neediness of want, desire for the partnered life Meredith ended without even consulting Jordan.

She'd never forget the morning Meredith left. How she hadn't even given her any warning. No discussions. No "Hey, I think we need to talk." Just a set of suitcases by the door, "I have to leave" on Meredith's lips.

She'd been in remission for two months.

That's all Jordan got with her wife after the hell they'd both been through. And a month later, divorce papers arrived in the mail.

Jordan had signed them. Meredith pretty much gave Jordan everything—the house, Jordan's truck, their cat—which Jordan assumed was supposed to be some sort of consolation for abandoning Jordan and every promise Meredith had ever made her.

"Well, fuck her," Jordan said out loud now.

But the problem wasn't Meredith. Not anymore. Jordan was no longer in love with her wife—she knew that. The problem was Jordan couldn't shake the aftereffects. Those bombs Meredith had dropped, they left scars. Deep ones, carved into Jordan's heart, lungs, brain, blood, and she'd spent nearly a year in therapy trying to heal them to no avail.

She pressed her nail gun to the right spot on a kitchen cabinet and fired.

Bam.

Bam.

Bam.

She continued until she ran out of nails. As she reloaded, her phone buzzed in her back pocket. She pulled it out, horrible, sticky hope rising in her chest without a single shred of permission. Astrid had her number. Granted, she'd never used it before, but she'd had it since the first day they met, when she bossily insisted Jordan hand over her contact information so Astrid could send her the dry cleaning bill for her stupid dress.

Jordan almost smiled at the memory now.

That is, until she looked at her phone's screen and saw Meredith's name in her notifications, the short message fully visible.

I'm in town next week. I'd love to see you.

"What the fuck?" Jordan said out loud. She shook her head and stuffed the phone back into her pocket, shoving nails at a reckless speed into her gun. Meredith didn't know she wasn't in Savannah anymore, and Jordan sure as hell had no intention of telling her.

She set her gun on its next intended spot on her cabinet, but before she could fire, someone knocked on her workshop door.

"Oh my god, leave me the fuck alone!" she yelled into the empty workshop, a little louder than she intended. It was probably Simon— he was the only one who would dare interrupt her work right now, and he'd forgive her surly tone.

"Well, you don't have to be so rude."

A feminine voice.

A familiar feminine voice.

"Parker?"

"Yes. Can you let me in?"

She glanced around at the slew of sage-colored cabinets around her, total contraband. "Um. Well."

"Oh, come on," Astrid called. "I already know you have your secret projects all over the place in there."

Jordan frowned. She set her nail gun down and went over to the door, unlocking the padlock and cracking the door open a few inches. Astrid stood there in the rain, a clear umbrella above her head. She was fresh-faced and dressed in sleek black pants and a plum-colored silk blouse, her shaggy hair a little frizzy from the humidity, and Jordan thought she was the most beautiful woman she'd ever seen.

Oh, Jesus Christ, Everwood, get a grip.

"How do you know that?" Jordan asked, trying to gird her out-of-control loins.

Astrid gave her a look. "Last night, you said you didn't have to make my job so hard, and I'm here to collect on that. I'm not going anywhere, Jordan. We both know I can't. So you might as well let me in."

Jordan took a second to consider, to get her Astrid-addled brain back into professional gear. She knew eventually she'd have to talk to Simon and Natasha about what she was doing, but that conversation would go a whole lot smoother if she had Astrid by her side . . . professionally speaking, of course. Astrid designed for a living. Astrid ran a successful business. Astrid wasn't a cosmic fuckup in Simon's eyes. So, yes, Astrid and Jordan could both make each other's lives a whole lot easier.

Jordan cleared her throat and opened the door all the way, watching as Astrid stepped inside and slow-walked toward her workbench, taking in the sage cabinets, the boxes of mullioned glass, the huge slabs of butcher block Jordan still needed to cut for the counters. Astrid's heels echoed through the space until she paused at the edge of the workbench where Jordan's laptop was carelessly perched. She set her umbrella on the floor and lifted her gaze to Jordan's, a question in her eyes.

Jordan nodded and Astrid tapped a key on the computer, bringing the device to life. The Everwood kitchen—the way Jordan had envisioned it, at least—filled the screen. Astrid's expression didn't give much away. Her dark eyes scanned the images, narrowing softly here and there before relaxing again. She clicked on the track pad and now Jordan's plan for the library sprang to life—that same sage color featured prominently, but now coating the existing built-in bookshelves, the mantel above the fireplace.

In fact, the sage green appeared in every room on the first floor, an accent color that paired well with Astrid's gray walls. There was one guest room on the main floor, a corner room with a cozy slanted ceiling that Jordan had covered with painted vines and flowers in her plan, turning the whole room into a soothing oasis. She had no idea what design rules she was following or breaking—she just knew what felt right for the house, and this was it.

Jordan stood on the other side of her workbench as Astrid clicked from one room to the next, her brow sometimes smooth, sometimes furrowed. Upstairs, there was the Lapis Room, of course, but then every other guest room had an identity too, a bold color or pattern that distinguished it from the others.

"I know it's not perfect," Jordan said.

Astrid didn't answer right away. Jordan watched as she went back and looked at each room, mouth pursed in thought.

"No, it's not," she finally said.

Jordan nearly laughed. This woman really did not hold back, and Jordan sort of loved it. She'd spent the last year with everyone in her life walking on proverbial eggshells around her, so careful not to upset her, so intent on keeping her calm. Astrid knew all about Meredith and didn't give two shits.

Or maybe Astrid simply believed Jordan could handle whatever life had to throw at her.

The thought made Jordan's throat ache. She swallowed and stepped around the workbench so she was standing next to Astrid, laptop between them.

"Maybe you could help make them perfect," Jordan said. "Or better, at least. I don't know all that much about design."

"I can see that," Astrid said, but she was looking right at Jordan, not her work, and there was a whisper of a smile on her mouth.

Jordan fought her own smile and shook her head. "Well, I guess I'm lucky you know oh so much."

Astrid laughed. "I guess you are."

Jordan looked back at the library design on her laptop's screen.

"But seriously. What do we do? I'd love your help with this, but not if you don't actually like what I've done here."

Astrid turned back to the screen as well. "What happens if I don't?"

Jordan felt a pang of hurt she wasn't prepared for. She'd put a lot into this design. Her love for her family and the childhood she'd spent here, the house's history, the town's love for Alice's story. The idea that a professional—no, not a professional—the idea that *Astrid* wouldn't like her creation stung.

But it didn't change anything.

"Then I guess we're back to subterfuge and paint jobs in the middle of the night," she said. She started to walk away, just back around to the other side of the workbench for some distance, physically and emotionally, but Astrid grabbed her hand.

"Hey," she said. "I'm sorry, I don't know why I even asked that. I love it."

Jordan froze. The whole world froze, in fact, as though the only thing that existed were those three little words and Astrid's warm fingers tangled with her own.

"You do?" she managed to say.

Astrid nodded. "I mean, it needs some work." She released Jordan's hand, but in a slow slide that kept their fingertips together until the very last minute, and nodded toward the laptop. "Texture is a big issue in most of the spaces, and I'm not sure that yellow-and-ivory stripe is really what you're going for, considering the mood of the rest of the rooms, but if you're open to—"

"I am," Jordan said, elation filling her up like helium. "I am so open."

Astrid smiled. "You don't even know what I'm going to suggest."

"I'm still in. I'm all in."

A blush bloomed on Astrid's face, possibly the loveliest thing Jordan had ever seen. Well, that, and the way Astrid's long lashes fanned over her cheekbones, those little vampire teeth coming out to bite her lower lip.

Shit.

Jordan shook her head to clear it.

"Okay," Astrid said. "Then we do this together. We go through each room, detail by tiniest detail, looking at your designs and mine, seeing if we can come up with something cohesive and thematic."

Jordan nodded vigorously.

"And we'll have to do it fast, because the base paint is already mostly finished on the first floor, so if we're going to incorporate this sage, we've got to put in that order with the painters pretty soon."

"Yes. Agreed."

"Which means we have to get approval from Pru, Simon, and Natasha before that."

Jordan wasn't so much concerned about her grandmother—she'd designed this whole house with Pru in mind—but Simon was trickier. Legally speaking, his name was on the contract with Bright Designs, along with Pru's, so Jordan knew Astrid had to get his okay before implementing anything. Still, Jordan was pretty confident Simon would go along with whatever Astrid advised. And Natasha . . . well. She'd already called Astrid's design "uninspired" once. She had a feeling that a woman who wore a clit necklace on a daily basis would be up for a little more intrigue in the design, particularly one that accented the house's history.

Jordan started to say yes to everything Astrid was proposing, but one thing gave her pause.

"Why?" Jordan asked. "Why are you doing this? Why not just fight me, go to Simon and tell him everything I'm trying to do since we both know he'll shut me down. Why work with me when you could just do your own plan like you wanted?"

Astrid looked away, tucked her hair behind her ear. Her eyes glazed over on the computer screen, her thoughts clearly going inward. Jordan couldn't help but wonder . . . what did Astrid Parker really want? She didn't strike Jordan as someone who backed down, not after the way she laid into Jordan during their first meeting, demanding her phone number for the dry cleaning bill.

But she was backing down right now. She said they'd do this together, sure, but Astrid was *compromising*.

"This feels right," Astrid finally said, gently touching the computer's keyboard before turning her dark eyes on Jordan. "This is your family home. Technically, you're an Everwood, and you're my client too. I want this project to make you happy."

Jordan just blinked at her, stunned. Astrid seemed nearly as shocked by her own words, because her blush deepened and she looked away.

"Plus," she said, laughing a little, "I don't think I can handle walking into another room with Natasha Rojas without knowing exactly what color will be on the wall."

Jordan winced. "I actually am pretty sorry about that."

"I don't want subterfuge," Astrid went on, meeting her eyes again. "I want . . . I want a partnership."

Her words fluttered between them, and Jordan suddenly had a hard time getting a full breath.

A partnership.

A partner.

"Yeah," Jordan said. "Me too."

They stared at each other for a moment before Astrid shook her head, bangs brushing her eyelashes, and rolled her shoulders back. "Okay, then."

Jordan held out her hand. "Partners."

Astrid's throat bobbed in a hard swallow. She slid her fingers over Jordan's—way slower than Jordan thought was necessary, but shit, she wasn't going to complain—and gripped her palm.

"Partners," Astrid said softly.

They stayed like that for a second, hand in hand, but then Astrid's slight smile dimmed. "There's still the question about the show."

Jordan frowned, pulling her hand free. "What about it?"

"What do we tell them? Are we co-designers now? And will they even be okay with that? We have all this footage where you're the grumpy carpenter and I'm the uptight designer. Natasha and Emery seem to like that dynamic, but if we're working together, it's only fair you get credit."

Jordan sliced a hand through her hair. Honestly, all this *Innside America* bullshit stressed her the hell out. She didn't care about camera crews and interviews. She didn't even care about credit. She was only doing this to make sure her family home remained true to its roots. Any other project, she'd just be following the contractor and designer's orders, building and hammering and nailing.

But her family needed the show to do well, and she wasn't willing to risk Natasha—or worse, the higher-ups at the network—getting pissed that Jordan and Astrid blew up the dynamic they'd spent weeks establishing.

Plus, notoriety was Astrid's thing. Natasha Rojas was her design icon, and she had an actual design business that could benefit from the kind of exposure the show would provide. Jordan just needed that exposure to save an inn, not make her a star.

"Can we just keep going like we have been?" Jordan asked.

Astrid's brows lifted. "As in . . . exactly like we have been?"

Jordan nodded. "Grumpy carpenter, uptight designer."

Astrid put her hand up. "Hang on, just so I'm clear. You want me to continue to act as lead designer, even if we use a lot of your design?"

The whole plan sounded a bit off when Astrid put it like that, but Jordan forged ahead. She was so close to locking this down. "Look, we both need this show. I see no reason to change things around now, especially when Natasha and Emery like what we've got going. We're already going to change up the design, which is probably going to push their limits a little. Anything more than that would just complicate things."

Astrid pressed her mouth flat, but Jordan could see her wheels turning. Jordan might not fully understand Astrid Parker, but she knew that working as the lead designer on the show was important to her.

And Jordan wanted to give that to her, which was perhaps the bigger revelation here.

This time, Jordan reached out and took her hand. "Just take it, Astrid. You're helping me; now let me help you."

Astrid squeezed her fingers and nodded. "Okay," she whispered, then louder, "Okay. So we're doing this."

Jordan grinned. "We're doing this."

CHAPTER

TWENTY

A FEW DAYS later, Astrid stood outside Iris's apartment door for an impromptu movie night with her friends. She was exhausted, she and Jordan pretty much burning all the midnight oil working on their new design plan. She was looking forward to a calm night with her best friends, a little wine, Iris's squashy couch, and a bad movie they could mock mercilessly on the screen.

She'd just lifted her hand to knock when she heard it.

Moaning.

Coming from inside Iris's apartment.

"Yeah," Iris's breathy voice said. "Right there. Oh, god, Jillian, yeah."

Astrid's hand flew to her mouth, and she all but stumbled backward. Still, Iris never did anything at half speed, including how loud she was when, apparently, having sex with her new girlfriend.

"Fuck, yes, oh god, your tongue, just . . . like . . . that."

This was what Astrid got for being perpetually early. Her mother had pummeled punctuality into her so fiercely that even when Astrid

was on time, her anxiety spiked and she went down a thought spiral
of disappointing or inconveniencing whoever might be waiting for
her. Hence, she was ever the early bird.

Now, though, she'd prefer being late to this awkward situation.
She didn't want to stand here and wait until Iris and Jillian finished,
dear god, but she also didn't want to turn around and leave, because
where would she go? When Iris had messaged her, Claire, and Delilah in their group text earlier, suggesting a movie night and tacos,
she had said six thirty. It was six twenty-five.

And yet, the moaning continued.

"You like that?" Jillian's velvety voice came through.

"I like that. Oh, fuck, I really like that. Please, I need your mouth
on my pu—"

Astrid bolted down the hall and toward the stairs before Iris
could finish that sentence. Her cheeks were flaming hot, her heart
pounding, and . . . oh, Jesus.

Her lower belly felt tight, a pressure between her legs she couldn't
ignore. Or she *could*, but god. She did not come here tonight expecting to get all hot and bothered. Iris had always been very open about
her sex life, but Astrid had never heard her sex life actively happening.

She stood at the top of the stairs, bottle of Riesling tucked under
her arm, squirming to try and make the throbbing at her center go
away. She closed her eyes, but nope, nope, that didn't help, as Jordan's
perfect rosebud mouth bloomed into her mind, and she started imag-
ining the carpenter's calloused fingers sliding over her—

Shit, she needed some air.

It was a nice night. She'd just wait on the street until Claire and
Delilah arrived, no big deal.

She was halfway down the stairs when Jordan Everwood came
bounding up from the first floor, a six-pack of craft beer in one hand.

Her phone rested in her other palm, eyes focused on the screen. Astrid felt a sudden swell of joy at the sight of her, which was ridiculous considering they'd just been together an hour ago at the inn.

They'd been together a lot in the last few days—the standard nine-to-five, plus several late nights in Jordan's workshop, scouring fabric samples and paint colors and Etsy, to-go food containers filling the space around them.

Somewhere in the back of her mind, she knew she should feel a little threatened or territorial over her work. Together, she and Jordan had gone over both of their design plans for the entire house, and for each room, Jordan's plan ended up being the base design. It was true, a lot of Astrid's plans trickled through as well—a herringbone feature wall here, black-and-white photographs of Bright Falls there—but sometimes it was hard to remember who actually came up with what idea.

At least, that's what Astrid told herself. She knew she was integral to this project's success—Jordan was horrible at organization, and when one was juggling orders and plans for a house this size, organization was key—and Jordan didn't make a move, didn't click a *complete order* button, without Astrid's input. Still, whenever she flipped through the images on the design software, Astrid couldn't shake this growing sense of unease, which paired inconveniently with the pure, unadulterated happiness she felt when she was with Jordan Everwood.

Now, as more dopamine flooded her system at seeing Jordan unexpectedly, that unease was still there, like a storm cloud hovering miles away. She swallowed and focused on the good, which was a lot easier said than done. Happy was not a word that entered her sphere of experience very often.

She blinked, focusing on Jordan's swoopy hair, her slow climb toward Astrid, and the unease ebbed a bit. Unfortunately, the feelings Iris's little encounter stirred up did not. At the sight of Jordan sauntering up the steps, *those* feelings rushed through her with the force of a river released from a dam.

"Hi," she said when Jordan was a few steps away.

"Holy shit." Jordan stumbled back a step, dropping her phone in the process so she could grab onto the railing.

"Oh, god, I'm sorry," Astrid said, bending down to pick up the phone. As she passed it back to Jordan, she caught a glimpse of a text conversation on the screen, the name *Meredith* at the top.

Her stomach plummeted to her feet, a touch of panic linking up with her myriad of emotions. Maybe she should just go home. Horny and anxiety-riddled was not a good combination.

"No worries," Jordan said, taking the phone and stuffing it into her back pocket. She had changed out of her normal work overalls and into a pair of black jeans cuffed at the ankle and a short-sleeved button-up, this one navy blue and covered in tiny green succulents.

Astrid put on a smile, made her voice bright and perfect. "I didn't know you were coming."

Jordan frowned and narrowed her eyes. "Are you okay?"

Astrid's smile dipped a little, but she managed to keep it in place. "Yeah. I'm fine."

Jordan watched her for a second, that frown still wrinkling her brow. Finally, she looked away, rubbed the back of her neck. "Iris texted Simon, who insisted on dragging me along. If he's not saving his reclusive sister, I don't think he knows what to do with himself." She jutted a thumb toward the building's main door. "He's parking the car."

Astrid nodded, wishing she'd been the one to invite Jordan to Iris's, but she hadn't seemed to be able to get the question out of her mouth. What if Jordan thought she was asking her out? What if she said no? Astrid didn't think she could handle that, not when all of her thoughts and feelings about Jordan felt so close to the surface lately. Jordan had already rejected her once, decreeing that Astrid couldn't kiss her unless she really wanted to kiss *her*, and Astrid was determined to honor her request. After all Jordan had been through, Astrid understood it. She even agreed with it. She knew she had plenty of soul-searching to do when it came to her motives.

But right now, after seeing Meredith's name on Jordan's phone, all she wanted to do was take Jordan's face between her hands and kiss her until she forgot Meredith's name altogether.

"I'm glad you're here," she said instead, except her voice was soft, her tone very . . . Jesus, very *eager*, and her cheeks grew warm with embarrassment at her admission.

Jordan canted her head, considering Astrid for a second. Her eyes traveled from Astrid's black espadrilles and up her legs to her black shorts, pausing on her chest and her sleeveless sky-blue blouse before trailing up to her face and settling on her eyes. Astrid's breath was locked in her lungs—no way she could breathe right now. Not with this unbearably sexy woman looking at her like she wanted to eat her for dessert.

But then Jordan's expression evened out, placid and totally neutral. She nodded and said, "Yeah, me too." But her voice wasn't soft or eager. It was normal. Unaffected. And Astrid felt the sudden urge to cry like a kid who just found out their birthday party was canceled.

"Hey, sweetie!" Claire's voice sounded from the bottom of the stairs, and Astrid shook her head to clear it. Claire and Delilah started up the stairs, grocery bags in their arms, Simon coming up behind them.

"Hey," Astrid said back, then turned and headed back toward Iris's apartment before her best friends could see how red her cheeks were.

THANKFULLY, IRIS AND Jillian were fully clothed and acting normal by the time the whole group arrived at her door, though Iris's face was a little flushed. Still, she poured wine and set out taco fixings on her tiny kitchen's island, opened up her turquoise cabinets to find this and that, all while chattering a mile a minute about a new planner she was designing, about Claire and Delilah's party this weekend, about how it wasn't really a housewarming since Claire already lived there, and on and on.

Astrid wondered how one recovered so quickly from what seemed to be mind-blowing sex. Granted, she'd never really had mind-blowing sex, but she felt like it would lay her out for a good hour.

She stood in the kitchen, filling mustard-colored bowls with lettuce, salsa, and guacamole, while Claire browned a skillet full of ground beef. Everyone else was in the living room with Jillian, who was, apparently, showing Simon the hundred-dollars-a-bottle bourbon she'd brought from Portland just that morning.

Jordan was with Delilah.

Astrid watched them as they sat on Iris's red couch, Jordan with a beer and Delilah with a few fingers of Jillian's bourbon, legs tucked up and chatting easily, as though they'd known each other for a long time.

"Do you think she's divulging all your deep, dark secrets?" Iris asked, hip bumping Astrid's at the sink.

"What?" Astrid said, freezing while she rinsed a bunch of cilantro. "Who?"

"Delilah and your mortal enemy," Iris said.

"She's not my mortal enemy," Astrid said, shaking the herbs dry and laying them on the cutting board. "Plus, I don't . . ."

She was about to say she didn't have any secrets, but that wasn't altogether true. She hadn't told Claire or Iris about her attraction to Jordan, and while Delilah knew about the sex dream, she didn't know Astrid had pretty much tried to make out with Jordan, only to be rejected.

No one knew that.

She had a sudden urge to spill everything to her friends, the need to get advice, or even some simple comfort, nearly overwhelming. But with Jordan a mere ten feet away, there was no way Iris Kelly finding out that Astrid had been experiencing extremely queer feelings was going to be a quiet affair.

"You don't what?" Iris asked.

Astrid shook her head as she chopped up the cilantro, making quick work of the small bunch. "Nothing. I . . . I don't think Delilah would say anything mean."

Iris scoffed. "Are we talking about the same woman? Tattoos? New York City attitude for days? A general disdain for clothes in any shade lighter than the ninth circle of hell?"

Claire wacked Iris's butt with a towel. "That's my girlfriend you're insulting."

"I'm not insulting her," Iris said. "I'm making simple observations."

"I can hear you, you know!" Delilah called from the living room. She lifted her bourbon in a mock toast. "And I like my black clothes, fuck you very much."

Iris flipped her off and Delilah laughed, and even Astrid couldn't help but smile at the comfortable—if a bit biting—way her friends and Delilah interacted. But when she caught Jordan's eye, her smile dipped.

Shit, she was a mess.

"I'm going to look for some books to borrow," she said, drying her hands on a towel and grabbing her wine. She just needed a second to get herself together, a moment of peace. Which, with this crowd, was hard to come by.

"Sure thing," Iris said. "Be sure to pick something really dirty."

Claire laughed, but Astrid just shook her head as she headed for the library, the only room in Iris's open-plan apartment that was separated by a couple of walls. She turned toward the spread of shelves spanning the entire back wall, spines arranged by color, which was such an Iris thing to do.

Astrid let her eyes scan the rainbow of books, wondering how the hell Iris ever found anything with this aesthetic system. It was a pulse-calming distraction, though, the pleasing swell of red to orange to yellow.

"This is the queerest bookshelf I've ever seen."

Astrid whirled around at the sound of Jordan's voice. She had a bottle of beer in her hand, and her eyes were on Astrid.

"Yeah," Astrid said. "Iris is anything but subtle."

Jordan laughed as she made her way toward her. "I gathered as much."

Astrid turning with her as they both faced the rainbow. Their shoulders brushed and Astrid felt herself loosen, something that seemed to happen naturally around Jordan Everwood. By all accounts, Astrid *should* be tightening up. Jordan made her first-crush nervous, and all she wanted to do around the other woman was giggle and make out, which was a stress-inducing identity crisis in and of itself.

So, yes, Astrid had plenty of reasons to lock up right now.

Instead, she all but melted at the feel of Jordan's body heat radiating into her arm.

"Do you like to read?" Jordan asked her, plucking a colorful paperback from the shelves—a romance, by the looks of the entwined couple with very little clothing on the cover—and reading the back.

"Yeah, I do," Astrid said. "I don't have much time lately, but when I was a kid, I read a lot."

Jordan put the book back and turned to face her fully. "What sort of books did you like?"

Astrid thought back, remembering how much she swooned over Gilbert Blythe, how her heart would beat faster when Darcy and Lizzie verbally sparred, the giddy excitement she felt when finishing one of the steamy romances her babysitter used to forget in the couch cushions.

Oh, how Isabel would've hated those racy novels, had she known about them.

"Romance, mostly," Astrid said.

Jordan's brows shot upward. "Really."

Astrid laughed. "Don't look so surprised."

"I am surprised. I thought you'd be into—"

"Whatever you're about to say, just don't." Astrid took a sip of wine, made sure she was smiling, but Jesus Christ, if Jordan said she assumed Astrid enjoyed the likes of *Heart of Darkness* or some other depressing white man literary shit, she'd throw her glass against the wall right now.

Jordan mimed zipping her lips, but smiled. "So tell me more about young Astrid Parker."

"Like what?"

Jordan shrugged. "Well, I know she liked romance novels. She had a very involved mother."

Astrid snorted. "An understatement."

Jordan's eyes narrowed softly. "What did she dream about?"

Astrid reared back, surprised. "Dream about?"

"Yeah. I mean, what did you dream your life would be like? Me, I wanted to be a Disney singer when I grew up."

A laugh flew out of Astrid's mouth. "A Disney singer."

"You laugh in the face of my dream?" Jordan placed her free hand on her chest. "I'll have you know, my grandmother said my living room dance routine to 'Part of Your World' was the best she'd ever seen or heard."

Astrid laughed even harder. "So you sing?"

Jordan winked. "That talent—or lack thereof—I reserve for my inner circle, so you'd have to torture my brother into submission for the truth."

Astrid rolled her eyes, but something like longing rose in her chest, which she promptly shook off.

"How'd you get into carpentry?" Astrid asked.

"My dad bought me one of those kid's tool kits when I was ten. I was immediately hooked. Smashing shit with a hammer? I was in."

Astrid smiled. "I like smashing shit too."

"I remember," Jordan said, winking at her.

Flutters. All through Astrid's belly.

"Really though," Jordan said, "I loved creating. Bringing something to life like that, something other people will love? Magic."

Magic. That's exactly what Jordan's design for the Everwood felt like.

"Okay, so," Jordan said after another swallow of her beer, "I've divulged my squandered dreams. It's your turn."

Astrid shook her head, smiling as she sipped her wine. "I didn't—"

"Don't you dare tell me you didn't have any," Jordan said, pointing a finger Astrid's way. "Let's start simple. Did you always want to be an interior designer?"

Astrid opened her mouth, the right answer right on the tip of her tongue.

Yes, of course.

But it wasn't true. Not even close. And she didn't want to lie to Jordan. She couldn't.

"No," she said softly, "I didn't."

Jordan nodded, as though this information didn't shock her in the least. "What did you want to be?"

"I wanted . . ." Her thoughts trailed back to a little girl, a tween, a teenager, who dreamed of being not only one thing, but many things. A journalist. A teacher. A baker.

She thought of those lovely lavender scones she and Jordan had at the Sotheby flea market, how they reminded her that she'd loved baking with Claire and Iris when they were growing up—trying out new recipes, laughing when something came out horribly, squealing when a batch of cookies or a cake was just right. She loved creating something people could enjoy too, something warm and impractical and fun.

She supposed she still did love it, though she hardly ever baked these days. It had been years. Ruby's eighth birthday, if she remembered correctly. The bakery in town had screwed up Claire's order for a strawberry cake, so Astrid had stepped up to the plate, needs must and all that.

The cake had been delicious. And she'd loved making it, especially for Ruby, whom she adored with her whole heart. That had been a sort of magic, she supposed. There was no better feeling than someone tasting something she made and loving it. She hadn't felt that in a long time. She was always satisfied when a client loved her work for them, but somehow, it didn't ring quite as . . . well, as magical.

"I wanted to be a lot of things," she said now, honestly. Then she told Jordan about how journalism—writing facts in beautiful ways—had always intrigued her, how her junior year English teacher made her think teaching could be fulfilling. She told her about baking with Iris and Claire, the strawberry cake for Ruby.

"So why didn't you?" Jordan asked.

"Why didn't I what?"

"Do any of that? Teach? Bake? Don't think I've forgotten about your wealth of lavender sugar knowledge."

Astrid shook her head. She should simply say her dreams changed, but had they? Or had they just dimmed as the years passed, as Isabel's expectations tightened like a noose. She didn't even remember choosing business administration as her major in college. That was simply *The Plan*, what she was always going to do.

She went for honesty again, meeting Jordan's eyes. "I don't know."

Jordan tilted her head, eyes searching Astrid's. Astrid felt raw, naked even, but she couldn't look away.

"Maybe one day I'll sing for you," Jordan said.

"You will?"

Jordan nodded. "If you bake a cake for me."

Astrid held her gaze, and she couldn't have stopped the smile that settled on her mouth right now if she'd tried.

"Maybe," she said.

Jordan grinned back, and that first-crush, effervescent feeling bubbled through Astrid again—her chest, her fingertips, her toes. Finally, she turned back toward the shelves and pressed the rim of her wineglass to her still-smiling mouth.

She stood there like that for a moment, pretending to scan the shelves while grinning like a teenager. Because she knew now. She knew it with one hundred percent certainty—she wanted to kiss Jordan Everwood. Not just any woman or person. Jordan. No one else would do.

The thought was freeing and terrifying and electrifying all at once. She was of half a mind to grab Jordan right now, but she had to think this through. Jordan had to know she meant it, that she wasn't caught up in memories or in some future scenario involving Disney songs and baked goods.

As she worked to even out her emotions, her eyes snagged on a deep blue spine featuring an illustration of two white women entangled in an embrace. She pulled the book out to see a larger version of the women on the cover—one redheaded and one blond—gazing at each other under the stars, the Seattle Space Needle in the background.

Her heart suddenly felt very large and very tender in her chest. She scanned the book blurb on the back—a *Pride and Prejudice* retelling, queer, a bisexual woman and a lesbian.

"That looks intriguing," Jordan said, leaning in to see the cover. Jasmine and pine wafted over Astrid—she fought the urge to inhale deeply.

"It does, doesn't it?" Astrid said. She met Jordan's eyes and swore she saw a challenge there.

She set her wine down on the turquoise coffee table and tucked the book under her arm, eyes scanning the shelves for more options while Jordan settled into one of the squashy leather chairs in the middle of the room and watched, lazily sipping her beer. After ten minutes, Astrid had three more paperback romances in hand—one featuring two Dominican women, another with a male Jewish rabbi and a bisexual female, and one with a female and nonbinary pairing that was all about a baking competition.

She spun on her heel, colorful books in her arms. Jordan lifted a single brow.

"Looks like you've got some reading to do."

Astrid just smiled. "Looks like I do."

THROUGHOUT THE REST of the night, all Astrid could think about were the books she'd stashed in her bag. Around eleven, Simon and Jordan were the first to say good night, and she took the opportunity to leave too—they had a big day tomorrow, after all, going over the new design plan with the Everwoods and Natasha. Really, though, she'd never been so glad to go home to her empty, white-walled house. She showered and settled into her bed with the novel about two women in Seattle, which she read until well after two in the morning, devouring the words, the swoons, the arc of the characters' relationship.

The sex.

Dear god, the sex.

Within the span of just a few hours and a couple hundred pages, she had to stop reading to get herself off. Twice. What's more, she didn't picture some nameless, faceless person when she slipped her hand into her underwear, as she circled her middle finger around her clit. She didn't picture the characters in the book.

She pictured Jordan Everwood, every single time.

CHAPTER

TWENTY-ONE

JORDAN WAS PRETTY sure she'd never felt this nervous. She stood in the inn's kitchen, her laptop resting on the piece of plywood they'd used to cover the counter-less island as a sort of makeshift desk for today's meeting. As she clicked through room after room on her laptop, checking for any last-minute irregularities in the design, her stomach threatened to reject the avocado toast she'd eaten for breakfast.

The morning had started out a bit differently. As soon as the light had shone through her window, she'd leaped from her bed, stretched luxuriously as though she were a Disney princess getting ready for the day, and *smiled*.

She smiled while she showered.

She smiled while she brushed her teeth.

She smiled while she put on her favorite print button-up, white with colorful merfolk of various races, ethnicities, and genders dappling the cotton.

She told herself that all this infernal smiling—which was honestly starting to hurt her out-of-practice face—was because the design for the inn was done, it was glorious, and she and Astrid were presenting it to her family and Natasha on film today after lunch. She knew what she and Astrid had created was breathtaking, the Everwood through and through, and for the first time in over a year, she felt pride in her work.

But as she had left her bedroom and made her way to the kitchen for some coffee, her work wasn't what kept tugging at her mouth. No, that honor went to a leggy, shaggy-haired, vampire-toothed pain in the ass, standing in front of a rainbow bookshelf and talking about cakes, whom Jordan could not seem to get out of her head.

She thought about Astrid a lot lately. Too much. It scared the ever-loving shit out of her, all these thoughts, but she couldn't stop them. She meant what she'd told Astrid back in the Lapis Room nearly a week ago—she wouldn't kiss her until she was sure Astrid wanted *her*. She knew herself, and she couldn't afford the heartache when—*if*—Astrid decided, *Oh, hmm, never mind, I don't like the ladies after all.*

But that didn't keep her from daydreaming, from pining, because goddammit, the way Astrid looked at her lately—the way she always seemed to make sure their shoulders brushed when they were both at the laptop, how the woman could not carry a tune in a bucket, but that didn't stop her from singing along to Tegan and Sara's latest in Jordan's truck when they ran errands, how she could think through every single moment of a guest's day to determine the best placement for a bed, a desk, a dresser—stirred up emotions in Jordan she'd missed so damn much. She'd *missed* liking someone, that flare of hope and terror in her gut whenever she thought of the person, the glances and smiles.

Hell, she wasn't even sure if *missed* was the right word. She re-membered bits of these emotions with Meredith, but they'd met in middle school, Jordan had all but followed Meredith to Savannah College of Art and Design, and then they just sort of fell into being lovers one night their senior year after prepping portfolios, kissing slowly over a box of leftover pizza.

She and Meredith had been a matter of course.

And that was what did it—that thought right there had halted her steps halfway down the cottage's hall that morning.

I don't want a best friend. I want a destiny.

She'd felt her smile slip down to her feet, where it stayed all through her coffee, through the toast she choked down while Pru eyed her worriedly, to right now as she frowned at the design plan, sure she was somehow going to crash and burn and fuck everything up.

"Hey," Astrid said, slipping in the back door and shaking out her clear umbrella. She was dressed to the nines, as usual: a black blouse, wide-legged ivory pants, and her standard three-inch black heels. Jordan had no clue how she traipsed around the Pacific Northwest weather in those shoes.

"Mm," Jordan said back, focusing again on the screen.

She felt rather than saw Astrid pause, take stock of her. She could feel the woman's eyes sliding over her, feel her brain working, assessing.

"I'm fine," Jordan said preemptively.

Astrid click-clacked closer to her, not stopping until their shoulders touched. She smelled clean, that ocean-breeze-and-laundry scent. She smelled like *her*, and Jesus Christ, Jordan's knees nearly buckled. She was suddenly so tired. Fuck the smiles, maybe what she really needed was to sob into Astrid Parker's lovely neck, feel her arms around her.

She shook her head, trying to get a grip. She hated that Meredith could still do this to her. One thought. One memory. And *kapow!* She was laid out on the floor, body parts strewn all over the fucking place. Emotionally speaking, that is. Suddenly, nothing felt right. She was going to blow this—the design was tacky, Astrid just wanted to fuck a woman, didn't matter who, and Jordan would never play any role in her own goddamn life other than the best friend. The pal. The—

"Jordan."

Astrid's voice.

Astrid's fingers on her cheek.

Jordan let Astrid turn her chin so they were facing each other.

"You're okay," Astrid said.

Not *What's wrong?* Not *Are you all right?* Nothing interrogative whatsoever. A statement. A beautiful declarative sentence. Jordan's eyes began to sting, legit tears threatening to swell, and Jesus, she would not cry and ruin her eyeliner right now, not with her family and camera crew due to arrive any moment for their meeting.

But she did circle her fingers around Astrid's wrist. Two wrists, as somehow both of Astrid's hands had come up to frame Jordan's face, thumbs swiping across her cheekbones.

"You're brilliant," Astrid said, the breath from her words whispering against Jordan's mouth. "And everyone is going to love what you've created."

Jordan leaned in until her forehead touched Astrid's. "What we created."

Astrid sighed, then nodded. "We."

"We."

"It's a nice word."

Jordan laughed. "Yeah. It really is."

They stayed like that for what felt like hours, fingers drifting over cheekbones and smoothing over wrists, almost like a dance. With Astrid this close, Jordan didn't feel like just any woman.

She felt like herself.

She felt like—

A knock sounded on the swinging door, and Jordan pulled back a second too late. Natasha's head was already through the opening, her expectant expression brightening into something else.

"Oh," she said as Astrid stepped away from Jordan and straightened her blouse, cleared her throat. "I'm sorry, I didn't mean to interrupt."

Except her tone said, *I am so glad I interrupted.*

"You're not," Astrid said, professional smile back in place. "Come on in."

"I was just so excited to see this final design plan," Natasha said. Emery, Darcy, Regina, and Patrick spilled in behind her, quickly turning on all the equipment they'd set up the day before for today's shoot.

"Welcome," Jordan said, waving her arm at the space, where a single sage-green cabinet, complete with mullioned glass, rested on the floor. She and Astrid had moved it in here yesterday afternoon, planning to use it as a talking piece for their presentation.

Or rather, Astrid's presentation.

Jordan saw the moment Natasha laid eyes on the cabinet—her steps halted, eyes widening.

"Well, that is . . . surprising."

"Yes," Astrid said, "I told you we . . . *I* had some changes to—"

"Hold on, hold on," Emery said, waving a hand at them from behind a camera. "Let's get this on film."

"Yeah, of course," Natasha said, then proceeded to fold her arms and stare down Jordan and Astrid so intently, Jordan was positive she could accurately call out their heart rates.

Astrid glanced at Jordan, and Jordan glanced back, and a slow smile spread over Natasha's mouth.

"Oh, this is too good," Natasha said.

"What's too good?" Jordan asked.

But before Natasha could say anything else, Simon and Pru arrived, and Emery announced they were ready to go. Regina counted off before Astrid could say a word of explanation to the family about the sage-green cabinet in the room, which, of course, was exactly what Emery wanted.

"Well, this is surprising," Natasha said again, and they were off.

Simon frowned, but then he spotted the cabinet. "Oh. What . . ." His frown deepened. "What's that?"

"I'd like to know the same thing," Jordan said, eyebrows lifted in Astrid's direction. They'd talked about this, practiced it even. Jordan, the curmudgeonly carpenter. Astrid, the elegant designer. Still, getting salty with Astrid Parker now felt . . . strange.

"I'm excited to show you exactly what this is," Astrid said, her professional voice smooth and bubbly. She was good at this part.

Pru, Simon, Natasha, and Jordan—her arms folded in a tight, skeptical knot—gathered around the island, where Astrid snapped Jordan's laptop closed and pushed it out of the way. Jordan nearly smiled. They hadn't rehearsed that bit, but it was effective, Astrid's *get this horrible thing away from me* attitude very clear as she set up her own iPad.

Astrid started off the presentation with the Lapis Room, since both Simon and Pru had already seen the blue paint. As the image filled the screen, Jordan's grandmother gasped.

"Oh" was all Pru said, her fingers trembling at her mouth. Astrid explained the design, the lapis lazuli stone, while Jordan watched Pru's eyes start to shimmer.

"Wow," Simon said, leaning closer from where he was standing between Jordan and Pru. "That's . . . wow, that's spectacular."

"Isn't it?" Astrid caught Jordan's eye and lifted her brows. Jordan lifted her own back at her, the conspiratorial spirit between them like a drug.

But then Jordan's gaze snagged on Natasha, who had most definitely caught the look between the two women. Jordan cleared her throat and smoothed out her expression again.

Astrid continued with the presentation, room after room. As she talked and pointed out certain features, words bubbled onto Jordan's tongue—things she would add, points she wanted to make, decisions she wanted to explain—but she swallowed them down. She and Astrid knew how these designs came about, Pru clearly adored what they'd created—if her radiant smile, clapping, and gasps of delight with each new room reveal were any proof—and that was all that mattered.

Wasn't it?

"I love it," Pru said when Astrid finished. "I love it so much. It's perfect."

She looked right at Jordan when she said this, her head tilted and eyes swimming.

Jordan scrubbed a hand through her hair. Showtime. "Okay, yeah, it's nice. But what about all the work we've already done? Why the sudden change?"

That last question hadn't exactly been planned, and Astrid's mouth opened in surprise, but a calm smile replaced it so fast, Jordan wondered if she'd imagined it.

"I did some thinking," Astrid said. "Spent some more time with Alice's history, and this feels right. This place is special, and it deserves an . . . inspired design."

She glanced at Natasha as she said this, and Jordan nearly laughed.

"So why now?" Jordan asked, widening her stance, arms still crossed. "Why not do all this before?"

Astrid's smile faltered again. Shit. This was going to be trickier than they originally thought. But it seemed like a question a grumpy carpenter would ask the designer, particularly if this change was going to create more work for her and the crew. No one but Jordan and Astrid knew her workshop was currently filled with nearly completed pieces.

Astrid sighed and looked back at the design. "Sometimes, it takes a while to get to know a space, to really understand the spirit of a house or room. I'm not perfect, and I can admit when I act too hastily on a design."

"Well, part of that's our fault too," Simon said, waving his hand from him to Pru. "We asked for a modern design."

Pru nodded. "We did. I thought that would help bring in business, but this"—here she grabbed Astrid's hand—"this is breathtaking. More lovely than I could have ever imagined."

Emotion bloomed in Jordan's chest. This was what she wanted for the Everwood, for her family. She had to force her mouth flat.

"I've already cut the countertops for the kitchen," she said. A lie. "We ordered the shakers." Another lie. "This piece you ordered to prove your point"—she pointed at the sage-green cabinet on the floor—"looks custom made."

"Are you saying you can't build something as lovely as that cabinet?" Astrid asked, mouth pursed.

Another smile threatened to split Jordan's mouth. "Oh, I can build something as lovely as that cabinet. I can build the shit out of it." She glanced at Emery. "Sorry."

They waved her off, then rolled their hand for her to keep going.

"All I'm saying," Jordan said, "is that we're on a time crunch."

"So we work longer and faster," Astrid said, taking a step toward Jordan.

"You mean the crew and I work longer and faster," Jordan said. She moved closer to Astrid as well. They were nearly nose to nose. Jordan could smell her minty toothpaste. "I seriously doubt you'll be in my workshop hammering into the wee hours."

Astrid narrowed her eyes, but Jordan could tell she was fighting a smile too. This was actually kind of fun.

And a little hot.

As they stared each other down, Jordan felt a definite thrum between her legs. She stepped back, swiped a hand through her hair. "What do you think, Natasha?"

The design star's judgment was the only way they'd move on from this scene, and suddenly, Jordan felt like she needed a shower.

A cold one.

Natasha didn't answer right away. Instead, her eyes flicked from Jordan to Astrid, back and forth, like she was trying to dig under their skin. Finally, she smiled. "I think it's brilliant."

"Really?" Jordan asked on instinct, pride curling around her voice. She cleared her throat. "I mean, you think we can pull this off? We have four weeks."

Natasha pursed her mouth and waved at the laptop screen. "With a design that good, you do whatever you have to do to make it happen."

CHAPTER

TWENTY-TWO

CLAIRE'S HOUSE WAS packed. Astrid didn't even know who half of these people were, but they'd shown up for Delilah and Claire's pseudo-housewarming party, wine bottles and *Hers and Hers* towel sets in hand, ready to celebrate the happy couple. Astrid was pretty sure Delilah's agent was here, as well as a few gallery owners whom Delilah had made connections with up and down the west coast in the last year, which must be why Astrid recognized only a handful of guests.

"This is wild, huh?" Josh Foster said, stepping next to her on the back porch where she'd retreated for some air. She'd been at the house all day, helping Claire set up for the party, arranging charcuterie plates, and cleaning spots off wineglasses.

Astrid shot Josh her usual scathing look, and he grinned. At this point in their relationship, their mutual disdain was almost a joke.

"I had no idea Claire even knew this many people," she said.

"I doubt she does. But when your girlfriend is a semi-famous photographer, I guess you're bound to run in some swanky circles."

Astrid glanced inside, then at the few people on the other end of the deck. They were mostly dressed in black, tattoos everywhere, a few bohemian styles right up Iris's alley. "I'd hardly call this swanky."

He tipped his beer bottle at her. "Ah, yes, I forgot only Parker-Greens were experts in sophistication."

"Go fuck yourself, Josh."

He stumbled back, clutching his chest like he'd been shot. "Astrid Parker f-bombed me."

She shook her head, but a smile threatened to curve her mouth upward.

"The Everwood is coming along," he said when he'd recovered. "Show's interesting."

"Hmm" was all she said. Josh's crew was currently working on reinforcing the front porch, which had a lot of rotting wood, and they'd soon move on to the other myriad structural issues, like the slanting turret and all-new exterior doors. Pru had approved everything on the design, and Jordan was hard at work restoring a lot of the original furniture pieces that they planned to place back into the finished rooms.

At least, that's what she assumed Jordan was doing. In the three days that had passed since their redesign meeting, they'd had only two scenes together—one that featured them arguing about the exterior paint color, and another that had Astrid explaining the changes to an incredulous Josh while Jordan slurped loudly on her coffee in the background, leaning against the front porch steps with her feet crossed lackadaisically at the ankles.

Emery loved it. Natasha loved it. And of course, designer and carpenter had planned every moment, but each time they shot a scene where she and Jordan went toe to toe, it still left Astrid feeling shaky.

There was also the fact that these tense, recorded exchanges were the only interaction she'd had with Jordan since their meeting. They'd both been swamped filming individual scenes—Astrid directing

Josh's crew, Jordan building and refinishing—and Astrid hadn't laid eyes on her carpenter at all today. She felt desperate to see her, talk to her without cameras around, particularly after their literal tête-à-tête in the inn's kitchen right before the meeting. The feel of Jordan's skin under her fingertips, the way Jordan's eyes had fluttered closed . . . Astrid hadn't stopped thinking about it since.

She rose up on her tiptoes, scanning the crowd inside for a half-shaved haircut and a printed button-up.

"I like the new design," Josh said, taking a sip of his beer. "Doesn't seem like you though."

She frowned at him. "What do you mean?"

He shrugged. "It's vintage. Spooky. You are neither of those things."

She rolled her eyes. While he was technically right, she was not going to let Josh Foster tell her who she was. "I'm a designer. I can design whatever I need to."

He presented a palm in surrender, but somehow, his mouth kept flapping. "You never have before."

"What is that supposed to mean?"

"I'm just saying we've worked on a lot of projects together in the last year. This one feels different."

She shook her head, but her stomach tightened. If Josh could tell this design wasn't exactly on brand, surely everyone else in her circle would be able to as well. She hadn't been very forthcoming about the nature of the project with Claire and Iris. It wasn't like she shared a ton of work details with her friends all that often anyway, but somehow, withholding her design partnership with Jordan was starting to feel like lying.

"Or," Josh said, turning around to face the house, "maybe it's the *who* that's different."

She froze. "What the hell are you talking about?"

He tipped his beer bottle toward the living room, where Astrid could see Simon and Jordan weaving through the crowd.

She wasn't sure which *who* Josh was referring to, Simon or Jordan, but from the shit-eating grin he now sported, she could guess. But if there was anyone on the planet she was *not* going to discuss her sexuality with, it was Josh Foster. Plus, there was no way he actually suspected anything. She and Jordan pretty much pretended to hate each other whenever he was around.

"Dad!" Ruby Sutherland's voice split through her thoughts, the twelve-year-old flying onto the deck and into her father's arms, all long limbs and brown hair. Claire and Iris trailed behind her, both of their eyes lighting up at the sight of Astrid.

"Hey, there's my girl," Josh said, lifting Ruby off the ground for a second before setting her back down. "You ready for a weekend with your old man?"

"Yes, please," Ruby said. "There's way too much kissing happening in this house right now."

"Hey, now," Claire said, swatting her daughter's arm.

Ruby just laughed, then leaned her head on her mother's shoulder. Astrid smiled and ran a hand down Ruby's hair in greeting. Ruby beamed at her, and then she and Josh started talking a mile a minute about their plans for the weekend.

Astrid was glad for the distraction. She looped one arm through Iris's elbow and used her other to direct Claire to a corner of the patio. "Remind me never to let your ex corner me again, okay?"

Claire laughed. "What did he do now?"

Astrid waved a hand. "Just being his charming self." She took a sip of her wine and looked at Iris. "No Jillian tonight?"

Iris's shoulder slumped. "No. She had to work this weekend. Some big corporation did something horrible."

Claire canted her head. "Is she defending or prosecuting?"

Iris winced. "Defending, I think."

Astrid and Claire caught each other's eye. Iris was pretty much a hippie, preaching the evils of Amazon and the need for composting services in every city in America.

"I know, I know," Iris said. "You don't have to say it."

"Say what?" Astrid said, feigning ignorance.

Iris popped a hand on her hip. "Look, when you're having the best sex of your life, things get a little hazy up here." She tapped her brain. "And Jillian is *sweet*. She recycles and gives to charities."

"Oh, well, if she recycles," Claire said, winking at Iris over her own wineglass.

"Fuck you," Iris said, but she was smiling.

"Hey, I won't judge you for having a little fun," Claire said. "Plus, best sex of your life . . ." She trailed off, and she and Iris clinked their glasses, then looked at Astrid expectantly.

"Um, yeah, right?" Astrid said, holding up her glass as well, but she knew she wasn't fooling her best friends. *Best sex of your life* didn't really apply to Astrid, considering she was almost positive she'd never had it. Good sex, okay. *Best?* If what she'd experienced so far was *best*, then she led a sad, sad life.

"Hey, you two," Iris said.

Astrid shook herself out of her depressing thoughts to see Simon and Jordan headed their way.

"Hey," Simon said. "Congrats on the cohabitation, Claire." He leaned in to kiss her on the cheek.

"Thanks," Claire said.

"Where's Jillian?" Simon asked.

Iris groaned, then started to explain where Jillian was again, but was cut off by a cell phone ringtone that Astrid had never heard before. Everyone froze as Celine Dion's "The Power of Love" filled the space between them.

"What the hell is that?" Iris asked, looking around.

"The nineties' sad attempt at romance?" Simon suggested.

She made a face at him but smiled. Still, the song played on, tinny and a bit muffled.

"It's your phone, Ris," Astrid said, leaning closer to her friend and hearing the melody get a little louder.

"*My* phone?" Iris frowned but dug her device out of her pocket. "That isn't my ring—"

She blinked at the screen and slid her finger over the surface, holding the phone to her ear. "Hello?"

Astrid glanced at Claire, both of them exchanging worried looks. Next to Astrid, Jordan shifted, her shoulder brushing against hers. Warmth flooded through Astrid like adrenaline, but she tried to focus on her friend.

"This is Iris. Who the hell is this?" Iris said, hand on her hip, but then her arm dropped and her mouth fell open. She glanced at her friends and held up a finger before turning on her heel and heading back inside.

"What was that?" Claire asked.

"I have no idea," Astrid said.

"I'm going to go check on her," Claire said.

"I'll join you," Simon said.

Astrid knew she should go as well—she was worried about Iris, but Jordan was here, finally, after three days of pretending to be annoyed with her on film and random sightings across the inn's yard, and she couldn't seem to make her feet move.

"Hey," Astrid said after the others disappeared inside.

Jordan smiled at her, but it was a tired smile. "Hey."

"How are you?"

"I'm well," Jordan said, a teasing lilt to her voice. "And you?"

"Great."

Jordan nodded and sipped her beer, looking around at the other guests while Astrid racked her brain for more to say. She had a lot to say, actually, most of which was some form of "Please hold my hand,

and could I maybe kiss you?" but Astrid didn't think she could just *say* that.

Or could she?

Shit, her pulse was sprinting. Had she always been so completely awkward when it came to liking someone?

A stream of people poured out onto the deck, bumping Jordan and Astrid closer together. Words and laughter enveloped them, and Astrid caught an irritated look cross Jordan's face at the man next to her who didn't seem to be aware that his elbow kept jutting against Jordan's arm.

Astrid grabbed Jordan's beer, then set both the bottle and her own wineglass on the patio table before taking Jordan's hand. "Come with me."

She didn't wait for Jordan to answer, just pulled her inside the house, through the packed living room and into the main hallway. She didn't stop until they got to Claire and Delilah's bedroom, which was currently being used as a coat closet, jackets strewn neatly all over the bed.

She ushered Jordan inside, then closed the door, pressing her own back against the white-painted wood. It was dim in here, a single reading lamp on one bedside table the only light. Jordan stood in front of her, hands in the pockets of her dark gray jeans, eyebrows lifted in expectation. She didn't say anything, and somehow, Astrid knew she wouldn't.

This was Astrid's show, her move to make.

And goddammit, she was going to make it.

"You're not the first woman I've ever been attracted to," Astrid said.

Jordan's eyebrows shot up even higher.

"I just didn't understand what it really meant before you," Astrid went on.

Jordan watched her for a second—a second that felt like years, Astrid's heart galloping against her ribs.

"Fair enough," Jordan finally said.

Astrid exhaled, and took a step closer. "I didn't *let* myself understand. My whole life, I've waited to feel like this."

Jordan's mouth parted. "Like what, Parker?"

Another step. "Like *this*. The way I feel when I'm with you. Like I'm twelve years old and going through my first crush. Like I might explode if I don't see you, talk to you. Like I don't care about anything else in this whole messed-up world but what you think about me. Feel about me."

Jordan still didn't say anything, but her chest moved up and down a little faster, her eyes locked on Astrid's.

One more step. They were so close now. Astrid could feel Jordan's breath on her face, the fabric of her light pink button-up covered in darker pink kiss prints brushing up against Astrid's own deep green sleeveless blouse.

She took a chance—because hell, she'd definitely passed the point of no return here—and ran her thumb over one of those kisses at Jordan's hip. Electricity shot through her entire body, just from that single, barely there touch, and she saw Jordan's own arm pebble with goose bumps.

"I want to kiss *you*," Astrid said. She let her other hand come up to Jordan's waist, both fists closing around Jordan's ridiculously serendipitous shirt. She didn't tug her closer though. Not yet. "I want to touch *you*, and not so I can know what it's like to be with a woman."

"Why then?" Jordan asked. Her voice was deliciously ragged, and Astrid couldn't help but smile a little.

"So I can know what it's like to be with *you*," she said.

Jordan sucked in a breath, her tongue slipping out to lick at her lower lip. Heat pooled low in Astrid's belly, but she didn't move. She needed Jordan to say yes to this, needed to make one hundred percent sure she was okay.

One corner of Jordan's beautiful rosebud mouth tipped up in a tiny smile. "I guess you better find out, then."

Joy spread through Astrid's chest, her arms and legs and stomach. That was the only word for this feeling that coursed its way through her body. Pure joy.

There was also terror.

What if she was a bad kisser? What if she did everything wrong, and Jordan didn't feel the same after this? Astrid was, after all, her mother's daughter. She was cold, unfeeling, dispassionate. Spencer had said as much during one of their last phone conversations as they dismantled their wedding last year. She was sure others had thought it. Hell, the reason she and her college boyfriend had broken up junior year was because she was too focused on her studies.

Because she wasn't any fun.

But she didn't feel any of that when she looked at Jordan Everwood. She didn't feel like the same woman who'd yelled at her outside Wake Up just a few weeks ago. She didn't feel powerless and hopeless like she did at her weekly brunches with her mother. She didn't feel like a failure like she did when she thought about Natasha Rojas's declaration about her original design.

She didn't feel miserable like she did when she thought about design at all.

She simply . . . felt. All the good things. Hope, longing, excitement, curiosity. She felt everything with Jordan Everwood.

She tugged at Jordan's shirt, pulling her flush against her body. Jordan let out a tiny gasp of surprise, but then smiled as Astrid trailed her fingers to Jordan's arms. Astrid wasn't going to rush this. She was going to take her time and enjoy every single second of this first kiss.

Jordan's own hands went to Astrid's waist, dipping under her silk blouse, thumbs swiping against her bare skin. Astrid nearly collapsed at the contact, it was such a relief, but she concentrated on her own journey, sliding her fingertips along Jordan's forearms, then to her upper arms, curling around her toned biceps for a second before drifting up her shoulders and over her exposed collarbone.

God, she loved this woman's clavicle. She danced her fingers along the delicate bone, then let them meet at that pretty dip at the base of Jordan's throat. Finally—*finally*—she traveled up Jordan's neck and framed her face between her hands. They stared at each other, their breathing loud and labored by this point.

"Shit, Parker" was all Jordan said.

Astrid smiled. She suddenly felt young and giddy, and she couldn't get enough. She loved the effect she was having on this gorgeous, amazing woman, and she leaned in slowly, letting their mouths brush, but just barely.

Jordan was like a drug—her jasmine-and-pine scent, the way her body felt under Astrid's hands. Astrid suddenly felt wild, ravenous, and let one palm circle around to cup the nape of Jordan's neck.

Still, she didn't hurry. She drifted her mouth over the side of Jordan's lips, then trailed up to her cheek, over to her temple, skimming her eyelids, her forehead, before coming back down the other side and settling her mouth just under Jordan's ear.

"Fuck," Jordan said, arching her neck to give Astrid more access. "As much as I'm loving this whole seduction, if you don't kiss me right now, I might lose it."

Astrid pulled back and grinned at her. "I think I can handle that," she said.

Jordan spread both of her hands wide on Astrid's bare waist and yanked her even closer. "You damn well better."

So Astrid complied.

She closed her mouth around Jordan's bottom lip, then turned her head and did it again . . . and again. Each time a little harder, each time a little more desperate. Jordan followed her lead, but then, as soon as Astrid's tongue touched hers, she let out a sort of growl that made Astrid's toes curl, and opened her mouth fully to hers.

Jordan tasted like summer, like beer and mint and something uniquely her, and Astrid couldn't get enough. She backed her up toward the bed, hands moving over Jordan's face, shoulders, waist. Jordan's hands were on their own mission, sliding up Astrid's bare back and around her ribs as they made out like teenagers.

That was the only way to describe it. Tongues and teeth, tiny breaths into each other's mouths, a desperation Astrid didn't remember ever experiencing fueling every touch.

The backs of Jordan's knees hit the bed and she fell back onto the sea of coats, pulling Astrid on top of her. Both women laughed, but when Astrid hooked her leg around Jordan's hip, the need to straddle her nearly unbearable, Jordan's expression turned very serious. She rolled them so Astrid was underneath her, then pressed her deeper into the mattress.

Astrid gasped, slipping her own hands under Jordan's shirt, the feel of her bare skin like heaven. Jordan kissed her again, tongue dancing with hers, teeth tugging on her lower lip in a way that made Astrid's clit throb.

"Do you know how long I've wanted to do this?" Jordan asked, mouth sliding to Astrid's neck, sucking gently at that spot under her ear.

"How long?" Astrid managed to ask.

"Since I saw you swing that sledgehammer." Kiss. "I wanted you right then. Maybe even before, I don't know." Kiss.

"Me too," Astrid said. She bucked her hips against Jordan's, seeking pressure. "Even in front of Wake Up that day—I was a bitch, I know, but there was something about you."

Jordan laughed against her skin. "You were a total bitch. A really hot, really sexy bitch."

Now Astrid laughed, tightening her leg around Jordan's hip.

"And that cherry stem," Jordan said. "Fuck, that was hot."

"Really?"

"Oh my god," Jordan said, before tugging at Astrid's earlobe. "I saved the damn thing, it was so hot."

"You did not," Astrid said, pushing on her shoulders to look her in the eyes.

"I most definitely did. It's on my dresser right now."

Astrid didn't know what to say. It was a silly thing—a cherry stem tied in a knot—but somehow, the sentiment behind it made her eyes sting. She cupped Jordan's face in her hands and pulled her down for a slow, deliberate kiss. A kiss that soon picked up speed, turning desperate and wild.

Astrid lost all track of time. There was only Jordan's mouth, Jordan's hands and stomach and thighs, the taste of her skin right below her ear that Astrid couldn't stop kissing, delighting in the little sounds Jordan made in response.

She was drowning in this woman, happily, blissfully, which was probably why she didn't hear the bedroom door open until Claire's voice filled the space.

"Oh, Jordan, I'm so sorry," Claire said. Jordan and Astrid froze. "I didn't realize you'd come in here. Have you seen Ast—"

But Claire cut herself off when Jordan turned to look over her shoulder, revealing Astrid underneath her, very clearly make-out mussed, her thigh still wrapped around Jordan's hip.

Claire blinked. "Oh my god."

"Um," Astrid said. "Hi."

"Yeah. Um. Hi," Claire said back, still blinking rapidly.

"Okay, this is a little awkward," Jordan said, untangling herself from Astrid and sitting up. Astrid got up too, straightening her shirt.

"I'm sorry, Claire, I didn't mean to go all R-rated in your bedroom," Jordan said.

Claire waved a hand, then laughed nervously before rubbing her hands over her face. "I just . . . wow, I don't . . . um . . ."

Astrid watched her best friend wrestle with her shock, waiting for embarrassment to wash over her.

It never came.

She wasn't embarrassed at all. She was just . . . damn, she was just *happy*. She slid her hand into Jordan's, squeezing once. Jordan glanced at her and winked, squeezing back.

Finally, Claire seemed to get a grip on herself. "We need to get over to Iris's," she said. "That's why I came to find you."

Alarm quickly mingled with her happiness. "Is she okay?"

Claire nodded. "Physically, yes, but something happened with Jillian."

It took a second for the words to process. "Jillian? Jillian's not even in town."

"I know. But when Simon and I went inside to find her, she was gone. Her car was gone too. She wasn't answering her phone, so Delilah went over to her place to check on her and . . . I don't know. She's upset, but won't say what happened until you and I get there. Said she doesn't want to say it more than once."

"What?" Astrid said. "Iris loves rehashing stuff."

"I know," Claire said, nodding, "which is why I'm pretty worried here."

"Right," Astrid said, scooting to the end of the bed and grabbing her sandals that had fallen off and onto the floor at some point. She caught Jordan's eye as she slipped them on.

"Go," Jordan said. "You need to see your friend."

"You'll be okay?"

Jordan grinned. "More than okay."

"Hand me your phone."

Jordan did and Astrid opened up her contacts, putting in her number. A little thrill went through her. So far, they'd only communicated through emails and the direct message feature of the design program they'd been using. Officially having each other's numbers—and in a much nicer context than demanding dry cleaning—felt somehow romantic.

"Text me, okay?" she said as she handed Jordan's phone back. "Or I'll text you after . . . I'm not sure how long I'll be over there."

"No worries, Parker."

Astrid nodded. She really wanted to kiss Jordan goodbye, but Claire was standing right there, watching them with this *Who the hell are you and what have you done with my best friend* expression on her face, so she resisted.

But as she joined Claire in the doorway, she did glance back to see a grin settle over Jordan's face as she looked at her phone, no doubt seeing the name Astrid had entered for herself in Jordan's contacts.

Semi-Decent Human Who Wants to Kiss You Again

CHAPTER
TWENTY-THREE

ASTRID SAT IN the front seat of Claire's Prius, hugging her bag to her lap while Claire drove through town.

"Josh said he'd handle the party," Claire said. "Lock up when everyone's gone in case we're here for a long time."

Astrid nodded.

"Ruby's headed to his house for the weekend anyway," Claire said.

"Good," Astrid said.

"I hope Iris is okay."

"Me too."

"I mean, I'm not Jillian's biggest fan, but still."

"Yeah."

Claire cleared her throat. Astrid knew her best friend wouldn't bring up Astrid's make-out session. She also knew Claire yammering on about other things was her attempt to get Astrid to talk about it.

Which she was not going to do.

Not that she didn't trust Claire with the information, but she still needed to process it all herself. She and Jordan had kissed. No, they'd made out. Heatedly. So much so that Astrid could feel how damp her underwear was right now. While it wasn't the most comfortable she'd ever been and she wouldn't mind putting on a clean pair, particularly now that the kissing was over, she couldn't help the smile that kept settling on her face as she thought about every single detail of the last half hour.

When Claire pulled up in front of Iris's apartment building downtown, Astrid wasted no time getting out of the car. Claire followed in silence, though Astrid could almost *feel* her questions.

"Hey," Claire said as they stopped outside Iris's unit.

Astrid braced herself, keeping her eyes on the door and rapping three times with her knuckles. "Yeah?"

"Um, well," said Claire. "You might want to—"

The door swung open to reveal Delilah holding a full glass of water, an unopened box of tissues tucked under one arm. Astrid started to ask how Iris was, but Delilah spoke first.

"Holy shit, what happened to you?" she asked.

She was looking at Astrid, her eyes wide and her brows lifted.

"What are you talking about?" Astrid asked.

"Um," Claire said, then circled her hand around her own face before pointing at her hair.

Astrid's hand flew to her head, a sinking feeling settling into her stomach. She stepped inside, all but shoving Delilah out of the way, and found the colorful framed mirror Iris had hanging in the entryway.

"Oh my god," she said when she saw her reflection. Her hair was a mess, sticking up and parted weirdly from Jordan's hands running through it, but that wasn't the worst part. The worst part was that her lipstick—a dark pink rose color she'd forgotten she even put on when she was getting ready—was smeared all over the lower half of her face.

All. Over.

She looked like a clown with a penchant for long-lasting lip stain. Working her hand over her mouth, she tried to remove the evidence, but she only managed to make it worse.

"Here," Claire said, heading over to the kitchen, wetting a paper towel under the sink and adding a dot of hand soap. "This should do it." She handed the towel to Astrid, who proceeded to clean off her still-swollen lips while Delilah watched her with a shit-eating grin on her face.

"Don't you say a word," Astrid said, wiping furiously.

"I wasn't gonna," Delilah said, still smiling.

"Wait, you knew about this?" Claire asked.

"About what?" Delilah said innocently.

"Babe," Claire said, a cute little whine to her voice.

"Hello?" Iris shouted from the bedroom. "Heartbroken best friend in here eagerly awaiting some succor!"

Claire threw one more annoyed look at her girlfriend before all but stomping off toward Iris's room. Delilah waggled her eyebrows at Astrid.

"I see you took that dream to reality level," she said.

Astrid finished cleaning off her mouth, which now had a definite rashy look to it. "I thought you weren't going to say a word."

"I changed my mind."

Astrid shook her head, but felt it coming . . . the smile.

"Uh-huh, there it is," Delilah said.

"Oh, shut up." Astrid balled up the stained paper towel and threw it at her stepsister, which Delilah deftly dodged, even with her hands full.

"At least tell me it was good," she said.

The smile spread into a grin. Jesus, her cheeks were starting to get sore. "So good."

"Oh my god!" Iris yelled again.

"Coming, my queen!" Delilah yelled back, then ticked her head toward the hall.

Astrid nodded, following her stepsister into Iris's room to find their redheaded best friend in bed and surrounded by a million balled-up tissues, her colorful mosaic-patterned quilt tucked around her, eyes red and puffy. What appeared to be an empty bottle of wine sat on her mint-green bedside table, no glass in sight, which wasn't a good sign.

"I'm wallowing," she announced as Delilah and Astrid entered the room. Claire was already settled on one side of Iris, so Astrid lay down on the other.

"I can see that," Astrid said, resting her head against one of Iris's many multicolored pillows and wrapping one arm around her friend's waist.

Iris sighed, sniffled, fresh tears welling in her eyes. Delilah cleaned up Iris's snot-rags, set the new box of tissues on Iris's legs, and replaced the empty wine bottle with the glass of water.

"That better be vodka," Iris said.

"You need to hydrate," Delilah said.

"Ugh, fine," Iris said, but took the glass of water and gulped down half.

Finally, Delilah settled on the bed at Iris's feet, resting one hand on her shins. Claire wrapped her arm around Iris's waist too, her fingertips brushing Astrid's elbow. Astrid met her eyes over Iris's body and winked. Claire smiled back.

They sat like that for a while, nothing but the sound of breathing and Iris's occasional sniffles filling the room.

"What happened, honey?" Claire finally asked.

Iris sighed, brushed a red strand from her face. She opened her mouth, closed it, and repeated this little dance several times. The other three women glanced at each other—Iris Kelly rarely had a hard time knowing exactly what she wanted to say.

"Sweetie," Claire said softly. "It's us. Whatever it is . . ."

She trailed off and Iris nodded, then dropped her face into her hands. "I just feel so stupid."

"You're not stupid. Jillian is stupid," Delilah said.

Iris released a watery laugh. "You don't even know what she did."

"Whatever it was, it's caused you to go all angsty-teen-dealing-with-her-first-breakup, so she's stupid."

"Agreed," Claire said.

Astrid just squeezed Iris tighter.

They waited.

And waited some more.

Finally, Iris sighed. "She's married."

The words echoed through the room like a sudden clap of thunder on a clear day, rendering them all shocked and silent. Of course, Delilah was the first to break.

"What the *fuck*?" she said.

Iris nodded. "Yep. Married. To a woman named Lucy. They have a goddamn *kid*. Elliott, age eight. He loves baseball and painting his nails purple."

"Oh my . . . oh my *god*," Claire said.

"How'd you find out?" Astrid asked.

"Jillian has my phone," Iris said. "And I, apparently, have hers, a highly inconvenient mix-up after she sailed into town this morning for some cunnilingus."

The other three women just blinked at each other.

"That Celine Dion disaster earlier?" Iris went on. "Yeah, that was her ringtone for her fucking wife, who had no clue Jillian was taking trips to Bright Falls to fuck a redhead she met on Instagram, and I then spent the next hour on the phone with the sobbing scorned spouse of my lover, trying to *soothe* her."

"Oh, honey," Claire said.

Iris just shook her head, fresh tears welling into her eyes as her anger morphed into sadness. "I thought I was over this."

"Over what?" Astrid asked.

"This . . . this *feeling*. Like who I am isn't what anyone else wants."

"Sweetheart," Claire whispered, pressing closer and swiping Iris's hair off her face. Astrid caught Claire's eye, a knowing glance passing between them. This past fall, Iris and her boyfriend of nearly three years had split up because Grant wanted to get married and have kids, and Iris didn't.

She'd never wanted kids, but Grant loved her and kept hoping she'd change. Finally, he gave up and left—or they mutually agreed that Grant needed to follow his dream and Iris needed to follow hers, but Astrid knew it was a blow to Iris, a judgment on the kind of woman she was, even if Grant never intended to make her feel that way.

"I just . . ." Iris said. "I want a partner, you know? I *do* want that. But I feel like people take one look at me, at my red hair and big boobs, and they hear my loud mouth, and they just think . . . well, she's good for a nice lay, but nothing else."

"Hey, that's not what they think," Delilah said.

"It's what Jillian thought."

"Grant didn't, though," Astrid said. "You two were just on different paths, and that's okay. It doesn't mean you're not partner material."

"It means something," Iris said. "That Jillian thought she could treat me this way. Doesn't that mean *something*?"

"It means Jillian's a dick," Delilah said. "And I will personally kick her ass when I drive to Portland tomorrow to get your phone back."

"You don't have to do that," Iris said.

"I'm doing it," Delilah said.

"Okay," Claire said, "but, like, babe, please don't kick her ass."

"By *kick her ass*, I mean kick her ass true lesbian style, where I glare at her with my mouth all twisted up like a butthole and give her the silent treatment."

They all laughed at that, even Astrid, and she found herself exhaling almost happily. Not that Iris was hurt—she hated what Jillian did to her—but that she had this wild group of women who would most definitely kick someone's ass for her if she needed them to.

They very nearly did when she was engaged to Spencer.

Suddenly, she felt overwhelmed and exhausted, so she let herself be this Astrid she so often ignored lately—this person who cuddled and laughed while she and her friends plotted an asshole's fiery end.

"Okay, enough of this," Iris said, tossing another used tissue onto the floor. "I'm done talking about it. What I do want to talk about, however"—she sat up and very dramatically aimed her gaze at Astrid—"is why our beloved Astrid Parker looks like she just made out with a lumberjack."

Astrid's eyes widened and she bolted upright. "What?"

Delilah clapped a hand over her mouth. Claire just lifted her brows in Astrid's direction.

"You have looked in the mirror lately, right?" Iris asked, circling her hand around her own mouth. "You've got some major beard rash going on."

"It's not beard rash," Astrid said. "My lipstick smeared."

Iris pursed her mouth. "And how, pray tell, did that happen? In the twenty years that I've known you, I've never once seen you with smeared lipstick."

Astrid opened her mouth to answer but had no clue what to say. If she confessed the truth to Iris, that was it. There was no going back. She glanced around the room. Delilah already knew. Claire was an eyewitness. But even more than all that, she didn't want to go back.

She liked Jordan Everwood. What that meant in terms of a label or how to define her sexuality, she didn't know. And honestly, she didn't care.

Still, kissing and telling had never been something she engaged in all that often—hypothetical sex dream sharing notwithstanding—and she didn't want to break Jordan's trust.

She snapped her mouth shut. "I think we need ice cream."

"Oh, hell no," Iris said, pointing at her face. "I know that look. That's the Astrid Parker doesn't want to talk about her feelings look. Which, I would think after last year's engagement debacle, you would've learned your lesson."

"Iris," Claire said.

"What?" Iris said. "You know I'm right."

"There's a difference between a secret and not being ready to talk about something," Claire said.

"Oh, you mean like when you were banging Delilah and lied to everyone about it?" Iris said.

Silence. Astrid's stomach twisted, and she glanced at Claire, whose cheeks were now very red. Delilah reached over and grabbed Claire's hand, lacing their fingers together.

"Shit," Iris said, rubbing her eyes. "Shit, I'm sorry. I'm being a real asshole."

"Yeah, you kind of are," Delilah said.

"I'm sorry," Iris said. "No excuse for that, I know, but Jillian has my mind all fucked up. Maybe we *should* eat some ice cream."

"I'll grab it," Astrid said, swinging her legs off the bed. She desperately needed a minute to get herself together. Her brain was a mess. A happy, still-slightly-horny mess, but a mess nonetheless.

In the kitchen, she found a pint of Ben & Jerry's, gathered four spoons from a drawer, and was about to head back to Iris's room when her phone buzzed in her back pocket. She fished out her device to find a notification from **Delightful Human Who Ruined Your Ugly Dress** glowing on the screen.

Astrid smiled and opened up her messages, as the name Jordan had put in her phone weeks ago was too damn long to reveal any part of the text in notifications.

Did you mean it?

Astrid quickly texted back, Did I mean what?
The little dots bounced, as did Astrid's leg as she waited.

That you want to kiss me again.

Astrid bit her lip. Yes. One hundred percent. You?
This time the dots bounced a little longer, and Astrid felt a sudden rush of doubt. But after a few seconds, the one hundred percent emoji popped up, three in succession.
So three hundred percent? Astrid texted.
A few more one hundred percent emojis.
That's a lot of percent, Astrid tapped out.

Damn right it is, Parker.

Can I see you tomorrow?

You better, Jordan texted. Did Claire have a lot of questions?
Astrid paused before typing, No, but you could've told me that my lipstick was pretty much all over my face.
Jordan sent a laugh-crying emoji. I didn't notice, I swear. I was too busy trying not to drag you back to your place cavewoman style and have my wicked way with you.
Astrid's belly fluttered. An event I'd be very much into at a later date, she texted.

Yeah?

One hundred percent.

You're not super into emojis, are you?

Astrid laughed. It was true she didn't use emojis very often, but for Jordan, she'd do just about anything. She scrolled through the sea of colorful images until one in particularly caught her eye. It a little flirty, maybe a little dirty too, which was not Astrid's usual way, but it felt right, so she tapped on the peach emoji and hit send.

PARKER, Jordan texted back, making Astrid laugh right there in Iris's kitchen, ice cream softening in her arms.

So what did you do about your lipstick problem? Jordan asked.

Made it worse, apparently. Now Iris says it looks like I made
out with a lumberjack. Beard rash or something.

And what did you say?

Astrid paused. She wanted to play this carefully. The last thing she wanted to do was make Jordan feel like she was ashamed to tell her friends about them. She wasn't. At all. But she also wanted to respect Jordan's privacy.

Nothing yet, she finally tapped out. I wasn't sure if you wanted people to know.

The three little dots bounced, then disappeared. Bounced, then disappeared again. Astrid pressed a hand to her stomach, jaw clenching as the dots resurfaced for the third time. Finally, Jordan's message came through.

I'm in if you are.

Astrid exhaled, what she was starting to think of as her Jordan smile settling back on her mouth. I'm in, she texted back. I'm very in.

Okay then.

Okay then.

Give Iris my best. Let me know if I can do anything to help.

I will. Good night.

Night, Parker.

Astrid clicked her phone dark and slipped it back into her pocket before pressing her forehead against the cool surface of Iris's retro turquoise refrigerator. After taking a few more deep breaths, she marched back to Iris's room. Inside, Delilah was fiddling with Iris's laptop, pulling up what looked like a horror movie on Netflix, while Claire shook up a bottle of bright blue nail polish, ready to give Iris an amateur manicure.

Astrid dumped her loot onto the bed, then put her hands on her hips.

"I didn't make out with a lumberjack," she announced.

Three pairs of eyes flew to her like bugs to a light.

"I made out with a lumber*jane*. Okay?"

For a second, the other women seemed frozen, their gazes shifting from her to each other and back again. Finally, Iris was the one to break the spell.

"Jordan-fucking-Everwood," she said, clapping her hands on each word before pointing at Astrid. "I knew it! I knew you two were eye-fucking each other over my rainbow shelves last week."

Then, before Astrid could laugh or protest or react at all, Iris grabbed her around the waist and pulled her onto the bed. She yanked both Claire and Delilah into her embrace as well, until the four women were wrapped up together on the bed, laughing and crying and swearing, everyone's hair and makeup ruined good and proper.

And no other moment in Astrid's life had ever felt so perfect.

CHAPTER
TWENTY-FOUR

A WEEK LATER, Jordan stared down at the card on her comforter, the colorful image of a person sitting in bed, their face in their hands in clear despair, nine swords placed horizontally above them, several of which looked like they might be piercing their back.

Jordan sighed and leaned against her headboard. For the last week, her daily card had been a source of extreme irritation. First, there was the Fool, which, fine. New journey, new paths. Jordan had come to Bright Falls to start something new, after all.

The next day, though, she'd pulled the Eight of Cups. Okay . . . leaving behind negative things and energy in one's life. Meredith's daily texts for the last week were certainly a negative thing. Jordan had half a mind to block her.

Then there was the Hermit. Ah, yes, good, being alone for some strongly needed introspection, but wasn't that what Jordan had been doing for the last goddamn year?

Next up was the Ace of Pentacles. Health, wealth, material prosperity, new jobs and opportunities, it was the card everyone starting off on a new financial venture wanted to see in their spread. But when Jordan drew it a few days ago, she couldn't help the scowl from settling on her face, unease she couldn't explain clouding in her chest.

Now today, here was the Nine of fucking Swords, which was just great. Impending betrayal. Lovely. Maybe her energy had gotten mixed up with Iris's, and this was actually referring to that dick Jillian and the stunt she'd been pulling on Iris for the last month.

It was possible. Energy was a strange thing. Who knew what it got up to when people crossed paths?

But what Jordan really wanted to know was, where the hell was her Two of Cups? The soul mates card. The perfect pairing card. The new relationships card. The positive partnership card. The card that she'd been pulling at least three times a week for the last two months. Where was *that* little asshole?

She tried not to let it bother her, but she hadn't seen the Two of Cups since the day before she and Astrid kissed at Claire's party a week ago. She liked Astrid. So much. Maybe too much. She kept feeling that old need rising in her, the same one that sent Katie, her one lover since Meredith, running in the other direction all those months ago. Except with Astrid, it was worse, magnified to the point that Jordan had to curl her hands into fists to keep from clinging to Astrid when she left her house every night, bite her tongue so she didn't ask to stay.

Not that any of these feelings were bad in and of themselves. She and Astrid were new. They clearly liked each other. And even though she got the impression that Astrid needed to take things slowly— emotionally and physically—she never failed to find Jordan at the inn when the workday ended, kiss her lightly on the mouth, and ask her what she wanted to do that night. Spending the evening together was a matter of course the past few days, so it wasn't like Jordan's feelings were one-sided.

She knew they weren't.

But they still scared the shit out of her. She couldn't stop thinking about destiny. About how Meredith, her first love, the person who knew her better than anyone, had looked at her after so many years together and said, *No thanks.*

Jordan wasn't destiny material. How could she be if even her wife, the woman she'd gladly given up everything to help nurse back to health, didn't want her? Astrid would figure that out eventually.

Wouldn't she?

Her phone buzzed on her nightstand, interrupting her spiraling thoughts. She stuffed the Nine of Swords back into her deck and grabbed her phone, swearing out loud when she saw the text from Meredith.

> I'm in town. Please answer me, Jo.

She swiped a hand through her hair and leaned her forehead on her palm. Meredith had been calling and texting all week long, including an extremely mercurial text yesterday that simply said, Where are you? Meredith had probably discovered Jordan no longer resided at their Savannah house in Ardsley Park, but she also didn't give a shit. Voice mail after voice mail stacked up in her inbox, but she didn't listen to them. She knew she was being childish—a healthily functioning adult would be able to deal with their ex in a civil manner, especially a *lesbian* adult, a lot of whom stayed BFFs with their exes for all eternity—but Jordan never claimed to be the picture of mental health.

Or the perfect lesbian.

Her phone buzzed again.

"Oh, my god, what?" she yelled, swiping at the screen, hackles raised. Hackles that immediately calmed down when she saw **Semi-Decent Human Who Wants to Kiss You Again** flash across the screen.

> Good morning! I'm grabbing coffee from Wake Up on my way to the inn. Do you want some?

Jordan smiled and sent back a zombie emoji.

I'll take that as a yes? Astrid texted.

Jordan found the tongue emoji, pressed it four times, and hit send.

Is that panting for coffee or . . .

Jordan laughed out loud, realizing too late the tongue emoji is often used in a dirtier context.

Use your imagination, Parker, she texted.

The three dots appeared, then disappeared. Jordan grinned, picturing Astrid's face cinnamon-candy red right now. The woman got right and truly flustered when it came to sex, and it was adorable.

They hadn't had sex yet. They hadn't even ventured below the waist in any capacity—mouths, fingers, nothing. There'd been a little over-the-bra action, but that was it.

What she and Astrid did do, however, was spend at least half the night, every night, making out to the point that Jordan felt like she was about the explode. She wasn't complaining. Despite her fears and the distinct lack of the Two of Cups in her daily spread, she was actually pretty shocked at how well she was holding her shit together.

She didn't want to fuck this up.

Now, her phone buzzed again, Astrid finally sending back a text.

My imagination is making it hard to walk right now.

Jordan's eyebrows shot up, a million wings taking flight in her stomach.

Maybe we should do something about that, she texted back.

Yeah. Maybe we should.

SO OF COURSE, after that little text exchange, Jordan didn't see Astrid all damn day.

She came into her workshop to find a cup of coffee from Wake Up already on her workbench, a series of x's and o's drawn on the cup with one of the Sharpies Jordan knew Astrid kept in her purse, but no Astrid.

Unfortunately, Jordan didn't have time to hunt her down, either. They were filming the installation of the kitchen cabinets today, and Jordan could not wait to see them in all their glory. They were beautiful, if she did say so herself, and she knew the effect of the deep sage green against the lighter gray wall was going to be striking.

She slugged down her coffee, sent Astrid a thank-you text, and was soon lost in her work. As she and Josh focused on the cabinets, Nick and Tess, two other members of Josh's team who had been working closely with Jordan this past week, installed the butcher-block counters and the white porcelain farmhouse sink.

Throughout the day, the kitchen came to life. It was like watching a sunrise, the image Jordan had only dreamed about slowly becoming real. By the time five o'clock rolled around, it was done. There were gaping holes where the appliances would go, as well as some decorative elements, but the skeleton was in place, the anchor for the whole room—the whole inn, really—and Jordan felt her throat swell as she took it in.

"This looks great," Josh said, wiping the sweat off his forehead.

"You think so?" Jordan asked. She stood with her hands on her hips, sweat dotting her own forehead and chest.

He nodded. "I had my doubts about this color, but yeah. It's perfect."

Jordan smiled so broadly her cheeks hurt. She opened her mouth to say *Thank you*, even to explain how this was exactly the kind of cabinets one might find in a 1930s kitchen back when Alice Everwood was alive, but then she remembered.

She wasn't the designer.

"Oh my god, look at this kitchen," Natasha said, stepping inside the room and putting herself in the shot, as she often did.

"Right?" Josh said, sending a grin in Natasha's direction that even a very gay Jordan could recognize as panty-dropping.

Natasha, for her part, was focused on the room. "It's breathtaking. It really feels like I might encounter a ghost in here, but not in a creepy way. It just feels . . . intriguing. That's the word for it."

Jordan noticed too late that she was grinning like a kid with a trophy. Natasha canted her head, and Jordan quickly smoothed it out. She was supposed to be neutral about the design, if not downright ornery.

"These cabinets were a pain in the ass to make, I know that," she said, and Emery snorted a laugh from next to a camera.

"I can see that, but what a payoff, huh?" Natasha said.

Pride swelled in Jordan's chest. Again. She never expected to feel like this . . . so tender about her work. She'd never been overly precious regarding her creations before, but this was different. This was an entire house's design, her own family's home.

Which was all that mattered. She didn't need credit or praise— she just needed to stay in her lane for a little bit longer, a carpenter who built shit and that was it. Nothing to live up to, no one to disappoint.

She repeated all of this to herself every time her pride threatened to spill over. Astrid was the sole designer. This arrangement was better for everyone involved. There was also the fact that Natasha didn't strike Jordan as a woman who put up with any amount of bullshit, and lying to her for the past couple of weeks about the origin of the design she found so inspired? Well, that sounded like bullshit to Jordan.

Plus, Astrid had been working just as hard as Jordan, mostly on administrative and logistical stuff, all the shit Jordan had no head for.

She was integral to this project, there was no denying it. Watching Astrid in action, her quick decision-making, the way she solved a problem before it became a catastrophe, like when their supplier sent the wrong clawfoot tub for the master bathroom—copper instead of bronzed nickel—was pretty badass.

And a little bit of a turn-on, if Jordan was being honest.

"And cut," Emery called out. "Okay, everyone, that's a wrap for today."

Jordan felt her shoulders drop, all that on-camera tension falling away. She said goodbye to Josh and his crew as they headed out the back door, while Emery, Natasha, and Regina retreated to a corner to go over details for Monday.

"Oh my god."

At the familiar voice, Jordan's heart did something semi-embarrassing, but she smiled at Astrid standing in the kitchen's doorway.

"What do you think?" Jordan asked, spreading her arms to indicate the space. "Not bad, huh?"

Astrid shook her head, gazing around the room. "It's . . . Jordan, this is amazing." Her gaze settled on Jordan, her mouth open. Something sad spilled into her eyes, something Jordan couldn't put a finger on. She honestly wasn't sure if she wanted to. She was well aware this professional arrangement, blended with what was going on with them personally, was a precarious mix.

"You okay?" Jordan asked.

Astrid nodded, but her throat bobbed in a hard swallow. Jordan watched her shake it off and walk over to her. She leaned in for a kiss, and shit, Jordan very nearly acquiesced, but froze when she remembered three members of *Innside America*'s crew were standing in a corner.

And they were all staring at Jordan and Astrid.

Jordan cleared her throat, and Astrid followed her gaze, inhaling a surprised breath when she spotted the other people in the room behind her.

Natasha had her arms folded, with what could only be described as a smirk on her face.

"Yeah," Emery said slowly. "Okay, I think it's time to head out."

"I'd say so," Regina said, who looked just as uncomfortable as Emery.

"I need to get home too," Jordan said, gathering her tools into her toolbox. She didn't need to get home. What she needed was Astrid's mouth on hers, but getting out of this kitchen felt more pressing at the moment.

"Same," Astrid said, smoothing her hands down her black shorts. "I—"

"Oh no," Natasha said, shaking her head. "You two aren't going anywhere."

Astrid and Jordan exchanged a look but didn't dare move. Jordan had the distinct feeling she'd just been called into the principal's office.

Emery and Regina didn't even bother dealing with the equipment, opting instead to bolt through the swinging door as fast as possible. Once they were gone, Natasha didn't budge. She simply stared at Jordan and Astrid for a solid minute.

"Anything you want to tell me?" she finally said.

Jordan didn't dare look Astrid's way, but she could feel her radiating stress like a furnace.

"Like what?" Jordan asked.

They had to be careful here. Jordan was sure Natasha was referring to the fact that Jordan and Astrid were clearly about to make out, and not that Astrid was pretending to be the lead designer in a major televised project, but still. Either truth felt suddenly disastrous when Natasha Rojas shot her glare your way.

"Okay, so we're going to play coy," Natasha said. "I'll just come right out and ask then. How long have you two been fucking?"

Astrid spluttered, then coughed, her hand flying to her chest like a southern damsel. Jordan would've laughed and given her shit for it had Natasha not been in the room.

"We're not fucking," Jordan said, which was actually the truth.

"Fine, sorry, maybe that was a bit too crass," Natasha said, waving her hand. "How long have you two been gazing longingly in each other's eyes and *dreaming* about fucking?"

Jordan glanced at Astrid, who was still tapping on her chest while she coughed and cleared her throat a dozen times. She needed Astrid to take the lead here—this was Astrid's baby, her name to either go down in infamy or rise in notoriety with *the* Natasha Rojas, and Jordan wasn't going to make any decisions for her.

"We're not . . . doing any of that," Astrid said when she got herself together. Jordan held her breath.

"Oh, really?" Natasha asked.

And then . . . Jordan saw it happen. The original Astrid, the one she'd met outside Wake Up that first day, took control. Astrid rolled her shoulders back, lifted her chin, a muscle tensing in her jaw.

"Really," she said coolly. "But we have become friends."

And goddammit, Jordan tried not to feel it, she really did. She tried to ignore that sinking feeling in her stomach, that vulnerable emotion of being cast aside, denied. But it wormed its way in there anyway, digging its claws into Jordan's exposed underbelly.

"Friends," Natasha said. Her gaze landed on the carpenter, and it took Jordan a few seconds to realize Natasha was waiting for her to give confirmation.

She cleared her throat, schooled her features.

"Absolutely," she said. "Um, you know, I just moved back, so Astrid and her friends took pity on Simon and me. Invited us to a few things and, yeah. Friends."

Smooth. Very smooth.

Fuck, she needed a minute. She needed Natasha out of this room now.

"Okay," Natasha said, but she didn't look convinced. Honestly, Jordan didn't give two shits if she was convinced or not. Her heart felt like it was four times its normal size, making an awful racket in her ears.

"I guess I was wrong, then," Natasha said.

"Maybe we could all hang out some time," Astrid said brightly. Jordan felt the need to growl.

"Maybe," Natasha said, then glanced at her phone. "Right now, I've got a Zoom meeting with my boss back in Portland, so I'll see you two on Monday."

Astrid nodded. "Have a great weekend."

Natasha just smiled, eyed the two of them again like she was waiting for them to jump each other's bones and prove her right, before she finally left out the back door.

There was a beat where neither woman moved, but finally, once they heard Natasha's car start up, Astrid's ice-queen demeanor melted, her shoulders dropping and a huge exhale flying from her mouth.

"Oh my god," she said, clutching her chest and breathing heavily. "That was close."

Jordan gritted her teeth. She knew she didn't have any room to be upset. Natasha finding out about Astrid and Jordan's romantic involvement could be a disaster for several professional reasons, jeopardizing everything they'd worked so hard to create here. She knew that. Her *head* knew that.

But.

Her heart didn't give a fuck.

"Yeah," she said tightly, turning away from Astrid and toward her tool bag on the island. She tossed her measuring tape inside, her hammer. She pulled out the case for her drill, dismantling the bit and slipping it into its assigned spot.

"Hey," Astrid said from behind her.

Jordan couldn't answer. Not quite yet.

"Hey," Astrid said again. Softer. Closer. She put a hand on Jordan's arm and tugged gently.

Jordan let herself be turned around, steeling her expression into place.

"You okay?" Astrid asked.

Jordan nodded, waved a hand through the air, made a sound like *psh*, which was perhaps two too many assurances, as Astrid's frown only deepened. Finally, Jordan gave up the pretense.

"I just . . . I wasn't expecting that," she said.

"Me neither," Astrid said. "I had no idea Natasha was even in the room, and I—"

"Not Natasha," Jordan said. "You."

Astrid took a step back. "What do you—" But she cut herself off, her eyes widening. "Oh. God."

Jordan shook her head. "It's fine. I get it. I just . . . it felt . . ."

"Shitty," Astrid said. "It felt really shitty, oh my god, Jordan, I'm so sorry. I wasn't even thinking about . . . I just . . . I didn't think we wanted Natasha to know. I have no idea how she'd react, or what that would mean for the show and—"

"You need the show," Jordan finished for her. It was true—Jordan needed it too—but bitterness laced through each syllable nonetheless. She swallowed hard, tried to be logical, reasonable.

But since when was her heart fucking reasonable?

They stood there, awkwardly, and Jordan had no clue what else to say. Astrid didn't seem to know either. In her back pocket, Jordan's phone went off, saving them from having to figure it out.

Meredith's name flashed across the screen.

"Goddammit," Jordan whispered, smacking the red button and all but slamming the phone down on the brand-new countertop.

"What's wrong?" Astrid asked. "Who was that?"

"No one."

Astrid didn't press, but she still looked worried.

"Jordan," she said, stepping closer. She hooked her finger through the belt loops of Jordan's overalls. "I'm sorry about what I told Natasha. Or *didn't* tell her. It's not you."

Jordan laughed. "Wow, that's some line."

"No," Astrid said, yanking Jordan against her body. "It's not. It's really not you. And it's not *us*. It's just . . . I don't know what I'm doing, okay? This has all been a lot. A *great* a lot—I'm not complaining, but I'm . . . I'm . . ."

"A baby bisexual?" Jordan said, letting a smile curl one side of her mouth. Fuck, this woman was adorable. Even when Jordan wanted to be a little pissed at her, she couldn't resist. And, in truth, this *was* all very new for Astrid. Jordan needed to remember that.

Astrid smiled back. "Well, I mean, yes, maybe I am, but I'm not even talking about the whole queer aspect of this. I'm talking about you. *You* are new to me. Feeling like this."

"Okay, now *that* is a line," Jordan said, but her heart didn't care one bit. She brought her hands up to frame Astrid's face between her hands. She didn't kiss her. Not yet, and mostly because Astrid was still frowning at her, with an expression that could only be described as desperate.

Astrid glanced toward the pantry door, which was slightly ajar. Grabbing Jordan's hand, she pulled her inside the empty space and closed the door after them.

CHAPTER

TWENTY-FIVE

IT WAS TRUE, Astrid had no idea what she was doing. But in this moment, shoving the girl she liked into a pantry after she'd made her feel like total shit seemed like a logical choice. If Jordan thought her words were lines, fine. She'd show her. She'd make Jordan *feel* everything Astrid felt for her.

"What the hell—" Jordan started, but never got another word out because Astrid pressed her against the door and kissed her. Jordan tasted like spring this time, like pine and rain. Astrid slid her hands inside Jordan's overalls, fingers dancing up her spine to her sports bra.

"Okay, hang on," Jordan said, pulling away and flicking on the light so she could see Astrid clearly. "Not that I don't love this, but you do realize we're alone in the house, right?"

Astrid laughed, relief at Jordan's light tone making her giddy, and kissed down Jordan's neck to her collarbone.

"I know," Astrid said, running her teeth over Jordan's skin. The other woman sucked in a breath, and Astrid grinned—she'd never get over the fact that she could pull that kind of reaction out of Jordan. The effect was drug-like, addictive and euphoric. "Pulling you into a pantry seemed like a good grand gesture after screwing up. I'm not saying it makes sense."

"It makes no sense whatso—"

Astrid used her tongue now, dipping it inside that lovely divot at the base of Jordan's throat.

"Fuck," Jordan said, arching her neck to give Astrid more room. "Not gonna argue with you. Ever."

"Works for me," Astrid said, fingers playing at the underside of Jordan's bra. She'd never touched a woman's bare breasts other than her own, but shit, she wanted to, even as nerves filled her stomach. They were the good kind of nerves though. The *wanting* kind of nerves.

"Jordan," she said, pulling back to look at her. "I—"

"Shh," Jordan said, running a thumb over Astrid's bottom lip. "It's okay."

"It's not," Astrid said. "I want you, okay? I need you to believe me." She might not know anything about being queer—whether she was bisexual or pan or something else altogether—but she knew without one single doubt that she wanted Jordan Everwood.

"I do," Jordan said, then she kissed her once, twice, and flipped them around so Astrid's back was to the door. The motion snapped the air from Astrid's lungs, but she loved it. Maybe this was what she needed—what they both needed—this glorious place where *design* and *inns* and *Natasha Rojas* and *Isabel Parker-Green* didn't factor into anything. They were just Astrid and Jordan, two women who wanted to rip each other's clothes off.

Jordan's hands sneaked under Astrid's plain white tee, calloused fingers drifting over her stomach and up her rib cage, closer and closer . . .

"Is this okay?" Jordan asked, thumb just barely skating the edge of her bra.

Astrid nodded so hard, her head cracked against the door.

"Ow, shit," she said, grabbing her head with both hands.

"Whoa, careful," Jordan said, huffing a soft laugh. "I like that head."

"Yeah, me too," Astrid said. She went to put her arms down, ready for more of Jordan's touch, but before she could, Jordan tangled their fingers together above Astrid's head. Jordan's knee slid back in between Astrid's thighs, putting pressure right where Astrid needed it.

Heat pooled in her center, and Jordan's kisses grew more fervent, tugging at Astrid's lower lip in a way that made her want to scream. Jordan's hips worked against hers in delicious, evil circles.

"God, Parker," Jordan said into her mouth. "I need to make you come." She released Astrid's arms and slid her hands down Astrid's back to her ass, pulling her harder against her thigh.

Astrid registered how amazing all of this felt, how much she actually needed to come, but something inside her froze at Jordan's words, and Jordan felt it.

She let her leg drop from between Astrid's and settled her hands on Astrid's hips. "You okay?"

Astrid nodded, more gently this time. "I just . . . I'm not sure—"

"Hey, we can stop," Jordan said so sweetly, Astrid wanted to cry. "We don't have to go any further."

"No," Astrid said, hooking her hands inside Jordan's overalls and pulling her closer. "No, I want to. So much. I just . . . I don't want you to be upset if I can't . . ."

Jordan raised an eyebrow. "Can't what?"

Astrid shrugged. Jesus. This was all she needed. How very *Astrid Parker* of her, to let her baggage ruin this moment when all she wanted was to prove to Jordan how much she wanted her.

"What is it, Parker?" Jordan asked seriously.

Astrid sighed. "If I can't . . . you know. Come."

Jordan's eyes went wide. "Is that what you're worried about?"

"I haven't always been able to with other people, that's all. I *can*, just not every time."

A wicked smile settled on Jordan's mouth, and Astrid could see that *challenge accepted* glint in her eyes she'd come to know very well.

"Oh, here we go," Astrid said.

"You're goddamn right here we go," Jordan said, yanking Astrid against her, lower lip brushing her own. "I bet I can make you come without ever touching your skin, Parker."

Astrid pulled back. "What?"

"You heard me."

"Are you talking about dry humping? Because I did that plenty in high school, and it never really worked."

"Probably because you were rubbing against an inexperienced teenage douchebag who was only concerned with getting himself off."

Astrid frowned. She'd never really thought about it like that before.

Jordan dropped her hands from Astrid's waist and took a step back. "Have you ever been with a guy who spent some real time trying to get you off? As in one hundred percent focused on you and not his own dick?"

Astrid opened her mouth. Closed it.

"Holy shit, you've been with some real assholes," Jordan said.

Astrid covered her face and groaned into her hands. "Oh my god, I have."

"You do realize they were the problem, right? Not you?"

Did she realize that? Astrid knew some people just weren't all that interested in sex, and that was totally fine. It also didn't describe her at all. She liked sex. She wanted to have it. A lot more than she had in her life, if she was being honest. She was attracted to men and had felt turned on when she was with them. It just usually took a lot of foreplay to get her to come, and most men weren't up for putting in the time. Spencer surely hadn't been, but then he'd get frustrated when she *didn't* come, and she could never bring herself to fake it. During the last couple of months of their relationship, she'd started watching porn in the bathroom before they had sex, just to try and get her own engine going a bit. Sometimes it worked. Near the end, though, nothing worked.

She'd always assumed that's just the way she was. No big deal—it was still fun most of the time, and she had very capable fingers to finish herself off after her partner hopped in the shower or fell asleep.

"Maybe?" she said to Jordan now, dropping her hands. "I don't know."

Jordan shook her head. "Well, we are going to fix this right the fuck now."

Astrid couldn't help but smile at this woman's determination. "We're going to dry hump in the closet?"

"Not exactly." Jordan grinned mischievously, and pushed Astrid back against the door. She pressed the whole length of her body to Astrid's, kissing her neck, below her ear, then her mouth. Astrid's pulse quickened, heat building between her legs again, just like that. "Is this okay? Can I try?"

"Yeah," Astrid said, her voice ridiculously breathy.

"Okay. No skin begins"—Jordan kissed her once more—"now."

Jordan pulled her body off of Astrid's and smiled at her.

Astrid frowned. "I don't get it."

"Just try and relax."

"I'm not the greatest at that."

Jordan laughed and set both hands on Astrid's waist, thumbs pressing into her shirt's cotton. "I've noticed. Trust me."

Astrid leaned her head against the door and tried to follow directions. Jordan's hands started a slow journey north, stopping at the base of Astrid's ribs, fingers curling and exploring and soothing. It felt nice, but not exactly orgasm worthy. Still, Astrid closed her eyes and focused on Jordan's touch.

Soon, the other woman's hands began moving upward again. She closed one hand, then the other, around Astrid's breasts, gently squeezing and massaging before her thumbs swept across Astrid's nipples.

Astrid sucked in a surprised breath, her tips instantly hardening, even though Jordan was touching her through two layers of cotton. She arched her back, needing more, and Jordan definitely delivered. Lowering her head, she closed her mouth around Astrid's left breast, one hand still working the other. Astrid could feel the heat of Jordan's tongue, even through the fabric.

"Oh," Astrid said on a gasp, then clapped her hand over her mouth.

Jordan looked up at her. "Are you okay?"

"Yeah. Totally fine." In truth, she had never been very vocal in bed, but she'd never really thought about why until this very second, with Jordan's hot mouth searing through her shirt. *Oh* was a proclamation. So was *yeah* and *right there* and *just like that* and whatever other words people might say during sex. They were tells. They revealed a piece of yourself, something soft and vulnerable and completely at the other person's mercy.

Astrid had never let people get that deep. Even when they did manage to make her come, she bit her lip and released, at most, a grunt of satisfaction, and then got up to go to the bathroom. But with Jordan, she wanted to go deep. She wanted to be vulnerable. What's more, she couldn't *not*, and found herself sinking her hands into Jordan's hair, gently pushing the carpenter's mouth back to her tits.

Jordan laughed. "You are one in a million, Astrid Parker."

Astrid smiled, hoping that was a good thing. She blew out a breath as Jordan continued to explore her body. But when Jordan sucked her nipple into her mouth again, cotton and all, she couldn't have kept quiet if someone paid her.

"Oh god," Astrid said. She only felt silly for a moment, because then Jordan hummed against her, sending vibrations straight to her clit. Her body writhed, arching into Jordan's mouth as she worked her tongue over the cloth in ways Astrid hadn't even known were possible. She opened her eyes to watch Jordan, the sight of herself between her teeth unbearably hot. She started to lift her shirt, needing skin on skin like she needed air, but then Jordan pulled back.

"Nope. No skin, remember?"

Astrid made a sound that was not unlike whining. "Seriously? Still?"

Jordan drew in close, but stopped before her mouth touched Astrid's. Her hands went to the button on Astrid's shorts.

She flicked it free.

"Seriously," she whispered.

Astrid's knees started to shake as Jordan unzipped the zipper.

"This okay?" Jordan asked, her finger tracing the top edge of Astrid's underwear.

Astrid nodded. Couldn't breathe. Couldn't talk.

"I need a verbal yes here, Parker."

"Yes," Astrid managed to get out on a sigh. "Yes, yes, yes."

"Thank god," Jordan said, then dipped her hand inside Astrid's pants.

She was serious about this no skin thing, staying on top of Astrid's underwear, fingers exploring gently, circling one way, then the other. Astrid widened her stance a little to give her better access, which Jordan took with enthusiasm. She increased her pressure, sliding two fingers from Astrid's entrance to just below her clit. Astrid could feel herself spreading, could smell her arousal clouding between them. Far in the back of her mind, embarrassment lurked, but she told the feeling to go fling itself into the sea and focused on the way Jordan's fingers felt sliding closer and closer to her clit.

"You're very wet," Jordan said. She rested her body along Astrid's side, but still didn't kiss her, didn't touch any part of her skin. She simply pressed in close and worked her fingers over Astrid's center, tight circles that drew small keening sounds from Astrid's throat. The double friction of Jordan's fingers and the cotton of her underwear was intense, more intense than Astrid thought possible.

The feeling built surprisingly quickly. Jordan increased the pressure, circling, then sliding, then rubbing. Astrid realized that Jordan was listening to the sounds she was making, adjusting her touch accordingly, and holy fuck, was it working. Astrid's thighs started to shake, the tension in her lower belly billowing like a volcano ready to blow.

And that's what this felt like—like she was literally going to explode. She'd never felt this wild with another person before, this desperate for release. She started grinding herself against Jordan's hand, gripping the other woman's shoulders for support. Jordan snaked her free arm around Astrid's waist, holding her up as her fingers did absolutely wicked things to Astrid's clit.

"Please," Astrid heard herself say. No embarrassment. No worries. If anything, she felt even more like herself. "God, Jordan, please, make me come."

Jordan lowered her head and bit Astrid's collarbone through her shirt, gently working her teeth while circling her fingers harder . . . harder . . .

A wave—no, an ocean—of pleasure slammed into Astrid, nearly knocking her off her feet. She made a ridiculous noise as she came, raw and primal, and she didn't bite her lip even once to stop it. Jordan tightened her grip on Astrid's waist, that magical hand still moving until Astrid finished shuddering.

"Oh my god," Astrid said once she was back on planet earth. She swiped at her sweaty forehead. "I mean, that was—"

Before she could get another word out, Jordan yanked Astrid's shorts down so they pooled at her ankles.

"Oh," Astrid said, but then Jordan's mouth was on hers, her hands under her shirt. They both groaned at the skin-to-skin contact. Astrid had the overwhelming urge to rip off Jordan's shirt. She was desperate to feel the woman's skin against hers, lick a stripe between her breasts. She unclipped both of Jordan's overall straps, her hands immediately pawing at her sports bra.

"Not exactly how I pictured our first time," Jordan said, lifting Astrid's shirt over her head and throwing it behind her. "Wouldn't you prefer a bed?"

"I don't care about a bed," Astrid said.

"Thank fuck," Jordan said, unhooking Astrid's bra, "because if I don't taste you right now, I might lose my mind."

Astrid pulled back for a second, her bra hanging on her elbows. "Like . . . you mean . . ."

Jordan smirked. "Yeah." She drifted her fingers across the band of Astrid's underwear. "Can I?"

Astrid swallowed. She'd never been great at receiving oral sex. Spencer hated going down on her, and with other guys, she'd always felt incredibly self-conscious, like they were only performing the act so she'd reciprocate. But this was Jordan.

Everything was different with Jordan.

"Okay," she said, letting her bra drop to the floor. "Yes."

Jordan stepped back, taking her in. Astrid wasn't exactly full-chested, but her tits were perky and she'd always liked them. From the way Jordan's pupils went dark, it seemed she liked them too.

"Shit, Parker," Jordan said, her hands cupping Astrid's breasts, rolling her nipples between her thumbs and forefingers. Astrid very nearly started panting. When Jordan lowered her head, circling her tongue over one of Astrid's hardened peaks, there was no cotton between them this time. Astrid yelled something unintelligible, gripping Jordan's hair as the carpenter slid down her stomach, her mouth exploring her belly button, the soft skin just below.

Jordan hooked her thumbs through the legs of Astrid's underwear and tugged. The slow slide of fabric down her legs was torture, and Astrid had zero patience for it. She kicked the lacy yellow boy shorts off—god only knew where they landed—and looked for something to hold on to, bracing herself for the feel of Jordan's mouth.

"I've got a better idea," Jordan said when Astrid gripped the empty shelves on either side of her. She slid her fingers down Astrid's arms, linking their hands and guiding them both to the floor. They'd recently repainted the shelves in here, so a drop cloth covered the hardwoods.

Astrid started to lie down next to Jordan, but Jordan shook her head. "Up here." She patted her chest.

Astrid frowned at her. "Where?"

Jordan grinned, then sat up and directed Astrid to straddle her stomach. "Slide up." She lowered herself back to the floor, pulling Astrid up toward her face.

"Are you sure?" Astrid asked, suddenly realizing exactly where Jordan meant and that she was very, very naked.

And soaking wet.

She clenched her thighs around Jordan, feeling a strange mix of desperation and embarrassment.

"You're gorgeous," Jordan said. She reached out and slid a thumb up Astrid's wet center, then . . . sucked that thumb into her mouth. "And I'm sure."

Astrid's jaw dropped and Jordan laughed, wrapping her hands around Astrid's ass and tugging her up to her mouth. Soon Astrid was straddling Jordan's shoulders, her knees pressing into the cotton drop cloth. Jordan curled both arms around Astrid's thighs, pulling her even closer.

Astrid leaned back a little, desperate to see Jordan's face, her tongue as it—

"Oh, fuck," Astrid said as Jordan's mouth closed around her sex. Jordan hummed in agreement and the vibrations nearly sent Astrid to the ceiling. Jordan kissed her softly, carefully, spending time in the creases where her legs met her hips before returning to her center. When her tongue dipped into Astrid's wet heat, Astrid gasped, bracing her arms on Jordan's hips behind her. She rotated her pelvis over Jordan's mouth, a movement she couldn't control if she tried. The noises she was making were animal, primal—she barely recognized her own voice. Astrid had never felt anything like this.

"You like that," Jordan said against her wet skin. It wasn't a question, and Astrid didn't answer. Instead, she shifted, leaning over Jordan and sliding her hands into Jordan's hair. Jordan's fingers played at the crease in Astrid's backside while she lapped at Astrid's pussy, her tongue dipping into her entrance before her lips closed around her clit and sucked.

"Oh, god, yeah, right there," Astrid said, not at all embarrassed at the way she was humping Jordan's face right now.

Jordan kept kissing, sucking, humming, and Astrid felt herself grow dizzy as her lower belly clenched, her orgasm building from her clit and radiating down her legs.

"Fuck," she said, then said it again and again as Jordan's mouth worked, slid, sucked. When Astrid finally came, she pressed herself even tighter against Jordan's mouth, a groan rumbling in her chest as she shuddered, fingers clawing so tightly into Jordan's hair, she worried she'd hurt her.

It felt like forever before the room stopped spinning and she could feel her limbs again.

"Okay," she said, once she could see straight. She scooted back on top of Jordan, straddling her hips now. "Okay, wow."

Jordan smirked and propped herself up on her elbows.

"Don't look so smug," Astrid said, but she was smiling.

"Oh, I'm going to look smug," Jordan said. "I'm going to look smug for about a month. No, make that a year. Maybe longer."

Astrid laughed and leaned down to kiss her. She could taste herself on Jordan's mouth, and she wasn't even appalled by it. In fact, she was, impossibly, turned on again.

"I want to do that to you," she said against Jordan's lips, gently dragging her fingernails down Jordan's neck. God, she could *eat* her.

"You do?" Jordan asked, her voice suddenly losing all its bravado.

"Yes," Astrid said with no hesitation. The care, the *effort*, Jordan had just put in, only to make Astrid feel good—*twice*—she truly had never been on the receiving end of that before. She knew a lover worth any time at all should do the same, but that was the thing—before Jordan, she'd never realized that at all. She'd never realized a lot of things, and she didn't think it was only that Jordan was a woman, her first queer experience. As she looked into Jordan's hazel eyes, all that green and gold, her emotions felt raw, tender like a bruise, and she knew she was completely gone on this person.

"Like, now," Astrid said. "Do you want to come over to my place?"

Jordan smiled, lovely lashes sweeping over her cheekbones. "Yeah, I think that would be—"

"Jordie?"

They both froze at the sound of Simon's voice echoing loudly through the house.

"Jordie, where the hell are you?"

"Shit," Jordan said.

Astrid scrambled off her, and they both spent a panicked twenty seconds locating all of Astrid's clothing. Jordan hooked her overalls back on—Astrid had the brief, inappropriate thought that she'd never gotten to see Jordan's breasts, a fact she'd have to rectify very soon—and they'd barely righted themselves when the pantry door flew open.

"What the hell?" Jordan said when Simon appeared in the doorway.

Simon looked from Astrid to his sister. "Yeah, I could ask the same, sis."

Astrid felt her cheeks go warm. This wasn't the most professional situation Simon could've found her in—she was almost positive she had a major case of sex hair right now, and the pantry . . . well, it reeked of sex. Simon had to smell it. Still, she knew, deep down, she wasn't doing anything wrong, and she was sure everyone at Claire's party last week knew exactly what had happened in Claire's bedroom.

"None of your business, bro," Jordan said.

He just rubbed the back of his neck. "I've been looking everywhere for you. Why didn't you answer your phone?"

"It's on the counter," Jordan said, nodding her head toward the pristine butcher block. "Now if you'll excuse us, I'm sure whatever this is can wait." She went to pull the door closed, but Simon guided it back open in one smooth motion.

"Except it can't," he said, and then he sighed—a tired, resigned sigh of someone who did not want to be dealing with whatever he was talking about right now—and looked off to his right.

Where what had to have been one of the most beautiful women Astrid had ever seen stepped into view. She was white and had shiny black hair, cut short to just below her ears, creamy skin, and eyes that could only be described as amber, as though she were a vampire who fed on animal blood. She was tall and lithe and somehow curvy all at the same time.

She felt Jordan go slack against her before uttering a single, horrifying word.

"Meredith."

CHAPTER

TWENTY-SIX

"HI, JO."

Jordan blinked.

Meredith smiled, that dimple Jordan used to kiss at night before they went to sleep pressing into her left cheek.

"What . . ." Jordan managed, but that was pretty much it.

"If you'd answered your phone, this wouldn't be such a surprise," Meredith said.

Jordan flicked her eyes to Simon, who looked like he wanted to both rip Meredith's head off and pull Jordan into his arms at the same time. He sighed and ran a hand through his hair, but he met her gaze, a million silent questions passing between them.

You okay?

Do you want me to stay?

I will kick her off our property right the fuck now, just say the word.

Honestly, Jordan wasn't sure about the answers to any of them.

Then Astrid cleared her throat, and everything sharpened and got really, really real.

"Shit," Jordan said. "Hey, sorry. Um, Meredith, this is Astrid."

"Hello," Astrid said coldly, the woman who'd yelled at a stranger in front of Wake Up back in full force. But Jordan kind of liked that woman right now.

"Nice to meet you," Meredith said, her amber eyes flicking to the pantry in which they were most definitely still standing. "I'm sorry to interrupt."

"It's fine," Jordan said, the words coming out of her mouth before she could stop them. It wasn't fine. Her head was spinning. Meredith was *here*. She was beautiful and healthy, and the very center of Jordan's chest wouldn't stop aching.

"I should go," Astrid said. "Give you two some time."

No. Don't. Please don't leave.

The protests flitted around in Jordan's mind, but she couldn't seem to get them onto her tongue. She just looked at Astrid and nodded.

Why the hell was she nodding?

But Astrid nodded back, her brown eyes clouded. She was clenching her teeth. Jordan could tell, that muscle in her jaw working furiously. But then, as Astrid stepped out of the pantry, Jordan saw her lower lip bob just a little before she pressed her mouth together, her jaw even tighter now.

And Jordan watched her walk away.

"I'll walk you out," Simon said when Astrid was halfway to the back door. "Okay?" he added, eyes on Jordan.

She nodded. Again. Jesus, someone needed to lock her neck into place.

She glanced at Astrid, hoping she'd look back as she stepped out the door, but somehow knowing she wouldn't.

The door closed, and Jordan got that horrible, dread-soaked feeling in her gut that she'd fucked up.

She'd fix it.

She could fix it.

But first, she had to figure out why the hell Meredith was in the

Everwood kitchen. She had to know why she'd just prioritized the woman who left her and made her feel like nothing over the woman she was currently falling for.

"So," she said, brilliantly.

Meredith just smiled at her, always so fucking calm. She was wearing a royal blue romper, a woven straw sun hat in her hands. Jordan knew she was sensitive to the sun since chemo, had to slather on a layer of sunscreen every hour if she was going to be outside. She looked good though. Really good. She'd gained weight, and her skin glowed with health and vitamin D. Her hair was longer but still barely reached her earlobes, a slight curl to the once-straight locks.

"What are you doing here, Meredith?" Jordan finally managed to ask. "How did you even know I was in Bright Falls?"

"Well," Meredith said, leaning against the kitchen's island, "I went to Savannah first. Got there yesterday morning. But then someone who wasn't you answered the door to our house—"

"My house."

Meredith's eyes narrowed softly. "Your house. That was my first clue."

"And your second?"

"Aside from the fact that I was your wife and know that this place is like your own personal Disneyland? You left a forwarding address with the new tenant."

Goddamn Simon. Jordan didn't leave shit.

"Did you sell it?" Meredith asked. "The house?"

Jordan shook her head. "Renting it out for now. But I will."

Meredith nodded. "Probably a good choice."

"I didn't ask for your approval."

"Jo. Don't be like this."

"Like what?"

Meredith waved her hand at her. "This. I wanted to see you. I'd hoped you'd want to see me. We're still us."

Jordan laughed. "That's the thing, Meredith, we're not. We're not us. At all. You left me for . . . what was it?"

"Jo."

"Ah, yes, I remember now. A destiny. Have you found that yet? Any destinies lurking in the Rockies or on top of the Eiffel Tower or wherever the hell else you've been for the past year?"

Meredith rubbed at her forehead, looked away. Regret crawled up Jordan's throat. Jesus, she did not want to get into this. It was done, and rehashing it—particularly with Meredith herself—just made her feel like shit.

She was so tired of feeling like shit.

"I'm sorry," Meredith said. "I'm sorry my decision hurt you."

Jordan laughed mirthlessly. "That's not an apology."

"Then maybe I'm not really making one," Meredith said, her voice rising. "I *am* sorry I hurt you, but I'm not sorry I left. I had to. For both of us."

"Both of us? Oh my god, so, what? You're the magnanimous decision-maker in our fifteen-year-long relationship because poor Jordan doesn't know what's good for her?"

Meredith sighed but said nothing.

"That's exactly what you think, isn't it?" Jordan asked, realization dawning like a blood-red sunrise. "Holy shit."

"Jordan." Meredith said, her voice soft now. "I love you. I will always love you, but you know I'm right."

Jordan shook her head. She put her hands on her hips, stared down at the plastic-covered floors, trying to get herself together without looking at the woman she once thought she'd be spending her entire life with.

There was no pull, no longing in her chest. She already knew she'd fallen out of love with her. Until recently, she'd thought anger had simply burned up every romantic emotion she'd once felt for

Meredith, but lately, she had wondered. She and Meredith met in middle school. They'd been best friends who fell into being lovers in college, and when it came time to enter the adult world, it just felt natural to do so with her oldest friend, the person who knew her the best. The person she was most comfortable around. Their sex life was good. They had mutual friends. They built a life together.

But sometimes, Jordan wondered how they ended up with that life. Who made the decision. She couldn't even remember which one of them brought up marriage, who asked who. She didn't think either of them actually asked. Once the Supreme Court legalized same-sex marriage, getting married was simply the next step, something they *should* do, the American Dream. They didn't even have a wedding. Not really. They got married at the courthouse on a Wednesday afternoon, had a small party for family and friends in their backyard a week later.

These thoughts were bitter, hard to swallow, but underneath all of that, there was this aftertaste of relief. Jordan didn't fully understand it—she clearly had a lot to process, a lot of anger still clouding her feelings about Meredith and their life together. A phone call to her therapist was probably in order.

For now, though, Jordan wasn't ready to talk about any of this with Meredith herself. No matter her reasons, no matter how right she thought she was, Jordan wasn't sure she could ever forgive her.

"Okay, sure, fine," Jordan said, tired of whatever this was and ready to be done with it. "I need to—"

"Tell me about this design of yours," Meredith said, spreading her arms to indicate the kitchen.

Jordan froze. "What?"

"The design," Meredith repeated, then walked around the room, sliding her hand over the new counters, running her fingertips over the edge of the mullioned glass in the cabinets.

"It's . . . it's for the reno," Jordan said.

Meredith rounded the other side of the island and braced her palms on the butcher block. "And it's yours."

Jordan blinked at her. "It's . . . yeah. I built the cabinets."

Meredith sighed and shook her head. "See, when I arrived at your grandmother's cottage, they couldn't find you. You weren't answering your phone, and the inn was empty." Here she smirked at the still-open pantry door. "Well, we thought it was empty. I know your family isn't exactly my biggest fan, so while we waited for you to call Simon back, it was really, *really* awkward. I asked about the reno that was clearly going on, and he told me. He also showed me the design plan on his laptop."

Jordan crossed her arms. "Get to the point." Except she wasn't altogether sure she wanted to know the point. Or rather, she had a feeling she already did. Unease slid through her like oil through water.

"My point, Jo, is that this whole thing is *your* design, but when Simon talked about it, he kept mentioning someone named Astrid Parker. The same Astrid, I'm assuming, I just met a few minutes ago."

Jordan's nostrils flared with the effort to keep her breathing even. "That's not . . . the design isn't—"

"I know you," Meredith said. "I know your style and your work, and this is it." She spread her arms again, letting them fall slowly back to her side. "My question is, why are you letting some blond bitch take the credit?"

"Hey," Jordan said sharply. "Don't you dare call her that."

Meredith pressed her eyes closed. "Okay, you're right. I'm sorry. But Simon seemed to think she was the designer. The lead designer."

"She is."

"Jo."

"My name is Jordan."

Meredith watched her for a second, sadness filling her expression.

She'd been calling her "Jo" since they were in eighth grade. "Okay. Jordan. I know you may not want to hear this, or maybe you just don't give a shit about yourself, but *I* still care about you. I'm just trying to understand, because—"

"It's not your business to understand anymore."

"—the design is breathtaking."

That gave Jordan pause. "Breathtaking."

Meredith nodded, her eyes shining with what Jordan could only describe as pride. "Breathtaking. Truly, Jordan. It's astounding. It's *you*. So sue me for wondering why you're handing over all the credit to someone else. And on a nationally televised show, no less."

"Because she *is* a designer. I don't want the credit, and she does. She needs it. And she's working just as hard as I am to make sure this all comes together. It's not like she's just sitting back and sipping mojitos while I sweat."

Meredith's mouth hung open. "So you're telling me that a woman you're sleeping with—"

"I'm not sleeping with her."

Meredith frowned. "Really? Because I'm pretty sure you just made her come in a pantry."

Jordan's face heated. "That's . . . that's not . . . okay, but that was the first time that happened, and . . ." She swiped a hand through her hair. "Fuck, this is none of your business."

"Okay, let me rephrase," Meredith said, clearly ignoring the part about what was and was not her business. "You're telling me that the woman you just made come in a pantry somehow convinced you to hand over your brilliant design for your family inn, stamp it with her name, and take the credit as lead designer for an episode in a major design show. Do I have that right?"

Jordan's stomach tightened into a coil. "You're twisting it around. When you say it like that, it sounds horrible."

"It is horrible, Jordan. How can you not see that?"

Jordan shook her head. It wasn't horrible, it was . . . a partnership. It was a mutually beneficial arrangement. It was . . .

Fuck, the look on Meredith's face—*her* Meredith, the girl who was constantly one-upping their math teachers throughout school, finding every hole in logic, the woman who soared through her architectural program and who always knew what Jordan was feeling a split second before Jordan herself figured it out. She knew that look.

But Astrid was . . . she was *Astrid*. The adorable, vampire-toothed baby queer who pulled Jordan into a room and told her she wanted to kiss *her*, who'd spent every evening of the last week with Jordan. She hadn't needed to do any of that. There was no way she actually manipulated Jordan into this whole scheme. There was no way she was using Jordan just to get what she wanted.

Was there?

Jordan knew Astrid was desperate for this project to go well. She knew her mother had some sort of emotional and professional hold over her. She knew Natasha Rojas's opinion of Astrid could make or break her.

Uninspired.

That's what Natasha had called Astrid's original design plan . . . right before Astrid came to Jordan suggesting a partnership. Before Astrid flat-out denied any romantic involvement when Natasha asked . . .

No. No, no, so much other stuff had happened before that, after that. There was no way this was all contrived.

Jordan's throat ballooned. Air. She couldn't find it. Couldn't breathe.

"Okay, okay, it's all right," she heard Meredith say. "Sit down. Put your head between your legs."

Suddenly, Jordan was on the floor, forehead pressed against her knees, Meredith's hand rubbing soothing circles on her back.

"It's okay," Meredith said again. "It's not too late. You can still fix this."

Jordan's head popped up. "I don't . . . this isn't what I want."

"What's not?"

She waved a hand at the kitchen. "I just want the Everwood to be the Everwood. I want something that feels true to its history."

"I know," Meredith said, sitting down across from her and folding her legs. "And your design is true to that. But you have to see that you can't let Astrid take that away from you."

"She's not. I don't want—"

"Jordan, all I see is a woman who put her heart and soul into something and is content to give it away. Maybe ask yourself why."

Jordan opened her mouth. Closed it. She wasn't giving it away. She had what she wanted. The Everwood taking shape like it should, a chance to save her family's business. She'd just make a mess of the spotlight. She worked best behind the scenes. Astrid was the front woman. Hadn't there been a million partnerships throughout the creative world that were just that? And she and Astrid *were* partners in all of this.

But now . . . she wanted so much more than a true design for the Everwood.

She wanted Astrid too.

"I need to go," she said, getting to her feet. The room spun for a second, but righted itself soon enough. Meredith got up too, a steadying hand on her arm.

Jordan pulled away.

"Wait," Meredith said. "At least let me take you to dinner."

Jordan shook her head. She needed to see Astrid, and she needed to see her now. "I can't."

She grabbed her phone off the counter and headed for the back door. Bag. She needed her bag. License. Keys to Adora. They were all in her workshop.

"At least tell me you've come to your senses," Meredith said.

Jordan froze in the doorway.

"Jo—Jordan. I care about you. You deserve—"

"You have no fucking right to talk about what I deserve," Jordan said. She didn't turn around to look at her ex-wife. She didn't wait for her response. She just pushed open the screen door, texted Simon to get Meredith the hell off their property as she hurried across the yard and into her workshop, and then peeled out of the driveway as fast as Adora would take her.

CHAPTER
TWENTY-SEVEN

RELIEF.

That's the only way Jordan could describe the expression on Astrid's face when she opened her door thirty minutes later to find Jordan standing on her front porch.

What's more, Jordan sort of . . . melted at the sight of her. Her shoulders—which had been tense for her entire drive over—loosened, and a loud exhale swooshed from her lungs.

"Hey," Astrid said, and she said it so softly, so sweetly—no trace of that prim coldness from before—that Jordan felt her chin start to wobble. Astrid noticed. Of course she did. She reached out her hand and pulled Jordan inside and into her arms, hands sliding around her neck and into her hair. Jordan slumped against her. She'd thought she was tired before, but now, all her Meredith-stress releasing, she felt like a balloon just relieved of all its air.

She let her own arms circle Astrid's waist. Astrid was a little taller than she was, so she could rest her chin right on Astrid's shoulder. Jordan squeezed her eyes closed and relaxed them, trying to figure out what to say about . . . well, everything.

"I'm sorry" was the first thing out of her mouth.

Astrid pulled back, a frown creasing her straight brows. "For what?"

Jordan shook her head. "For just letting you walk out earlier. I wanted you to stay, I just didn't—"

"Hey," Astrid said, moving her hands to cup Jordan's face. "It's fine. We were both a bit shocked."

Jordan let out a bitter laugh. "Yeah."

"Are you okay?"

Jordan nodded, but even as she did so, tears welled in her eyes. She couldn't stop them—it was like every emotion she'd felt lately about the inn, about Astrid, about Meredith, finally spilled over.

"Oh," Astrid said, looking alarmed.

For a split second, everything in Jordan froze. She looked away, shuddering breaths rattling her chest. This was one of those moments in a new relationship—discovering how someone handled it when you completely lost your shit. Jordan already knew Astrid was a complicated woman—raised like an heir to a throne, buttoned up to within an inch of her life. And now, with Meredith's theory about Astrid floating through her brain, Jordan really needed Astrid to—

"Come here," Astrid said softly. She tangled her fingers with Jordan's and led her to the giant white sectional in her very white living room. She sat them down, still holding her hand, one leg propped up on the cushion like a true bisexual. Jordan almost laughed and made a comment about it, but then Astrid leaned into Jordan, thumb moving against her palm in slow, calming circles.

This.

Jordan needed Astrid to do this.

"Do you want to talk about it?" Astrid asked.

Jordan sat back, turning her head so she could look Astrid in the eyes. She stayed silent for a few seconds, searching for any sign of the manipulative woman Meredith painted her to be, but all Jordan saw were soft brown eyes gazing back, her mouth slightly parted in concern.

"I forgot how it felt," Jordan said.

"How what felt?" Astrid said.

Jordan swallowed hard. "Seeing her. How she makes me feel. I mean, I didn't *forget* forget. It's always there, you know? But these past few weeks, I've been so busy. Distracted. Maybe even happy, I don't know."

Astrid nodded. She had one arm over the back of the couch, her hand tangled in Jordan's hair, thumb swiping against her forehead. "How does she make you feel?"

"Like . . ." Jordan exhaled. There were so many feelings, but one really stood out. One, she suspected, had driven nearly every decision she'd made in the last year. "Like somehow, whatever I do will never be enough. Like I don't deserve to be happy or get what I want. She just reminds me of everything I'm not, everything she saw and knew about me and left anyway. And then she said all this shit about you, and I just—"

"About me?" Astrid said, alarm filling her features. "What about me?"

Jordan sighed, letting her head fall back on the cushion. She hadn't meant to say that. Hadn't meant to bring up what Meredith thought about Astrid at all.

"Hey," Astrid said, squeezing Jordan's shoulder. "Please. Tell me."

Jordan debated refusing, but a part of her didn't want to. More than a part, if she was being honest. A huge, tender, scared part of her wanted some reassurance here. She focused on her hands in her lap, couldn't meet Astrid's eyes as she said it.

"She knows a lot of the inn's design is mine."

Astrid's brows dipped.

"I didn't tell her," Jordan said. "She just knows me. Knows my style."

"Okay," Astrid said. "And . . . she didn't like that, did she?"

Jordan finally looked at Astrid, who was still tucked against Jordan's side, her brown eyes wide and concerned. "Tell me this is more than the job."

Astrid blinked. "Is what more than—"

"Us. This . . . whatever we're doing. It's not about the job, is it? The show?"

"Jordan—"

"I'm not saying we have to have some big define-the-relationship talk or something," Jordan said, her palms starting to sweat. "I just . . . I need . . . I don't think—"

But Astrid pressed a finger to Jordan's mouth, stopping any more words from flowing.

Astrid left her hand in place, dark eyes roaming Jordan's face. "You listen to me," she said firmly. "I know you and I are complicated. The inn. The show." She waved her hand between them. "Us. But I like *you*, Jordan Everwood. I wanted to kiss *you*, remember?"

Jordan nodded, Astrid's fingers still gentle on her mouth.

"You deserve every good thing, okay?" Astrid went on. Her voice actually sounded sort of teary. "You deserve . . ." She trailed off, the tiniest of smiles crooking up one corner of her mouth. Jordan held her breath, heart pounding and desperate for whatever Astrid was about to say.

When Astrid finally spoke again, her voice was a low, intense whisper. "You deserve a destiny, Jordan Everwood."

Jordan blinked, the word settling into her brain, her heart. *Destiny*. Those seven letters had always been this nebulous concept, this thing that she *wasn't*. She'd never once thought about her own destiny.

But now, hearing it from Astrid Parker, of all people, the word suddenly felt . . . real. It felt sun-soaked and bright and warm, this shimmering feeling deep in her gut. Every doubt in her mind—her heart—vanished. They felt so silly now, sitting here with Astrid, this woman who pretended to be so tough and cold, but who was actually the kindest, most open-hearted person Jordan had met in a long time. She just didn't show that to everyone, and Jordan felt a sudden rush of gratitude that for some reason, Astrid had picked her. Had *seen* her.

"Astrid," she said softly, because that's all she could think to say.

Astrid's smile widened. "Say that again."

Jordan frowned. "What . . . your name?"

Astrid nodded. "You always call me Parker. You've only called me by my first name one other time. When you told me I couldn't kiss you."

Searching back through all their interactions, Jordan realized Astrid was right. She had no idea why she'd favored Astrid's last name, but right now, all she wanted to do was say this woman's name over and over again—whisper it against her skin.

She slid her arm around Astrid's waist and hauled her onto her lap. Astrid gasped but her legs parted, straddling Jordan's hips. Jordan settled her hands on Astrid's lower back, pulling her in tighter, looking up into her eyes as Astrid's hands raked through Jordan's hair, short nails scraping across her scalp.

"Astrid," Jordan whispered, pressing a kiss to her throat. "Astrid." A kiss below her ear. "Astrid." A scrape of her teeth against her collarbone.

Astrid hummed softly, tilting her head back, but soon, her fingers in Jordan's hair tightened, pulling the two of them apart long enough to get her mouth on Jordan's.

The kiss was soft at first, as though Astrid was sealing the promise of everything she had just said, but soon it changed. Astrid's tongue slipped into her mouth, teeth biting at her lip, a groan rumbling in her chest. Astrid's legs tightened around Jordan's thighs, her hips circling and seeking pressure. Jordan sought back, the ache in her center already at crisis levels. They might have had amazing first-time sex back in the pantry, but Jordan still hadn't come.

"Astrid," she said again, but this time her name was a plea, need lacing through each letter.

Astrid pulled back. Jordan nearly whined in protest, but then, for the second time today, Astrid's fingers went to her overall buckles, setting them free with a gentle clink of metal. Jordan watched, heat pooling between her legs, as Astrid slid the denim down to her waist, then swung her leg off Jordan's lap to stand in front of her. She tugged at Jordan's clothes until Jordan lifted her ass off the cushion, letting Astrid strip her down to her purple sports bra and black boxer briefs.

Astrid's eyes trailed over her for a second, overalls still dangling from one hand. Her tongue darted out to lick at her lower lip, and Jordan couldn't help but smile up at her. Finally, Astrid laughed nervously, before she dropped the overalls and shoved all of her spa-blue and ivory pillows onto the floor.

"Lie down," she said.

Jordan lifted a brow, but she complied. Nerves fluttered through her belly as she watched Astrid undress, pulling her blouse over her head and tossing it behind her, unzipping her little black shorts to reveal those lacy boy shorts Jordan barely had time to fully appreciate back in the pantry, considering how quickly she'd removed them.

"Jesus, Astrid," she said, and she started to sit up. She had to touch this woman now. Taste her. Bury her face between her legs again and hum.

Astrid, however, had other plans. She straddled Jordan's hips and placed a hand on her chest, pushing her back down.

Jordan groaned and Astrid laughed.

"Just let me make you feel good," Astrid said, hovering over her.

"Okay, yes, I'm all for that," Jordan said, putting her hands on Astrid's hips. "But you can't strip in front of me like that and expect me—"

"Yes, I can," Astrid said, removing Jordan's hands and then stretching both arms above Jordan's head. "It's my turn."

Jordan started to protest again, but then Astrid bent low and scraped her vampire teeth over Jordan's collarbone.

"Shit," Jordan said, hissing as Astrid did it again, bucking her hips.

Astrid released Jordan's hands, but hell, at this point, Jordan would do anything this woman asked, so she left her arms above her head and let Astrid have her way.

Which was a very, very nice way.

Her hands came down to cup Jordan's breasts, thumb swiping over her already hardened nipples. She wasted no time in pulling the bra over Jordan's head, then yanking off her own. Jordan barely had a second to ogle her perfectly pert tits again, complete with large, brown nipples already hard and swollen for her, before Astrid was pressing them against Jordan's own chest, pulling a moan out of both of their throats.

"Fuck," Jordan said, writhing on the couch. "You feel amazing."

"Yeah," Astrid said breathlessly. She undulated on top of Jordan, her center seeking friction, sliding her nipples very deliberately over Jordan's. "This is . . ." But apparently she couldn't get the words out, her eyes slamming closed, moans tumbling from her gorgeous lips.

Jordan was about ready to explode. She needed her hands on Astrid now, needed to get her off, get herself off, and as Astrid was new at being with people with pussies, Jordan felt she needed to take the lead here.

Which Astrid one hundred percent would not let her do. As soon as Jordan's fingertips grazed Astrid's swaying breasts, Astrid opened her eyes, stopped humping her, and slammed Jordan's arms back above her head.

"Christ, Astrid," Jordan said, but she was smiling. She kind of loved this I-am-the-fucking-one-in-charge-here attitude.

Astrid grinned evilly, kissed her once—Jesus, that tongue—and started a slow journey south. She stopped at Jordan's breasts, kissing the underside of one while palming the other, humming against her nipple in a way that made Jordan yell a couple of expletives to the ceiling, before sucking that same nipple into her hot mouth.

More expletives. More sucking.

Astrid moved lower, pressing kisses and trailing her tongue over Jordan's stomach, before finally spreading Jordan's legs wide and settling between them.

"Hang on," Jordan said, her breath ragged like she'd been running a marathon. She propped herself up on her elbows. "Are you sure?"

Astrid frowned up at her. "Do you not want—"

"No!" Jordan chanced a touch, sliding her hand over Astrid's hair. Astrid allowed it. "I do. Shit, I do, but this is your first time doing . . . well, you know."

"You."

Jordan grinned at that. "Yeah. And I want you to feel comfortable."

"I am. I want to." She kissed the inside of one of Jordan's thighs, then the other, but then froze and looked up. "Are you worried I'll be bad at it?"

"What?"

"I mean, I've never done this before. What if I suck at it?"

Jordan laughed, scraped her nails over Astrid's scalp. "Well, sucking is half the point."

Astrid laughed, but her cheeks went pink. It was so adorable, Jordan nearly groaned.

"And I highly doubt you'll be bad at it," she added.

"I've been reading up on it," Astrid said matter-of-factly, leaning on one elbow. "And I'm pretty sure I can do a good job. I think—"

"Wait, wait, wait," Jordan said, waving her hand through the air. "You've been reading up on it?"

Astrid bit her lip and scrunched up her nose, nodding.

"Reading up on cunnilingus?"

"Well, I mean, not like I googled directions or anything, but it's featured in most of those queer romances I've been reading, and when I watched a few videos, it looked—"

"Holy shit, wait, you watched porn for this?"

Astrid's already pink face deepened to red, and she pressed her forehead against Jordan's thigh. "Maybe," she said against her skin.

Jordan guffawed.

"I don't like feeling incompetent, okay?" Astrid said, but she was laughing too. "And now that I know how incredible it feels when done right"—here Jordan couldn't help but smirk—"I want to do that for you too."

Jordan adored this woman. Fucking adored her. Astrid Parker, watching porn so she could please Jordan in bed. It was funny, hilarious even, but it was also unbearably sweet, and Jordan could not help but angle Astrid's chin up so she could look at her.

"You'll be amazing," Jordan said, not for one second wanting to negate the thought Astrid had put into this moment. Then she obediently put her arms back above her head and lay back.

Astrid laughed softly, took a few breaths, and then got back to work.

And fuck, she took her work very, very seriously. She started over Jordan's underwear, gentle fingers and warm breaths, thumbs sliding along the crease where Jordan's leg met her hips. Then she kissed her, right on her center over the cotton, gentle and firm at the same time, and Jordan nearly levitated off the couch. She was already so wet, soaked as far as she could tell, which only increased when Astrid's tongue came out to play, swirling over Jordan's pussy in random patterns.

By the time she tugged Jordan's underwear off her legs, Jordan was dizzy with want. Once she was totally bare, she felt Astrid pause, as though studying her. Jordan resisted the urge to squirm, letting Astrid do this at her own pace.

She was tentative at first, and yeah, it was a little clumsy for a few seconds, Astrid's mouth pressing too softly, her tongue a little too hard. But she must've simply needed a few practice rounds, because suddenly, Jordan couldn't keep her hands in place—she had to touch Astrid's hair, pull on the silky tresses as Astrid locked her mouth around Jordan's sex, angling her head to kiss her this way, then that way, then gliding her tongue up from her entrance to her clit. Still, she stopped short of that small bud of nerves every time like a god-damn pro.

"You're a very quick learner," Jordan managed to croak out, words that quickly became a moan and a *fuck* as Astrid's tongue dipped inside her.

"You taste . . . wow," Astrid said. "I never . . . this is . . ." But she didn't finish and Jordan didn't care, because Astrid fucked Jordan with her tongue, her mouth, and—holy shit—her teeth. Pretty soon, her fingers joined in the fun too, her thumb dipping in and out of Jordan's entrance to the point that Jordan felt like she was on the verge of hyperventilating.

Low keening sounds rumbled through Jordan's chest as she got closer. Both hands plunged into Astrid's hair, but she didn't direct her. Every movement was all Astrid, every hummed vibration and slip of her fingers. Finally—fucking goddamn finally—she closed her mouth around Jordan's clit, alternating between sucking and flicking her tongue.

"Fuck, Astrid," Jordan yelled, thighs clenching around Astrid's head as she came hard. Astrid kept working her tongue, albeit a little gentler, waiting until Jordan stopped shuddering and her hips pressed back into the couch to break contact. Even then, she stayed put,

kissing Jordan's thigh, her mound, before sliding back up her body—
stopping briefly to tongue one nipple in a way that nearly had Jordan
screaming again—before settling next to her, her own breath shallow
and quick.

Astrid leaned on one elbow and alternated between looking at
Jordan and biting her lip. Her cheeks were red, and Jordan reached
out a hand to cup her face.

"That was unreal," Jordan said.

Astrid exhaled heavily. "Yeah? Really?"

Jordan pulled her in close and kissed her, and Jordan loved the
scent, the taste, this shared intimacy of oral and its aftermath.

"You'll have to show me which porn tutorials you watched so I
can pick up some tips," she said, her limbs still trembling like they'd
been blasted with lightning.

Astrid smacked her lightly on the arm but laughed and kissed her
again, settling her head on Jordan's shoulder. "You don't need any.
Trust me."

"Did . . . did you like it?" Jordan asked, feeling herself go a little
tense as she waited for Astrid's answer.

Astrid didn't make her wait long, though. She pressed a kiss to
her shoulder, then her neck, murmuring, "I loved it," against Jordan's
skin.

Jordan exhaled and sank her fingers into Astrid's hair, rubbing
her scalp in slow circles. It was nice, this post-orgasmic cuddle, but
Astrid's hands curled into the skin at Jordan's waist, her hips moving
just enough to let Jordan know she was horny as hell.

Luckily, Jordan really didn't think she needed a tutorial to take
care of that. Still lying down, she nudged Astrid's leg apart, slipped
her hand between her thighs and into her wet heat, and proved it.

CHAPTER

TWENTY-EIGHT

EIGHT.

That's how many orgasms Astrid had had so far, and it was only Saturday afternoon, the day after their pantry sex and Astrid's maiden voyage into cunnilingus with Jordan Everwood.

Not that she was keeping count.

Except that was exactly what she was doing, because *eight*? She hadn't had that many non-self-induced orgasms in the last eight *years*.

Yet here she was, Astrid Parker, naked and sprawled on her bed, sheets a tangled mess, breathing heavily at the ceiling as she came down from that wondrous number eight. She was pretty sure she was one touch away from needing to ice her clit.

The thought made her laugh, the sound bubbling into her chest and bursting out of her mouth before she could stop it. The last twenty-four hours had been . . . well, she didn't think she'd ever had so much fun.

"What are you laughing at?" Jordan asked. She was lying next to Astrid, gloriously naked and propped up on one elbow, trailing her fingertips along Astrid's stomach, that smug-satisfied look on her face because Astrid hadn't exactly made her orgasm tally a secret.

Astrid rolled over and propped herself on one arm too, shaking her head. "I can see why Natasha Rojas wears a clit necklace, that's all."

Jordan laughed. "I mean, it is pretty amazing."

"So amazing. Did you know the clitoris has eight thousand nerve endings in the tip alone? That's double the number in the penis."

"I—"

"And it's made up of eighteen parts, this intricate mixture of erectile tissue, muscles, and nerves."

Jordan just blinked at her for a second. "You did clit research."

Astrid bit her lip. "I may have looked up a few things."

Jordan slung her arm around Astrid's bare waist. "A *few* things?"

"It's a fascinating organ, having nothing to do with reproduction whatsoever. It literally exists for pleasure. The clit is badass."

Jordan grinned. "'The clit is badass.' Can I get that stitched on a pillow?"

Astrid smacked Jordan's arm, which quickly turned into a glide around her neck, a deep inhale of Jordan's skin.

"This is nice," Astrid said, pressing her nose to Jordan's throat.

Jordan kissed her on the top of her head. "It is."

"I've never done this before."

Jordan laughed. "Yeah, we've established that."

"No, not . . . not sex. *This.*" She waved her hand around the room, where half-drunk glasses of wine dotted her nightstands, clothes dappled the floor, and towels could be seen on the tile through the bathroom door where she and Jordan had taken a shower together.

Twice.

"Spent all weekend with someone like this," Astrid said. "Having sex, eating delivery food, not caring about anything else."

Jordan tucked a strand of hair behind Astrid's ear. "I haven't either, actually."

Astrid's eyes went wide. "Never? Not with . . ." She couldn't say the woman's name and suddenly had a very strong urge to change the subject. With Meredith's thoughts about the inn's design hovering in the back of Astrid's mind all night long, she worried they were still hovering in Jordan's too.

She wanted to silence those thoughts, every word Meredith said to her. Because they weren't true. Not even a little bit. Astrid wasn't using Jordan. She wasn't. She *liked* Jordan.

Maybe she even more than liked her.

She opened her mouth to talk about something else, but Jordan frowned and flopped onto her back, staring at the ceiling. "We didn't even have a real honeymoon. We stayed in a condo in Tybee Island for a couple of nights, but even then, it was like . . . I don't know. We'd have sex, maybe twice a day. And it was good, but it was almost like . . ." She blinked, as though she was just realizing whatever she was about to say for the first time. "It was like we were just checking it off our list. Something we *had* do because we were married."

Astrid wasn't sure what to say to that. She'd be lying if she said she wasn't a little bit happy that this sex marathon they'd been running was Jordan's first time too, but another part of her ached for Jordan, for all the memories that made her feel like some item on a list.

"Well," she said, aligning her body with Jordan's. She danced her fingers down Jordan's breasts, down her stomach, until she found the curls between her legs still wet. "I don't feel like I *have* to do this at all."

She slipped one finger inside.

Jordan's eyes fluttered closed.

"Or this," Astrid said, inserting another finger and pressing her palm against Jordan's clit.

"Fuck," Jordan hissed, her hips bucking against Astrid's hand. "Did you read up on that little trick too?"

"Maybe I did. And I definitely didn't have to." And then Astrid proceeded to do truly wicked things with her fingers that had Jordan clutching the sheets so tightly, her hand ached for an hour after she came.

⁓

BY THE TIME Sunday morning arrived, the orgasm tally was up to ten. Astrid came out of her bedroom in such a sex haze, it took her a second to realize that Jordan had covered her kitchen counter with all manner of baking supplies.

Astrid approached slowly, wearing a pair of black yoga pants and a pale green cropped T-shirt that showed her midriff, something she thought she may have bought for actual yoga but was positive she'd never actually worn.

Jordan stood at the coffee maker, her back to Astrid, and she wore nothing but her own sports bra and a pair of Astrid's pajama shorts, the sight of which sort of turned Astrid on.

Astrid watched her for a second, Jordan's fingers tapping on the granite counter, a little braid plaited through her golden brown hair right at the part, waiting for the coffee to finish brewing.

Something giddy bubbled up in Astrid's chest.

"What's all this?" she asked when she'd finally gotten a grip and could walk into the room without a ridiculous grin on her face.

But then Jordan turned and smiled, and Astrid's mouth rebelled.

"Hey, you're up," Jordan said.

"I'm sore," Astrid said, walking over to Jordan and capturing her mouth in a quick kiss. She opened the cupboard above the coffee maker and took down two mugs.

"Me too. Who knew Astrid Parker was so obsessed with sex?" Jordan smacked her on the butt.

"Hey, now, that was a two-way street."

Jordan hooked an arm around her bare waist and yanked her close. "It certainly was."

Astrid went in for another kiss, sort of ready to go for orgasm number eleven, if she was being honest—shit, maybe she *was* obsessed with sex—but then Jordan released her and angled away.

"Nope, nope, we have other plans this morning," she said.

"We do?" Astrid eyed the counter covered in flour, vanilla extract, white and brown sugar, eggs, baking chocolate, and myriad other sundry items, all of which looked brand-new. Astrid had a lot of baking supplies in her pantry, but she was pretty sure most of it was expired.

"Did you go out and buy all of this?" she asked.

Jordan nodded, chewing at one corner of her lip. "I might have gone a little overboard."

Astrid blinked. "But . . . why?"

Jordan smiled shyly. "I want you to bake something for me."

"Bake something."

Jordan nodded. "You told me baking used to be your dream."

Astrid thought back to that conversation at Iris's. She scanned the ingredients Jordan had collected, her heart suddenly in her throat, her fingertips tingling.

"If I bake you a cake, will you sing for me?" she asked, collecting on the promise Jordan had made her in front of Iris's rainbow shelves.

Jordan narrowed her eyes. "You remember that, huh?"

"I'm not one to forget."

Jordan laughed. "No, you're not. Okay. You bake me a cake, I'll sing you a love song."

Astrid's brows lifted, a picture taking shape in her mind. Jordan Everwood holding her close, her husky voice in her ear, singing a melody.

A love song.

She really wanted that love song.

"Deal," she said.

———

THE MORNING SPILLED into the afternoon, light brightening, then fading, and by four o'clock Astrid's kitchen counters were covered in confections.

She'd baked Jordan her cake. A simple yellow cake with chocolate icing, which apparently was Jordan's favorite. But then, once Jordan had tasted it and proceeded to pretend to pass out from how good it was, Astrid sort of . . . bloomed.

That's what it felt like. A closed-up flower that the sun had finally found. It was as though she forgot everything that came before this weekend—she forgot about her mother's expectations, she forgot about the Everwood, she forgot about *Innside America*, she forgot about the rolling sense of dread she'd felt lately when she did think about all of those things.

Instead, she remembered what it felt like to work hard on something she truly loved. There'd been glimpses of this at Bright Designs—a particularly creative accent wall, or that feeling of satisfaction she got when a client really loved the end result, but all of those moments were nothing compared to this . . . this *bliss* that zinged through her veins as she dipped her hands into a knot of dough, as she measured the right amount of sugar and butter and yeast and then watched it all come together into this brand-new creation.

It felt like magic.

Jordan was her dutiful taste-tester and assistant that afternoon, wearing a green-and-white gingham apron and passing her ingredients and washing out bowls and measuring cups, pressing kisses to her temple with her hands on Astrid's waist while Astrid whipped egg whites into a French meringue.

Soon, her kitchen was covered in three whole cakes, a dozen pumpkin-apple muffins—the flavor of which had Jordan emitting orgasmic sounds that made Astrid feel like she could fly—a batch of dark chocolate–cinnamon brownies, and two dozen oatmeal-butterscotch cookies.

"Shit," Jordan said, polishing off a cookie. "I'd say you definitely earned yourself a love song."

Astrid grinned at her, aching hands on her hips. Flour dusted her arms, her cheeks, and every muscle in her body felt like it wanted to curl into a cramp, but *shit* was right. She surveyed her work and took a bite of a cookie.

"We should take some of these to Claire and Iris," she said, chewing and tapping her finger against the cookie's golden-brown edge. "We used to make these as kids."

Jordan nodded and hopped off the stool where she'd been perched for the last hour, drinking white wine and stealing treats as soon as they came out of the oven. "Let's do it."

Astrid opened a drawer to search for some Tupperware, but as soon as her fingers closed around one container, the doorbell rang.

"I'll get it," Jordan said, dusting off her hands and swallowing another cookie. "You pack up the goods." She bounded off toward the entryway, while Astrid settled her cookies into the container. She smiled, thinking about how Iris and Claire would react. They hadn't eaten these cookies in years, maybe since high school, even. It would be—

"Hello. And who are you?"

Isabel Parker-Green's voice filtered through the hallway like ice spreading over verdant plants.

Astrid froze, her mind quickly cataloging just how many of her mother's calls she'd been avoiding for the past few weeks.

She heard Jordan give Isabel her name, heard Isabel offer nothing other than "I see" in response. No "Nice to meet you" or even "I'm Astrid's mother." Nothing.

Astrid knew she needed to save Jordan from whatever cold hell her mother was probably dragging her into, but her feet felt glued to the floor, her hands stuck to the kitchen drawer's handle.

"Um, Astrid's in the kitchen," Jordan said.

No response. Just the quick click-clack of Isabel's heels over the hardwoods. Soon she appeared, dressed pristinely in a pair of black cigarette pants and a dusky pink silk blouse, dyed blond hair perfectly in place.

Astrid blinked. For a split second, she swore the figure in the doorway was *her*, just with a few more lines on her around her mouth and eyes. Would Astrid fight those, too, when the time came? Botox her face until it could barely express emotions?

"Mom, hi," she managed to say, shaking her head to clear it.

Isabel lifted her brows in response, eyes taking in the mess. Sugar and carbs everywhere, flour dusting the floor, sink piled with the last round of batter-covered bowls and spoons.

"Astrid, what is going on with you?" her mother asked. "This is the second weekend in a row you have failed to show up for brunch, and this week, you didn't even bother to lie about why you couldn't come."

Oh shit. It was Sunday. And she'd completely forgotten about brunch.

"I thought you were dead," Isabel said. "I called your phone, but I was sent straight to voice mail."

Her phone. Astrid didn't even know where her phone was, much less who had tried to call it in the past forty-eight hours.

"I'm sorry," she said, wiping her hands on her apron.

Jordan appeared behind Isabel, eyes wide in concern.

Jesus. Jordan. She was still dressed in nothing but a sports bra and Astrid's shorts and she'd . . . she'd answered the door like that. No wonder Isabel was in full bitch mode.

"Let's talk out on the back porch," Astrid said to her mother. "Do you want something to drink?"

"No," Isabel said, then glided toward the back door, knuckles white on her tiny Prada purse.

Astrid swallowed around the knot in her throat. Or tried to. That knot was on a mission to cut off all her air, and Astrid had half a mind to let it.

"You okay?" Jordan asked. "Sorry, I didn't know what to say to her."

Astrid just nodded, trying to smooth her hair into place, which was also a losing battle. She'd washed it in the past couple of days— or rather, Jordan had—but then she'd just let it air dry into a half-straight, half-wavy mess.

"I'll be right back," Astrid said. Jordan reached out to squeeze her hand as she passed, and Astrid let her, but she couldn't look at her. Dread had replaced every bit of happy, and she didn't want Jordan to see that side of her.

Outside, the sun was just starting to sprinkle gold over the grass. Sunset was still hours away, but the day was fading. This was usually Astrid's favorite time of day, when everything started to change color and slow down. Now though, with her mother standing at her back porch's railing, looking out over Astrid's tiny backyard, she felt anything but slow.

She felt frantic, panic she didn't even fully understand spreading through her limbs.

"I'm sorry about brunch," she said. "I lost track of time and—"

"Who is that woman?" Isabel asked.

Astrid froze. Isabel knew exactly who she was. "Jordan Everwood."

"And why is the woman you're technically working for in your house dressed like she's at a slumber party?"

This was not how she envisioned this conversation going. Granted, she hadn't really envisioned it at all. She knew she'd eventually come out to her mother as . . . as whatever she was, but she hadn't thought about the logistics yet. She hadn't had time. She and Jordan were just starting out. Between the inn and this weekend that had left her in a complete daze, she hadn't factored her mother into her queerness quite yet.

She wasn't ready for this moment.

But it was here nonetheless. She could lie, but then there was no way she could face Jordan if she did, no way she could face herself.

"Because we're seeing each other," she said before she lost her nerve.

Isabel turned around, one eyebrow raised. "Are you."

It wasn't a question. But with those two little words, Astrid felt like her mother had just made some sort of existential declaration.

"And you really think that's appropriate given the current state of your business?" Isabel went on. "Your reputation in this town as a serious businesswoman?"

Astrid swallowed. "I—"

"She's an Everwood, Astrid. You are redesigning the Everwood Inn. On national television. How do you think that will look? Do you really think you'll attract other clients when they find out?"

"When they find out what, Mother? That I'm seeing a client or that I'm seeing a woman?"

Isabel pursed her lips. "When they find out you're seeing the woman who's the true designer of the Everwood project."

Her mother's words took a second to land, like shrapnel in slow motion.

"What?" Astrid finally managed to ask.

"You heard me, Astrid. And the horrified look on your face confirms it. I was right."

"How . . . how did you—"

"I co-own Bright Designs. I have a right to know every move you make."

"You . . . you have access to my design plan?"

"I've *always* had access to your design plans, Astrid."

Of course Isabel had access to the cloud, the drive where Astrid stored everything for the business. When they were first starting out, Isabel had overseen every move, everything Astrid spent money on, every spreadsheet. But in the last several years, her mother hadn't offered her input on anything, so Astrid assumed she was checked out, that she finally trusted her.

Turns out she was wrong.

She'd always been so, so wrong.

"You still check every design I create," Astrid said quietly. "Don't you?"

"Of course I do," Isabel said, her tone incredulous. "Why wouldn't I? I'm your mother. It's my job to protect you, make sure you succeed."

Astrid nodded, but tears threatened to spill over. When Isabel put it like that, it almost sounded endearing, but all Astrid heard was that she wasn't good enough on her own. That without Isabel's micromanagement, she'd fail.

"Which was why," Isabel went on, "I was extremely shocked when I looked over things today and saw a completely different design than the lovely plan I approved a few weeks ago."

"Approved? When did you—" But Astrid cut herself off. If Isabel says nothing corrective about a design—about anything in Astrid's life—that's approval. Isabel Parker-Green style.

"What is going on, Astrid?" Isabel asked. "That design, which I assume you're executing, is not yours. You've never in your life come up with something so . . . gaudy."

Astrid's shoulders tightened. "It's not gaudy. It's beautiful. It's what the Everwood Inn needs, and I—"

"But it's not yours, is it?"

Astrid could lie. She should. But her mother already knew the truth. In fact, Isabel didn't even wait for her to answer. She simply shook her head, that disapproving press of her mouth like a gun shot through her daughter's chest.

And then . . . Astrid felt it happen. The old Astrid—the Astrid before Jordan, before Delilah, before breaking up with Spencer, before ten orgasms and baking until her fingers cramped—took over. She slid right into place, like a key in a lock, that young, scared, sad, desperate-for-her-mother's-love Astrid.

"I'm still the lead designer," she said. "On film, on paper. It's still me."

Isabel narrowed her eyes. "And that woman is fine with this arrangement?" She spit *woman* like it was a four-letter word.

Astrid hated it.

She hated the person she became in her mother's presence. But she didn't know how *not* to be this person. Her mother . . . she was all Astrid had. Her only family. Her only everything for most of her thirty years.

"Yes," she heard herself say, her voice robotic. "Jordan is fine with this arrangement."

A knot lodged itself in her throat as she finished the sentence, everything in the center of her chest screaming, *No, no, no, no.*

Because Jordan shouldn't be fine with it. Meredith was right. It was so goddamn clear now, this unease Astrid had felt growing since the second the two of them decided on this plan. Astrid wasn't simply the front woman to an equal partnership. This wasn't *equal*. This was . . .

God, she couldn't even get the thought to form clearly in her brain. Because if it did, what then? What would happen to this whole deal she and Jordan had, this whole ruse that they both needed?

That's what Astrid had to remember. This was for Jordan, for the Everwoods, as much as it was for her.

Wasn't it?

Isabel huffed a breath through her nose. "Well, I certainly hope you know what you're doing. I don't have to tell you the kind of disaster that would ensue if anyone were to find out the truth."

Astrid nodded. The good little girl. The dutiful daughter.

"As far as this"—Isabel flicked her eyes toward Astrid's living room, where Astrid supposed Jordan was perfectly visible—"relationship is concerned, I don't care who you spend your time with, Astrid. I really don't. You made your choice with Spencer and I honored it, but this is your *life*. The world is not as kind as you think it is, and I certainly hope you're not letting novel, fleeting emotions cloud your judgment. Your reputation is who you are, and you need to get it together before you lose yourself completely."

And with that, Isabel Parker-Green brushed past her daughter without another word and left.

CHAPTER
TWENTY-NINE

JORDAN WATCHED ASTRID'S mother glide out the front door, no *goodbye* or *fuck you* or anything. The woman seemed like an utter delight. She knew Isabel Parker-Green was a piece of work, but shit. Jordan's own hands were shaking, and she had barely spent two minutes in the woman's presence.

Jordan sat down on Astrid's couch, watching Astrid on the back porch. She hadn't come in yet, nor had she really moved at all since her mother left ten minutes ago. Whatever they had discussed outside, it had been short and, given the way Astrid's shoulders curled inward right now, not so sweet.

Jordan stood up from the couch. Sat back down. She wanted to go to Astrid, but she wanted to give her space too. She knew what it was like to have someone hovering when she was losing her shit, thanks very much to her twin brother.

Then again, as annoying as Simon's concern was at times, it was still *care*. It was love, and goddammit, Jordan wanted to give that to Astrid right now.

She stood up again. Squared her shoulders and started toward the porch, then decided it was probably a good idea to bring a little liquid courage, so she jogged into the kitchen and filled two glasses with pinot grigio. Properly armed, she opened the back door as quietly as she could. Stepping outside felt like stepping into another world. It was spring-warm, clouds gathering overhead, but they held back their rain, a gentle blanket of calm over the fading day.

Astrid didn't turn around. She stayed facing the backyard, but Jordan saw her shoulders come down just a little.

"Hey," Jordan said, stepping up next to Astrid and offering her one of the glasses.

Astrid took it, then gulped down half, shuddering as she swallowed.

"Damn, that bad?" Jordan asked. She went for a light tone, hoping they could have a laugh about Jordan answering the door in little more than her underwear, only to find her lover's mother standing there like Meryl Streep with a stick up her ass.

Astrid just released a trembling breath, took another swig.

"What can I do?" Jordan asked.

Astrid shook her head. "I told her. I told her we were seeing each other."

Jordan sent a hand through her hair. "I take it she didn't warm up to the idea?"

Astrid shrugged, her eyes still glazed on the backyard. "She didn't care. That's what she said. 'I don't care who you spend your time with, Astrid.' Those were her exact words."

This time Jordan took a gulp of wine. As far as coming-out-to-your-parents experiences went, it wasn't horrible. Hell, she'd heard horror stories from her queer community in Savannah, particularly among the Gen Xers, people whose parents kicked them out, sent them to conversion camps. She knew that still happened and hit kids of color and trans kids a lot harder than anyone else.

Still, when a parent reacted with *I don't care* to a pretty huge life confession, it wasn't great.

"Shit" was all Jordan could think to say.

Astrid nodded. "She did care, however, about my reputation."

"As in, what will people think of you dating a woman?"

"As in . . ." She trailed off, her gaze going inward. Jordan suddenly felt Astrid was miles away.

"Hey," Jordan said, pressing her shoulder into Astrid's. "Dating someone you like isn't going to ruin your career. It's—"

"She's not talking about my dating choice," Astrid said, pushing off from the railing and starting a slow pace around the deck. She held her wine, but she seemed to have forgotten the glass was in her hands, pale yellow liquid sloshing around as she moved. "She's talking about me. Who I am. And maybe she's right. I mean . . ." She waved her hand at herself. "Look at me. I'm . . . I'm a mess. I'm not focused on work, my designs are *uninspired*, the inn is my only project right now because I don't care enough. It's all falling apart, and maybe it has been for a long time, but I thought I could . . . I thought I could save it with the inn. But lately, I'm just . . . I'm—"

"Happy," Jordan said, and Astrid froze. "That's what you've been lately. Don't you see that?"

Astrid shook her head. "You don't get it. You don't—"

"What? Have a job?" Jordan felt her temper swelling. She tried to stay calm, but she was witnessing the woman who watched porn videos just to make sure Jordan had a good time disintegrate right in front of her eyes. "Have a bitchy mother to please?"

"That's not fair."

"Oh, it's not? But it's fair to declare that spending time with me, partnering with me, doing things you clearly fucking love"—she flung her arm behind her, toward all the desserts currently swallowing the kitchen—"is a mistake. Just because your *mother* doesn't like it?"

"That's not what I meant."

"See, I think you did. I think you are so fucking lost, you don't know who you are or what you want. And you're letting your mom call the shots like a coward."

All Jordan could hear was her own blood rushing in her ears. Regret tightened in her chest, but she couldn't take it back. She wasn't even sure she would. These last few days with Astrid had been a revelation. Seeing Astrid come alive only pointed out how miserable the woman had been before with almost everything in her life. Work, family. Her friends were the only thing that ever pulled a genuine smile from Astrid's mouth, the only thing that revealed Astrid's big heart and caring spirit. She hid all that away in literally every other aspect in her life, and for what? For a mother who didn't even seem to *like* Astrid very much. Jordan hated it. She hated watching it happen.

Jordan didn't want to lose this Astrid.

But already, the Astrid before her was different. Tighter. More reserved. A dispassionate woman in an ivory pencil dress. She stood still as stone, fingertips white on her wineglass.

"Fuck you," Astrid finally said so quietly, Jordan almost didn't hear her. "You don't know what the hell you're talking about. You had two parents growing up. You have a grandmother who adores you. You have a twin brother who would die for you. I know you had your own share of family struggles, Jordan, but you had multiple people to help you through them. I had my mother. That's it. Me and her, from the time I was three years old to now."

When she spoke, she did so with clenched teeth, her jaw so tight it looked ready to snap, sparks glinting in her brown eyes. Jordan could only stare, like she was watching a phoenix light itself on fire.

"My mother lost two husbands in seven years," Astrid said. "I lost two fathers. I watched her dissolve into grief, terrified she'd disappear too and leave Delilah and me alone. Then Delilah was too fucking sad to be a sister to me, so yeah, I was a little dependent on my mother. And she worked hard to make sure I became who I was supposed to be. She made sure I was *great*. Because when you're great, when you're a success, no one can take that from you. That doesn't die. Your name, your reputation, that doesn't leave you, as long as you're careful. You can control it. You can mold it into the exact companion you need it to be. It will never, ever disappoint you. It will never let you down."

Tears poured down her cheeks, though Jordan didn't think Astrid even knew she was crying.

"So fuck your lost theory, Jordan. I'm only lost if I fail. I'm only lost if everything I've worked for goes up in flames, because my mother's right. It's my *life*. Who the hell am I without it? Without her? If my own *mother* doesn't think I can succeed, that I can be someone important, then who . . ."

"Astrid," Jordan said softly. She wanted to say other names too. *Baby* and *sweetheart*, but Astrid backed up when Jordan tried to come closer, her hand up in warning.

"Without a mother who believes in me, who am I? Who is anyone without that one, most basic thing, Jordan? What the hell is the point of all of this?" Her breathing came out ragged, growing rougher and more stuttering by the second. Her eyes were wide, like a terrified kid's. "Who . . . who . . . am I? Who am I, Jordan? Who . . ."

Jordan saw the panic spill over. Astrid inhaled a painful-sounding breath, as though a fist were trying to punch all the air out of her body at the same time.

"Hey, hey, hey," Jordan said, hurrying toward her to grab her wineglass and set it on the patio table. Then she took the trembling, gasping woman into her arms, hoping Astrid would go willingly.

She did, falling against Jordan like a rag doll, choked sobs wedging themselves through her constricted throat, her hands covering her face. Jordan held her, rubbing circles on her back.

Astrid's outburst flitted through Jordan's mind on repeat, all this anger and sadness mingled together, and Jordan had no clue what to do about any of it. She had no idea how to help Astrid, except to simply hold her and wait.

Soon, Astrid's breathing regulated. She pulled back and Jordan let her go. Astrid's eyes were red and puffy, her hair a complete disaster by Astrid's normal standards. But even like this, she was still beautiful. She still made Jordan's insides feel soft and light, gauzy like a fairy's wings.

And just like that, Jordan knew. She knew like she knew Simon was her brother, or the moon's gravity pulled at the sea.

She was in love with Astrid Parker. She was one hundred percent, wildly, make-stupid-ass-decisions in love with her.

"I think I owe you a love song," she said gently, everything in her body shaking. Still, she held out her hand.

Astrid's shoulders slumped, her still-glistening eyes going soft, fresh tears spilling. She took Jordan's hand and Jordan pulled her close, slipping one arm around her bare waist, using her other to press Astrid's palm to her heart. Then she started dancing, swaying in slow circles as the first love song that popped into her head flowed out of her mouth, Elton John's "Your Song."

Astrid smiled against Jordan's neck. "You sound just like Ewan McGregor in *Moulin Rouge!*"

"Damn right I do."

"You really can sing."

"Shh," Jordan said, spinning them around, her mouth pressed to Astrid's jaw. "I'm singing to my girl."

CHAPTER THIRTY

FOR THE NEXT week, Astrid worked.

She worked like she'd never worked in her life.

Every morning at seven a.m., she'd arrive at the inn, deal with paperwork and orders. Then, once the crew arrived, she'd film. She filmed the kitchen appliances going in; she filmed painting a delicate flower on the slanted ceiling in the downstairs guest room; and she filmed a grim conversation with Josh and Jordan about how the back porch, half of which they were transforming into a solarium, had major foundational problems and they'd have to build the thing up from scratch.

She did it all with her smile in place—except for when she was expected to frown—and her breath perfectly calm and even in her chest.

She filmed, and she lied.

I need this mantel to work, Josh.

I think these flowers will create an English garden feel guests will love.

I know you doubted this bronzed nickel tub, Natasha, but I was right, wasn't I?

Lie. Smile. Lie some more.

Of course, she and Jordan had been lying for weeks now, playing a part on camera, and a very different role after hours. But now, after their weekend together and Isabel's visit, everything going on with the inn felt fraught. Every word, every decision, every planned-out frown.

Astrid told herself she and Jordan were doing this together. She told herself that she was lying for Jordan, for the Everwood's success, as much as she was lying for herself. But each day—when she wandered the house as it transformed under her eyes into something she never could've imagined, when she caught Jordan gazing at her laptop screen, fiddling with the design, a wistful expression on her face that vanished as soon as Astrid made her presence known—this too started to feel like a lie.

So she worked.

She worked, and when work was done, she worked some more.

At five p.m., she'd find Jordan and kiss her rosebud mouth. She'd breathe the other woman in, desperate to stay there, but she had so much work to do. She'd go to her office and draft newsletters to send out to current and prospective clients. She scoured the Internet for projects on the horizon, prepared pitches, made list after list of people to call, to email, to pursue.

Finally, she'd make it home around ten, where she'd shower and try not to think about Jordan, think about what Astrid was doing to her, taking from her, and she'd try not to call her just to hear her voice.

She usually failed.

And as soon as she called, Jordan would hear how small her voice was—because Astrid had spent the last eighteen hours trying to hide that tiny, desperate sound, and she just couldn't do it anymore, not with Jordan's soft, gentle, trusting words in her ear—and Jordan would come over and take her to bed, and Astrid would finally get her first real breath of the day.

"You're working too hard," Jordan said that Thursday night, smoothing her hand over Astrid's hair as they lay tucked under Astrid's white duvet. Ten minutes before, Jordan had come in the house and found Astrid sitting in her shower, totally asleep. Now, dried and dressed in a plain white tee, Astrid could barely keep her eyes open to respond.

"I'm fine," she said.

Jordan sighed, pressed a kiss to her head. "No, you're not."

Astrid didn't respond. She pretended to have drifted off already, but Jordan's words lodged themselves in her mind.

She *was* fine.

This was who she was. She worked hard and long. She succeeded. She'd already booked two new projects for the summer—a new office for a gynecologist who wanted a spa-like feel, and a tiny bungalow over on Amaryllis Avenue—and she was poised and professional during her hours at the Everwood job.

But was this even her?

She wasn't sure anymore.

When she felt Jordan go limp against her, her breathing evening out with sleep, she turned to face her lover just as she had every night this week, tracing her elfin face with her fingertips. Sleep eluded Astrid. Instead, she watched Jordan's eyes flutter with dreams, the woman she was almost positive she was in love with, whose design she was claiming as her own, and she cried.

BY FRIDAY MORNING, Astrid was so exhausted, she could barely stand up. She knew she looked terrible and relied a little too much on Darcy, who was absolute magic with under-eye circles. Today's filming schedule was packed. They were starting in the Lapis Room for the installation of the rugged wooden beams that were going to arch over the ceiling, as well as the herringbone feature wall. After that, Natasha and the Everwoods were heading to the historical society in town to get some shots of a few Alice Everwood artifacts they kept under glass.

Astrid was in the Lapis Room already, going over the design one more time, checking that all the materials were accounted for. Her iPad shook in her hands. She'd probably had one too many cups of coffee that morning already, but caffeine was the only thing that kept her alert these days.

"Hey," Jordan said as she came into the room carrying her tool bag.

"Hey," Astrid said, keeping her eyes on her screen. She felt rather than saw Jordan pause, as though she were waiting for Astrid to look at her.

She didn't.

She couldn't.

Eye contact was hard lately. Not that it had ever been easy for Astrid, but she could hardly meet Jordan's gaze this last week without her throat swelling.

Astrid hated it, but she didn't know what else to do. They just had to get through this reno, all this filming. Once that was done, she and Jordan could really start. Once all this was over, everything would go back to normal.

The thought should've been comforting, but somehow, it only made Astrid want to scream. Her lower lip threatened to wobble, so she clenched her jaw so tight, she knew she'd have a headache by noon.

"Hey," Jordan said again, but this time, she was right next to Astrid. Jordan set both hands on her shoulders, turning her so Astrid had no choice but to look her in the eye.

God, she was beautiful. Astrid drank her in, and almost against her will, Astrid's lungs heaved a deep, shuddering breath.

Jordan frowned and brought her hands up to frame Astrid's face. "Baby," she said, and that was it. Just that single, soft word, but it was enough to nearly break Astrid in half.

"Let's go somewhere this weekend," Jordan said.

Astrid struggled to keep her voice even. "Like where?"

"Anywhere. Winter Lake, maybe. I bet Josh could hook us up with a cabin to rent. We'll go on a proper date and watch horrible rom-coms." She wrapped her arms around Astrid's waist, pressed her mouth to her neck. "Sleep until noon. Drink cheap wine. Have sex on the porch."

Astrid laughed. "The porch?"

Jordan's teeth nipped at her neck. "We'll get a secluded cabin."

Astrid closed her eyes, let herself drift. That sounded perfect. That sounded like the kind of life she wanted.

"Okay," she heard herself say.

Jordan pulled back. "Okay?"

Astrid nodded and Jordan kissed her. Astrid curled her arms around Jordan's neck and kissed her back. She kissed her harder, then harder still, as though the press of their mouths was the solution to every problem.

Maybe it was.

Astrid was ready to call it a day and drag Jordan home with her when a throat was cleared in the doorway. The two women leaped apart, but relaxed a little when they saw it was Simon.

"Sorry to interrupt," he said. "Natasha just got here and she wants to meet with all of us downstairs in the library."

"About what?" Jordan asked, one hand still holding on to Astrid's hip as though she were afraid Astrid might float away.

"I don't know, but she's got that scary calm look in her eye she gets when she doesn't like something."

Astrid felt her stomach flip over once . . . twice. She glanced at Jordan, but only for a second. It was probably nothing. Natasha was famously meticulous. Most likely, there was some detail in the crown molding that wasn't up to snuff, a scuff on the newly painted walls.

Still, even those scenarios sent Astrid's mind whirling. *She* was the lead designer. *She* was supposed to be meticulous, make sure everything was perfect.

The three of them headed downstairs, Astrid bringing up the rear. Natasha was already in the library, frowning down at her phone. Pru was there too, as well as Emery, but no other crew member was present.

There were also zero cameras.

Natasha liked to film everything—every interaction, positive or negative, the juicier, the better. So the fact that she clearly had no intention of filming this meeting set Astrid's pulse racing.

"Good morning," Natasha said when they were all inside the room. There were no chairs, no furniture to even lean against, so everyone stood in a wonky circle. Simon offered Pru his arm, and Astrid stood next to Jordan, the heat of her shoulder grounding Astrid to the floor.

"I'll get right to it," Natasha went on. Except then she simply pressed her hands together, phone in between her palms, and touched her fingertips to her mouth.

"I received a very interesting email yesterday evening," Natasha finally said. "I've spent all night trying to figure out what to do about it, but the only thing I can think of is to simply ask."

"Ask what?" Simon said. "Who was the email from?"

"No one I know," Natasha said. "Her name is Meredith Quinn."

Jordan sucked in a sharp breath. Astrid blinked at Natasha, half expecting her hair to morph into snakes or something else fantastical, anything to indicate Astrid was dreaming right now.

"Meredith Quinn emailed you," Simon said, glancing at Jordan. "Why?"

"You know her?" Natasha asked, her voice tight and terse.

"She's my ex-wife," Jordan said, a frown pushing her brows low.

Natasha's eyes popped wide at that. "Your *ex*?" She tapped her fingers on her phone's screen. "Well, that *is* very interesting."

"Why would Jordan's ex be emailing you?" Emery asked.

"Excellent question, Emery," Natasha said. She was clearly pissed, but Astrid couldn't think why. Why *would* Jordan's ex be emailing Natasha?

Unless . . .

Astrid's stomach plummeted to her feet. Her gaze darted to Jordan, who suddenly looked very green.

"Why don't you read it out loud for us, Jordan," Natasha said, "so we can all try and make sense of it." She held out her phone, which Jordan took with a trembling hand.

For a second, Jordan just stood there, eyes on the screen as she read it to herself. She closed her eyes, a muscle jumping in her jaw.

"Come on now, Jordan," Natasha said, "don't keep something this intriguing to yourself."

Astrid's breathing had suddenly become very loud, and she had to press her lips together to keep from panting.

"*Dear Ms. Rojas,*" Jordan began, her voice raspy. She cleared her throat. "*It is my understanding that you are currently filming the Everwood Inn renovation in Bright Falls, Oregon. I've long admired your show and your work, and I know you value talent and effort. Because of your integrity and reputation, any designer who was featured on your show would receive countless opportunities for growth in their field. It's truly a once-in-a-lifetime chance. Therefore, I urge you to investigate the fidelity of the Everwood Inn design. Sincerely, Meredith Quinn.*"

Silence echoed through the room.

"What the hell?" Simon finally said, breaking the shocked spell.

"That's exactly what I'd like to know," Natasha said as she took back her phone. "Jordan?"

Astrid watched her, held her breath. She knew what Jordan would say. She knew Jordan would fix this. She'd make it right, ensure they could all go on with their day, their work, the show's success. Astrid could almost see the words forming in Jordan's mind, and she knew— she *knew*—she needed those words. They all did. They all needed this show to keep them afloat.

But Astrid didn't want those words.

Her mind grabbed for them—the lies that had become her bread and butter—but her heart shoved them away. She watched Jordan struggle. She'd watched Jordan struggle for *weeks*, trying to reconcile her role as the lead carpenter with her reality as the lead designer. She'd watched Jordan give and give and give, and Astrid had let her do it. And for what?

For *what*?

For a mother who would never really see her?

For a career Astrid didn't even like?

She didn't want to be this woman, someone who let the person she loved fade into the background, when they deserved to shine. She didn't want to be the kind of daughter who clamored so desperately after her mother's approval, she lost herself.

Because Jordan was right.

Astrid was lost.

And she had to find herself. She had to find herself now before she disappeared completely.

"I don't know what she's talking about," Jordan said. Her voice sounded calm, but Astrid knew better. She heard that slight tremor. "Meredith is . . . she's my ex. We didn't part amicably, and I . . . I guess she's just trying to stir up trouble."

Natasha lifted a brow. "So this is a scorned lovers' quarrel?"

Jordan nodded. She held out her hands, but they were shaking. Astrid saw Pru frown.

"I'm so sorry," Jordan went on. "I'll talk to her. She won't bother you again. I assure you, the fidelity of this design is—"

"Stop," Astrid said. Her voice was quiet, but it halted Jordan in her tracks. Astrid lifted her eyes to Jordan's. "Just stop."

CHAPTER
THIRTY-ONE

JORDAN STARED AT Astrid.

"Stop . . . stop what?" she asked.

Astrid closed her eyes. Still, Jordan didn't move. No one moved. No one said a word. Finally, Astrid squared her shoulders, nodding to herself as she took a deep breath.

Shit.

Jordan knew that look.

"Astrid, wait—"

"Jordan is the lead designer on this project," Astrid said. "Not me."

There was a horrible span of silence before Natasha canted her head. "I'm sorry?"

"She deserves the credit," Astrid went on, "and she deserves every opportunity featuring on this show will provide."

"Astrid," Jordan said, her voice a whisper. Shock pushed her emotions over the edge. She couldn't breathe, but she could fix this. She would just deny it. That's all she had to do to make this right. "What are you talking about?"

"Don't," Astrid said to her now. She didn't look at her. "I'm so sorry I let it go on for this long. I don't know . . ." She shook her head, pressed a hand to her mouth.

And with that, Astrid turned and walked out of the room. No one stopped her. Not even Jordan, while she tried to process what had just happened and what it would mean. She caught Simon's gaze, who was looking at her as though he'd never seen her before. Tears glistened in Pru's eyes, both hands laced together and pressed to her mouth. Natasha just stared with her mouth slightly open, as though she was trying to figure out what the fuck to say or do.

Jordan went after Astrid.

"Hey," she said, catching up with her in the foyer. "Hey, hey, hey, slow down."

Astrid didn't. She barreled toward the front door, and Jordan had to run the last few steps to catch up with her. She grabbed her arm and whirled her around.

"Don't say anything," Astrid said. "Please don't."

"Of course I'm going to fucking say something," Jordan said. "What the hell were you thinking? Why did you do that?"

"You know why. I can't . . . I'm so sorry, Jordan."

"Sorry for what?" Jordan asked, spreading her arms wide. "We're partners in this."

Astrid shook her head. "Partners don't do this. They don't steal credit and opportunities. They don't lie."

"Astrid," Jordan said. "You weren't . . . you didn't . . ."

But she couldn't finish that sentence, and they both knew it.

Astrid heaved a dry sob. "I was so close. I was so close to taking everything away from you. And you know what? I would've done it. I really think I would've gone through with it all if Meredith hadn't emailed Natasha. That's what scares me the most. That's what . . ." She rubbed her forehead, sighing into her hands. "I can't do this."

"Do what?"

Astrid waved her hand between them. "This. Us."

"Hang on," Jordan said, panic clouding into her chest. Surely Astrid didn't mean *them*. She was talking professionally.

Wasn't she?

"We can fix this," Jordan said. "Just slow down, okay? Let's think for a second."

"I don't want to fix it," Astrid said, her voice shaking. "Don't you see? This is what needs to happen. Everything needs to fall apart so you can start over. Do this project as the lead designer, just like you were supposed to."

"Astrid, I don't want it," Jordan said, anger rising to join with her shock and worry. "I told you from the beginning I didn't want it."

"But you do," Astrid said softly. "I see the way you look at what you created. You love it, Jordan. You've just convinced yourself that you don't, because you think you don't deserve it."

"I . . . that's not what I'm doing," Jordan said, but something in her—something hard and tough she'd built up inside her the second Meredith slammed the door on their life a year ago—started to crumble.

Astrid took a step closer and took Jordan's face between her hands. She pressed their foreheads together. "You *do* deserve it, Jordan. You deserve every good thing."

A sinking dread filled Jordan's stomach. "Wait . . . Astrid, hang on. What are you—"

But Astrid didn't let her finish. She kissed Jordan on the mouth, once . . . twice . . .

Then Astrid let her go.

And for the second time in Jordan's life, she watched a woman she loved walk out the front door.

⌣

JORDAN STOOD THERE, staring through the empty doorway of the Everwood Inn, for a long time. So long, Simon had to come out and get her.

"Jordie?" he said, placing a gentle hand on her arm.

She turned to look at him. She felt how slack her face was, how void of any emotion, but she couldn't seem to react.

Astrid left.

She'd left her.

"Is it true?" Simon asked.

Jordan turned away, blinked at the muddied front yard. The landscapers were coming in two weeks.

"Is what true?" she asked.

"The design. Is it yours?"

She heaved a shaky breath, lifted her eyes to look at the foyer, which they'd painted the same Twilit Stars blue as the Lapis Room. It was dark and lovely, pulling guests into the intrigue of the Everwood Inn. Later, they'd add an ivory area rug patterned with navy and goldenrod circles, armless chairs in similar colors set underneath domed amber sconces.

Astrid was right.

Jordan loved what she'd created.

She'd loved creating it.

In the last few weeks, she'd tried not to. It was too hard, loving something you made that you had to give away, but that was the very nature of art. She'd done it before, with every piece of furniture she'd ever created, and she was prepared to do it with this project too. It was the only option that made sense, the only way *Innside America* could happen for all of them.

Jordan wasn't a designer.

She was just a carpenter who loved her family's home, who fucked up everything she touched.

Including the Everwood Inn. Because she knew this was over. Natasha would never continue filming Astrid as lead designer now, and they'd lost too much time, the reno was too far along to start over with Jordan.

"So is it?"

The new voice startled Jordan out of her thoughts. She turned to see Natasha in the library's doorway, Emery right beside her. Pru stood behind them, and Jordan's heart nearly broke at the sight of her. They'd have to sell. No way they'd ever recoup the money her grandmother had borrowed to do this renovation without *Innside America*'s exposure.

Even if Jordan lied right now, what was the point? Astrid was gone—she'd never walk back into this inn ever again, Jordan knew that for a fact. She'd be too humiliated, and Simon, once he realized the scope of everything that had gone on with the design, would be too pissed to let her.

"Yeah," she finally said. "It's true."

For a second, hope bloomed. Maybe Natasha—who Jordan knew loved the design—would figure out how to make this work. Maybe they had enough footage without Astrid to cobble together some semblance of an episode. Maybe not *Innside America*'s best, but wouldn't that be better than wasting all the footage they did have, all the money the network must have spent on crew and lodging and equipment? Maybe—

But as Simon uttered a soft "Fuck" next to her, as her eyes met Natasha's and she saw the disappointment there, the resignation, all of those maybes popped like soap bubbles drifting through the air.

CHAPTER
THIRTY-TWO

THE EMAIL OFFICIALLY terminating Astrid's contract with the Everwoods came the next day. Astrid had turned her phone off—Jordan had called several times after she had left the inn and there was no way Astrid could talk to her yet—so the curt missive from Simon had pinged into her email when Astrid had opened her laptop to turn on a bad movie to watch in bed.

Dear Ms. Parker,

Per the terms of our agreement, this is written notice to inform you that Everwood Inn is dissolving our partnership with Bright Designs based on clause 3.1, which stipulates the client may terminate the contract on the basis of project dissatisfaction. Thank you for your time.

Sincerely,
Simon Everwood

She snapped her laptop closed, then pulled the covers over her head, where she stayed for the next ten hours.

SHE DIDN'T REMEMBER hearing the doorbell. But knowing Iris, she hadn't even rung it. Both Claire and Iris had keys to Astrid's house, a decision she was now regretting when she opened her eyes after a Tylenol PM–induced sleep to find her two best friends and her stepsister staring down at her with concerned expressions on their faces. She groaned and rolled over, hoping presenting her back communicated a clear message of *Get the hell out of my house.*

But of course, it didn't. Not with this crew.

"We brought supplies," Iris said, plopping down on the bed. Astrid heard the crinkle of a paper bag, but she didn't turn around.

"Ice cream, chips, and a giant box of really bad wine," Iris went on.

"Go away," Astrid said.

"Not happening, sweetie," Claire said. She came around to the other side of the bed so she could see Astrid, then knelt down on the floor and rested her forearms on the mattress.

Astrid sighed and rolled onto her back, staring at the ceiling. "What day is it?"

"Sunday."

Two days since everything went to hell, and Astrid was positive she'd only left her bed to pee.

"How much do you know?" she asked.

"All of it," Delilah said. "Simon told Iris, and then Iris told us, and then Iris called Jordan, who totally ignored her five million messages."

"I'm a bit hurt, if I'm being honest," Iris said, but her tone was light, joking.

Still, Astrid didn't feel like joking. She had to resist the urge to pull the sheet over her head like a pouting kid. Embarrassment clouded into her chest, that hot, slimy feeling of shame she'd worked her entire life to never, ever feel.

She'd been fired.

She'd failed.

She'd hurt Jordan. She'd *been* hurting her for weeks. She just hadn't seen it clearly.

Now, though, everything was painfully obvious—each grotesque and craggy detail of the past month of her life bloomed in full color for all the world to see.

"Honey," Claire said, smoothing a hand over Astrid's hair. "Are you okay?"

Astrid sat up, rubbed at her puffy eyes. She didn't even think she'd washed off her makeup from Friday. And also, she didn't give one single fuck.

"None of you have talked to Jordan?" she asked, looking at each of her friends.

Iris shook her head. "Simon said she's been holed up in her room. She hasn't even talked to him all that much."

"What about the show?" Astrid asked. "Is Natasha really angry?"

Iris and Claire exchanged a glance, both of their mouths open. No words came out, though. Astrid looked at her stepsister pointedly.

Delilah sighed. "The show's done, Astrid. Crew left yesterday morning."

"Shit," Astrid said, dropping her head into her hands. "That wasn't supposed to happen. They were supposed to . . ." But even as she thought it, hoped for it, she knew Jordan simply stepping in as lead designer on a show that had been filming a renovation for five weeks now was impossible.

So she'd fucked that up too.

Jordan must hate her. Jordan *should* hate her.

She closed her eyes, trying to hold back all these emotions, the messy ones, the ones that Isabel had spent the last thirty years teaching Astrid how to control. But she was so goddamn tired of keeping it together, of knowing every next step and exactly how to execute it. She was *lost*, for fuck's sake. She was ready to act like it.

So she did something she'd rarely done in front of her friends.

She cried.

As the warm saltwater streaked down her cheeks, she realized she'd only ever really sobbed in front of one other person—Jordan Everwood, on her back porch, as she fell apart, and then Jordan put her back together again with a love song.

The thought only made her cry harder, and soon, she was sobbing into her hands, her shoulders shaking with deep, bone-breaking breaths.

"Holy shit," Delilah said, but Astrid only dimly registered her voice. All that mattered right now was getting everything out, every single thing she hated about herself, her life, what she'd done to Jordan. Her tears were like a detox, coursing through her body and wiping it clean.

At least, that's what it felt like.

That's what she hoped it was, but it all felt so impossible— starting over. What did that even mean for a person who'd already walked on the earth for thirty years?

Soon, she felt her friends' arms around her, all three of them— Delilah included—wrapping her up and holding her while she right and truly broke down.

"It's about time," Iris said, but not unkindly. She said it gently, lovingly, as she pressed a kiss to Astrid's forehead. "It's about damn time."

MONDAY MORNING, ASTRID finally left her room. She showered, washed her hair, even put on a little makeup. But standing in front of her closet, rows of black and white and ivory hanging in front of her, she couldn't seem to force herself to put on a suit or a dress.

She found a pair of black jeans stuffed in the back of her dresser and slipped them on, followed by a plain white tank top. She paired that with a few gold chains, some gold hoops in her ears. As she stared at herself in the mirror—eyes still red and puffy, hair wavy because the idea of blasting herself with a hair dryer felt unbearable right now—she thought she recognized the woman in the reflection.

Exhausted.

Heartbroken.

That's what this was. For the first time in her life, Astrid's heart was shattered. Or had it always been like this and she'd just never let herself feel it? She wasn't sure, but it felt right. It felt *real*.

She poured a tumbler full of coffee, got in her car, and drove to the Bright Designs office downtown. If this were any other day, she'd have a lot of work to do, and she wasn't sure if the dread she felt at the prospect of more projects, more designs, smiling for clients, was all part of this *real*, or something else.

She'd spent most of Sunday with her best friends and Delilah, watching bad movies and sleeping, but after her breakdown, she hadn't talked much. It wasn't that she didn't want to—she simply wasn't sure what she needed to say yet.

The *real* Astrid was still all tangled up with the one from before, the one her mother had made in her own image.

Once settled behind her desk, she finally turned on her phone. The screen lit up with dozens of notifications.

Delightful Human Who Ruined Your Ugly Dress

Astrid's throat tightened at Jordan's name, the one Astrid couldn't bring herself to change for some reason. She knew she was still **Semi-Decent Human Who Wants to Kiss You Again** in Jordan's phone, and shit, how true that first part had turned out to be.

Jordan had made all of her calls on Friday, pretty soon after Astrid left the Everwood. She hadn't left any voice mails, but she'd sent several texts. Astrid's hands shook as she opened up her messages.

Don't do this, Astrid.

Please answer me.

Let's talk about this, please.

Why are you doing this?

Baby. Call me back. Please.

And that was the last one. That sweet, soft plea. Astrid could almost hear Jordan's voice wrap around the words. The hurt.

"Fuck," Astrid said out loud, tears clouding her eyes. She pressed a hand to her mouth, stared at Jordan's last message. She hadn't texted or called at all on Saturday or Sunday. Which meant Astrid had really fucked up.

Panic rose in Astrid's chest, and she hovered her finger over Jordan's number. One tap. That was all she needed to do.

She set her phone down.

She'd meant what she said to Jordan in the Everwood foyer— Jordan deserved every good thing, and Astrid was a fucking mess.

She looked around her tiny, gray-walled office, abstract paintings placed just so, white sofas in the waiting area, white desks. She closed her eyes and thought of deep, midnight blue; sage green and goldenrod and silver; clawfoot tubs and delicate flowers painted on a ceiling.

"So you are alive, then," a voice said.

Astrid snapped her eyes open to see her mother standing by the front door, regal in ivory pants and a black silk blouse. Astrid had a few versions of the exact same outfit in her closet.

Isabel slid off her sunglasses and folded them in her hand, then walked to one of the white chairs in front of Astrid's desk. She sat primly, calmly, but her mouth was pinched, skin tight around her eyes.

Astrid slumped back in her chair. She didn't even cross her legs. Instead, she propped one leg up on the seat and wrapped her arms around her knee.

One of Isabel's brows lifted, but she said nothing about Astrid's lackadaisical pose.

"Well?" her mother asked instead. "Are you going to explain your-self?"

"Explain what, Mother?"

Isabel laughed humorlessly. "You honestly think your little stunt with the Everwood Inn isn't common knowledge by now? Has your office phone rung this morning, Astrid? What about your email? How many notifications of canceled projects do you have waiting in your inbox?"

A familiar flare of panic. Astrid let her leg drop to the floor as she leaned toward her computer and opened her email. She sifted through her normal mix of design subscriptions until she found some familiar names.

The two clients she'd managed to procure this past week, both of them writing Astrid to inform her that they'd decided to go in a dif-ferent direction. She sat back, all the breath leaving her lungs.

Isabel sniffed. "I can't believe you let the situation at the Ever-wood spiral out of control like that. I warned you what would happen if people found out, and I was right. Now, what we need to do . . ."

Her mother kept talking, but Astrid barely heard her. She sat there, staring at her computer screen, at her complete lack of clients, Simon's email terminating her still sitting in her inbox, and she knew this was the moment.

Complete, notorious failure.

She'd finally done it.

Her reputation, her integrity as a designer, all gone.

It was over.

She knew she should be fanning that little spark of panic, she should be losing her shit, planning and scheming how to fix it. She should be listening to her mother.

But she wasn't.

She was . . . relieved.

That's what this was, this big, open space in her chest. Astrid Parker had fucked up her professional life good and proper, and she was goddamn thrilled.

She was *happy*.

". . . will go a long way to restoring your reputation," her mother was saying, tapping away at her phone. "We'll host the dinner at Wisteria House on Wednesday, which means we have a lot to do between now and then. I'll email you a list of who you need to—"

"Stop," Astrid said.

Isabel's eyes widened. "Excuse me?"

"Just stop," she said. She'd said the same words to Jordan three days ago, just two tiny words that subsequently blew up her entire life.

And she meant to blow it up a little bit more.

"I'm done, Mother," she said, pushing back from the desk.

"You're . . . done," Isabel said. It wasn't a question. More like an accusation.

Astrid took a deep breath and leaned forward, her elbows propped on her knees. "Yeah."

"With what?" Isabel asked.

"All of it. Bright Designs. Sunday brunch. Dinner parties and these"—she waved her hand between them—"strategy sessions on how to fix me. I don't need fixing, Mother."

Isabel looked offended. "Astrid. Don't be ridiculous. I'm not try-ing to fix you. I'm trying to help you."

Astrid shook her head. "No. You're trying to *make* me, and I don't need to be made. I thought . . . I thought things would change after Spencer. I thought you'd see that I'm my own person and I'm *okay* just how I am, but you didn't. And I can't even blame you because *I* didn't see that in myself. I let you keep fixing and meddling and shaping because I wanted you to love me and accept—"

"Love you?" Isabel's mouth hung open, and for the first time in years—maybe ever—Astrid saw genuine hurt flicker in her mother's eyes. "Astrid, of course I love you."

Astrid closed her eyes. She wanted it to be true. Her mother was the only family she had—but even as she thought it, she knew it wasn't the case. Claire was her family. Iris. Delilah, even. She'd spent her whole life trying to gain her mother's approval, her mother's love, and she'd barely noticed anything else around her. Of course, she knew her friends were there for her, but again, it was as though her head and heart were in constant dissonance—she knew they loved her, but she hadn't let them love her the way she needed to.

She hadn't let it be enough.

But it was.

Astrid Parker was loved, no matter what her mother thought of her. No matter what choices she made.

And that love gave her the courage to choose herself.

"I believe that you believe that, Mom," she said, her voice sud-denly shaky with emotion. "But all I feel is your love for an Astrid you've created in your mind, and I don't like that woman. I don't want to be her anymore."

Isabel's mouth still hung open, eyes blinking rapidly. "Astrid, what are you saying?"

Astrid stood up. She didn't run her hand down her jeans. She didn't straighten her shirt or smooth her hair. She simply took her keys out of her bag and worked the one for the Bright Designs offices off the ring. She placed it on the desk in front of her mother.

"I'm saying I quit."

And then she walked out the door, tears of relief, joy, and a little sadness spilling freely down her cheeks as she went.

CHAPTER

THIRTY-THREE

THE GODDAMN TWO of Cups.

Jordan couldn't believe it.

After two weeks of pentacles, swords, and wands, Empresses and Hanged Women, that little bitch chose Wednesday morning after Jordan's entire life imploded—again—to pop back up like a jack-in-the-box from hell.

She tore the damn thing right in half, something she probably should've done months ago. It might've saved her a lot of heartache. Or, at the very least, it would've saved her a lot of useless thoughts and feelings about love and partnerships.

Still, hours later, while she installed the herringbone feature wall in the Lapis Room, she couldn't stop thinking about it.

Soul mates.

A perfect pairing.

Well, fuck that.

She slammed the nail gun into a slanted piece of espresso-colored wood a little harder than necessary.

After Astrid's declaration, Natasha, Emery, and the rest of the

Innside America crew left on Saturday morning without much fanfare. In the driveway, Natasha had hugged Jordan. She'd apologized that things had gone down the way they had, but she hadn't once offered any alternatives, any ideas for how they might fix this mess and continue filming.

Jordan couldn't tell if she was devastated or relieved. Maybe she was both—they'd have to sell the inn now, but she also didn't think she could just go back and film as the lead designer. Not with Astrid haunting every room, every design choice.

Now, the plan—drawn up by Simon, of course—was to finish the reno and try to get as much money for the house as possible. A real estate agent had come in yesterday, ecstatic over the possibility of selling such an American treasure. Her name was Trish. She had very blond hair that didn't move when she walked, and Jordan had to fight the urge to toss her out a window.

Still, Trish estimated a seven-figure sales price, which should've made anyone happy.

All it did was send Jordan back to her bed, staring at her recent one-sided text thread with Astrid, fighting the urge to call again.

She wouldn't do it. By now, she was a goddamn expert in women she loved walking out without even discussing it with her, and she wasn't about to go chasing after someone who clearly didn't want her. A decision that would've been a lot easier to focus on without that infernal Two of Cups card, which was exactly why it was now in pieces in the cottage's kitchen garbage.

She jabbed at the wall again with her nail gun.

Bang.

Bang.

Bang.

She tried to push Astrid's face from her mind—Astrid smiling, baking, slow-dancing, coming—but the only thing that seemed to really block the woman out was the slam of her nail gun. She'd just placed a new slat of wood against the outline on the wall when her phone rang.

She dropped the tool, her heart catapulting into her throat. Just like that, her hands were shaking, that goddamn *hope* zipping through her chest like a comet. She fumbled her phone from her back pocket, still unsure what she would do when she saw Astrid's name across her—

But it wasn't Astrid.

It was Natasha Rojas.

Jordan blinked at her screen while she gave herself a second to get her breath back to normal. Then she slid her finger over the glass.

"Jordan, hey," Natasha said after Jordan mumbled a confused greeting. "I didn't catch you at a bad time, did I?"

"Um, no. I was just working on the herringbone."

"Ah. That's going to be really lovely."

"Yeah."

Natasha sighed heavily, buzzing the connection. "Listen, I'll get right to the point. I hate the way things went down."

"You and me both."

"I know. Your work is extraordinary, Jordan. I hope you know that."

Jordan sat back down on the bench, forehead resting on her palm. She was still getting used to this—compliments. Compliments she could actually accept.

You've convinced yourself you don't want it, because you think you don't deserve it.

She shook her head, trying to dislodge Astrid's words, even though she knew, deep down, Astrid was right.

Now, on the phone with Natasha Rojas, she sighed and simply told the truth. "I don't know what I know, honestly."

Natasha was silent for a beat. "Well, I'd really like to try and convince you."

Jordan straightened. "What do you mean? The show's a non-starter. Isn't it?"

"Oh, completely. And the higher-ups are pretty pissed. We lost a lot of money. A lot of time."

"I'm sorry," Jordan said, because she hadn't said it yet. To anyone.

"Me too," Natasha said. "Luckily, they pretty much do what I want these days."

"Wait, so . . . the show's back on?"

"Oh, no, honey. I'm good, but I'm not magic. Canceling your episode was my call."

"Right. Shit. Sorry."

"But I didn't call you so we could boo-hoo about best-laid plans for an hour."

Jordan huffed a laugh. "Fair enough."

"I called you to offer your renovation a feature in *Orchid*."

It took a second for Natasha's words to sink in, but even when they did, Jordan wasn't sure she'd heard correctly.

"*Orchid*," she said.

"Yes."

"As in your design magazine that I see on every grocery store checkout line I've ever been in."

Natasha laughed. "And every major city newsstand across the country."

"You want to feature the Everwood."

"I want to feature *you*, Jordan. We've got enough still shots for the before and during photos. All we'd need to do is come out for a shoot once the reno is finished. And, of course, an in-depth interview with you about the design, your inspiration."

Jordan stood up and glanced around the Lapis Room. The thought of seeing her design, her beloved family home in the glossy pages of *Orchid*—it was almost too much to process.

"I . . . I don't know what to say," she said.

"There's more."

Jordan sat back down. "Oh?"

"As I mentioned, the network execs weren't happy about the canceled episode."

"Yeah. I'm sor—"

"But," Natasha cut in, "I showed them your design plan for the Everwood. They lost their minds over it, Jordan."

"Like . . . in a good way?"

Natasha laughed. "Yes. In a good way. And they want to bring you in as a junior designer."

"They . . . I'm sorry, they what?"

"You heard me."

"What does that mean?"

"Well, at first, it basically means you do whatever they ask you to do. That might include consulting on various shows behind the scenes, but if they like what you bring to the table, you could be a featured designer on shows like *Housemates* and *Duel Design*, where there isn't one regular designer, but several who cycle through episodes."

"I'd . . . I'd be on TV?"

"Yeah, you'd be on TV. And a designer for the network. And, if you're as good as I think you are, it could all lead to your own show one day. Hell, you could be the next me, Jordan Everwood."

Jordan laughed at Natasha's teasing tone, but there was an echo of truth to her words.

"So what do you say?" Natasha asked.

Jordan stood up again and scrubbed a hand through her hair. Then she just left her fingers tangled in her locks, tugging a little, hoping the sting might jolt her back into reality.

But this was real.

Natasha was on the phone, offering her the opportunity of a lifetime.

Offering her a way to save the Everwood.

Offering her . . .

Jordan let her hand drop to her side. This was what she wanted. Natasha was offering Jordan what she *wanted*. She wanted the credit for this design. She wanted the world to know *she* did this, she made this happen. It felt like such a selfish thought, but she couldn't help herself. She wanted to build kitchen cabinets and bookshelves and coffee tables, but she wanted to design too. Rooms, apartments, whole houses. She wanted to transform the spaces where people lived and loved, just as she'd done with the Everwood.

And more than that, she deserved it.

Even if she made a mess of it all.

Even if she had no idea what she was doing.

Even if.

She deserved to be happy.

"Yes," Jordan said to Natasha now. "Yes to all of it."

JORDAN RAN DOWN the Everwood stairs, then bolted out the door and across the lawn to the cottage. In the kitchen, she found both Pru and Simon sitting at the table, eating turkey sandwiches and sipping iced herbal tea.

"Sweetie," Pru said, looking at her through royal-blue glasses, "are you all right?"

"I'm great. I'm amazing." She fell into the chair across from her brother. "Call Trish what's-her-name, Simon. Tell her we're not selling."

"What?" he asked. "Jordie, we have to."

Jordan shook her head, then told them about Natasha's phone call, about the opportunity for Jordan to design for the network. Pru started to gush, but Jordan cut her off, saving the most important news about the *Orchid* feature for last.

"It's not an episode on *Innside America*, but it's something," she said. "It's enough. Right?"

Pru beamed at her, tears shining in her eyes, but Simon frowned. Because of course he did.

"Jordie, this is amazing," he said without looking at her. "Really, I'm so proud of you. But I'm not sure it'll be enough to keep the Everwood up and running. We need a whole new business plan. We need a new manager, a new cook."

"So we make a new plan. We find a new manager. It can't be that hard," Jordan said. "There has to be a way."

Simon shook his head, but Pru reached across the table and took her hand. "We'll find a way. We've found a way for over a hundred years. We'll find a way now. You did it, sweetheart. I knew you could."

Jordan frowned at Pru, something in her tone giving her pause. "Did you . . . Grandma, did you know the design was mine?"

Pru sighed and sat back. "I suspected. I know you, and the design . . . it felt familiar, like family."

"Why didn't you say anything?"

"Maybe I should have." Pru picked up her tea and took a sip. "But I could tell you and Astrid meant something to each other, and part of me didn't want to interfere, because she made you happy. Also, I wanted to give Astrid a chance to do the right thing. And she did. In the end."

Jordan shook her head, eyes stinging. "Without even discussing it with me."

Pru reached across the table and squeezed her hand. "I know that hurts, honey. But love doesn't always think through the details. Sometimes, love just *does*."

That word—*love*—lodged itself in her throat. Love had nothing to do with her and Astrid. If it did . . . well. She'd be on her way to Astrid right now to share her news. She'd be *with* Astrid. And she wasn't.

Before Jordan could think on it a second longer, Simon pushed back from the table so suddenly, the plates and glasses rattled. He mumbled an apology and left the room.

"What's wrong with him?" Jordan asked.

Her grandmother took off her glasses, polishing them on her blue sweater. When she placed them back on her nose, she tented her fingers and smiled at Jordan. "He's a big brother."

Jordan frowned, then stood up and went looking for her twin.

SHE FOUND HIM on the front porch, leaning against the railing and gazing out at the overgrown rosebushes.

"What's up with you?" Jordan asked, settling next to him and nudging his shoulder.

He sighed and shook his head. "Sorry. I just needed a minute."

"For what? Simon, I know you're worried about Grandma and money stuff, but we'll figure it out. And I—"

"I know we will," he said, then he turned to face her. "I know *you* will."

She tilted her head at him.

"Jordan, I owe you an apology. A few apologies, in fact."

"Simon, you—"

"No, let me get this out." He stuffed his hands in his pockets. "I love you, Jordie. Probably more than any other person in my life. And after Meredith, I was so worried about you. I think . . . I think I just got used to worrying, you know? I forgot who you are, that you're this amazing, strong, capable person. I wanted to take care of you, so much so that I forgot to believe in you. I should've recognized the design as yours. Now that I know, it's so obviously *you*, but I couldn't see it before because I didn't think you could . . . fuck. I'm sorry, Jordie. Please know how sorry I am."

She blinked sudden tears away, but they just kept on springing into her eyes. "Simon. You . . ." She didn't know what to say. She couldn't say *It's okay*, because they both knew it wasn't. But neither was she angry. She was hurt, yeah, but mostly, she was grateful. She was so goddamn grateful for this moment, for a brother who loved her enough to care so much, even if he took it a little too far sometimes.

She looped her arms around his neck and pulled him close. "In your defense," she said into his shoulder, "I *was* a big fucking mess."

He laughed and held her tightly. Her twin. Her best friend.

"I'm proud of you, sister," he said. "I'm so proud of you."

She squeezed him one more time before letting him go. They both wiped at their faces, laughing at their matching red and watery eyes.

"So," he said once they'd recovered. "What are you going to do about Astrid?"

Jordan's smile slipped right off her face. "Nothing. There's nothing *to* do, Simon."

Because Astrid was right—Jordan *did* deserve every good thing. And maybe, as much as Jordan felt like her heart was going to tear itself to shreds at the thought, Astrid wasn't good for her.

Jordan deserved someone who wouldn't run away. She deserved someone who would talk through things, figure it out, give Jordan a chance to talk too.

Jordan deserved a great love.

She deserved a destiny.

And goddammit, she wasn't going to settle for anything less.

CHAPTER

THIRTY-FOUR

WEDNESDAY EVENING, ASTRID called an emergency coven meeting. They gathered at Claire and Delilah's, where the four of them were now huddled around the kitchen table, laptops and papers and pens spread across the wooden surface, along with cans of bubbly water and a barely touched bowl of popcorn.

Astrid had spent the last two days since she quit her job ignoring her mother's calls and making lists. She had a list for her financial situation—she had a good bit of savings, along with the money from her father that she couldn't access until she was thirty-five, so that didn't help much right now. She had a list of real estate agents who weren't in her mother's pocket—if she got a job quickly, she wouldn't have to sell her house, but more and more she was feeling like she wanted to sell it. Just start the hell over. And, of course, she had a list featuring possible career paths, which included anything and everything she could think of.

"Jesus god, if you get your real estate license and put a billboard with your Stepford wife smile up on I-5, that's it," Iris said, looking over the latter list. "I will cease to be your friend."

Astrid groaned and dropped her head into her hands. "I don't want to be a real estate agent."

"Then don't be one," Delilah said. She picked up a pen and scribbled the option off the list.

"Receptionist?" Claire asked, looking at another bulleted item. "Not that there's anything wrong with that, honey, but I don't think it would make you happy."

Astrid lifted her hands in defeat. "I need money, Claire. Being happy—"

"Is the whole point," Iris said. "That's why you quit your job. It's why we're sitting here. Not everyone gets that chance, and it's an incredibly privileged position to be in, my darling."

"You're right. I know you're right," Astrid said. She was lucky. She had a solid savings account and friends who would do anything for her.

"So what do you *want*, Astrid?" Iris asked.

She opened her mouth to beg off again—lucky or not, the question still scared the shit out of her—but Iris put up her hand to silence her.

"No. Full stop. If you could do anything, what would it be?"

A name flitted through her mind. A backyard with a hammock under the stars, calloused hands on her hips while she whipped up something in the kitchen. A rosebud mouth on her neck.

Astrid shook her head and focused on jobs. There was something there, way in the back of her mind and covered in cobwebs. But it was as far-fetched as Astrid herself becoming a Disney singer. "That might not be possible."

"So what?" Iris said. "It's a starting point."

Astrid sighed and looked over her list. Her cobwebbed dream wasn't written on here. She hadn't had the courage.

But she *was* brave enough. She'd told the truth about the Everwood design, even though it crushed her heart to do so. She'd confronted her mother. She'd quit her job. No, not her job. She'd quit her career. All for the tiny flare of hope in her chest that there was something more for her, something that would actually make her happy. Something that made her feel like herself, even when it was hard.

She picked up a pen and added another option to her list.

Claire, Iris, and Delilah all leaned in to read it.

Iris's head snapped up first, her eyes shining on Astrid's. "Yes. Hell yes."

Astrid winced, but a smile worked itself onto her mouth. "Yeah?"

"Yeah," Claire said, reaching out to grab her hand. "One hundred percent."

Delilah nodded. "I vaguely remember your cookies being pretty damn good."

Astrid exhaled and looked down at her writing.

Baking.

There it was in black and white. Her dream.

But dreams needed reality if they were to ever come true, and the reality was she had no training, no previous experience, and no capital to start her own business. She said as much to her friends.

"Okay, so we just need to find the right opportunity," Iris said. "Doesn't Wake Up make their own pastries?"

"I think so," Claire said.

"Let's check with them to see if they have an opening."

"And if they don't?" Astrid asked.

"We go to Winter Lake. Sotheby. Graydon," Iris said. "Wherever. That Sugar and Star place with the amazing scones an hour away. There has to be somewhere willing to give you a shot. All you'd have to do is bake a single cake for them and you'd be in."

Astrid grabbed Iris's hand and squeezed. This was terrifying. This was what she'd been afraid of for years, why she'd settled for the life her mother carved out for her. But it was also liberating. It was thrilling, to make these choices, to say what she wanted and actually try to go after it.

"Wait a sec," Iris said, yanking her hand from Astrid's and holding out her palms. "What about the Everwood?"

Astrid's stomach flip-flopped at the name. "What about it?"

"Iris," Delilah said, her voice tight.

Iris didn't heed whatever warning was there, though. She rarely did. "They're looking for a new cook and a baker since they're not selling because of Jordan's feature in *Orchid*, and oh, holy shit, I was not supposed to tell you that."

Iris winced. Claire rubbed her forehead, while Delilah just shook her head.

Astrid's flip-flopping stomach launched into full-on somersaults. "Jordan . . . Jordan got a feature in *Orchid*?"

Claire nodded. "It just happened today. Simon told Iris. We weren't going to tell you right away. You know, give you a few days to adjust to everything that's been going on."

Astrid nodded, her throat tight and aching. As she processed this new information, she tried to parse how she was feeling.

Jordan had landed an opportunity that Astrid would've killed for a few months ago. But she wasn't jealous. Not one bit. Instead, she felt like sobbing because she was so fucking happy for Jordan, and she wished she could tell her that. She wished she could pull her into her arms, hold her face in her hands, and tell her she was magic, that Astrid was proud of her.

But she couldn't.

Jordan had been through so much, and Astrid couldn't hurt her again. She couldn't risk it.

"It's not a bad option," Delilah said carefully.

Claire nodded. "It's pretty great, actually. With your business experience, you could probably turn that place around. Maybe even manage it, too, while you got your baking stuff in order, and—"

"I can't," Astrid said. "I doubt I'm the Everwoods' favorite person right now." Plus, being around Jordan without being *with* Jordan? She wasn't that brave.

"Have you tried talking to her?" Claire asked softly.

"No," Astrid said firmly. "I can't. I almost ruined her life, Claire. She deserves so much better."

"Why don't you let her be the judge of that?" Iris said.

Astrid shook her head, picking up her pen and tracing *Baking* over and over again on her list. She could feel her friends staring at her, but luckily, the front door opened, halting any further romantic plots from forming.

"I'm home!" Ruby's voice sounded from the entryway.

"Hey, Rabbit," Claire said when Ruby appeared. She pulled the girl into her arms and kissed the top of her head. "Have fun at Tess's?"

Ruby nodded and handed over a padded envelope covered in yellow smiley faces to Claire. "This was outside. Something from Grandma." She eyed the mess on the table. "What are you doing?"

"Just trying to convince Aunt Astrid to go after the woman she loves," Iris said.

"Iris!" Astrid said.

Iris just smirked at her.

"Wait . . ." Ruby said, looking at Astrid. "Aunt Astrid, you like girls?"

Astrid sat back and smiled weakly. "Yeah. I do. Well, one girl right now, but . . . yeah."

"Cool!" Ruby said, taking a handful of popcorn from the bowl and lobbing a piece in her mouth. "Me too."

Astrid's eyes went wide. "Really?"

Ruby nodded. "Yep. I think I might like *only* girls, but Delilah says I don't have to label it yet, you know? I'm only twelve."

Astrid's smile broadened. She adored this kid. "Yeah. I do know. That's great, Rubes."

Ruby grinned, then ambled off to her room to do some home-work. Astrid leaned across the table toward Claire. "When did *that* happen?"

Claire smiled, and Delilah took her hand. "Last week? She came home all starry-eyed, talking about this new girl in her class, and then she just sort of . . . came out to us. I had my suspicions, so it was honestly a relief."

"We're thrilled," Delilah said. "But, you know, the world can be pretty cruel, so we're talking her through it."

"Ruby is badass," Iris said. "And she has badass adults in her life. She'll be fine."

"Turns out, every single one of us is extremely queer," Delilah said, tossing the subtlest of winks at her stepsister.

"Thank the goddess," Iris said, and Astrid smiled.

She wasn't exactly sure what label fit her the best quite yet. *Bisexual* felt right, but for now, she was happy to simply know who she was and be with her friends who understood.

Claire laughed as she opened the package from her mother. She took out a small box featuring an illustration of a Black woman in a white dress and red robe holding out a wand. "Oh god, it's another Tarot deck. I've got about ten of these already."

Claire's mom, Katherine, traveled a lot with her husband and was very into Tarot, along with oracles, crystals, and herbs. She was constantly sending Claire something new to try, books or decks she thought the bookstore could stock.

"Any cards with apples on them in here?" Delilah asked, leaning over and pressing a kiss to Claire's neck. Claire blushed and actually giggled.

"Oh, inside jokes between lovers are my fave," Iris deadpanned, and Claire stuck out her tongue.

"This one might be cool, though," Delilah said, taking the box from Claire and reading the back. "Looks pretty diverse—not everyone is white, and there are all women or nonbinary people on the cards."

"Nice," Iris said, grabbing the box to take a look. She opened it up, and out spilled a bevy of brightly colored cards.

Cards that looked vaguely familiar.

"Hang on," Astrid said, picking up a few and inspecting them closely. They were all illustrated, simple, but something about the drawings, the colors, scratched at the back of Astrid's brain. Where had she—

Jordan. In the Andromeda theater. Jordan had shown her a card in the exact same style and talked about how she'd drawn that same card for months.

The Two of Cups.

The soul mates card.

"How does this work?" Astrid asked, taking the little guidebook and flipping through it for some sort of directions.

"What, you want your cards read now?" Iris asked.

"Just tell me how it works." Astrid's voice was low but shaky, and her friends noticed. Suddenly, she could feel her pulse everywhere.

"Okay, sweetie," Claire said. She took the cards from Astrid and shuffled them, explaining how she should ask an open-ended question as she did so. Then, she cut the cards into three stacks, put them back together, and drew the top card.

A Four of Wands.

Iris took the guidebook from Astrid. "This card means celebration, prosperity, the gathering of kindred souls." She grinned at her friends, then looked back at the book. "Could also mean marriage."

Claire choked and glanced at Delilah, who simply smirked.

"Just saying," Iris said.

"Want to try it?" Claire asked, clearing her throat and looking at Astrid.

Astrid nodded. She had no clue why, but it had to mean something, didn't it? That she was in Claire's house at the exact moment this package arrived, that it just happened to contain the exact Tarot deck that Jordan used? Astrid didn't believe in this kind of thing—she was practical to a fault, type A, believed your choices were your own.

Or your mother's, as the case may be.

And she still believed all that.

But what if . . .

"Yeah," she said. "I want to try it."

Claire handed her the cards, instructing her to knock on the deck once to clear the last reading. Then Astrid held the cards in both hands, trying to think of an open-ended question.

Will my mother hate me forever?

Did I do the right thing?

What do I need to know right now?

She settled on that last one, which felt like exactly the right mix of practical and woo-woo.

"Remember, it's not predictive," Claire said. "Tarot is just supposed to help you understand what's already in your heart, choices you're facing, stuff like that."

"When did you become such an expert?" Iris asked.

Claire waved a hand. "Since my mother insists on reading my cards—and Ruby's and Delilah's—every time she comes into town."

Astrid shuffled and cut the deck into three stacks, put them back together—*instinctively*, Claire had said—and then she froze. She stared down at the top card, fingers resting on the glossy blue surface. Maybe this was silly. Maybe this was—

She flipped over the card before she could finish the thought.

There, shining up at her in all its ridiculous, impossible glory, was the Two of Cups.

CHAPTER
THIRTY-FIVE

JORDAN LAY IN bed, clutching her phone in her hands. It was well past midnight, and the cottage was quiet.

Too quiet.

The kind of quiet that made one make very stupid decisions.

She should've given her phone to Simon, told him that under no circumstances was she allowed to have it back for, oh, the next month. But like every heartbroken person, a little masochism lingered under her skin, and she couldn't seem to stop waiting for Astrid's name to pop onto her screen again.

The first call had come around nine p.m. Jordan was brushing her teeth and heard her phone buzzing on her nightstand, so naturally, she vaulted herself over the obstacle course of junk all over her bedroom floor—scaring the shit out of her poor cat in the process—and reached her phone just in time to see a missed call notification from **Semi-Decent Human Who Wants to Kiss You Again**.

She stared at the screen, toothpaste dripping from her mouth and onto her shirt, waiting for a voice mail to ping into her mailbox.

It didn't.

But Astrid did call again thirty minutes later.

This time, Jordan was ready for it. She'd been sitting at her desk, laptop open to her design program, but she only pretended to work on some ideas. Really, her mind was whirling, visualizing how she'd answer the phone calmly, and then tell Astrid in no uncertain terms that she didn't want to talk to Astrid ever again.

It was a good plan.

But when her phone finally buzzed, Astrid's name appearing, Jordan couldn't do it.

She couldn't answer the call. If she did . . . then what? She doubted she'd actually have the strength to tell the woman she was madly in love with to fuck off, and god knew what would happen to her already bruised heart if she listened to whatever Astrid wanted to say.

So, ignoring and denying was really the only way to go here.

Now, though, Jordan couldn't slow her brain down enough to sleep. She couldn't stop hoping Astrid would call again, pursue Jordan until Jordan couldn't ignore or deny anything ever again.

But that wasn't Astrid's style.

Jordan knew that.

She rolled over, Catra purring happily and tucked against her chest, and resolved to think of other things. She had a reno to finish, a swanky magazine feature to prepare for, a possible career at a major design network on the horizon. She didn't need Astrid. She didn't need any sort of romance right now. It was too messy, too hard, and she'd just end up—

Her phone interrupted her thoughts.

She snatched it up, heart already halfway into her throat. So much for her steely resolve.

But it wasn't Astrid.

It was Meredith.

Jordan sighed and pressed the phone against her forehead, the vibrations rattling her thoughts even more. Since Meredith's life-exploding email to Natasha Rojas a week ago, she had called, texted, or emailed at least once a day. Lately, she'd taken to trying Jordan long past any normal time human beings spoke on the phone.

Jordan was tired of seeing her ex's name on her screen . . . but she wasn't angry. She knew she should be—Meredith had crossed every line in the book by contacting Natasha, but Jordan just didn't have the energy to fan the emotion. In fact, she felt very little when it came to Meredith lately.

Before she could think better of it, she hit the green button.

"What?" she said.

"Jo? Oh my god, you actually answered."

"Yeah, well, I figured best get this over with."

Meredith sighed into the phone. "Look. I'm sorry. I didn't realize they'd cancel the show."

"Been talking to Simon, have you?"

"Your grandmother, actually. She knows I care about you."

"Care?" Jordan couldn't believe this woman. "Meredith, these are not the actions of a person who *cares* about someone else."

"You created that design, Jo, and you—"

"I'm not talking about the inn."

There was a beat of silence, and Jordan knew if she didn't say all this now, she might never say it at all. And she needed to. She needed Meredith to understand *why* her leaving had crushed her.

And then she needed to say goodbye.

"You left me," Jordan said.

"Jo, I—"

"You left me because you weren't in love with me, and I get that, Meredith. I actually, really, really get that. And fuck, you know what? You were right that we weren't the best fit for each other. You were right that we needed to separate, that there was something more out there for us. But what you don't seem to understand is that we were partners. *Partners*, Meredith. And you fucking made that final decision for me. Not a word about your doubts in all the years we were married, nothing while you were sick, and then you just walk out the door the second you were in remission. And that's what I'm pissed about. That's what hurts the most, that you didn't think enough of me—*care* enough about me—to have a conversation. Then again, I guess that's proof enough that it wasn't love, right?"

Her throat tightened on her last words, and someone other than Meredith floated into her mind. A shaggy-haired pain in the ass, but she shoved the image away.

"You're right," Meredith said after a beat of silence. "God, you're right, Jordan. I should've talked to you first. I just . . . I didn't think . . . fuck. Honestly? I was worried you wouldn't be able to handle it. I was scared that you'd say all the right things, and I'd stay, and then I'd be unhappy and unable to make you happy, and the cycle would just repeat itself over and over."

Jordan rubbed her forehead. There was some truth swirling through Meredith's words, but it still hurt to hear that her own wife didn't think she was strong enough.

"Well," Jordan said, "I guess we'll never know."

"I'm sorry, Jo. Jordan. I'm really sorry."

Jordan nodded, even though Meredith couldn't see her. "Okay."

And, in the end, that's all there was to say. Jordan asked for some time, for Meredith to give her some space, and Meredith agreed to do so.

Then they said goodbye.

Jordan dropped the phone on her chest and pulled Catra closer. Tears welled in her eyes, and she let them fall into her hair. They felt good, a release she'd been waiting to feel for the last year.

Being happy was about more than love and romance. It was about more than a vampire-toothed bombshell who stormed into her world in a flurry of coffee and anger and changed her entire life. Happiness was about purpose, it was about self-awareness and acceptance. So that's what Jordan would focus on. That's what Jordan—

Plink.

Her thoughts froze, and Catra stiffened in her arms, lifting her head with her ears perked up toward the sound coming from the window.

Plink.

"What is that, girl?" Jordan asked Catra.

The cat slinked off the mattress and hid under the bed.

"My hero," Jordan grumbled as she tossed the covers back and walked toward the window, pulling back her curtains to peer outside. The moon was full and cast a silvery glow over the grass, but she didn't see much of anything past the rosebush blocking half her view.

Plink.

This time, Jordan reared back as what had to have been a pebble smacked against the glass.

"What the hell?"

She unlocked the window, but no matter how hard she tugged, the damn thing wouldn't budge. God only knew the last time it had been opened.

Plink.

She sighed, grabbed her *Y'all Means All* sweatshirt from the end of the bed and shoved it over her tank top and sleep shorts, stuffed her feet into her boots, and headed toward the kitchen's back door. She grabbed a knife out of the block by the stove before opening the door as quietly as possible. She certainly didn't need Simon or her grandmother waking up and freaking out about what was probably nothing but a bug zapping against the window.

Outside, the air was cool, the grass already dewy. She crept along the side of the house until she reached her bedroom window, but once she got there, she didn't see anything. She didn't hear anything, either, other than the slight rustle of rosebush leaves in the summer breeze, a soft *shh* sound that must've been her own feet over the grass.

She'd just turned around, ready to go back into the house, when she saw it.

A small rectangle lying on the grass, the moon's light reflecting off the surface, turning it bright and silver.

She walked over to the spot and picked up the item—a card—and angled it into the light so she could see it clearly. It took her a second to register what it was.

A Tarot card. But not just any Tarot card.

A Two of Cups.

She'd never seen this one before—the art was bohemian in style, two hands intertwined and facing downward, colors pouring off their joining hands and into two golden bowls. She glanced up, confused as all hell as to who could've left this here. She was about to call out, when she saw the second card.

It was about fifteen feet away, lying in front of her workshop. She ran to pick it up and was greeted by another Two of Cups. This one was a black-and-white sketch, the only color from the red petals of two roses crossed over two goblets. She stared at it, her breathing suddenly so hard and fast, she started to feel dizzy. She tucked this card with the first, then scanned for any sign of who—

There.

About twenty feet away from her workshop door, in the direction of the inn, was a third card. Her legs felt like water, her fingertips fizzing with too much oxygen as she picked up another Two of Cups, this one with two women's faces in profile, stars dappling the background.

Jordan's mouth was dry. She was shaking, and something that felt very much like tears clouded into her chest. She dropped her knife in the grass and gazed up at the inn.

A light was on in the Lapis Room. Or, at least, some kind of light.

It was amber-colored, soft and flickering, but she kept walking, heart crashing like a cymbal against her ribs.

On the front porch steps, she found a fourth Two of Cups—all white except for a delicate charcoal illustration. When she pushed open the inn's front door, which was disturbingly unlocked, she turned on her phone's flashlight and found a fifth Two of Cups in the foyer, a sixth halfway up the staircase, a seventh in the hallway, and an eighth right outside the Lapis Room.

She scooped this latest one into her hands—a watercolor illustration of two lovers entwined on a misty beach—and joined it with the others. The barest glow of what had to be candlelight flickered from the space underneath the Lapis Room door.

She placed her hands on the refinished wood—closed her eyes, breathed—and pushed.

INSIDE, JORDAN TURNED off her phone's light. She didn't need it, as there were at least ten candles illuminating the room, all various shapes and colors, some in jars, some dripping wax onto their holders.

And in the very center of the room stood Astrid Parker.

Jordan knew she'd be here. Maybe she even knew after picking up that first Two of Cups, but she was scared to trust it.

She was scared to trust it now, like this was all some dream or hallucination.

But shit, Astrid looked real. She also looked gorgeous, dressed simply in a pair of dark jeans and a heather-gray T-shirt, her hair shaggy, bangs just brushing her lashes. Her eyes were bright, candlelight turning them almost amber—she didn't look nearly as wraithlike as she had the last time Jordan had seen her.

She looked different somehow. Less haunted.

And she was staring at Jordan with a card in her hands.

"Hello," she said, her voice soft and a little raspy.

"Um . . . hi," Jordan said. She tried to breathe normally, but she was huffing and puffing as if she'd just run a marathon.

"Do . . . do you need some water?" Astrid asked, canting her head.

Jordan laughed. "I mean, if you've got it. Some lady just sent me on a wild Tarot card chase in the middle of the night."

"Sounds weird," Astrid said, smiling as she turned and dug a bottle of water out of her bag. "Sorry it's not cold."

Jordan waved her hand, then gulped the water down her parched throat. She was grateful for the emotional reprieve, a second to get her head on straight. She drained the bottle and set it on the floor, then waited for Astrid to say something . . . anything.

"Are you really going to make me start this conversation?" she finally asked.

"Shit, no, I'm sorry," Astrid said, taking a step forward. "I just wanted to give you a minute . . . to make sure you really want to be here."

Jordan lifted her chin, trying to exude more nonchalance than she felt. Why, she wasn't quite sure, but it seemed the safer route. "I haven't decided yet."

Astrid nodded. "That's fair."

Jordan didn't say anything to that. She wasn't going to give anything else. She couldn't.

Astrid took a deep breath, took another step toward Jordan. "I had this whole speech planned," she said. Her smile was wobbly, her voice thick. "But now that you're here, I . . ."

Without her permission, Jordan's feet moved her forward. "You're what?"

Astrid swallowed hard, looked at the card in her hand.

"You're what, Astrid?" Jordan said again, more firmly this time, even though her insides felt as though they were melting.

"I'm scared," Astrid finally said. She met Jordan's gaze. "Earlier tonight, I was at Claire's, thinking through my next steps. And her mom sent her this Tarot deck in the mail. *Your* Tarot deck. The same one you showed me at the Andromeda. And I just . . . it felt like some sort of sign, you know? And so I drew a card and I got this."

She turned the card around in her hands. Jordan knew what it would be before she saw the familiar colors, the two women facing each other, the golden cups in their hands.

"Holy shit," Jordan whispered.

"Yeah," Astrid said, feet moving closer. "I don't believe in this kind of stuff. I never have, but I couldn't . . . I didn't *want* to ignore this. So I called you, but you didn't answer, and then I knew you deserved so much more than just me freaking out on the phone about a Tarot card."

"I do?"

Astrid nodded. "You deserve a grand gesture."

Jordan's stomach fluttered, a million wings spreading and taking flight. "Is that what this is, Astrid? Are you grand-gesturing me?"

Astrid laughed. Tears shone in her eyes, spilled over, but she didn't wipe them away. "I am."

Another step. The space between them was mere inches now, and Jordan didn't move away. Couldn't. Didn't fucking want to. Astrid's eyes were locked on hers, cementing her into place.

"I love you, Jordan Everwood," Astrid said. "That's what it comes down to. I thought I didn't deserve you, that you deserved better, and that still might be true. I put you through hell these last few weeks. I used you. Even if I didn't really understand what I was doing at the time, I still used you. And I'm so, so sorry. After everything. If you don't feel the same, I'll understand, but I had to tell you. I had to tell you that I *want* you, more than I've ever wanted anything in my whole life. And it might sound silly or childish, but I don't care. *You* are my destiny, Jordan. Not because of a card or the stars or some sort of magic, but because I choose you. And I—"

But Jordan didn't let her finish. She bridged the space between them and took Astrid's face in her hands, cutting off her words with a kiss. And not a soft kiss either—a wild, frantic, tongues-and-teeth, hands-raking-through-hair kind of kiss. A kiss that communicated a hundred words Jordan couldn't possibly say coherently right now.

Astrid dropped that fated Two of Cups and wrapped her arms around Jordan's waist, hands dipping under her sweatshirt and tank top, nails dragging down the bare skin of her back. She moaned into Jordan's mouth, the sound so close to a sob, Jordan kissed her harder, held her tighter. She could feel the tears on Astrid's cheeks, and she swiped them away with her thumbs.

Eventually, their kiss grew gentler, softer, and soon they were simply standing in the middle of a half-finished room, their arms wrapped around each other, foreheads touching.

"Would it be a cliché to say that you had me at hello?" Jordan whispered.

Astrid laughed. "I don't care if it is a cliché. Tell me anyway."

"You had me at hello," Jordan said, pressing a kiss to her neck and spinning them around. Astrid laughed—her real laugh, her real smile—and Jordan had never heard such a beautiful sound in her life.

"Okay, I have to ask," Jordan said, once they stopped twirling. "Where the hell did you get all these Tarot cards?"

Astrid grinned. "Claire had a lot of decks on hand. She and Iris and Delilah helped me put all this together. Placing the cards outside, the candles."

"And throwing rocks at my window?"

Astrid covered her mouth with her hands, speaking through her fingers. "Sorry. That was Iris. She also might've been hiding in your rosebush when you came outside."

Jordan laughed. "Holy shit, Parker. This was quite the production."

Astrid's expression went serious. "You deserve it."

"You keep saying that."

"Because it's true. I want to make sure you know that."

"I do," Jordan said, pressing her forehead to Astrid's again, her throat going tight with emotion. "I finally do."

Astrid tipped her chin up and had just set her mouth on Jordan's when the Lapis Room door slammed shut.

Both women startled, clinging to each other and watching as the door . . . creaked open again.

Astrid just laughed. "It looks like Alice Everwood agrees."

CHAPTER

THIRTY-SIX

AFTER JORDAN PACKED a bag and left a note for her brother and grandmother on the kitchen counter, Astrid took her home.

She'd barely locked the door behind them before they were tearing off each other's clothes. They didn't make it to the bedroom either. Instead, Astrid pulled them to the couch, bras and underwear falling to the floor. She didn't want tongues or fingers. She needed to feel Jordan's skin on hers, Jordan's mouth against her mouth, breathing each other's air and words.

So she laid Jordan down and straddled her, aligning every part of their bodies.

"Fuck," Jordan gasped when their pussies met. She sank her hand in Astrid's hair, tugged the already messy strands to the point that Astrid cried out too, the mix of that gentle sting with pleasure like nothing Astrid had ever felt before. She pumped her hips against Jordan's, desperate for contact, for sensation, rubbing their clits together until they both came in a string of swears, fingernails digging into skin, mouths dragging over throats and shoulders.

She collapsed against Jordan's chest, her own lungs heaving, her limbs filled with that perfect, postorgasmic weight.

"Shit," Jordan said, her breath ragged.

"Yeah," Astrid said.

Jordan lifted Astrid's chin and met her eyes, gazing at her for so long, Astrid started to squirm.

"Are you okay?" Astrid asked.

Jordan nodded, smiled. "I love you too. I didn't say it back at the inn."

"You don't have to—"

"It's true."

Astrid let those words wrap around her heart. She let them be true. She let them *feel* true. Then she kissed the woman she loved. The woman who loved her. She kissed her on that couch, then she kissed her in the bedroom, in the shower, on the back porch. She kissed her until the sun started to peek through the curtains, and they finally fell asleep.

———

"HEY, I HAVE something for you," Jordan said late the next morning.

They were sitting at the kitchen table while rain sluiced down the window, a fresh batch of apple cider muffins cooling between them, as they'd slept right through breakfast.

Astrid looked at Jordan over her coffee cup. "What's that?"

Jordan wrinkled her nose, like she did when she was feeling shy about something. It was so damn cute, Astrid very nearly swiped everything off the table and took her again right there.

"It's . . . well, I ordered it for you before . . ."

Astrid nodded. She knew what *before* was. They'd spent half the night, in between sex and more sex, hashing out what had happened with the inn, how they both felt about it. Astrid shared with Jordan everything she'd done since then—quitting her job, essentially breaking up with her mother, at least for the time being. She told Jordan about her lists, about how she wanted to try baking for a living.

And Jordan told Astrid about Natasha's phone call, her offer regarding *Orchid*, the network. Finally hearing the news for herself from Jordan, Astrid searched herself for any jealousy or bitterness, but it still wasn't there. She just felt happy. Proud. And she told Jordan so with her words . . . and then with a few actions that left Jordan gasping her name.

Now, Jordan got up and walked into the living room, which was as far as her bag had made it last night. She rifled through the contents before finally bringing out a small white box. She made her way back over to Astrid, scooting her chair closer. She placed the box in front of her.

Astrid's eyes went wide. "Um, what—"

"It's not a ring," Jordan said, her expression completely serious. "I know the joke about lesbians bringing a U-Haul to the second date, and that's not what this is."

Astrid laughed. "Oh my god, that is not what I thought."

"Sure you didn't."

"I didn't!"

Jordan leaned in and kissed her. "Just open it."

Astrid shook her hair out of her face and took the box in her hands, lifting the lid. There, on a little bed of cotton, sat a gold necklace. The chain was delicate, as was the small charm, which was—

Astrid gasped as she recognized that double wishbone shape, her eyes darting to Jordan's.

Jordan just grinned.

"It's a clit necklace," Astrid said.

Jordan nodded, then rushed to explain. "I wanted to get you something after the whole thing with your mom on the back porch, something that made you feel strong. I saw this on Etsy and thought of you."

"You . . . thought of me when you saw a clit necklace?"

Jordan laughed. "Not like that."

Astrid lifted her brows.

"Okay, yes, when I think of you, I want to bang your brains out, but that's not why I got you the necklace."

Astrid grinned and tangled her free hand into Jordan's hair, then let her fingers rest on the back of her neck.

"You admired Natasha for being bold enough to wear something like this," Jordan went on, "and I wanted you to feel that bold. I wanted to get you something that reminded you that you're brave and capable and you can choose yourself, you can prioritize what *you* want, and you deserve to be loved no matter what those priorities end up being."

Astrid released a breath, then pulled Jordan closer until their foreheads met. God, she was so gone on this woman. She was amazed by her more and more with each passing second.

"I love it," Astrid said, then sat up to take the necklace from the box. "It's perfect."

"You don't have to wear it. I know it's a little edgy."

"I can be edgy," Astrid said, circling it around her neck and then turning so Jordan could hook the clasp. The charm fell right below the hollow of her throat.

Jordan laughed, but then grabbed Astrid's legs and turned her back around, sliding her hands up Astrid's thighs. "You can be anything you fucking want to be."

And Astrid believed her.

THE DOORBELL RANG at five o'clock that evening. Astrid assumed it was probably her friends, though Claire had promised to try and keep Iris at bay for a few days to give Astrid and Jordan some time together. Still, as Astrid walked toward the door in a tank top and yoga pants, she found she didn't mind the intrusion. She had a lot to tell her friends, and now was as good a time as any.

And god, Iris would love her clit necklace. Astrid was pretty positive they'd all have matching charms by the start of summer. She smiled at the thought but felt her expression go flat as she opened the door and came face-to-face with her mother.

Isabel Parker-Green looked rough. Well, as rough as Isabel could look, which meant a little less makeup, her hair a little duller than normal, and she was wearing linen pants and a matching top as opposed to her normal silks. Still, as she met Astrid's gaze, a black umbrella above her head, her eyes weren't quite as sharp as they usually were, always searching for flaws. No, this was an expression Astrid wasn't sure she'd ever seen before. She couldn't even put a name to it.

For the past several days, Astrid had been ignoring her mother's calls, texts, and emails. She knew they'd have to talk eventually, but she needed time to figure her own self out before she invited Isabel back into the mix again.

"Mother," she started, but then her throat seized up, a sudden swell of emotion, maybe even fear. She wanted to call out for Jordan, but her girlfriend had gone out to pick up their dinner. It was just as well. Besides, Astrid could handle this on her own.

She straightened her clit necklace and took a breath.

"I'm not ready to talk, Mother," she said. Her voice only wobbled a little.

"I know you're not," Isabel said. Her voice was soft but came out a little stilted, like her usual stoicism was fighting against something gentler.

"Then why are you here?" Astrid asked.

Isabel's knuckles whitened on her umbrella, the most un-poised Astrid had ever seen her. "I just wanted you to know that I'm here.

When you're ready, I'd like to ta—" She shook her head and took a deep breath. "When you're ready to talk, I'd like to listen."

Astrid's eyes went wide. Her mother was a horrible listener. Astrid couldn't think of a single moment in her life when she'd felt heard.

And maybe her mother had finally realized it.

"Okay," Astrid said. "I'll let you know."

Isabel nodded, straightened her pocketbook on her shoulder with her free hand, and turned to go.

She came face to face with Jordan Everwood.

Astrid held her breath, but she also took a step forward. No way in hell was Astrid going to let her mother say one derogatory thing to Jordan. Not today, not ever.

The other two women both froze, a bag of sushi dangling from Jordan's elbow and Astrid's clear umbrella over her head, rain plinking onto the surface.

"Um, hi," she said.

Isabel rolled her shoulders back. "Hello, Jordan," she said. "It's . . . it's nice to see you again."

Jordan's brow soared into her hair, and she caught Astrid's eye over Isabel's shoulder.

"I saw your work for your family's inn," Isabel said. "It's lovely. Truly."

"Oh," Jordan said, blinking. "Thank you."

And with that, Isabel slid past her, got into her BMW, and drove away.

"Holy shit, did I just get a compliment from Isabel Parker-Green?" Jordan asked, walking up to Astrid. Once under the porch's covering, she closed the umbrella and set it against the house.

"I think you did. Not that you need it."

"Oh no, of course not." Jordan made a *psh* sound and waved a hand, making Astrid laugh. "Seriously, though. You okay?"

Astrid didn't answer right away. Honestly, she felt a little raw and exhausted, those few words with Isabel completely sapping her of all energy. But her mother was . . . her mother. A part of Astrid would always be desperate for approval, for love. She didn't think that was wrong, for a daughter to want that from her own parent, especially one who raised Astrid all alone. She wanted Isabel in her life.

But for once, Astrid was going to do something on her terms, and Isabel knew it. That knowledge made her feel strong.

She nodded, then tapped her chest. "Maybe it's the power of the clit necklace, but yeah. I think I am. I feel sort of . . . badass."

Jordan laughed, hooking an arm around Astrid's waist and pulling her in for a kiss. "Astrid Parker, you are the biggest badass I know."

CHAPTER THIRTY-SEVEN

TWO MONTHS LATER

THE EVERWOOD INN glowed. Soft amber sconces lit every hallway, every room, and strategically placed candles made all the glasses of champagne in the room glitter. A very queer band Astrid had found in Portland called the Katies played in the library, guitars and mandolins crooning in a perfect Brandi Carlile sort of style.

Astrid Parker stood by a sage bookshelf packed with all manner of romances and books most definitely *not* penned by dead white men. She sipped her champagne and watched as the crowd—which was significant, people coming from as far as New York City to celebrate the grand reopening of the Everwood Inn—fussed and fawned over her girlfriend.

Jordan looked amazing. She always did, but tonight, dressed in a tailored black suit, white dress shirt open at the neck, her ruby-red lipstick perfectly in place, her golden-brown hair swooping over her forehead, Astrid's breath caught every time she caught a glimpse of her.

"So she's a total rock star," Iris said from next to Astrid, tipping her glass toward Jordan, who was gliding through the crowd with

Natasha Rojas, hands in her pockets, stance wide and confident each time they stopped to talk to someone who wanted to meet the designer.

"Yeah," Astrid said. "She really is."

The *Orchid* piece featuring the astonishing and groundbreaking transformation of the Everwood Inn had just been released earlier that week. A month ago, when Natasha had been in town with her *Orchid* photographer and writer for the final shoot of the recently finished inn, she'd given them the piece's release date, so of course, Astrid knew the perfect time to host a reopening party would be soon after, capitalizing on the buzz the magazine feature created in the design world.

And she'd been right.

Since taking over management of the Everwood Inn five weeks ago, Astrid had worked hard to prepare for an onslaught of business. It was a guess, but it was an educated guess, and she assured Pru and Simon that the money they were investing in linens, a new computer for the concierge area, and new software to manage online reservations and payroll would all be worth it.

Now, a mere three weeks after the *Orchid* feature released, they were booked solid for the next three months.

Astrid had also spent a lot of time in the kitchen. While the array of muffins, cakes, and scones she and Jordan had brought with them during their initial meeting with Pru and Simon had convinced the Everwoods she could handle the baking, cooking was a very different thing, so they'd also hired a chef—a young Black woman named Rhea who'd studied at a culinary school in Seattle—and Astrid was excited about the partnership. She knew she could learn a lot from Rhea, who was both organized and talented. Astrid had never tasted anything in her life as delicious as the woman's spinach and rosemary frittatas.

As for housekeeping, they'd kept on Sarah, who'd been working at the Everwood for about a decade before the reno and was thrilled about all the changes.

"This place is completely gorgeous," Claire said as she and Delilah joined Astrid and Iris, their own glasses sparkling in the light. "We're totally going to book a night here, aren't we, babe?"

"Hmm," Delilah said, nodding as she swallowed a mouthful of champagne. "Honestly, the idea of Astrid bringing me some pillows is too good to pass up."

Astrid smacked Delilah's arm, but she was smiling. She'd happily bring Delilah a pillow. She'd turn down her bed too, leave a mint on the cool sheets. She'd do it all and love every second of it. She adored being here, in the Everwood's cozy hallways and rooms. She didn't think she could love a place more. Even when the job got tedious— working on budgets or placing orders for the little soaps and a variety of shampoos for different hair types they stocked in each bathroom— she knew this was where she belonged right now.

The Everwood made her happy, plain and simple.

She spotted her mother in the crowd, elegant as always in an ivory pantsuit. About a month ago, Astrid had finally called her mother to talk. She didn't go to Wisteria House, but asked Isabel to meet her at Wake Up—neutral ground—where she proceeded to tell her mother how she felt, everything that led up to her quitting Bright Designs.

And her mother listened.

At certain moments throughout the conversation, Isabel had looked horrified. She'd also looked sad, confused, and hopeful. She hadn't said much in response, but Astrid simply needed her mother to hear her, and she believed Isabel had. Two weeks later, they met again for coffee, where they talked about Astrid's new job and how Isabel was putting Bright Designs up for sale.

It was slow, sometimes uncomfortable work, but Astrid was willing to do it. More surprisingly, she knew Isabel was too, and that was all that mattered right now.

From across the room, she caught Jordan's eye. Her girlfriend winked at her, sending Astrid's stomach fluttering like a preteen. She smiled and bit her bottom lip, and apparently that was enough to cause Jordan to make her excuses to Natasha and head toward Astrid.

"You two are gross," Iris said, witnessing the whole exchange.

"Oh, you love it," Astrid said.

"Love what?" Jordan said when she arrived. She wrapped an arm around Astrid's waist and gave her a quick kiss.

"Us," Astrid said, leaning into Jordan. "We're breathtakingly gorgeous together, you know."

"Oh, are we?" Jordan said, smiling at her.

Astrid nodded, her grin impossible to prevent.

"Gag," Iris said.

"You're just saying that because you're not dating anyone right now," Claire said. "Are you jealous?"

"I most certainly am not," Iris said, taking a sip of her drink and staring out at the crowd. "I've given up dating, thanks very much."

Astrid glanced at Claire and Delilah. Iris had been oddly silent on the romance front ever since Jillian's betrayal a couple months ago.

"Taking a break is totally fine," Delilah said.

Iris didn't say anything in response. Instead, she spotted Simon across the vestibule at the buffet table set up in the dining room. She squeezed Jordan's shoulder and pressed a kiss to Astrid's cheek, then made her way over to him. They'd been spending a lot of time together lately, Iris and Simon, though she swore they were just friends. Plus, Simon had started dating Emery from *Innside America* a few weeks ago, right after they'd come with Natasha for the final *Orchid* shoot.

"We're going to walk around a bit," Claire said, tangling her fingers with Delilah's and giving Astrid a kiss on the cheek.

Astrid nodded, then pulled Jordan into a somewhat shadowy corner by the fireplace.

"Alone at last," she said, kissing her girlfriend's neck. Then she looked around the bustling room. "Sort of."

Jordan tugged Astrid closer. "Just a few more hours, and then I'll have my wicked way with you."

"Well, I *am* wearing my lucky dress."

Jordan laughed and pulled back enough to look Astrid up and down. She was wearing her ivory pencil dress, the very one Jordan had spilled coffee all over during their first fateful meeting. Her clit necklace, gleaming from the hollow of her throat, was the only jewelry she wore, and instead of black heels, she had on a pair of absolutely killer cherry-red stilettos.

She lifted Astrid's arm and spun her around. "I'm the lucky one— have you seen your ass in this dress?"

Astrid giggled. "I have, actually."

Jordan whistled, then pulled Astrid close again as the Katies started up a slower song. Astrid looped her arms around Jordan's neck, and they started swaying to the mellow rhythm of a mandolin.

"No one else is dancing," Astrid whispered.

"I don't care," Jordan said, spinning her around. They were attracting some glances, most of them smiling.

"I don't either," Astrid said, smiling against Jordan's hair as she realized it was one hundred percent true.

"God, we must be in love or something."

"It's like it's fate."

"Astrid Parker, are you saying that you're my destiny?"

Astrid's eyes went to a piece of art on the wall by the fireplace.

Settled in between off-white matting and surrounded by a square, sage-green frame, were nine Tarot cards.

Nine Two of Cups.

She smiled and kissed Jordan softly on the mouth. "That's exactly what I'm saying, Jordan Everwood."

ACKNOWLEDGMENTS

First and foremost, thank you to everyone who read and reviewed and talked about *Delilah Green Doesn't Care*. I have so enjoyed connecting with readers over the first Bright Falls book, and I sincerely hope Astrid's story did not disappoint. This one was a very personal one for me, and I'm so honored to share it with you.

As always, none of this would be possible without Rebecca Podos, my incredible agent and friend. Their insight and compassion and fierceness will never cease to amaze me. Thank you to my editor, Angela Kim, whose keen eye helped shape this book into exactly the story it needed to be—I'd still be swimming in a vast ocean of over-writing without you!

Thank you to the whole team at Berkley, including Katie Anderson, Fareeda Bullert, Elisha Katz, Tina Joell, and Beth Partin. Endless thanks to Leni Kauffman, whose cover illustration for Astrid and Jordan is like something right out of my dreams.

Thank you to my dear friends, Meryl, Emma, and Zabe, whose humor, wisdom, and insight help every step of the way in this process. Courtney Kae, thanks for reading *Astrid* early on and offering excellent feedback that helped Astrid and Jordan find each other in even more meaningful ways. Thank you to Brooke Wilsner for reading Astrid first and helping me feel confident that it wasn't total crap.

Thank you to Alison Cochrun and Courtney Kae for their wonderful words about Astrid. I'm a forever fan of both of you, as authors and humans!

Thank you, authors, who offered your kind words to endorse Astrid. I appreciate your time and praise more than you know!

As always, thank you to C, B, and W, who create a safe space for me to write every day and love me even when I disappear into my mind for a while.

Lastly, and again, and always, thank you, readers. Without you, Astrid and Jordan would live only in my head, and I'm so thankful you've helped bring them to life.

ASTRID PARKER DOESN'T FAIL

Ashley Herring Blake

DISCUSSION QUESTIONS

1. Jordan's and Astrid's first impressions of each other aren't the greatest, to say the least. Have you ever met someone in a similar way? Did you end up liking each other?

2. Do you think Isabel, Astrid's mother, is redeemable? Why do you think it took Astrid so long to stand up to her?

3. Jordan regularly does Tarot readings for herself, while Astrid isn't a big believer in it. Are you interested in Tarot? If so, have you found that the results apply to your life?

4. Would you rather have Astrid or Jordan design your home? And why?

5. If you were Astrid, would you have agreed to Jordan's plan to pretend the design is yours, or would your conscience stop you?

6. Have you ever had a drastic career change like Astrid? If you were considering one, what would your dream job be?

7. For a long time, Astrid tried to conform to another person's idea of who she should be. Have you ever experienced conflict with what someone else expected of you? How did you handle it?

8. Astrid realized certain things about her sexuality after she turned thirty. Do you think sexuality is fluid? Have you ever experienced an "awakening" about your own identity or personality?

9. Jordan spends much of the novel feeling like she's not good enough for anyone in her life, and eventually learns that she has to be good enough for herself first. Does this resonate with you? How does the way you view yourself affect your relationships?

10. In the end, Astrid and Jordan both believe in some sort of destiny—while it's true we make our own choices and those choices shape our lives, do you believe there are certain things that are fated?

Keep reading for an excerpt of

IRIS KELLY DOESN'T DATE

The next romantic comedy by Ashley Herring Blake.
Coming soon from Piatkus!

IRIS KELLY WAS desperate.

She paused on her parents' front porch steps, the June sun feathering evening light over her bare shoulders, and took her phone out of her pocket.

Teagan McKee was desperate.

She typed the words into her Notes app, staring at the blinking cursor.

"Desperate for what, you little minx?" she asked out loud, waiting for something—anything that didn't feel overdone and trite—to spill into her brain, but nothing did. Her brain was a terrifying blank slate, nothing but white noise. She deleted everything except the name.

Because that's all she had for her book. A name. A name she loved. A name that felt right. A name that Teagan's best friends shortened to *Tea*, because of course they did, but a solitary name nonetheless. Which meant, in terms of her second full-length romance novel her agent was already up her ass about, that her publisher had already bought and paid for, that her editor was expecting to land in her inbox in two months' time, Iris had nothing.

Which meant Iris Kelly was the one who was desperate.

She glanced up at her parents' front door, dread clouding into her belly and replacing the creative panic. Inside that house, she knew what awaited her, and it wasn't pretty. Her mother's dentist, perhaps? No, no, Maeve's gynecologist more likely. Or, maybe, if Iris was really lucky, some poor sap who wanted to be there even less than Iris, because Maeve Kelly was nearly impossible to resist once she set her mind on something, and Iris and the aforementioned sap could commiserate over the absurdity of their situation.

Hell, maybe Iris could get some content out of it.

Teagan McKee was on a date. She hadn't planned the date, nor did she recall being asked out.

Iris froze with one foot on the step and opened up her Notes app again. That actually wasn't too bad . . .

"Honey?"

Iris dragged her eyes from that infernal blinking cursor—*why the hell don't you want to go on a date, Teagan?*—and smiled at her mother and father, now standing in the open doorway, arms around each other, marital bliss causing their faces to glow in the summer light.

"Hey," she said, tucking her phone away. "Happy birthday, Mom."

"Thanks, sweetheart," Maeve said, red and gray-streaked curls bouncing into her face. She was a round woman, with soft arms and hips, a hefty bosom Iris herself had inherited.

"More gorgeous every year, she is," Iris's dad said, kissing his wife on the cheek. Liam was tall and lithe, pale red hair ringing the shiny bald spot on top of his head.

Maeve giggled, and then—and *then*—Iris watched as her parents started full-on making out, which including a flash of Liam's tongue and the definite, not-so-surreptitious slide of his hand down Maeve's ass.

"Jesus, you two," she said, stomping up the stairs and averting her eyes. "Can you give it a rest at least until I get in the house?"

They pulled away from each other, but kept the obnoxious grins.

"What can I say, love?" Liam said, his Irish accent still fully in place even after forty years in the States. "I can't keep my hands off the woman!"

More kissing noises commenced, but Iris was already passed them and heading into the house. Her younger sister, Emma, appeared, her four-month-old hidden under a nursing wrap and, Iris assumed, attached to one of her boobs.

"God, are they at it again?" Emma asked, chin-nodding toward the front door where Maeve and Liam whispered sweet nothings in each other's ears.

"Are they ever not?" Iris said, hanging her bag on the hook in the foyer. "But at least it's distracting Mom from—"

"Oh, Iris!" Maeve called, pulling her husband into the house by the hand. "I have someone I want you to meet."

"Fuck my life," Iris said, and Emma grinned.

"Language," Maeve said, then hooked her arm through Iris's.

"Isn't there a dirty diaper in need of changing?" Iris asked as her mother dragged her toward the back door. "A filthy toilet I could scour? Oh, wait, I just remembered I'm late for a root canal—"

"Stop that," Maeve said, still tugging. "Zach is perfectly nice."

"Oh, well, if he's *nice*," Iris said.

"He's my spin class instructor."

"Oh fuckity fuck."

"Iris Katherine!"

Maeve shoved her onto the deck, which was how she found herself sitting next to Zach, who, thirty minutes later, was busy extolling the virtues of CrossFit training.

"You never really know how far your body can go, what it can do, until you push it to the edge," he was saying.

"Mmm" was all Iris had to say back. She sipped at a Diet Coke, cursing her mother's habit of saving the wine for the meal, and looked around for a savior.

Liam was silent at the grill, a stalwart of *That's none of my business,* so he'd be absolutely no help. She loved her father, but the man was complete trash for his wife, bending heaven and earth for the woman whenever possible. Which meant Maeve got to spring these "dates" on Iris whenever the family got together, and Liam would just smile, kiss Maeve on the cheek—or make out for ten minutes as the case may be—and ask what she wanted him to grill for said blissful occasion.

Emma was currently sitting across from Iris at the redwood patio table, her red hair cut into a sensible, advertising executive bob, grinning at the whole situation. Iris knew Emma thought her mother's setups were hilarious, as she also knew Iris would never, in a million years, go for someone Maeve dragged home.

Mostly because Iris hadn't gone for anyone at all in over a year.

"Have you ever done HIIT?" Zach asked now. "Feels like you're going to die while you're in the throes, but whew, what a rush!"

Emma snorted a laugh, then covered it by patting her newborn on the back.

Iris flipped her off under the table.

Meanwhile, Aiden, Iris's brother and the eldest of the three Kelly siblings, was running around in the backyard growling like a bear, chasing his twin seven-year-old daughters, Ava and Ainsley, through the dusky golden light. Iris seriously considered joining them—a good game of tag or whatever they were doing seemed like a better way to spend an evening than this current tenth circle of hell.

Of course, Iris had expected this. Just last month, at a gathering to celebrate Aiden's move from San Francisco to Portland, Iris had found herself seated next to her mother's hairstylist at dinner, a lovely lavender-haired woman named Hilda who led off the conversation by asking if Iris was a fan of guinea pigs. Iris then spent the next week wasting at least five thousand words of her novel writing about Teagan looking for love in a PetSmart. She'd ended up scrapping the whole thing, then promptly blamed her mother for the horrible inspiration.

"You know that stuff will kill you," Zach said, nodding toward her soda and smiling at her wryly, showing all of his perfect teeth. He was a white guy—blond hair, blue eyes—but he was also vaguely . . . orange. Iris had to bite back a reply about tanning beds and skin cancer.

"Oh, see if you can get her to drink more water, Zach," Maeve said as she came out the door with a tray of homemade veggie burgers for the grill.

"Water is really the only thing I drink," he said, leaning his elbows on his knees, admittedly impressive biceps flexing. "That and the occasional cup of green tea."

"Jesus Christ," Iris said, chugging back some more soda.

"What was that?" Zach said, leaning closer to her. His salty-piney cologne washed over her—a tsunami rather than a gentle wave—and she coughed a little.

"I said cheese and crackers," Iris said, slapping the table and standing up. She tugged at her cropped green sweater, which just barely covered her midriff. "I think we need some."

"Cheese and crackers, cheese and crackers!" Ava and Ainsley both chanted between giggles and squeals from the yard, where Aiden had them both hoisted over his broad shoulders. Their long auburn hair nearly brushed the grass.

Aiden deposited the girls on the top porch step, and Iris immediately pounced, grabbing their tiny hands with her own. She moved so fast, she imagined she looked like a vulture descending from the sky, but honestly, she didn't care. She would one hundred percent use her adorable nieces to get her out of this situation.

"I can get it, honey," her mother said, depositing the platter of burgers into her husband's hands and moving back toward the door.

"No!" Iris yelled. Yes, yelled. She slapped on a smile and softened her voice. "I can do it, Mom, you take a load off."

And with that, she pulled Ava and Ainsley into the house, moving so fast their gangly legs nearly tangled with hers. She managed to get all three of them inside without ending up in a heap on the floor, and bustled the two little girls into the kitchen through an array of carefully curated tickles.

Aromas of baking bread and sugar greeted them. Emma's husband, Charlie, was mashing potatoes in a giant blue ceramic bowl, forearms flexing, while Aiden's wife, Addison—resplendent in a belted shirtdress and ruffly apron—laid strips of pastry over what looked like a rhubarb-strawberry pie. It was like a fucking Norman Rockwell painting in here.

Iris waved at her siblings-in-law, then quickly located the charcuterie platter her mother had already prepared on the butcher block island. She immediately stuffed a rectangle of cheddar in her mouth, then spread a smear of brie onto a sesame seed cracker before dipping the whole thing into a tiny stainless-steel cup full of locally sourced honey.

"Easy," Addison said as the twins reached for their own snacks. "Don't ruin your appetites."

Iris stuffed another delectable, meal-ruining square of bliss into her mouth. Addison was nice and Iris had always gotten along okay with her, but the woman still dressed the twins in matching outfits, braided their hair in the same styles, and ran a mommy blog about how to balance style with efficiency in the home.

Not that there was anything wrong with any of that, but Iris, whose apartment was an amalgam of mismatched furniture and housed a drawerful of various sex toys in both of her nightstands, was never quite sure how to bond with her sister-in-law. Especially when Addison said shit like *Don't ruin your appetite* to kids eating tiny cubes of cheese.

She made a point to slather the honey extra thick onto her next cracker, which, conveniently, meant her mouth was practically glued shut when her mother bustled into the kitchen, eyes aglow and fixed on Iris.

"So?" Maeve said. "What do you think?" Behind her, both Aiden and Emma, along with baby Christopher, spilled into the kitchen, which meant her poor father was stuck outside with Zach and his fitness advice.

"Yeah, Iris, what do you think?" Aiden said with a smirk, popping a square of pepper jack into his mouth.

Iris glared at him. Growing up, she and Aiden had been pretty close. He was only two years older than she was, and he'd worked as a designer at Google, until this past summer when he moved his family to Portland to be "closer to the grandparents," as he put it. He and Iris were both creative, both prone to dreaming, but ever since he married Addison and became a dad, they hardly ever talked except at family events like this one.

Not that Iris didn't understand—he was busy. He had a family, kids to feed and mold into responsible human beings, a spouse. He was *needed*, while Iris spent most of her time lately staring up at her dust-covered ceiling fan wondering why the hell she ever thought *writing* was the correct career choice after her paper shop closed down last summer.

"What do I think about what?" Iris said, playing ignorant.

"I think he's cute," Emma said, swaying while Christopher dozed in her arms. He squirmed, wrinkled eyes closed, mouth still puckered from his meal.

"You would," Iris said to Emma. Emma was . . . well, she had her shit together. Always had. Three years younger than Iris, she'd married the perfect man at twenty-four, already worked her way to junior executive at a lucrative advertising agency in Portland by twenty-six, and popped out a kid at twenty-seven. Incidentally, this timetable had always been her plan, from age sixteen when she skipped her sophomore year and made a perfect 1600 on her SATs.

"There's nothing wrong with being health conscious," Emma said. "I think someone like that would be good for you."

"I can feed myself, Em," Iris said.

"Barely," she said. "What did you have for dinner last night? Hot dogs? A Lean Cuisine?"

Needless to say, Emma and Addison were BFFs and co-chairs of the Perfect Women Who Have It All Club. Iris imagined it as an elite group that probably met in an opulent, password-guarded penthouse apartment, where all the members brushed each other's gleaming hair and called one another by nicknames like Bunny and Miffy and Bitsy.

"Actually," Iris said, popping a green olive into her mouth, "I fed on the repressed tears of uptight women who need to get laid, thanks very much."

Emma's mouth puckered up in distaste, and Iris felt a tinge of guilt. Unlike Aiden, she and Emma had never been close at all. As a kid Iris had relished the idea of being a big sister, and there were myriad pictures of the precious Emma—the youngest, the surprise blessing, the completing jewel in the Kelly family crown—cuddled in Iris's arms. As the years passed, their roles shifted, the line between older and younger sister blurring, as Emma always seemed to know the answer, the right behavior, the correct choice, a split second before Iris did.

If Iris figured it out at all.

"Iris, really," her mother said, taking Christopher from Emma and kissing his bald head. "Your father and I worry about you," Maeve went on. "All alone in your apartment, no roommate, no steady job, no boyfriend—"

"Partner."

Her mother winced. Maeve and Liam Kelly, both longtime

survivors of staunchly Irish Catholic upbringings, had always accepted
Iris's bisexuality with open arms and hearts—even going so far as to
set her up with Maeve's queer, guinea pig–loving hairstylist—but they
still got trapped in heteronormative language sometimes, particularly
when all of Iris's siblings were straight as fucking arrows.

"Sorry, honey," Maeve said. "Partner."

"And I have a job," Iris said.

"Writing those SEAs or whatever you call them that you don't
even experience?" Maeve said.

Iris gritted her teeth. No one in her family had read her first
novel yet. It wasn't out until the fall, and Iris's family members
weren't exactly the romance-reading types. *Fantasy*, her mom called
the genre back when Iris first fell in love with the books as a teenager. "Real romance takes work," Maeve had said, then promptly
stuck her tongue down Liam's throat.

"*HEA*s, Mom," Iris said. "Happily Ever After."

Maeve waved a hand.

"Shittily Ever After," Aiden said, getting a couple of beers out of
the fridge and handing one over to Charlie.

"Daddy said shit!" Ava said.

Aiden winced while Addison glared.

"Syphilis-ly Ever After," Charlie said, because he had half a sense
of humor, unlike the rest of this miserable lot.

Aiden guffawed. "Septically Ever After."

"Aiden," Addison said.

"Fuck you both very much," Iris said.

"Iris!" Addison said.

"Barn animals, all of you," Maeve said, covering one of Christopher's tiny ears. "Iris, I just worry sometimes. That's all I'm saying."

"I'm fine," Iris said. Her voice shook a little, belying her words,
but that's what a family ambush would do to a person. She *was* fine.
Sure, she'd had to close her paper shop last year—she still designed

and sold her digital planners out of her Etsy shop, but no one bought paper anymore. Or, at least, they didn't buy it enough these days. And once Iris started offering digital planners, the brick and mortar aspect of her business suffered. It was a difficult call, but it was also exciting. After a few months of feeling a bit adrift, Iris decided to try her hand at writing romance. She'd always loved reading the novels, and had long dreamed of penning one of her own. Turns out, she was a pretty decent writer. She banged out a story about a down-on-her-luck queer woman who had a life-changing encounter with a stranger on a New York subway, then keeps running into the same woman all over the city in the unlikeliest of places. She got several offers from agents and went with Fiona, who was the perfect blend of ruthless and nurturing, and sold *Until We Meet Again* to a major romance publisher in a two-book deal. Granted, she didn't sell it for a killing or anything, but she had enough money in savings to keep her afloat, and her Etsy sales brought in a steady stream of cash.

But of course, the dissolution of her business only made her mother freak out even more about her *future*, and Maeve considered writing a hobby more than a stable job. The fact that Iris hadn't dated anyone seriously in over a year didn't help. Iris imagined Maeve dedicated many hours a day to envisioning Iris dying poor and alone.

For Iris, the blatant lack of romance in her life was wonderful.

No drama.

No heartbreaks from partners who couldn't deal with the fact that Iris didn't want to get married or have kids.

No lies from people who claimed Iris was the most wonderful creature they'd ever met, only to find out from their sobbing spouse that they were fucking *married with children*.

Iris shook off the memory of the lying, cheating, asshole Jillian, the last person she'd let into her heart thirteen months ago. Since then, she contented herself with writing about romance and had simply removed dating from the equation, along with conversation, phone number exchanges, and any sort of scenario that left room for *I'd like to see you again.*

There was no *again*. No second date. Hell, what Iris had been doing with people she met on apps and in bars for the last several months wouldn't even qualify as a first date.

Which was exactly the way Iris wanted it.

Because, if she was being honest, romance novels *were* a fantasy. Not that she'd ever admit that to her mother, but that was what she loved about them. They were an escape. A vacation from the harsh reality that only zero-point-one percent of people in the world actually got a for-real HEA. Stories like her mom and dad's, a romance that lasts forty years, meet cutes where the couple accidentally picks up the other person's luggage after an international flight to Paris—that shit wasn't *real.*

At least, it wasn't real for Iris Kelly.

For Teagan McKee however . . .

"Iris!" Maeve screeched, jolting Iris out of her brainstorming and startling poor Christopher awake.

"Sorry, Jesus," Iris said, then took Christopher from her mother. He reached a hand toward her, yanking on her long hair. Iris smiled down at him. He *was* fucking cute.

"See?" Maeve said, beaming at Iris. "Isn't it wonderful to hold a baby in your arms? Now just imagine your own—"

"Oh my god, Mom, stop," Iris said, then handed Christopher back to Emma.

"Fine," Maeve said. "But all I'm saying is that someone who's ready to settle down might be good for you. Zach told me he's *tired of dating.*" She widened her eyes like she'd just revealed government secrets. "So are you!"

Iris rubbed her forehead. As usual, her well-meaning mother hit the mark just left of the bullseye. "I'm doing fine by myself, Mom."

"Oh, honey," Maeve said, looking at her with big *you poor thing* eyes. "No one is fine by themselves. Look at Claire and Astrid. They're happy now, aren't they?"

Iris frowned. "Just because they both have partners who make them happy doesn't mean they weren't happy before."

"That's exactly what it means," Maeve said, and Emma nodded, because of course she did. "Since she and Jordan got together, I've never seen Astrid Parker smile so much in the twenty years that I've known her."

"That's just Astrid," Iris said. "She was born with resting bitch face."

"Point," Aiden said, jutting a carrot stick into the air before biting off half. He was well-acquainted with Astrid Parker's fierceness, as she'd eviscerated him in their high school debate club when he was a junior and she a mere freshman.

"And *my* point," Maeve said, grabbing the second half of the carrot stick out of her son's hand and throwing it at him before fixing her Concerned Catholic Mother eyes back on Iris, "is that all this gallivanting around, seeing a new person every week, avoiding adulthood, isn't healthy. It's time to get serious."

Silence filled the kitchen.

Get serious.

Iris had grown up hearing one version or another of that very phrase. *Get serious* when she got suspended her junior year of high school for getting in a verbal match with the assistant principal in the middle of the cafeteria about the archaic dress code. *Get serious* when she told her parents she wanted to study visual art in college. *Get serious* when Iris dreamed of turning the doodles in her journals and notebooks into a custom planner business. *Get serious* for the entirety of her three-year relationship with Grant, enduring constant questions about marriage and babies.

See, Iris was *promiscuous*, which, even with her parents' best efforts at progressive thinking, still made her mother's mouth pinch and her father's fair Irish cheeks burn as red as his hair. Not that she shared many details with them about her personal life, but Iris was never very good at keeping her feelings or opinions to herself.

"Honey," Maeve said, sensing Iris's hurt. "I only want you to be happy. We all do, and—"

"Here's where you're all hiding," Zach said, his blond head appearing in the doorway. He stuffed his hands in his jeans pockets, which were so tight, Iris was amazed he could fit one finger in there, much less four. "Can I help with anything? Liam said the burgers are nearly there."

"Wonderful," Maeve said, brightening. She eyed Iris meaningfully. "Iris, will you and Zach set the table for us?"

Another thing Iris wasn't very good at? Subtlety. Call it the product of a childhood as the quintessential middle child, call it a flair for drama, call it an inability to be *serious*, but if Maeve wanted Iris and Zach to couple up, then who was she to deny the woman her dearest wish on her birthday?

"Oh, we absolutely will," Iris said. "But first, I have a very important question for Zach."

He lifted a blond brow, a sly grin on his face. "Yeah? What's that?"

Iris smoothed a hand over her long hair, tugging on one of the tiny braids plaited through her dark red locks like she did when she was nervous, a tick her mother knew full well.

Maeve tilted her head.

Iris took a deep breath.

Then she yanked the moonstone ring from her left index finger and went down on one knee, presenting the ring to Zach with both hands.

"Here we go," Aiden said.

Ava and Ainsley giggled.

"Zach . . . whatever your last name is that I will happily take as my own upon our union," Iris said, "will you marry me?"

"Iris, for god's sake," Maeve said, dropping her head into her hands.

"Um . . ." Zach said, backing up one step, then another. "Wait, what?"

"Don't break my heart, Zachie," Iris said, making her eyes as wide as possible, lifting the ring into the light.

"Iris, come on," Emma said.

Behind her, Iris heard someone snort-laugh. She was pretty sure it was Charlie, as Addison would never deign to snort in public in a thousand years.

"I . . . well . . ." Zach continued to splutter, his orange-toned skin deepening into russet. He took another step toward the living room and fished his phone out of his back pocket, squinting at the screen. "You know what?"

"Early meeting tomorrow?" Iris asked from her place on the hardwood floor. She stuck out her lower lip in a pout. "Family emergency?"

"Yes," he said, pointing at her. "Yes, exactly. I'm . . . this has been . . . yeah." Then he turned and bolted out the front door so fast, a cologne-soaked breeze fluttered the ferns in the entryway.

The sound of the door slamming shut echoed through the kitchen as Iris got to her feet and calmly slipped her ring back into place.

Her family just watched her with partly amused, partly annoyed expressions on their faces, which was pretty much her childhood captured in a single scene. Wild-haired, nail-bitten Iris, up to her usual antics.

Despite this familiarity, Iris's cheeks went a little warm, but she simply shrugged and reached for another cube of cheese. "I guess he wasn't ready to settle down after all."

Her mother just threw her hands into the air and finally—dear god, finally—opened a bottle of wine.

Don't miss Delilah's story . . .

'I loved Delilah Green'
TALIA HIBBERT

Available now from

PIATKUS